THE TERRIFYING QUESTION

Fiona stared at Simeon. She shook a red curl out of her eye and her lips compressed into a straight line. "Dr. Halstead," she said, trying to keep her voice calm, "my son Andy has something the matter with his vision and I'm really scared that it could be something serious. All I'm asking you is to tell me what the problem is and what we need to do about it."

Simeon looked blankly at her; then, as if he'd been caught thinking about something entirely different, he blinked. "Yes, of course. I'm sorry," he said, genuinely upset to see the anger in Fiona's expression. "I ... I don't know what is causing Andy's problems. As I said, we need more tests." He smiled a tight but real smile, and Fiona wondered whether maybe he had occasional moments of being human.

Pulling the doctor aside, so Andy wouldn't hear, Fiona asked Dr. Simeon Halstead to answer the question that haunted her: "Could it be a brain tumor?"

THE DR. JEAN MONTROSE MYSTERY SERIES
BY C. F. ROE

Francis Roe

SECOND OPINION

A SIGNET BOOK

SIGNET
Published by the Penguin Group
Penguin Books USA Inc., 375 Hudson Street,
New York, New York 10014, U.S.A.
Penguin Books Ltd, 27 Wrights Lane,
London W8 5TZ, England
Penguin Books Australia Ltd, Ringwood,
Victoria, Australia
Penguin Books Canada Ltd, 10 Alcorn Avenue,
Toronto, Ontario, Canada M4V 3B2
Penguin Books (N.Z.) Ltd, 182–190 Wairau Road,
Auckland 10, New Zealand

Penguin Books Ltd, Registered Offices:
Harmondsworth, Middlesex, England

First published by Signet, an imprint of Dutton Signet,
a division of Penguin Books USA Inc.

First Printing, December, 1995
10 9 8 7 6 5 4 3 2 1

 REGISTERED TRADEMARK—MARCA REGISTRADA

Printed in the United States of America

PUBLISHER'S NOTE
This is a work of fiction. Names, characters, places, and incidents either are the product of the author's imagination or are used fictitiously, and any resemblance to actual persons, living or dead, events, or locales is entirely coincidental.

BOOKS ARE AVAILABLE AT QUANTITY DISCOUNTS WHEN USED TO PROMOTE PRODUCTS OR SERVICES. FOR INFORMATION PLEASE WRITE TO PREMIUM MARKETING DIVISION, PENGUIN BOOKS USA INC., 375 HUDSON STREET, NEW YORK, NEW YORK 10014.

I have been fortunate in having a number of highly qualified friends and colleagues who have helped with various aspects of this story, and I hereby thank them all, and at the same time retain responsibility for any factual errors that may have slipped through their nets.

Neurosurgery is a fast-moving discipline, and I thank Dr. Mark Erasmus, MD, FACS, who specializes in pediatric neurosurgery, for his help and expert advice. Foster Bam, lawyer and renowned underwater photographer, was kind enough to review the diving sequences, and in addition checked the legal aspects of the story. Linda Ann Smith, MD FACS, again provided penetrating observations on today's medical scene. Tasha Mackler gave her usual careful reading and insightful commentary, and finally, I would like to thank Bentley Lyon, musician, author, and friend, for advising on Simeon's music.

Writing a novel is a team effort, and it has been my privilege to have such talented people as Michaela Hamilton, my editor, and Matt Bialer, my agent, on the team. Between them they have taken care of many of the problems, and added greatly to the pleasure and productivity of authorship.

Who shall decide, when doctors disagree?
—ALEXANDER POPE

Part One

Chapter 1

Andy Markle stood with his back to the fence, swinging his bat and scrunching up his eyes against the sun. In the bottom of the ninth, the Vikings were playing the Stonington Bears, who were one run ahead. Andy watched his friend Kevin, the team's lead pitcher, walk up to the plate. Kevin could throw a mean curve but he couldn't bat worth beans, and Andy knew he'd be back soon.

Mike Brennan, their coach, also stood with his back to the fence, clapping his hands. "Knock 'em dead, Kevin!" he shouted, but he kept glancing over at Andy. For the first few weeks of the season, Andy had been the team's top hitter, then in the last couple of games he had run into a serious slump. It seemed to be his timing that was at fault, and Coach Brennan, who always liked a chance to talk to Fiona, Andy's mother, had mentioned it to her, wondering if maybe Andy had been staying up late at night or was worried about something.

Brennan glanced around. Sure enough, Fiona was sitting over to his right, talking to her friend Wilma Parkinson. Fiona's long curly red hair blew about in the late-afternoon breeze coming in off the sound. She noticed his glance, grinned, and gave him the thumbs-up sign. She was a slim, pale-complexioned woman in her mid-thirties, still freckled, quick and enthusiastic about everything she did. Mike thought of her as a siren, a mermaid with long auburn hair. Fiona Markle taught school at New Coventry High and had never missed a game that Andy played in. He remembered seeing her at the school concert last Christmas, alone on the stage, playing her guitar, first a feisty piece by Villa-Lobos, then accompanying herself in a couple of country-western songs, finally bringing the house down with her own funny arrangement of "He Got the Gold Mine, and I Got the Shaft . . ."

There was something lively and exciting about Fiona Markle, although she seemed to have quieted down a lot in the last few months. That was probably because of her divorce from Victor, thought Brennan. He shrugged to himself. Everybody had known for years what an asshole that Victor was, except for good old loyal Fiona herself.

Brennan watched Kevin take a couple of practice swings at the plate. There were maybe twenty parents and students in the home stands, but aside from a few encouraging shouts from Kevin's parents, there wasn't much noise when he raised his bat and faced the pitcher. They knew that it would be a miracle if Kevin's bat even touched the ball. Sure enough, three wild swings later Kevin was out. He walked back to rejoin his teammates, threw his bat disgustedly against the fence, and sat down on the bench.

Andy, feeling very tense now, took a deep breath and walked out, his bat tucked under his arm the way Willie Mays used to hold it. He tested his eyesight by looking at the pitcher, then at the scoreboard. Everything seemed okay. In the last game, he just hadn't been able to see the pitches coming, the ball seemed to split into two balls as it approached him, and he'd felt momentarily dizzy when he looked from the pitcher to the fence behind him. Reaching the plate, Andy glanced at the catcher, scraped at the dust with his foot, stepped back and swung his bat a couple of times. The pitcher, a long, lanky kid by the name of Dave Moss, stood on the mound, loose-armed, gangly, right hand behind his back, watching Andy, trying to intimidate him with his stare.

Andy stepped up to the plate and raised his bat shoulder high. He fixed his eyes on Moss, who had a rep for throwing fast and unexpectedly. And then it happened again. Moss became two identical people, standing on the mound, his hands together, swinging, preparing to deliver the ball, and the wire fence behind him lost its posts and became a gray blur. Andy stepped back, closed his eyes and shook his head. The late April sun was bright, and luminous red stars and dots floated on a light blue background in front of his closed eyes. When he opened them again, there was

Moss, and although he seemed a bit fuzzy and out of focus, at least there was only one of him. Andy stepped up, and before he knew it a ball had come whizzing past him and landed with a smack in the catcher's glove. Andy hadn't seen it, not even for a moment.

"Take it easy, Andy! Take your time!" His mother's voice, soaring like a bird, came to him from far away. The visitors, in the other stands, suddenly smelled blood, and they shouted encouragement to their hero, Dave Moss. If he could get Andy Markle out now, the game was as good as over. The home crowd picked up and shouted back, Fiona's voice high above the others. Moss smiled, a big, triumphant, toothy grin, and the catcher said under his breath to Andy, "You're dead meat, kid!"

Andy put his bat up, nice and steady, and stared at Moss. He could feel the sweat running down the sides of his face, and his palms were wet. Moss tossed the ball from his left hand to his right and wound up. This time Andy saw it, but too late. He swung, but he wasn't even close. Two strikes. Again Andy stepped back, away from the plate. He'd been feeling desperate before, but now he was scared. What was happening to him? He looked over in Coach Brennan's direction, but he couldn't see clearly enough to identify him. The noise from the crowd was swelling loud as Andy stepped up to the plate. His head was throbbing now, and the sunlight, coming from the right over Moss's shoulder, wasn't just bright; it hurt. Knowing that if he managed to hit whatever pitch Moss sent down it would be a pure accident, Andy stood facing the pitcher like a gladiator at bay. Everything was blurry now, and Moss was just a moving black shadow against a luminous yellow background. The ref shouted "Strike!" at the same time as the ball smacked into the catcher's mitt, and Andy was out. A few minutes later the game was over.

Fiona, hiding her anxiety, smiled and said to her friend Wilma, "Andy's going to be tough to live with for the next couple of days."

"Maybe the sun got in his eyes," suggested Wilma. She was a large, big-boned woman of about the same age as Fiona, a physical education teacher at the same school. She looked at her watch. "I have to run," she said. "Call me tonight, okay?" For a moment Fiona watched Wilma stump back toward her car, then she went over to talk with the other parents while she waited for Andy. She found that several were angry with him, and even with her.

"What's Andy's problem?" growled Big Ed Woviotis, Kevin's father, a burly man with a big belly and arms like tree trunks. He owned and operated a small private garbage collection company, and he occasionally helped Mike Brennan coach the team. "He looks like he's not interested, or just not paying attention."

"He certainly *is* interested and he *is* paying attention," replied Fiona, her eyes flashing dangerously. "He's just in a slump. Same as Kevin was earlier this year. Or don't you remember that?" Her voice was crisp and a shade louder than her usual conversational tone. Fiona never took long to rise to a challenge.

Big Ed, who said he never took no crap from nobody, not even from a woman as attractive as Fiona Markle, went suddenly red in the face and seemed to swell up. Fiona grinned at him and put a hand on his massive arm. "Take it easy, Ed," she said. "It's only a game, right?" After a moment he grinned back, and just then Andy and Kevin came up. She glanced quickly at Andy before addressing Kevin.

"Good pitching, Kev," she said. "That fast ball's a killer." Kevin blushed, grinned self-consciously, mumbled something, then went past her to join his dad. Fiona put a hand on Andy's shoulder. "Are you okay?" she asked quietly. He nodded, but didn't look her in the eye.

On the way home Andy found he could see clearly again, although his head was still throbbing a little. He figured that he must have got stressed out, and that was why he'd played so badly.

"Can we go to McDonald's?" he asked.

"No," replied Fiona in a faraway voice. She was feeling anxious about him, although as she'd told Big Ed, she knew that athletes of any age could have off-days, even off-weeks or months. "For one thing the Seidels are coming to dinner."

"Why?" asked Andy.

"Because I invited them," replied Fiona. "And because

we went to a cookout at their house two Saturdays ago, remember?" Fiona wasn't looking forward to the Seidels' visit either, but she was meticulous about her social obligations. Marty Seidel was the principal at New Coventry High School, where Andy was a freshman, and although Wilma and her other colleagues told Fiona that Marty was more than a little interested in her, she herself hadn't noticed anything. Well, hardly anything.

"Is anybody else coming?"

"No. But your father's picking you up at eight-thirty tomorrow, so you'll have to get up early and be ready when he comes, okay?"

For the rest of the trip home Andy said nothing. Fiona was about to ask him about his homework assignments when, as she turned into their driveway, he suddenly yelled, in a voice that sent chills down her back, "Mom I can't see anything! I'm blind!"

Chapter 2

In her fright Fiona almost drove through the closed garage door, but she stopped just in time, yanked on the emergency brake, and turned around. She had a quick, terrifying glimpse of Andy's eyes staring at her, wide open but obviously not seeing anything; then his eyes seemed to clear, he blinked and shook his head, and everything seemed all right again. The episode had lasted only half a minute or so, but Fiona wasn't about to let it pass.

"I'm taking you straight to the emergency room," she said. She still couldn't breathe properly and had gone white with anxiety. Before backing out of the driveway, she made Andy open and close each eye in turn and made sure that he could see out of both eyes.

Andy didn't argue. It had been a weird and scary feeling, so unexpected that he thought he was imagining it, or that it had suddenly got dark outside or something.

By good luck, Fiona found a parking place right outside the emergency room entrance, next to the big sign that said, NEW COVENTRY MEDICAL CENTER. Now Andy was feeling embarrassed and didn't want to go in. He protested that he was just fine and he could see much better than he ever had in his whole life and please couldn't they just go home and forget about it?

Fiona wouldn't even discuss it. "Out," she said.

After a nurse behind a desk looked at Andy and decided that he wasn't dying, they were directed across the corridor to the waiting room, a long, dreary-looking place with battered old chairs lined up along the wall. A wall-mounted TV was on, flickering so badly nobody could watch it. Eventually Andy was seen by Dr. Bennett, a tired-looking young man with spiky black hair who looked as if he'd just come out of the shower. He examined Andy briefly, then sent him for X rays. Fiona looked at her watch. The Seidels would be coming in about an hour, and nothing was ready. Twenty minutes later, Dr. Bennett came over to where they were sitting, a buff-colored X-ray envelope in his hand.

"Nothing here," he said to Fiona, indicating the X-rays. "Everything looks normal. And his vision seemed just fine when I examined him." He turned to Andy and smiled. "I guess it was just the stress of the game, huh, Andy?"

Andy nodded, and Fiona stood up, relieved.

"Come back and see us if it happens again," said the doctor.

There was a crowd of people around the main exit, and Fiona and Andy stepped into the line to get out through the revolving doors. Standing next to her was a small group of medical students gathered around a tall, slim, serious-looking doctor in a carefully laundered and ironed white coat. Without paying particular attention, Fiona noticed a pair of gray, expressionless eyes in a stern, rather narrow face. He glanced at her as she stood there, as dispassionately as if she'd been a brick in a wall. She glimpsed the name on his tag: Dr. Simeon Halstead. Standing behind Andy, Fiona tried to recollect where she'd seen that name before, but it wasn't until she'd taken a few more slow steps toward the door that she remembered. Dr. Halstead was a neurosurgeon, well known in the area, and his name had been in the local paper about a year before when one of his lab technicians had accused him of sexual harassment. The fuss had died down almost as soon as it surfaced, but like many people who lived in the shadow of New Coventry Medical Center, Fiona remembered things like that.

He doesn't look as if he'd make uninvited passes at women, she thought, feeling a slight, ridiculous resentment that he hadn't even noticed her. Fiona was not used to being ignored so completely. She shook her head. The line moved on, and they approached the automatic exit doors. Fiona hoped her car hadn't been ticketed or towed.

A minute or two later, Dr. Bennett, coming along the same corridor, stopped to tell Dr. Halstead about a head injury case they'd had in earlier. "By the way," he said as an afterthought, "I just saw a kid who complained of an episode of total blindness. It only lasted about thirty seconds, and everything seemed okay when I examined him. Both visual fields were normal, pupillary reflexes normal, all the rest of it. Would that be something you might want to follow up?"

Dr. Halstead nodded. "Yes, it is," he said.

"Right," said Dr. Bennett, scribbling on the back of a card. "I'll call them and tell them to make an appointment with you."

Fiona got home at the same time that Marty Seidel's shiny new black Infiniti drove up, and Andy, who hadn't seen it before, hopped out of the wagon and went over to look at it.

"Hi, Andy," said Marty, emerging carefully from his car. "Sorry I missed the game. How did it go?" Marty Seidel was around fifty, six feet tall, hair thinning on the top and graying at the sides. As always, he was formally dressed in a dark suit, and he wore a friendly, serious expression.

"We lost," said Andy simply. "Sorry."

"Well, better luck next time," said Marty, looking over at Fiona, who was getting out of her car.

He went to greet her, walking a little stiffly because he'd strained a leg muscle playing tennis, and gave her a hug. At school he was careful not to show his partiality; he made it a point never to touch her when on school premises.

"You're looking a bit frazzled," he said, standing back and looking at her. "Is everything all right?"

"No," replied Fiona, "it isn't. I'm two hours behind schedule, and I still have to make dinner. Where's Doreen?"

"She has one of her headaches and wasn't feeling too great, so she decided not to come," replied Marty quickly. "I tried to call you, but you weren't home."

"Shouldn't you stay with her if she's not feeling well?" asked Fiona, looking squarely at him. She hadn't really expected to see Doreen, who was very fat and avoided every social engagement she could get out of.

"To tell you the truth, I think she was glad to get me out of the house," replied Marty, smiling but obviously uncomfortable.

Fiona started to walk toward the front door, key in hand,

holding on to Andy's shoulder, and Marty followed them in. "I'm just going to throw something together from the freezer," Fiona said over her shoulder to Marty, "so don't expect a Cordon Bleu dinner."

"I know what a great cook you are, Fiona," said Marty, walking behind her. "I'd rather have one of your thrown-together dinners than a banquet at the Four Seasons."

"Yeah, sure," said Fiona, smiling at his clumsy compliment.

"We could still go to McDonald's," murmured Andy.

Thank God for frozen food, thought Fiona. Within half an hour she had an aromatic-smelling *boeuf Bourguignon* heating in a glass dish, almost ready to serve with new potatoes in butter with parsley and green beans with little white onions dotted among them.

Andy was watching the little TV in the kitchen, and Fiona had to ask him twice to go and set the table. He seemed to be completely back to normal. The doctor had said that it was probably stress, but she'd never heard of stress causing blindness. Andy was maybe quieter than usual now, but that might be because he was worrying about the ball game, or maybe it was Marty's presence. Not that Andy didn't like Marty; he did, and was in some awe of him, but he was always very protective and watchful when any man seemed interested in his mother.

Marty stayed in the kitchen with Fiona, talking about school, about the new teachers joining the staff, the baseball teams, projects that he was planning to introduce in the next school year. He seemed to enjoy talking to Fiona about his work; she figured he probably didn't get much opportunity at home. He tried not to follow her with his eyes as she moved around the kitchen, but it was difficult; Fiona had a neat way of moving, and under the practical blue-and-white-striped butcher's apron, her trim figure somehow exactly matched her movements.

"We've been asked by the state to participate in a gender equity program for schools," said Marty, "and I'd like to put you on that committee. Are you interested?"

Fiona hesitated. "I'd love to," she said, "but with all the extra stuff I'm already doing at school plus that exchange program with the South African townships . . . I'm not getting enough time with Andy."

"Think about it, Fiona," urged Marty. "You'd meet some of the senior education hierarchy people up in Hartford, and that wouldn't do you any harm professionally."

Fifteen minutes later, they were in the middle of dinner and Fiona was passing the dish to Marty for a second helping of *boeuf Bourguignon,* when the phone rang. Andy jumped up and grabbed the wall phone in the kitchen. At this time of day calls were usually for him.

"It's Dr. Bennett from the hospital," he said to his mother. "He wants to speak to you." He brought the phone over, stretching it to the limit of its cord.

Fiona took it, listened, and after asking Andy to bring her the pen and pad, wrote down a name and a number. "Thanks, Dr. Bennett," she said. "I'll call him first thing on Monday morning. Thanks for taking the time to do this." She handed the phone back to Andy, who hung it up.

"What did he want, Mom?"

Fiona was about to reply when they heard a car turn into the driveway. "That's Dad," said Andy. He looked at his mother. "I thought he was coming tomorrow."

Fiona sighed and put her napkin down on the table. This had happened before, and it always meant trouble.

The car door banged, and a moment later the doorbell rang insistently several times. Andy hesitated for a second, then got up silently and went to open the door.

Victor Markle was a big man, and he filled the doorway. Just the way he stood told Fiona that he had been drinking, and a familiar anger rose up in her.

Victor ignored Andy. "So, we're entertaining, are we?" he asked Fiona, coming into the room. "Am I interrupting something?"

"Victor, we didn't expect you until tomorrow morning," said Fiona firmly. If Marty hadn't been there, she'd have had him out in a second. Victor was big, but she was fast, and knew how to outmaneuver him.

Marty stood up. "Hi, Victor, I don't know if you remember me," he said, making an attempt at a friendly smile. "Marty Seidel. Fiona works with me at the school . . ."

"I bet she does," interrupted Vic, looking Marty up and

down. He turned to Fiona. "When did you start bringing your work home with you?"

Vic looked huge, towering above them. His eyes moved to the sideboard. "Where's the bourbon?"

Marty licked his lips, and for the first time that evening he wished Doreen had come with him.

Fiona took a deep breath. "There isn't any." She felt her body tense as she watched him, because Victor had been known to tear the place apart when he thought she was hiding liquor from him. "And now I'd like you to leave without making any more trouble. Andy'll be ready at eight-thirty tomorrow morning."

"And let you get on with your little tête-a-tête here?" said Victor, advancing further into the room. "Don't forget this is still my house; half of it, anyway, right?" His voice rose on the last word, and his face went bright red.

Fiona held her ground. Andy, embarrassed and desperate to avoid a confrontation between his parents, spoke up from the door. "I had to go to the hospital," he said. "We just got back an hour ago."

That stopped Victor. He swung around to face Andy, who was still standing by the door. "Why? What was the matter?"

Andy looked at the floor. "Nothing much," he said. "I couldn't see anything for a while."

Victor looked at Fiona, who told him briefly what had happened.

As soon as Fiona stopped talking, Marty stood up, hurriedly thanked her for dinner, nodded at Victor, and headed for the door, glad to escape without injury.

"So what did the doctor say?" asked Victor, ignoring Marty's departure. Fiona told him, and also said that he'd recommended that Andy see a neurosurgeon.

"Did he suggest anyone in particular?" asked Victor in that infuriating way he had, as if he knew them all and could pick and choose the best one.

"Dr. Halstead," replied Fiona.

"Halstead? Huh. I don't know him," he said. "But I'll check him out. In any case, if there's a real problem, Andy should go up to Mass General in Boston. They're the best."

"They're just as good here," replied Fiona. "And at this

point I don't see any need to take him anywhere else." She stood up. "I want you to leave now, Victor. You can come to pick Andy up tomorrow at eight-thirty as I said, but I'm telling you here and now that if there's any sign that you've been drinking, he's not going anywhere. I don't want to have to go back to court about this."

"I have rights too," said Victor. "And I haven't drunk a drop all day. You want to go back to court? Go ahead. I'm already paying you too much money, so I'll be happy to renegotiate that." He came and stood close to her, and Fiona tensed. "Don't for one minute think you've seen the last of me," he said. Then he turned and went out, slamming the door so hard the house shook.

Later that evening, after Andy had gone to bed, Fiona went downstairs to tidy up the kitchen, then remembered she'd promised to call Wilma. She picked up the phone and told Wilma about the events of the evening.

"Probably just stress," said Wilma, referring to Andy. "I get kids sometimes who actually faint before a competition." Then she laughed, a deep, chuckling laugh. "I guess Victor's just as much of a pig as he always was," she said. "Poor Marty, he must have been wetting his pants."

"It was very embarrassing," said Fiona. "Andy was mortified, especially with his principal sitting right there."

"Yeah, it's tough having a dad like that. I should know, I had one. Listen, I have a couple of Long Wharf tickets for next Friday," Wilma went on. "You wanna go? There's a whole bunch of people going ..."

"Are you trying to fix me up again?" asked Fiona, smiling. She twisted a lock of hair around her index finger.

"Well, not exactly, but there is this guy ... He's very nice, he's a professor at Conn College, and he wants to meet you ..."

"Wilma, we've been through this already. Thank you, but no thanks. I don't have time, for one thing, what with school and Andy, and honestly, I'm not interested."

"Okay, okay." Wilma's voice was tinged with resignation. "But you know, Fiona, you're letting your whole life get absorbed by other people. You have to think about yourself occasionally, have some fun once in a while. For God's sake, woman, when did you last even buy yourself some clothes? Hey, why don't we go up to Warwick Mall on Saturday and get you some decent threads? We could have lunch ..."

"Yeah, okay ... No, I can't. I'm taking my kids up to Boston, to the Peabody. Maybe the week after, huh? Anyway, my clothes aren't that bad ..."

"Try donating them to Goodwill," retorted Wilma. "*They*'ll tell you."

Later, after Fiona had washed the glasses, scraped the pots, and put everything in the dishwasher, she wiped the counter and thought about what Wilma had said. She went upstairs and looked at herself in the long mirror in her bedroom. She didn't look so bad ... maybe a bit of makeup might help. And her clothes ... She looked at the plaid skirt. Sure it was old, but it was top quality and still looked pretty good. She didn't have much in the clothes closet, that was true, but what she did have was all good, long-wearing stuff. And she didn't go out often enough to need a big fancy wardrobe. She shrugged and tiptoed across the hallway to check Andy. He was asleep, and she crept quietly into the room to be certain that she heard him breathing. She watched him for a long moment, her eyes getting accustomed to the dark, and she could feel her heart tighten again with anxiety for him. She went back down into the living room, across to the big bookshelf, and took down a thick volume. Eyes ... Blindness, transient ... Fiona checked under several different headings in the index, but the *Home Medical Encyclopedia* didn't have any answers for her.

Her guitar was there, propped up against the bookshelves, its black case grayed and tattered with age. She took the instrument out gently; the wood had a cold, reproachful feel about it, and Fiona realized that she hadn't played it for months, not since the Christmas concert. She gazed at it for a moment, then put it back into the case with its worn red velvet lining.

When she finally went to bed, she lay there with her eyes open in the darkness, and the events of the day came rushing back at her, especially that terrifying wide-eyed look that Andy had had in the car during the brief moments when he couldn't see.

"Please, God," she said silently, over and over again, "don't let anything bad happen to him."

Chapter 3

"There *is* something almost inhuman about him," agreed Edwina Cole, one of the medical students in Dr. Simeon Halstead's group. It was Monday, clinic day, and they had just finished seeing patients with him and were walking back toward the cafeteria, pushing their way through the throng of visitors coming into the hospital.

"All neurosurgeons are weird," replied Terry Matson, a small, round young man whose black hair was already thinning. "They have X-ray eyes, and they're trained to see right through your skull into your brain, every lobe and convolution."

"I can see why that would bother you," grinned Nina Muldrew, coming up close behind them. "How embarrassing!"

They turned left before the cafeteria, heading for the stairs that went down to the connecting tunnel between the hospital and the medical school.

"Aren't you doing some research with him?" Terry asked Edwina as they clattered down the concrete steps.

Edwina, a well-built, straight-backed, confident-looking, and strikingly attractive woman with thick dark hair tied at the back of her head, nodded. "I'm doing my thesis with him," she replied, but there was a note of exasperation in her voice that they all noticed.

Terry and Nina exchanged a glance. "So what's the matter?" asked Terry.

"He started this great project," said Edwina, pushing the metal bar on the door to the tunnel. "A new way of dealing with certain types of brain tumor."

"Big deal," said Nina dismissively. "Every neurosurgeon in the world has a project to deal with brain tumors."

"Well, I thought this one was different, and that was why I wanted to work with him. But he's hardly ever in the lab, and his techs don't know what they're supposed to be doing. I'm thinking of going to work with Paula Cairns or Dr. Winter instead."

Their footsteps rang on the floor of the tunnel, which stretched out in front of them, lit by a long string of bare bulbs hanging from the ceiling.

"You don't have time to start a new project," said Nina after a pause. "Our theses have to be handed in before the end of this year."

"I know," replied Edwina.

"Have you ever seen him operate?" asked Terry.

"Yes. He's incredible." Edwina pushed open the door at the end of the tunnel, and Terry held it for them. "His results are better than those of any other neurosurgeon in the country. Last week there were two South African neurosurgeons who came over from Cape Town just to see him operate, and the week before, a bunch of professors were over from France. The guy is really a technical genius."

"Yeah, but you're supposed to be doing research with him," said Nina. "And he's not a real, dyed-in-the-wool researcher, not like, say, Felix Cadwaller."

"What do you mean?" asked Edwina.

"Well, the real research gurus have a different mind-set," replied Nina. "They understand about money, about funding, about networking, pushing each other's work, and so on. They're a bunch of sharks, but they hang together, and in that field Dr. Halstead's just an amateur."

"Was there anything to that story about Dr. Halstead and his lab technician?" asked Terry. He looked around curiously at Edwina.

"Who knows?" Edwina's voice was distracted. "Some-body said that she was trying to make it with him and he wasn't interested, so she complained out of spite."

"Figures. He doesn't seem the type. Why would he bother? Half the women around here are crazy about him."

"Including our very own Edwina," said Terry slyly.

"Nah," said Edwina after a brief pause. "I like him a lot, but I'd rather have a guy I can joke with, who likes to

eat pizza and go country dancing once in a while. I like
smart people, but I think I'd get cerebral indigestion with
him."

Simeon Halstead left his students and walked back alone
through the E.R. toward his lab. He was tall, with a deliberate, precise way of walking, as if the length and duration
of every step had been carefully calculated in advance.

Two unexpected visitors were waiting for him outside the
lab. He recognized them immediately, and his face lit up.
He stuck out his hand.

"Well, Bob! Richard! Great to see you! What are you
guys doing here?"

Bob Kleinfelt and Richard Posner were his two oldest
friends. They had all gone to medical school together, but
Simeon hadn't seen either of them since his wedding, exactly two years before. Bob was an internist in Seattle, and
Richard, who had been Simeon's best man, had gone into
administration and now ran a major health care project
in Houston.

"We're here for conferences," Bob said. "Mine's on
practice management, and Richard's ... I can't remember
what he's here for." Bob was tall and very good-looking;
Simeon remembered the wide swath he had cut through
the female hospital staff in his medical student days.

"I'm actually here to play golf," said Richard, who had
become more rotund than Simeon remembered him.
"Bob's been spending all his time up at Foxwoods, gam-
bling his fool head off instead of learning how to squeeze
more money out of the insurance companies."

"Richard's giving the keynote speech to his group," said
Bob, not without pride in their friend's accomplishments.
"What's the title again, Rich?"

"We're talking real high-level stuff here, fellas," drawled
Richard, sticking his thumbs in his waistband and putting
on a spurious Texas accent. "They told me to talk about
the future of medical care in the twenty-first century."

"Richard's also got a new job," said Bob. "In Washington. Tell him, Richard."

"I saw something about it in the *Times,*" said Simeon.

"Congratulations. Aren't you going to be in charge of a new investigative division at HHS?"

"Pharmaceutical Oversight," said Richard, nodding. "Conflicts of interest in the outside research funding practices of the industry."

"He's got the drug companies petrified," said Bob. "They've gotten away with unbelievable stuff for years, and now they could get really canned. I told Rich he should call his group the Pharmaceutical Investigation Subcommittee, Section Of Financial Fiddling. Just for the acronym, you understand."

Simeon thought about that for a second and then grinned. "When do you start, Richard?"

"In a month. If the pharmaceutical companies' hit men don't get me first."

Richard put a hand on Simeon's arm. "Man, it's great to see you! My God, I don't even want to think how long it's been! The last time I saw you was at the wedding. And how is the beauteous Elisabeth?"

Simeon replied calmly, "Elisabeth is just fine, thanks," but he didn't elaborate.

"Great." There was something about Simeon's tone that made Richard feel he was treading on dangerous ground. "You should keep in touch, damn it, Simeon, and let us know how things are going with you," he grumbled, a little annoyed with his old friend. "All we hear is when we read in the papers that you've operated on some Saudi Arabian prince, or somebody like that."

Bob saved Simeon the trouble of responding. "How about if the three of us went out for a drink this evening, or dinner?" he asked.

Simeon grinned at them. "What's the matter with you guys? Don't you remember what day this is? Or rather, what day it was two years ago?"

There was a moment's pause while they looked at him. "Your anniversary," said Richard, in sudden realization. "Oh, my God, was that really two years ago?"

"Best wedding I ever went to," said Bob. "I woke up two days later without any idea of how I got home. And if you remember," he went on in an awed voice, "I was living in Minneapolis at the time."

"Why don't you two stop by for a drink before dinner?" suggested Simeon. "Elisabeth would be glad to see you."

"No," said Bob, rather too quickly. "We won't interrupt your celebrations. But give Elisabeth a big hug from both of us, okay?"

Richard nodded in agreement. "Right," he said. "Do that for us, fella."

"How long are you going to be in town?" asked Simeon.

"We're both leaving tomorrow," said Bob. "Damn it, Simeon, we were hoping you could set us up with a little excitement while we're here."

Richard grinned. "Right. Nothing out of the way, just some designer drugs, maybe, or an orgy, if you can arrange one on short notice. Or have you given up all that stuff since Elisabeth came on the scene?"

They sounded just like they had in the old days, thought Simeon, smiling. The three of them had teased and joked and cheered each other up all the way through med school.

Bob's eyes gleamed. "That's a great idea," he said. "God, I haven't been to an orgy, for, let's see, it must be weeks. How about it, old buddy? Can you arrange one for us?"

Simeon laughed. "Sorry," he said, "no orgies, but if you can come back next week, I'm doing a special on prefrontal lobotomies, and I know you could both use one. That is," he added, "if your Blue Cross covers it." He grinned at them. "Hey," he said, "it's really good to see you. Why didn't you let me know you were going to be in town? We could have set something up. Not just a simple old-fashioned orgy, but something really special."

Bob looked at his watch. "We'd better get out of here," he said to Richard. "We don't want to get Simeon off his schedule—or get him chewed out for being late for his anniversary dinner, right?"

"Right," said Richard. "Let's go."

They all shook hands.

"Give me a call if you're ever in Seattle," said Bob to Simeon.

"Or in D.C." Richard clapped Simeon on the back.

Simeon smiled as he watched them go along the corridor. It was tough, growing up, he thought. Not that med school had been easy, far from it, but there had been a camaraderie between them, a bonding that could never be duplicated in the real world. For a moment he recalled the escapades and wild times the three of them had had, way back when, then shook his head. Everything was different now. He thought again about how emphatically they'd both been against his marrying Elisabeth. That had put a barrier up between them. And that, he felt sure, was why they hadn't told him ahead of time that they were coming up to New Conventry.

He opened the door and went into the lab. Denis Popham, his senior lab tech, was there, talking with Sonia Goldenberg, the other technician.

Denis, with his ever-courteous British manners, stood up when Simeon came in. He was tall, gangly, with a hank of long blond hair that hung down over one eye. Large nostrils and a long face gave him a gentle, horselike appearance.

"I'm so glad you came in, Dr. Halstead," he said. There was an anxious look in his eye. "Dr. Wayland from the Neuro Institutes called again." He hesitated, and glanced uncomfortably at Sonia. Simeon got the message and nodded at the inner office. Denis followed him in and closed the door.

"Dr. Wayland says that the interim report on the astrocytoma project is more than two months overdue, sir," he said. He paused, looking at the floor. "She said that they'll have to cut off the funding if the report doesn't get to them within the next week."

"Yes . . ." Simeon thought for a moment. "I thought you were doing that report," he said.

"I did, Dr. Halstead." The way Denis pulled his hand through his hair showed his frustration. "But you were going to review it with me before we sent it in . . ." He let the sentence tail off. They both knew that Denis had made appointment after appointment with Simeon, but each time something had come up and Simeon had canceled.

Pushing aside the urge to throw up his hands, let the funding be terminated, and be rid of the lab and all the aggravation that went with it, Simeon said, "Okay, Denis, let's do it now."

Denis hurried back to the lab, grabbed a folder, and

came back into the tiny office as if he were scared that Simeon would simply vanish. An hour later, they had hammered out a passable interim report on the computer, and while Denis printed it out, Simeon sat back, thinking about how and why he had lost interest in the project.

It had started off well enough, about three years back, before he was married. At the time Simeon was doing research on certain types of brain tumors at Queen Square Hospital in London and there had conceived an entirely new method of destroying them. The other researchers in his group were trying different anti-tumor chemotherapy compounds and more precise forms of high-voltage radiation therapy. Simeon, who didn't have a license to practice in the U.K., had been earning a little extra money by being a ringside doc at various boxing matches around London. One night he was at the White City Stadium, thinking more about ways of destroying brain cancer cells than about boxing. A particularly bloody heavyweight bout was nearing its end; the contestants had slugged it out for eight grueling rounds without either gaining much advantage. Then one of them summoned up his last reserves and smashed his opponent hard in the midriff.

"In the solar plexus!" shouted the announcer excitedly. "Gomez has set him up! Now here comes the Sunday Punch!" And sure enough, once his opponent's guard was down, Gomez slammed in a powerful uppercut and put an end to the bout.

After the count of ten, the fighter hadn't moved, so Simeon clambered into the ring and checked the rolling eyes of the concussed boxer. It was then that he had his unexpected moment of discovery. He would do with the cancer cells what Gomez had done with his opponent, set them up with a pretreatment to make them vulnerable, then administer the Sunday Punch with a second killer drug and wipe them out.

Back home in the States, he spent weeks in the library, following up every known treatment for different types of brain cancer, and found that apparently no one had had the same idea, or if someone had, nothing had been published. Full of enthusiasm, he set up his lab to follow up his brainstorm, obtained a small grant, then a larger one, but in the ensuing months, several factors conspired to make him lose interest in his research. First, the group of British researchers he'd been working with at Queen Square published a preliminary report of a new cancer-killing technique that seemed to make his own idea redundant. Then there was that business with the lab tech. After that, he'd had to force himself even to go into the lab.

But the main reason his mind wasn't on his research was that his private practice was taking off; he had quickly developed a reputation as a conservative, meticulous surgeon, and his technical skill had become legendary. His breakthrough came when he successfully operated on a young Saudi Arabian prince with a brain aneurysm, and after that he had become *the* neurosurgeon in a medical center famous for its neurosurgeons.

After reading the printout of the interim report and asking Denis a few cursory questions, Simeon left the lab and looked at his watch, feeling a sense of relief to be out of there. It was just before noon, and for once he had no appointments until his office hours, which were scheduled to start at two.

He had to pick up his anniversary gift for Elisabeth at the jewelry store at the far end of Elm Street, and that was too far to walk. Five minutes later he left the store with a small package in his hand and got back into his car. Somehow the presence and feel of the package made him feel cheerful, as if it might have the power to reverse the downhill trend of his marriage. Elisabeth, who made large-scale sculptures in bronze and stainless steel, and occasionally sold one, was not an easy person to get along with.

Aside from a number of short-lived relationships before he was married, Simeon hadn't had very much experience with women, and when Elisabeth appeared in his life, her cool beauty and elegance had carried him away. To think he'd got married because he wanted a family . . . Simeon shook his head. When he had raised the topic some weeks after their wedding, Elisabeth was quietly emphatic. She wasn't interested, she said, not at the moment anyway. Maybe in a few years—maybe—but right now she was too busy with her sculpting to start a family. No, not even one, she said sweetly but firmly. Not now. Please, dear, let's talk about something else.

Simeon decided to go home and either have a sandwich with Elisabeth or take her out for a quick lunch, and in a few minutes he was on his way, leaving the clogging traffic behind as he turned onto the I-95 connector. They lived in a modern two-level home in Harbrook, about ten minutes away from New Coventry, on an inlet of the sound. Simeon turned off the highway, down a tree-lined street, just as a new gray Lexus with gold trim came around the corner. He saw it just long enough to recognize it as Nick Barry's, and his lips tightened. Nick, who had been an accountant before he branched out into big construction projects and got rich, lived with his wife, Sandra, on the other side of town. What a coincidence, he thought grimly. Maybe he has clients on my street ... Yeah, sure. He'd had his suspicions about Nick and Elisabeth for some time, although she coolly denied any involvement with him. They had first met Nick and Sandra at some fund-raising party, and Elisabeth had followed up. They went out to dinner a few times, then the four of them went on a brief skiing vacation together, and that was when Simeon's suspicions first started, though the evidence was very tenuous. After that, Elisabeth had insisted on continuing to see the Barrys, although he was not enthusiastic. "They're both wonderful people," she said, "and you enjoy them as much as I do."

"I doubt it," he'd replied, although he had to admit that the Barrys were good company. Both of them. Nick had worked as a purser on a cruise line for a couple of years and had a limitless fund of risqué stories. Simeon thought Elisabeth would not like Nick's tales of shipboard intrigue, but she did. And Sandra Barry, who wrote most of the art criticism for the *Register,* was a very attractive, sensuous blonde, with a spectacular figure and a way of walking that turned heads everywhere. Simeon liked her, because she had a tough, no-nonsense kind of humor, but that was all. His sights were fixed on Elisabeth; he had no interest in straying elsewhere.

Simeon turned the car into the short semicircular driveway in front of his house, stopped, and sat there for a moment, trying to decide what to say to Elisabeth. He didn't want to get into an argument, but on the other hand he had a right to know what was going on. Of course, Nick might have just been dropping off something; in fact, the last time they'd gone out he'd promised to send them a brochure about Martinique.

He went around to the back, to the long teak deck that ran the length of the house, past the closed french doors of the master bedroom. To his right, the property dropped off sharply down to the water, which lapped quietly on the thinly sanded beach twenty yards away. His neighbor, Ian Wylie, was out on his pier, working on the motor of his dinghy. Simeon walked along the deck toward the rear entrance, which was ajar. At that moment, Elisabeth came out, dressed in a white terry-cloth Cunard robe, and stopped dead with surprise when she saw him. Elisabeth was tall, willowy, beautiful, with straight, almost black hair that came down in a glossy mass over her shoulders, a fine figure and a determined, rather stern expression. Some people thought her eyes were cold; they were very pale blue with large black pupils. Now they looked startled.

"You're back early," she said.

"I thought we might have lunch together," he said, watching her, thinking how beautiful she looked, and feeling saddened to the bottom of his heart. "Either here or down at Giulio's."

"I can fix us a sandwich, if you like," she said. There was something in her voice, a little tremor that betrayed her nervousness.

"Great." Simeon could feel the gulf between them widen as they stood there. They had been married after a brief romance, but things had deteriorated quickly. What he had taken as a charming nonchalance soon became a coolness. Simeon was a very intense, passionate, focused man, but he was never quite able to get an emotional handle on Elisabeth. She was like a wraith; he put out his hand and somehow it seemed to go right through her without ever touching. And each time that put him off balance. Then she would reappear, tantalizing, elusive.

He stepped forward awkwardly and was about to give her a hug, or a little kiss, something, but without seeming to reject him, she slipped past him and went inside. Sometimes, but not always, she seemed to have an uncanny ability to avoid his physical presence. Over her shoulder she said, "If you'd called ahead, Simeon, I could have had something ready when you came."

Lunch was not a relaxed event. Elisabeth was always very precise about everything, and today there was an extra, uncompromising exactitude about the way she placed the napkins and silverware, to the point that Simeon hesitated to pick them up, as if they were sterile surgical instruments on a tray. Although she tried not to show it, it was clear that Elisabeth was seriously put out by his unaccustomed and unexpected appearance. She was an expert cook and had the ability to drum up an appetizing meal from whatever happened to be in the refrigerator. Within moments she put together a shrimp and egg mayonnaise, with tomatoes and parsley and raw onion rings and capers, served very elegantly on a lettuce leaf. Simeon would rather have had a piece of plain bread served with a little love, but there it was. As soon as the meal was over, he stood up, remembering that he had left the box with the sapphire bracelet in the car. He thought for a second, looked at Elisabeth's unyielding face, and decided not to give it to her now.

Simeon got ready to return to the hospital, but he couldn't stop himself from asking her the question that had been occupying his mind since he came in. "Did Nick come by today?" he asked casually. "I passed a car that looked like his on my way here."

Elisabeth turned to hide the sudden color that came into her face. She busied herself at the sink so she could keep her back to him. "No," she said, "he didn't come here. Why? Were you expecting him?"

"No," replied Simeon, his heart sinking, the rumblings of serious anger beginning to form. "But the last time we went out to dinner, he said he was going to drop off some brochures about Martinique or Guadeloupe, I forget which."

He was leaving it open for her to say, "Oh, yes, I forgot, he did stop by for a second. I put the brochures on your desk." But Elisabeth did no such thing, and Simeon's cold rage gathered momentum. One of the things he'd thought he knew for sure about her was that she was a straight shooter, and this obvious lie rocked the whole basis of his belief in her.

"I'm taking you out to dinner tonight," he said. "You may recall that it's our anniversary." He wasn't quite able to hide the coldness in his voice, and she turned her head to look at him for a long moment before replying.

"That'll be nice," she said, matching his tone.

"We can leave as soon as I get back from the hospital," he said. "About seven."

"I'll be ready," she said.

Simeon left, feeling her eyes watching him all the way to the car.

Chapter 4

Simeon always liked to see his new patients first, and when he passed the open door to the waiting room, he got a quick glimpse of a teenage boy sitting next to a rather striking red-haired woman who he assumed was the boy's mother. Vaguely he remembered that Dr. Bennett had mentioned a boy he'd seen in the E.R. who had complained of a brief episode of blindness. He figured this was the boy in question. Maria, the clinic secretary, was at her desk. "You have twelve patients this afternoon, Dr. Halstead," she said. "Three new ones." She stared at him for a moment. "Are you feeling all right?" Maria had worked at the medical center for many years and took a grandmotherly interest in her doctors.

"I'm fine, Maria, thank you." He smiled. "Do we have referral letters on the new patients?"

"Not the first one. His name's Andy Markle. There's just a note here from Dr. Bennett with a copy of the E.R. sheet and the X-rays. He says he discussed the boy with you yesterday."

"Doesn't he have an internist or a family doctor?" Simeon sounded annoyed. He was doing his best to keep his mind on his work, but his anxieties about Elisabeth kept surfacing, and the solid ground of his life seemed to be crumbling under his feet.

Maria shook her head, still watching him. "No, Dr. Halstead; at least there isn't one listed here. Sorry."

"Okay, then," said Simeon, glancing through the chart. "Ask Susan to take the boy into the exam room."

Fiona let Andy go ahead of her as the nurse held the door of the examining room open. Inside, it was austere, all white, with a table with a long strip of paper covering the sheet and pillow. A green curtain separated the table from the rest of the room, which contained two chairs, a standard floor lamp with a flexible neck, a small desk, and a metal table with a shiny steel tray on which rested an ophthalmoscope, a reflex hammer, and some other instruments that Fiona didn't recognize.

"Have a seat," said the nurse. "The doctor will be with you in a minute." She smiled and closed the door. Fiona could feel her heart pounding and constricting at the same time. All her anxieties about Andy came back.

The door opened, but it was only the nurse bringing in another chair. Fiona felt restless and wanted to walk around, but she forced herself to sit quietly next to Andy, who was staring curiously at the tray with the ophthalmoscope.

"Don't touch it," she said, observing his look, although he hadn't made any move to pick it up.

Andy stared at her. "I didn't . . ."

"I know." Fiona felt unaccountably close to tears, and kissed him quickly on the cheek. "I'm sorry." She felt that if the doctor didn't come in very soon she would explode.

When he did come in, it was like a chilly wind blowing through the door. His white coat was as immaculate as when she'd first seen him down in the emergency room, but there was a cold, almost frightening look on his face that hadn't been there then, even in the brief glimpse that she'd had of him.

"Hi," he said to Fiona. "I'm Dr. Halstead." He didn't even look at Andy, and Fiona was about to tell him that Andy was the patient when he said to her, "Please tell me what happened to him, from the beginning."

Fiona glanced at Andy. She wanted to go along with the doctor as much as possible, although her instincts as a teacher told her he should ask Andy first.

He read her mind. "I'll get to him in a minute," he said, watching her. He didn't crack a smile, and Fiona, who rarely felt a lack of confidence in herself, felt suddenly intimidated by this man.

"Andy was playing in his junior varsity game yesterday," she said, "and on the way home he had a sudden attack of blindness that lasted, oh, less than a minute." She glanced again at Andy, who, his eyes fixed on his mother, nodded. "And he hasn't been playing well for the last couple of weeks."

Dr. Halstead made a notation. "Both eyes?"

Fiona remembered Andy's wide-eyed, blind stare in the car, and, repressing a shiver, said, "Yes, I think so."

"Any previous similar episodes?"

"He never mentioned it if there were."

Andy was about to say something, but without even looking at him Dr. Halstead shook his head slightly, indicating that he didn't want to hear from him, not yet anyway. Andy glanced at his mother; he could feel the tension rising.

"How come the boy's father isn't here?" Simeon asked suddenly, after several more questions.

"He's a commercial pilot, and he's away a lot," replied Fiona, not wishing to answer any more directly. "And anyway," she added, "we're divorced, and I have custody of Andy."

Simeon nodded and made a notation. His lips tightened almost imperceptibly as he wrote, and she wondered if he had some religious opposition to divorce.

She clasped her hands together to keep them from tapping on her knee and wondered when he was going to start diagnosing Andy. She looked at the clock; maybe he charged by the minute. That would explain everything.

Without looking at her, Simeon said, "Mrs. Markle, thank you for your patience. I'm sure you're wondering why I was asking you these questions, which you probably thought would be better answered by Andy."

This guy speaks like a recording, thought Fiona. As if he practices everything he says in front of a mirror.

"That had crossed my mind," she said, turning slightly to wink surreptitiously at Andy, who, quick as a flash, winked back without any change of expression. It pleased her, that little confirmation of their unity.

"Temporary blindness in children this age is uncommon," he said, sitting back and looking somewhere over Fiona's head. "It may be hysterical . . ." He raised his hand palm outward when Fiona opened her mouth for an indignant reply. ". . . and when it is, the family, parents in particular, usually have a lot to do with it. Hysterical parents often have hysterical children." He lowered his eyes and looked, for the first time, it seemed to Fiona, directly at her. "You don't strike me as being particularly hysterical."

"Thanks," replied Fiona, matching his gaze. "Now that we've established that, can we get on with finding out what's the matter with Andy?"

"That's what we've been doing," replied Simeon calmly. "Now I need to know something about your family history. Have you any relatives that you know of who suffer from inherited neurological or other diseases?"

Fiona thought for a moment about her mall-crazy Aunt Helen, but as far as she knew Helen's mental problems were limited to occasional shoplifting. Her mind passed to Victor. She'd read somewhere that alcoholism was sometimes an inherited trait . . .

"No," she said.

Simeon turned to Andy and spent the next five minutes asking when he'd first noticed problems with his eyesight, whether he'd had headaches, attacks of dizziness, numbness, inability to move his arms or legs—a host of questions that made Andy feel dizzy just trying to answer them, because Dr. Halstead used a lot of terminology that he didn't understand.

Dr. Halstead must have pressed a button on the desk, because a nurse, the same one who had shown them in, appeared. She helped Andy take off his clothes, to his embarrassment, and put them neatly on the chair while Dr. Halstead wrote on the chart.

Fiona was surprised that he didn't dictate his notes or put them straight into a computer. Maybe he was just old-fashioned. Watching him, she wondered if he had some other heavy problems of his own to deal with; she noted the fixed expression on his face and the obsessive but impersonal way he was concentrating on Andy's case.

As long as he found out what was the matter with Andy, she thought, she didn't care if he had problems, was obsessive, or rode to work on a monocycle.

"We're ready, Dr. Halstead." The nurse's voice was quiet and very respectful, not the kind of tone that could be faked. Dr. Halstead had evidently earned that respect, and Fiona wondered how. Was it some extraordinary operation that he'd performed? Had he taken care of her, or a relative of hers?

Dr. Halstead uncoiled his long, spare frame, stood up, and went over to the examining table. Andy was sitting on the edge, wearing only his skimpy shorts, his shoulders hunched protectively forward. When Andy felt unsure of himself or was in a strange environment, he became silent, and now his face was watchful but otherwise quite expressionless. Fiona watched as Dr. Halstead started to examine him.

"I'm going to start by testing your cranial nerves," he said to Andy in a toneless, impersonal voice. Andy had no idea what the doctor meant, and he glanced at his mother, wondering if this was going to hurt.

Simeon opened a test tube with some fluid in it and asked Andy if he could smell what was inside. Andy sniffed, wrinkled up his nose, and said, "It smells rotten."

Dr. Halstead nodded. "It's a substance called asafoetida," he said. "Now smell this . . ."

After that, he checked Andy's eye muscles. As he said, "Look up, now down, now to your left . . ." Andy noticed something about this doctor, a different quality, something different from his father, different from Mr. Brennan, his coach, or the principal, Mr. Seidel. For one thing, he thought, although this Dr. Halstead never seemed to smile and his face didn't look as if it *could* smile, there was something real about him, like a person you could totally rely on. Unlike his dad. Feeling disloyal that he'd even thought that, Andy concentrated on what the doctor was saying to him. At least he wasn't trying to be friendly and win him over, and Andy liked him for that.

Twenty minutes later, after Simeon had examined Andy's retinas through the ophthalmoscope, tapped out his reflexes with the triangular red rubber hammer, checked his sensory perception with a sable-hair brush and a little pointed instrument, and made him stand on one foot, then the other, with his eyes closed, he finally finished his examination and nodded in a preoccupied way at Andy before going back behind the desk. The nurse stood by while Andy dressed, and Fiona felt her heart pounding. She searched Dr. Halstead's eyes for a clue to what he was going to tell her.

"Mrs. Markle," he said finally, holding on to the reflex hammer with both hands, "I was not able to find any sign of any neurological or neuromuscular lesion at this examination, but before we can consider him completely clear we'll need to do a series of investigative tests that will include ..."

"Dr. Halstead, can you tell me why he went blind like that?" Fiona interrupted in spite of herself. She was so uptight that she couldn't bear to hear any more of this medical jargon. She had to know *now* if Andy was suffering from some kind of illness, what the outlook was, and what could be done about it. "What caused it? Can you tell me?"

For a moment Simeon stared at her. He was obviously not accustomed to being interrupted. "As I was saying," he went on in the same tone, which made Fiona feel like a naughty schoolgirl, "before we can tell definitively what the cause of his blindness is, we need to do a series of tests that will include a CAT scan, PET scan ..."

"What's that?" Fiona felt she was taking her life in her hands by interrupting again. She reached into the canvas holdall at her feet and took out a pen and a notebook. She needed more than a vague, half-remembered mush of medical terms to take away with her.

Simeon sighed, looked at the wall clock. "I'd really like for you to have an LMD for Andy," he said. "It's difficult to ..."

"What's an LMD?" asked Fiona. "I'm sorry, but I'm a teacher, not a doctor, and I don't understand your acronyms and terminology."

Simeon's eyebrows went up fractionally, and in spite of her tension, she wondered if he practiced doing that in front of a mirror. "An LMD," he said, "is a Local Medical Doctor, usually a general practitioner or family doctor. I would like you to have one because he could explain much of this to you, and no doubt in simpler terms. My usual practice is to write an explanatory letter to the referring LMD, who then passes the information on to the patient."

"Well, I don't have one," she said, thinking she might ask Sam Seidel, Marty's brother, to be Andy's doctor. Sam was a general practitioner in New Conventry who did some pediatrics. "Our pediatrician left town about six weeks ago. You were going to tell me what a PET scan is."

Simeon smiled, barely. " 'PET' stands for Positron Emission Tomography," he said.

Fiona stared at him, her gray eyes beginning to turn green. She shook a red curl out of her eye, and her lips compressed into a straight line. "Dr. Halstead," she said, trying to keep her voice calm, "my son Andy has something the matter with his vision, and I'm really scared that it could be something serious. All I'm asking you is to tell me what the problem is and what we need to do about it."

Simeon looked blankly at her, then, as if he'd been caught thinking about something entirely different, he blinked. "Yes, of course." He seemed to be making a big effort to return to this planet. "I'm sorry," he said, genuinely upset to see the suppressed anger in Fiona's expression. "I was ... Okay. I don't know what caused Andy's blindness, or even if there is an organic cause for it. It could be caused by stress, something like that, but I doubt it. Right now I don't know, and I don't think it would be useful to guess. As I said, we need more tests." He scribbled something on several forms and passed them over to Fiona. "These are for a series of blood tests and X-rays and other imaging techniques to see inside the skull and brain. Please call the number at the top of the forms to make the appointments for Andy," he said. "I'll send the requisitions over to the lab and radiology departments."

The nurse opened the door.

"And, please," said Simeon to Fiona, "remember to get a family doctor." He smiled, a tight but real smile, and Fiona wondered whether maybe the guy had occasional moments of being human.

At the door, Fiona remembered a young woman, a former pupil of hers, who had died just over a year ago. She turned and said to Dr. Halstead, quietly, so that Andy wouldn't hear, "Could it be a brain tumor?"

He looked at her thoughtfully for a moment. "Mrs. Markle," he said, "I'm sorry to have to repeat this, but until I can make a precise diagnosis, I'm not going to make any guesses."

Chapter 5

Andy walked with his mother through the hospital corridor toward the main entrance. It wasn't noisy, but both of them felt they couldn't talk until they were outside. And because of the lump in her throat, Fiona knew that she couldn't say anything to Andy or even look at him until she collected herself a little better. A brain tumor. She was certain that Dr. Halstead thought Andy had one, although of course he wouldn't admit it was anything more than a possibility until he had proof.

When they got home, the phone was ringing. It was Marty Seidel, who wanted to know how the consultation had gone.

Fiona told him, then asked, "Is your brother Sam taking on new patients?"

"I don't think so," replied Marty. "Why?"

Fiona told him what Simeon Halstead had said. "I guess Dr. Halstead doesn't like to deal with patients directly," she went on. "He needs somebody to translate his medical jargon for us poor earthbound creatures."

"Sam'll take care of it," said Marty. "I'll give him a call. He'll take Andy on, I can guarantee it. No problem." He held the phone tight. Fiona's voice, with its lilting overtones, a legacy from her Scottish mother, always did something to him, but now, when she was in trouble, it brought out his protective instincts like nothing else could.

"Are you sure?" Fiona didn't like to be indebted to anyone. "I don't want to ..."

"No problem," repeated Marty, already thumbing through his Rolodex for his brother's office number. "Stay right there, and I'll get back to you in a couple minutes."

He pushed the disconnect button on his phone and, as

soon as he got the dial tone, tapped out Sam's number. Sam was with a patient, but Marty, knowing better than to ask him to call back, told the nurse he'd hold. For a minute he listened to the recorded medicine ads and shook his head. Sam was surely the most commercially minded person he'd ever met, but he was generally considered a pretty good doctor, or he certainly wouldn't have recommended him to Fiona. Fiona, Fiona, Fiona.

Outside his office, the school bell rang and the walls shook as the kids erupted out of their classrooms to yell and fight and push in the corridors until the next class started. Marty liked to leave his desk and walk down the corridors between classes, partly because it was a good thing to be seen there, but mainly in the hope that he would meet Fiona going on break or heading for the library. He loved to watch her walk, with that free-spirited, long-limbed stride and that wonderful head of curly red hair, threading her way through the crowds of kids. He would hear the greetings as she marched along. "Hi, Mrs. Markle, love that skirt" or "Can I come to see you after class?" And she'd smile and say something back, something that might cause a yell of laughter, but the kids knew not to stand directly in front of her because Fiona Markle was always in a hurry and didn't slow down for anybody.

Not even for Marty. So many times he would turn to talk to her, but she would just grin that open, slightly preoccupied grin and walk on without a pause. When he was walking the same direction, he'd find himself walking fast to keep up with her, and somehow that didn't seem dignified for a principal, as other people would certainly notice, because normally he walked at his own pace whoever he was with.

"Yeah?" Sam's voice was brisk; Marty always had a vision of his brother watching a clock with the seconds marked out in dollar signs. "What's up, Marty?"

Marty told him.

"They got insurance?"

"Mrs. Markle has the standard school health plan policy. Same as mine. It covers just about everything."

"You have a copy?"

"Of the policy? I'm sure I could find one."

"Fax it to me. I got burned on those before. If it checks out, sure, I'll be happy to see her kid."

"Great. Sam, take specially good care of this boy, okay?"

There was a brief silence. Very brief, because time was money.

"He one of the kids in your school?"

"Yes, he is. His mother's a teacher here on my staff, and she's . . ."

"Yeah. So it's the mother, huh?"

Marty felt his ears go red. "Sam, thanks for doing this. I appreciate it."

"Yeah, right. Anyway, you should make a few points with her for this. Okay, I have to go. Give us a call this weekend. No, why don't you and Doreen come over for brunch on Sunday, okay? And if Doreen can't make it, come by yourself." He grinned. "Or bring Mrs. Markle."

Sam put down the phone. Gloria Mandelbaum, his secretary, a middle-aged, efficient woman with black hair and a bouffant hairdo, came in with a stack of folders in her hand.

"Vitamin B-12 time," she said. "You have seven."

"That's all?" he asked. He sighed and rubbed the side of his nose. It was large and pore-covered, with little purple veins running around the bulb. Far from being sensitive about it, Sam would even make jokes. "When there's a power failure," he'd say in his gravelly voice, "there's no problem with lighting at *my* house."

"Okay, Gloria, I'll be right through. Listen, a Mrs. Markle's going to call for an appointment for her kid. Get her in this week sometime, okay? Fifteen minutes, first visit. There should be a fax coming through from Marty about her insurance. Make sure I see it before I see the kid."

Vitamin B-12 shots were something Sam liked to administer himself, although he was perfectly aware that they did his patients no more good than a sugar-pill placebo. And it wasn't because he particularly enjoyed the sight of flabby naked white butts quivering in fearful anticipation. The patients preferred to have the doctor do it; it gave the treatment an authenticity that a nurse, however competent, could never bestow.

Business wasn't getting any easier, though. He was seeing

fewer kids, and even his adult practice was down. In the old days, he'd have dozens of people, mostly women, coming in every week for their shots of B-12 and various other vitamins, allergy medication, antibiotics to ward off infection—you name it. Maybe these women were now reading warnings about such useless treatments in their women's journals, or maybe they'd gotten smarter, but for whatever reason, that side of Sam's operation was down. Herbal medications were getting more popular, though, and Sam was investigating that, although the profit margins were much lower. As he was fond of saying to Gloria, if you wanna stay in business, you gotta move with the times.

On the way to the treatment area, he passed the waiting room and caught a glimpse of a well-dressed, middle-aged woman with straggly blond hair, holding a large, multicolored purse. The parts of her that Sam could see, her face and hands, were a puffy, yellowish bronze color, as if she'd overdosed in a suntan parlor, and her ankles seemed thick and puffy.

"Who's that woman in there? The yellow one?" Sam asked Gloria, who was walking ahead of him with the charts.

"Mrs. Locarno. She says she's itching like a son of a gun and wants something to fix it."

"Jesus. Carla Locarno? Are you sure? I wouldn't have recognized her."

For the next twenty minutes, Sam gave his injections. He was always jovial with his patients, a bit crude or roughshod sometimes, but he remembered their names, and they liked his loud, almost raucous laughter. It took the edge off the rather scary business of being in a doctor's office, and it showed them that he was human too, with a good sense of humor, not like some of the more scientific doctors one heard about.

The last one for the B-12 shot was Thelma Walters, a woman in her sixties, carefully dressed in a dark blue suit and a silk blouse. She had immaculately coiffed white hair, and was lying on her stomach, her skirt pulled up and her pale buttocks exposed. She turned her head and peered as Sam and Gloria approached. She didn't seem to recognize

Sam until he was a couple of feet away, then she smiled rather primly at him.

"I thought the B-12 would have prevented this cold sore," said Thelma, pointing at her upper lip, which indeed had a substantial herpes simplex lesion.

Sam pursed his meaty lips and grinned at her. "Thelma," he said in his loud, master-of-every-situation voice, "don't tell me. I know exactly how you got that sore."

Thelma's penciled eyebrows went up, and Sam leaned down to whisper something in her ear. She went bright red. "Oh, my!" she said. "Certainly not! Oh, you're just terrible, Dr. Sam." She peered over at Gloria, who knew what he'd said and was grinning from ear to ear, and Thelma gathered confidence from her presence. "In any case, Doctor, I don't even *know* any black men, let alone do anything like that with them. For heaven's sake!" She giggled and put her head down on the pillow.

"Well, you can always hope, Thelma," said Sam jocularly as he rubbed the skin of her bottom with an alcohol sponge. "Anyway, the B-12 takes a while to act, you know."

"I've been taking it for seven months now," said Thelma, her voice muffled in the pillow. "Ouch!"

"Okay, that's it," said Sam briskly, putting the empty syringe back on the tray with the others. "See you next week." He paused. "The B-12 *is* making you feel better, right?"

"Oh, yes," said Thelma, sitting up and rubbing her sore buttock. "It seems to be making my skin softer, too, didn't you think?"

"Nah," said Sam, watching her. "They're making the needles sharper." Then he asked, "Thelma, how's your vision?"

"Not too good, Dr. Sam," she said. "You know I have cataracts."

Sam nodded. "A lot of times Vitamin A shots'll help that," he said. He had spoken this lie so often he almost believed it himself. "You know, it's the stuff in carrots that improves your vision."

"Then why don't I just eat carrots?" asked Thelma pertly.

"Don't you get smart with me, Thelma Walters," replied

Sam. "You want to eat forty raw carrots a day? Okay, go right ahead, do it. Then you'll look in the toilet bowl and think you're bleeding to death!" Sam's grin showed his large teeth, brownish yellow around the edges.

Thelma sighed and pulled down her skirt. "Okay, when do I start?"

"Next week," replied Sam. "Gloria, make a note. Let's see ..." Sam stared at Thelma and put his hand under his chin as if he were making some complicated mental calculation. "Let's start her off with fifty milligrams," he said, "and work up from there."

Ten minutes later, Sam was looking over the sketchy medical file of his next patient, Mrs. Carla Demarest Locarno. Carla, reputed to be very wealthy, was interested in alternative medicine, read various herbal and health magazines, and had been enthusiastically taking Sam's vitamin injections for several months, requesting even more than he recommended. "If a little bit's good for you," she told him in her husky voice, "more has to be better, right, Doc?"

"So, how's it goin', Carla?" Sam's eyes didn't miss much, and he was feeling a little apprehensive about her puffy, unhealthy, yellow appearance. "Been vacationing in the sun, huh?"

Carla's eyes seemed glazed, and her response was slow. "No," she said, pushing back a lock of straggly blond hair. "I ain't been in the sun or anywhere else. I'm so tired I could hardly get out of bed to come here."

"Need a tonic, from the looks of you," he said, almost reflexively, but he was taking in the way Carla was sitting back in the chair with her stomach bulging, quite unlike her usual trim self. And that color on her skin ...

"Have you been taking any more medicines?" he asked, pointing a spatulate finger at her. "I mean, aside from the ones I've been giving you?"

"Just a few additional vitamins and minerals," she said. "I've been feeling rotten—headachy, swollen up, even vomiting once in a while—so I thought I needed some more to pick me up a bit." Carla paused to catch her breath and moved uncomfortably on her chair. "There was an article in *Natural Health* about megadoses of lysine, so I thought why not try it. And I've been run-down, and anyway after menopause you need more of everything, right?"

"Like what? What have you been taking?"

"All the fat-solubles, A, D, E, and K, plus calcium and phosphorus, iron, thiamine, and some niacin . . . I can't remember. Except it takes me ten minutes every morning just getting all those darn pills and capsules down."

"How much are you taking? Do you have the bottles with you?"

"No. But I wrote their names down . . ." Carla turned and rummaged in the leather purse beside her, pulling out a crumpled sheet of paper, which she handed to Sam.

"You're taking all this?" he asked after scanning the list. "On top of what you're getting here? Jesus Christ, woman, you're lucky to be still alive!" He paused for a minute. "Listen, Carla, you need to go away someplace to get all that stuff leached out of your system. Lying around here in town isn't going to do you any good."

"I know, but I don't feel well enough to go anyplace," replied Carla. "All I want to do is sleep." And in fact Carla didn't look as if she could make her way unaided to the nearest health food shop, only a block away.

Sam gazed thoughtfully at her, as if he were trying to figure out the very best way of dealing with her uniquely complicated problems. "There's a great clinic near Puerto Vallarta in Mexico that's in business to take care of patients like you," he said finally. "It's a beautiful place, full of tropical flowers, a really modern medical facility with all the staff and equipment you could wish for, a private beach, masseurs, all that kind of stuff."

Sam paused to see if Carla was showing any interest, but it was hard to tell. "The medical director's a man by the name of Antonio Vargas," he went on. "You'll love him . . . Look, Carla, we'll take care of the arrangements. I have a travel agent who'll give you a real sweet deal. You'll be traveling first class, right?"

Carla nodded.

"Okay then, I'll give Dr. Vargas a call this evening. I just hope he has a bed available. There's always a long waiting list of people who want to get into that place. I'm sure you've heard of it—the Maya Clinic."

Carla frowned, her eyes dull. "I've heard the name, sure. I know it's famous, but I always thought it was somewhere here in the States. I didn't realize . . ."

"Yeah, right," said Sam without blinking. "It's pretty famous. I knew you'd heard of it."

"When do you wan' me to go?" she asked, after taking a few moments to make up her mind.

"As soon as possible. How about Wednesday? That'll give you a day to straighten stuff out, pay your bills, that kind of thing, okay? And we'll order a limo to take you to the airport." Sam looked at Gloria, who nodded and made a note. This wasn't the first time she'd made this kind of arrangement.

Carla agreed and was about to get up when Gloria said, "We'll need some blood tests before you go, Mrs. Locarno. Now just roll up your sleeve for me. Here, I'll help you . . ."

Later, after all the patients had gone, Gloria locked the front door. This was the time Sam liked to make his phone calls.

"You wanna call Puerto Vallarta, Sam?" she asked, when he was back sitting at his desk.

He nodded, and she reached over him, picked up the phone, and dialed a long number. Sam glanced at the clock; calls to Mexico were very expensive, even at this time of day. As usual, he figured how long he wanted the call to be and how much it would cost, although there were other factors to take into consideration. Gloria was still leaning over him, and he idly slipped his hand under her skirt and up between her thighs.

"Dr. Vargas on the line, sir," she said with a big grin, and Sam took the phone, simultaneously swinging his chair around until it was at right angles to the desk.

"Buenos tardes, amigo," he started. "¿Como está usted? ¿Bien? Bueno, bueno!" Having exhausted his vocabulary in Spanish, Sam turned to English. "Listen, Antonio, I've got a woman I'm sending down to you on Wednesday for detoxification. She's an overdose, mostly Vitamin A, but probably other stuff too. You got a bed?"

Gloria had gone down on her knees in front of him and was undoing his zipper.

"Of course." Vargas had done a year's internship in New

York, where the two of them had met, and his command of English at least equaled Sam's. "Yes, Sam, unfortunately we do have plenty of beds. I'll be happy to accept her. I assume that her insurance coverage is satisfactory?"

Gloria was having a little problem with access, so he used his free hand to undo his belt.

"Don't worry about that," he said to Antonio, grinning at Gloria. "Her name is Carla Locarno, and she has enough money to buy the entire clinic plus you and me." Sam grinned. "And she writes checks. No American Express or Visa cards."

Gloria now had everything the way she wanted it, and Sam slid forward in his chair. This was all very relaxing, and it didn't distract him at all from his conversation.

"Good. Sam, I'm very glad you called, because we have a real problem here at the clinic, and as you're part owner you should know about it. We're in trouble. We barely have enough patients to keep the place open. You have to send us more patients."

Gloria was getting into her stride now, and a pleasantly warm feeling spread over Sam's entire body.

"I'm doing my best, Antonio."

"Sam, another problem is that we're getting too many terminal patients. On average, they don't live more than about three weeks, and that has a major financial impact on our operation. You know how hard it is getting the U.S. insurance companies to pay up, and there's a lot of paperwork and telephone work just getting things set up with every new patient that comes in. And then there's the problem with transportation of the bodies back home ... Sam, if your average stay could be, say, three months, it would make a huge difference to us. I could get rid of half my office staff."

Gloria's face was flushed, and her rhythm was accelerating, so he put a warning hand on the top of her head. He didn't want to come in the middle of this conversation.

"If they lived any longer, you wouldn't have the excuse that they were already terminal," he said. "But seriously, Antonio, I'm working on it. I've talked to most of the docs around town and offered them a kickback for every patient they refer, but most of them already have deals going. I

have a couple of patients you should be getting soon, an
old guy with a rectal carcinoma and a young woman with
some kind of neuromuscular disease. Her family's taken
her everywhere—Lourdes, you name it."

"That's exactly what I'm saying, Sam. We need to get
these patients first, rather than last ... Anyway, tell me
that woman's name again, Carla. . . ?"

"Locarno. I'll put her medical history, X-ray and lab test
results in an envelope and she can bring it with her. No
point wasting money on the mails. We're getting her a
ticket to fly out of here the day after tomorrow, before she
changes her mind."

Sam said good-bye, hung up, and turned his undivided
attention to Gloria.

Chapter 6

The next morning, while Andy gulped down a hurried breakfast before going off to school, Fiona said, "How would you like to take the canoe out this afternoon after school? We could go up to Mystic and see the Seaport from the water."

"Great," said Andy. His voice was indistinct because he was stuffing great mouthfuls of dry Cocoa Puffs into his mouth and washing them down with a glass of milk. "Don't you have a staff meeting or something today?"

"I'm going to skip it," said Fiona firmly. Andy stared at her. His mother was the most conscientious person he'd ever met, and he was sure this must be the first meeting that she had deliberately planned to miss. Ever.

Fiona heard a faint rumble from outside. "That's your bus," she said.

"I don't know how you can hear it," said Andy. "Anyway, I'm going on my blades."

"I hear the bus because I don't deafen myself every day with rock music," replied Fiona.

"I'll race you to school," suggested Andy. On his rollerblades, Andy could usually travel the mile and a half in about as long as it took Fiona to drive it. But Andy didn't slow down for traffic lights or pedestrians or anything else.

"No, Andy. You know that's dangerous."

"Why don't *you* get a pair of blades?" He grinned, put his head back, and shook the almost empty carton into his mouth. "Mr. Seidel would love it. You could start a craze . . . Can you imagine Miss Hepplewhite or old Mr. Mullins zooming along to school through the traffic?" Andy made a weaving motion with his hands and a noise that was supposed to sound like a race car.

"Yeah, right. It's a great image. Now drink your juice before you go. I'm leaving." Fiona turned to the sideboard and picked up her big L. L. Bean canvas bag by its leather straps. It was bulging with corrected papers, books, magazines, computer printouts, pens and pencils, and various odds and ends, like rubber bands and adhesive tape, that were occasionally useful in the course of her daily work.

She came around the table, kissed Andy on the forehead, then opened the door to the garage. Her gray Escort was squeezed in between the lawnmower and a pile of boxes of stuff that belonged to Victor. He kept promising to pick them up, but they were still there.

She had barely backed out of the garage when she noticed that the steering felt strange, and the car was pulling to one side. She got out and found the left front tire flat. Andy, coming out of the house, walked over. He didn't waste a second; he set the handbrake, took the spindly little jack out of the trunk, and slid it under the front axle. "Here, Mom," he said, "wind it up until the tire's off the ground. Oops. Wait a minute . . ." He took the big wrench and loosened the wheel bolts. "You have to do that first or the wheel just spins around."

Fiona felt very proud of Andy, and watched his muscles as he worked. He was strong for his age, and there was a litheness, an agility, about his movements that marked him out as a natural athlete. He took the spare out of the trunk, bounced it so hard it came up and almost hit him on the chin, and grinned self-confidently at his mother as he rolled it out. This was man's work that he was doing. In seconds the flat was off, the spare was on, and he leaned into the long wrench to make the bolts secure while Fiona picked up the flat and dropped it in the trunk.

"Let's go wash our hands," she said and followed him back into the house. Andy was feeling very macho, and it showed in the way he moved. Strange, thought Fiona. There's something about automobiles that really affects men. And here was Andy, almost a man, although he was only fourteen. Watching him, she remembered him as a toddler, holding her hand with a grasp of iron and putting his legs up without being told when she changed his diapers . . .

"What are you thinking about, Mom?"

"You don't want to know. Thanks for changing the tire. Now get going or you'll be late and you'll say it was my fault."

"Remember to take the flat to Charlie's," said Andy. He sat down to put on his blades.

On the way to school, she kept looking for his speeding figure ahead of her, but he was gone. That Andy—he was the light of her life, and the thought that there might be something seriously the matter with him made her feel sick. It was strange how unlike Victor he was, in both appearance and personality. Whereas Victor was heavyset, Andy was slim and muscular. Even when Victor was a teenager he hadn't looked like that—not judging by his photos anyway.

And Andy was a naturally modest kid, although he was looked up to as a hero at school because of his prowess in sports. Again, not at all like Victor. But when she had first met Victor, he had just seemed supremely self-confident, not arrogant or a loudmouth or a know-it-all. God, maybe I did that to him, she thought. Did I change him from a basically good person into a boastful drinker and a womanizer?

The lights went red in front of her, and she pulled up and looked at her watch. She was okay, she had plenty of time. Even when they were first engaged and Victor had moved into her apartment, he had other women on the side, as she found out later. He was a junior pilot at the time, so dashing he made her heart stop, but his assignments took him away a lot, and the phone kept ringing. Sometimes they hung up when they heard her voice, sometimes not.

One time a woman with a very soft voice had asked to speak to Victor, and Fiona, irritated with the repeated calls, told her in no uncertain terms that Victor was her fiancé, and that she'd better go look elsewhere. The woman had laughed, a tinkly laugh that made Fiona think she was Asian. "Good luck," said the woman and hung up. Several times in the next couple of years, the phone rang and no one spoke when she answered, and Fiona had the strong feeling that it was the same woman, just checking. After

Victor finally moved out, there were no more hangups. Well, that wasn't exactly accurate, because there was always some kid at school who had a crush on her, sometimes a boy, sometimes a girl, but although the kids were very intense and often called and hung up several times in an evening just to hear her voice, they never did it for more than a week or two.

Fifteen years ago. That was when they'd got married. Fiona couldn't imagine how she'd taken it all that time. Nor did her friends. She could laugh now, thinking about Wilma's carefully acidulous comments about him. Finally, a year ago, Fiona had enough of the lipstick on his collars, enough of his absences, enough of his sarcasm and continual put-downs. What really brought it to a head was when it started to rub off on Andy, and he began to talk to her in the same way. Then suddenly she got mad. Really mad, when she finally realized the crap she'd been taking for all those years. She was working so hard, what with taking care of Andy and her job, that maybe she just hadn't noticed how Victor was treating her.

When Fiona decided to end the marriage, she told him so, but he just laughed. "Be grateful for what you have," he said. "Anyway, who's going to give you a second look, at your age, with a fourteen-year-old kid?" Especially when he had had too much to drink, Victor had a terrifying temper; now Fiona had to figure out how to get him out of the house without any bloodshed. As it turned out, circumstances played into her hands, mostly because Victor didn't have the good sense to keep his philandering out of town.

Fiona used to work out at least a couple of times a week in a health club near the school. She had made friends with a number of the regulars, including Austin Ford, a senior detective with the New Conventry Police Department. Austin was in his late thirties, a very big guy, strong enough that people would come over just to watch him lift weights. Austin was something of a byword around town, cheerful, friendly, a man whose mere presence had stopped many a fight. Lately, however, he'd got a reputation among his friends for not being too observant.

One afternoon at the club, Austin came up to where Fiona was working on the stationary bicycle, balancing a book on Renaissance artists on the handlebars. She didn't notice him until she felt the heat of his body next to her. He was wearing a Lycra cycling suit, leather wristlets, and a weight-lifting belt, and he smelled of sweat. The black armpit hairs that she could see were matted. There was nobody else in the immediate vicinity.

"Hi, Fiona."

"You're looking good, Austin."

"Fiona," went on Austin in a conversational tone, "did you know that Victor is fucking my wife?"

Fiona stopped pedaling and put the book down. "No," she said, "but I'm not surprised."

"I'm going to teach that asshole a lesson he won't forget," said Austin, flexing his massive arms. "I don't need your help, but I thought you might enjoy participating."

"Sure, as long as Andy isn't involved," said Fiona.

"Can you send him away this weekend?"

"He won't be here. He's going to the Cape with some of his baseball buddies."

"Good. I'll let you know."

Two days later, on Saturday around noon, when Austin Ford was on duty for the weekend and the coast was clear, Victor's car pulled up round the corner from the garden apartment where Austin lived with his pretty wife, Colette. Victor and Colette had met and bonded at a party given by a mutual friend, and as Victor didn't have the kind of schedule that keeps husbands faithful, when he was in town he could drop in during the day to see her.

Victor hurried up to the door, where Colette was waiting for him, nude inside a black and red Chinese silk robe.

Ten minutes later they heard a noise at the door, and Austin unlocked the door, jolted the chain off its metal plate, and walked in. Colette screamed, and Austin advanced on Victor, roaring. Victor was big and strong, but even in his normal condition he would not have been a match for Austin. Now, in his terror, he offered no resistance. Austin smashed him hard in the face with his fist, breaking his nose and knocking out a tooth, and after venting his fury with a few more well-placed and damaging blows, he caught him by the scruff of the neck and threw him out, buck naked, down the two steps into the street.

Hurting everywhere, Victor picked himself up and looked around desperately. Home was about three miles away, so he couldn't walk. He had almost decided to go down the street and ring the nearest doorbell, hoping to find someone who would lend him enough clothes to go home in, when a police car pulled up at the curb right in front of him.

Victor knew better than to run, so he stood there, spitting blood, his hands covering his genitals, while the two cops switched on their roof lights and the siren and got out slowly. Very slowly. Local people were already stopping in the street and looking curiously at Victor. One of the cops brought out a brown-colored blanket, and Victor gratefully wrapped it around himself.

"Get in," said the driver. "In the back."

The other officer put his hand on Victor's head so he wouldn't bump it, because both his eyes were puffing up and he couldn't see too well.

"We're taking you home, Mr. Markle," said the driver once he'd pulled away from the curb. Victor noticed that the lights and the siren were still on.

"Please," he said desperately, "don't take me home. I can go to a friend's house. My wife's having people over for lunch . . ."

The police car pulled up outside Victor's house. It had started to rain, a thin, cold new England drizzle. The driver got out, opened the rear door and helped Victor out, then went with him to the door and rang the bell. Then he said, "The blanket, sir," and flicked it off him. So when Fiona opened the door, Victor was standing there naked, bloody-faced, and shivering. With the door on the latch, she coolly asked what he wanted.

"Let me in, goddamm it!" he yelled. But she didn't. The police car was still parked at the curb, so he didn't dare try to kick the door down. Fiona slammed it shut, then sat down on the floor and laughed. Victor was finally rescued by a neighbor at the end of the street, who let him in and lent him some clothes, but after that, Fiona was adamant and refused to allow him into the house. Finally Victor took a room in a hotel, and Fiona had the divorce papers and the court injunction served on him there.

Victor came back eventually to gather his belongings.

Surprisingly, after a few weeks he seemed inclined to forget his humiliation. But of course he didn't know that Austin and Fiona had carefully planned the entire episode in advance.

Fiona turned in at the school parking lot, a forbidding place with a high fence topped with barbed wire. She made her way through the throng of students and was in her classroom when the bell rang and the kids came pouring in. Once she succeeded in establishing a semblance of calm in her class, she said, "Okay, yesterday we were talking about the causes of the Renaissance, and today we're going to talk about how those changes were reflected by the artists of that time. Can any of you give me the name of a Renaissance painter?"

Chapter 7

Andy had got to school about the same time as Fiona, but he went in through a different door.

"How you doin'?" Kevin asked him. They had lockers next to each other, and Kevin had to yell above the din from the other kids. The evening before, Andy had told him on the phone about his visit to the hospital.

"Okay," replied Andy. "I guess. It was all a bit scary at the time, though."

Kevin asked, "What was it like when you couldn't see anything?"

"Weird. Like, well, it was like having a black curtain over your eyes. I thought my eyes were closed, so I put my finger up to check, and that hurt, because they were open all the time."

"Wow! Last night, after I talked to you, I tried going around with my eyes closed, like I was blind ... It's not easy. You bump into things and can't remember where things are supposed to be. Can you see okay now? Hey, I could be your guide dog ..." Kevin raised his head and let out what he thought sounded like a canine howl, and Andy punched him good-naturedly. They slammed the locker doors as hard as they could, trying as usual to knock them off their hinges, and were about to set off down the corridor with the crowd of other students to their first class when Andy stopped and sat down abruptly on the floor, his back against the wall. He put his hands up to his head.

"Go ahead," he told Kevin. "I've got a headache ... I'll be okay in a minute."

Then, to Kevin's horror, Andy's eyes rolled up, and he slid slowly sideways. The flow of traffic stopped, and a bunch of kids gathered around.

"Go to the office!" said Kevin to one of the kids. "Tell them to get Mrs. Markle!" The kid darted off, zigzagging through the crowd.

Kevin stared helplessly at Andy, not knowing what to do. Then he pulled him so he was lying on his back and put a couple of books under his head. He kept looking down the corridor for someone to come and help him.

It didn't take long. Marty Seidel came running down the corridor, followed by the school nurse, Mrs. Drummond.

Mrs. Drummond knelt down and checked Andy's pulse, looked up at Marty and nodded. It was strong and regular. At this moment Andy opened his eyes, took a few moments to refocus, and started to struggle to get up. "Don't you move," said Mrs. Drummond sternly. "We've sent for an ambulance, and it'll be here in a minute."

Fiona appeared. She knelt next to Mrs. Drummond, who stood up, recognizing that a hierarchy exists in responding to childhood emergencies, with the mother at the top.

"Are you all right?" Fiona asked Andy, trying not to show the panic she felt. Andy nodded and tried to get up again, but Fiona put a gently restraining hand on his forehead. "Just lie back, sweetheart," she said. "I don't want you to get up just yet."

"Go along to your classes now," said Marty, turning to the kids who were still standing around watching. Reluctantly they shuffled off.

Fiona turned to Kevin. "What happened?" she asked, and Kevin was starting to explain when a clattering of wheels announced the arrival of the ambulance crew, a thickset black man and a younger, tough-looking woman with short hair who looked as if she'd been squeezed into her tight brown uniform shirt and pants.

"Go with him," said Marty to Fiona, knowing that Fiona would accompany Andy whether she had his permission or not. "I'll get someone to cover your class." Marty so badly wanted to take her in his arms and hold her, comfort her, that it was like a physical pain. "I'm sure he'll be all right," he added. "I'll call Sam and tell him. You'll let me know what happens, okay?" One of Marty's strongest rules was never physically to touch any of the teachers or students, but he took Fiona's arm for a moment and gave it a gentle squeeze, trying to put all his feelings of love and tenderness into it.

Within moments, the two ambulance people lifted Andy up onto the stretcher, covered him with a red blanket, and trundled back along the corridor at what seemed to him to be a terrifying speed. Even Fiona had trouble keeping up.

The ambulance ride was a blur of noise and movement for both Andy and Fiona, and it seemed only a matter of seconds before they were at the emergency room of New Coventry Medical Center. Hands reached up to open the doors, and within moments they were inside the building.

"Booth seven!" someone shouted, and the ambulance crew pushed the stretcher along the corridor, then through the last door on the left.

Andy looked at his mother as they lifted him onto another stretcher. He was feeling all right now and didn't understand what all the fuss was about.

The ambulance driver said good-bye, the young woman in the tight uniform patted Andy briefly on the head. "You'll be all right, kid," she said.

A nurse appeared, pushing a lock of blond hair out of her eye. "What's the problem here?" she asked, looking from Andy to Fiona.

"This is my son, Andy," said Fiona. "He was at school when he ... I guess he fainted. He was here two days ago because he suddenly went blind for a minute or so."

"How're you feeling now?" asked the nurse, looking at Andy. "Can you see all right?" She held up two fingers. "How many fingers?" she asked.

"Two," replied Andy. "I'm really okay." He could tell that his voice didn't sound normal. "I can see, but I have a headache, but it's not as bad as it was ..."

"Did you fall or get hit on the head?"

"No. It just came on. I don't remember. Then I was in an ambulance."

"You get migraines? Ever?" The nurse asked several more questions, then as it became crystal clear that Andy wasn't a victim of domestic trauma or other injury, her interest seemed to wane. "The doctors are very busy," she said. "It'll be a while before they can get to you."

The nurse then asked Fiona to go to the business office to arrange for payment.

"I don't want to leave him alone," replied Fiona. "I'll go when the doctors get here."

The nurse looked doubtful. "You have insurance? That covers him too?"

"Yes. I'm a high school teacher here in town."

Reassured, the nurse left.

After waiting about five minutes, Fiona, feeling increasingly impatient, stood up and went to the door, opened it, and looked out. The corridor was crowded with people, nurses, students, dazed-looking patients in wheelchairs. Then she recognized the spare, tall, white-coated figure of Dr. Simeon Halstead, standing at the main desk and talking to one of the secretaries.

"There's Dr. Halstead," she said, turning to Andy. "I'll tell him what happened. I'll be right back." With a determined step she marched down the hall.

"Dr. Halstead?"

He turned his head, and to her surprise he smiled. Not a big smile—one that barely turned up the corners of his mouth, but a smile nevertheless. "Mrs. Markle," he said.

"Andy's here," she said. "He fainted at school. He's okay now, but I'm really worried about him ..."

"Somebody'll be down to see him shortly," said the secretary loudly from behind the desk. She glowered at Fiona.

"That's okay, Martha," said Simeon. "I'll take a look at him."

The secretary's mouth opened slightly, and she stared at Fiona again. Fiona knew that such a break in protocol in this institution was considered a major crime, and if Dr. Halstead hadn't been standing right there next to her she would have been in serious trouble. She had a vision of Martha leaping over the high desk at her, teeth bared, going for her jugular ...

"He's in room seven, Dr. Halstead," said Martha, still fixing Fiona with an annoyed stare. "We've sent for his chart, but it isn't here yet."

Simeon nodded and started to walk toward booth seven. Fiona went with him, quickening her step so as not to fall behind.

At that moment somebody behind them, a man, called out, "Hey! Dr. Halstead!" in a loud, high-pitched voice, and something about the tone made Fiona turn around quickly, as did Simeon. A small, round man was running along the corridor toward them. There was another shout, from further back, and Fiona saw a security guard come from the main entrance and start after the man.

It took only a second for the chubby man to catch up with Simeon and Fiona. He was red-eyed, his longish, graying hair was sticking out all over the place, and he was out of breath.

Staring at Simeon with the most malevolent look Fiona had ever seen, he screamed at him, "Get in there! You too, lady!" He pointed at the open door of an empty examination room next to them.

Both Simeon and Fiona did as he asked, because he was holding a large black automatic pistol, aimed at Simeon's stomach.

Chapter 8

The man pushed them into the room and kicked the door closed behind him just as the guard came running up. Then he locked it with his free hand.

"Get over there against the window," he shouted at Simeon, his face bursting with hate. "I'm going to kill you, you fucker, and you know why."

Somebody rattled the handle, then banged on the door. Then a male voice shouted, "Open up! Are you all right, Dr. Halstead?"

"Yes," Simeon replied calmly. "We're fine, but we can't open the door right now. And please stop banging on it."

The noise stopped.

"No, I do not know why you're going to kill me, Mr. Garvey," replied Simeon, fixing him with a neutral, uninvolved stare. Simeon didn't move, and his voice was so composed that Fiona was astounded. She felt ready to faint, although she'd never done so in her life, and she put a hand up to her chest.

"Are you his patient?" said the man to Fiona. "Because if you've any sense, you'd better get yourself another doctor."

Fiona's mouth was dry. She shook her head, watching the man, looking at the gun, waiting, petrified, for the bullets to start spraying out. His hand was tightly clenched around the weapon, as if he were already pulling the trigger.

Simeon felt as calm as he ever had. At this point in his life, he certainly wasn't afraid of death. As long as he wasn't crippled or paralyzed.

"You killed my boy," said Garvey. "You *killed him*!" His round face went a shade darker red, and both Simeon and Fiona thought that the moment had come.

"This is Mr. Ted Garvey," said Simeon, speaking to Fiona but keeping his eyes on Garvey. "His son, Michael, was a patient of mine," he went on. "He died here of a brain tumor two weeks ago."

Somebody started to bang on the door again, this time hard enough to rattle it on its hinges. The sounds of people gathering outside the door could be heard. A radio crackled.

"Everything's all right in here," called out Simeon, loudly enough to be heard in the corridor. His eyes still didn't leave Garvey's. "Please go away. *Everything is all right,*" he repeated, emphasizing each word.

"Can I sit down?" asked Fiona in a quiet voice. Her face was white.

Garvey nodded, and Fiona turned and sat down in one of the two chairs next to the desk.

"Don't touch that phone," Garvey shouted at her.

Fiona put her hands together in her lap.

It was clear that the man was too distraught to think coherently and was getting more agitated by the minute. Simeon's assessment was that Garvey was very likely to shoot as long as he was in this state of mind. He had a strange, otherworldly feeling, as if he were watching and even controlling this scenario from a command post far above them.

"Let's talk about Michael, then, Mr. Garvey," said Simeon in a quiet, collected voice.

"Yeah, now you're doing the reasonable, compassionate doctor routine, when you have a gun pointed at you," said Garvey. He had small, beady teeth. "How come you never had time to talk about Michael to me or his mother when he was alive?"

Simeon spread his hands. "Michael's problem was hopeless, Mr. Garvey, as you very well know. His tumor had spread, he'd developed a paralysis, and the pressure inside his head was increasing. All we could do for him was try to make him a bit more comfortable. There was no way he could survive more than a few weeks at most."

It seemed to Fiona that Simeon was talking to her as much as to Garvey.

"It was *not* hopeless," said Garvey, raising his voice

again. "I know the statistics on the kind of tumor he had. More than half of the kids who get it survive. And this is supposed to be the best neuro institution in the world, so the numbers should be better. Jesus Christ . . ." He raised his gun again and pointed it, shaking, at Simeon, then at Fiona. She didn't think he was going to shoot her, but when that gun barrel was pointing at her, she felt a heart-stopping fear that she'd never experienced before.

"Look, Mr. Garvey," said Simeon, apparently unmoved by the gun, "your son had the best possible attention here, and I took care of him as best I could. But he had a particularly malignant situation, as we told you . . ."

"*You* didn't tell me anything!" shouted Garvey. "Your *resident* finally came and told us, after the operation was over. After we'd been in the waiting room for *six hours* without any news, nothing!"

"When I took on Michael's case," said Simeon, "I told you that I wouldn't be giving you interim reports on his condition. After the operation I called your referring physician and told him what the situation was, and he . . ."

"Michael wasn't *his* son. Michael was *my* son. Why didn't *you* tell us? We should have been told first. Or is it that you're just not human?"

A change was coming over Garvey. He was shaking, seemingly close to tears, and his gun was now pointed harmlessly at the floor. Fiona could sense that his first rush of fury and frustration was over, and he was drained, shaking and afraid for what he'd almost done, and for what he *had* done.

Someone banged on the door again, and a muffled voice said, "What's going on in there? Are you all right, Dr. Halstead?"

"We're *all* all right, thank you," replied Simeon, looking put out, as if this were an unwelcome interruption in the conversation. He took in Garvey's expression and came to a decision. "We'll be out soon," he said.

Garvey looked up when Simeon said that, and he brought his gun up again.

"Listen, Mr. Garvey," said Simeon, sitting down in the other chair and stretching his long legs out in front of him, "you're potentially in a whole lot of trouble here. I'm sure half the New Conventry police force is out there waiting for you in the corridor, and they'll probably have snipers outside ready to blow your head off as soon as you appear."

"I don't care," muttered Garvey. "They can do what they like to me."

"I'm going to call the hospital administrator," said Simeon, but he didn't make any move toward the phone. "I'll get him to call off the police and the security people. Once I've told him you are unarmed ..." Simeon held out his hand for the gun to Garvey, who shook his head, looking at Simeon as if he were in a trance "... and that you aren't going to make any trouble, I think we have a fair chance of getting you out of here in one piece."

At that moment the phone rang. Simeon looked at Garvey.

"Don't touch it," he said. The ringing seemed to galvanize him into action again. "Before I kill you, I want you to know that I think you're the most inhuman, heartless son of a bitch that ever lived," he said. His lips pulled back over his teeth, and slowly he raised the gun. The phone stopped ringing.

Simeon sighed. There was a fatalism about him that unnerved Garvey. In the several days since he had bought the gun, he'd fantasized about how Halstead would be on his knees, screaming for mercy, still pleading with him when his brain exploded ...

"Fine with me," said Simeon. "It's a lot better than dying of cancer."

There was a pause. Garvey's gun began to shake from the tension in his muscles.

"But before you do that," Simeon went on, "there's a couple of things you should know."

Fiona, a mere observer of this scene, watched with weirdly detached fascination. She felt paralyzed by the threat of sudden death, but at the same time she had an unnaturally clear understanding of both sides and sympathized with each. Simeon's control was something she marveled at. She had never seen anyone like him before.

Without giving Garvey a chance to say anything—and coldly aware that he was less likely to shoot while something was being explained to him—Simeon went on. "You have to know a bit about what my job is like," he said, addressing Garvey. "I'm a doctor, of course, but I am principally a technician. I have developed special surgical skills for dealing with tumors and other problems inside the brain. *The brains of living people,*" he went on, emphasizing his last words. "Can you imagine what that's like, Mr. Garvey, working inside someone's brain?" Again he didn't give the man a chance to say anything. "Especially when you know that many of these people are going to wake up after their surgery with paralysis, or unable to speak, or to see ..." Simeon glanced for the barest second at Fiona.

"When I was in training," he continued, still playing for time but with his voice reflecting the most intense sincerity, "there was a guy ahead of me in the program who spent every available minute with his patients, got to know them and their parents, helped the therapists with the rehab, brought his patients little gifts." Simeon paused, and his eyes, still on Garvey, seemed to glow. "He never finished the program. He committed suicide after one of the kids he'd operated on died."

"WHAT THE FUCK DOES THAT HAVE TO DO WITH MICHAEL?" Garvey screamed suddenly.

"He was a good surgeon," said Simeon, ignoring the outburst. "And all that skill and training was wasted. I didn't want that to happen to me, so I had to either go into some other specialty or learn not to get involved with my patients. If I got attached to them, I'd be thinking about them as people, and I wouldn't be able to do what was medically best for them. Eventually I wouldn't be able to function. What a patient does get from me is the best possible surgical care. Friendship, comfort, if that's what they need, that has to come from somewhere else. That's why I like my patients to have a family doctor who can provide that."

Simeon took a deep breath, while Fiona watched him, spellbound by this explanation of his clinical attitude. The man wasn't afraid of Garvey, but he *was* afraid of getting attached to his patients.

"To come back to Michael," Simeon went on. "He had a fast-growing, highly malignant tumor that was building up the pressure inside his brain, and that was why he was having those terrible headaches ..."

Now that Simeon was talking directly about his son, Garvey's face took on an expression of fascinated pain, as if he couldn't bear to hear about Michael because it hurt to think about him, and he couldn't bear not to because of the unanswered questions he had about his son.

"We operated simply to give him a little more time, by reducing the internal pressure ..."

"I know that," replied Garvey, hissing between his teeth. "And he died that night. He didn't wake up. AND YOU DIDN'T HAVE THE ORDINARY HUMAN DECENCY TO CALL AND TELL US YOURSELF! You gave the job to one of your flunkies ..."

Dr. Halstead interrupted, and his voice was hard. "First, Mr. Garvey, Dr. Penrose is not a flunky. He's a highly trained doctor who helped me on the case. Secondly, I wasn't there. I had to fly to London that night ..."

"Abandoning your patients! You did the operation and ran," sneered Garvey. A huge sob suddenly hit him.

"He was left in the care of the best neurosurgical team in this country," said Simeon, his voice suddenly gentle. "If Michael hadn't died then, he'd have died screaming in pain a few days later. And my resident did tell your wife that I was leaving."

Garvey, who had his back to the wall, slowly slid down until he was in a sitting position. He dropped the gun on the floor, put his head between his hands, and started to sob, loud, harsh sobs that seemed to rack his soul.

Someone knocked again on the locked door.

"Five minutes," said Simeon, and the knocking stopped. He stood up, went over to pick up the gun, put it in the pocket of his white coat, then lifted the phone and dialed a five-digit internal number.

"Marshall?" he said when the hospital administrator, Marshall Prince, was on the line. "This is Simeon Halstead. I'm sure you know about the situation down here in the E.R. No, everything's under control. There's a Mrs. Markle here, too ..." He glanced at Fiona. "Yes, well, everything's calmed down. Mr. Garvey, who ... wanted to talk to me is very distraught about his son, who died here two weeks ago. No, I don't think we want to do that. If everybody leaves ... yes, the police too, please. Then we need to get some help for Mr. Garvey. He'll need to be admitted to the psych unit. I'm sure he'll agree. No, we don't want a big fuss about this. Bad for him, bad for us too. Okay? We'll come out in ..." Simeon looked at his watch. "In exactly five minutes. That'll give everybody time to clear out of the way. Do I have your assurance...?"

Garvey had raised his head and was watching him.

Simeon nodded. "Good. Thanks, Marshall. I think that'll be best. I'll come over to your office after I've had a chance to talk to the psych people. Try to find Dr. Rosenfeld, and ask him to come down to the E.R."

Fiona stood up and went over to Garvey, who now looked as small and pathetic as he had looked threatening before. She stretched out her hand and helped him up from the floor, then, impulsively, put her arms around him and held him. His arms hung limp at his sides, and he started to weep.

Chapter 9

When Fiona left to go down the corridor, Andy lay back, wondering why he couldn't recall what had happened at school although he remembered the ride in the ambulance.

After a few moments he heard some shouting and the noise of people running, and then a breathless young woman of about seventeen, in a pink and white candy striper uniform with a coat over it, came in, closed the door, and quickly locked it. She stood panting with her back to the door, one hand on her chest.

Andy watched her. She was pretty, with a little nose, big brown eyes, and sexy, half-open lips.

"Hi," she said, smiling at him. Maybe it was her voice, or the way she looked at him, but Andy lost his heart instantly. "My name's Susie." She stood with her ear to the locked door and listened.

"What's happening?" asked Andy. Outside, the P.A. system was booming something about a code yellow, then there was the sound of heavy doors slamming closed.

"I was just going home ..." she said, looking at her watch. "That'll teach me to go out through the E.R. I should know better, huh?" She hesitated, then took off her coat and hung it on the hook on the back of the door. "What's your name?" she asked.

Andy told her. He was taking in the way she moved, her trim figure, and he marveled that anyone so beautiful could have just walked into the room and into his life.

"What's a code yellow?" he asked, sitting up. His head started to throb, so he lay down again.

"Oh, that's what they call an intruder alert. There's some guy out there making some kind of disturbance ... They told me to go in here, lock the door, and stay with you until the security people catch him."

"Where's my mother?" Andy asked, suddenly realizing that she'd been gone longer than he'd expected.

"She probably got put in another room," said Susie. "Nobody's allowed in the corridors while there's a code in progress."

Susie went over and stood by the stretcher and smiled down at him. She looked so wonderful in her neat uniform that Andy could feel his heart beating at double speed inside his chest. He had a sudden aching desire to get to know her—he'd never felt like that about anyone, ever, not his on-and-off girlfriend Stephanie, nobody.

"So what are you here for?" she asked.

"I passed out at school. I suppose that's what happened, anyway, because I don't remember anything about it. I was talking to my friend Kevin in the locker area, and the next thing I knew was I was in an ambulance." There was more noise outside and the sound of heavy feet running by. A radio crackled.

"Who's your doctor?" asked Susie. "I hope this code doesn't last much longer," she added.

"Dr. Halstead, I suppose. I saw him a couple of days ago," replied Andy, thinking that the code or alert or whatever it was could last until the end of time, just as long as she stayed with him.

Susie's eyebrows went up. "Dr. Halstead? Wow. Big time." She stared at Andy for a moment. "What school do you go to?"

"New Coventry High," replied Andy. "My mother teaches there too."

"My brother's in New Conventry Middle School," said Susie. She gave a little laugh and shook her head. Something about the way she did that, the way her hair fell back around her face, made Andy feel weak. "It sure is a small world," she went on. "What did you say your name was again?"

"Andy. Andy Markle."

"Oh, my," said Susie, with a tinkling laugh. "Matt won't believe this. He talks about you a lot. You play for the J.V. baseball team, right?"

Andy nodded.

"Well, Matt thinks you're great. Do you know him? He's in sixth grade. Matthew Seidel."

Andy shook his head. "I don't think so. Seidel's the name of our principal, though."

"He's my uncle. My dad's a doctor . . ."

There was a noise outside and the door rattled. "Andy? Are you there? Are you all right?" Andy had never heard his mother's voice so panicky. And right now he wasn't at all happy to hear her voice, because all he wanted to do was go on talking with and looking at and being with Susie. Susie Seidel. A wonderful, musical name.

At the same time they heard the voice on the P.A. system saying, "Code yellow is now completed."

Susie went to the door and unlocked it. Fiona ran past her to Andy and hugged him.

"What happened?" asked Andy, round-eyed.

"Oh, everything's all right now. I'll tell you the whole story later." She turned around. "Hi," she said to Susie, "I'm Andy's mother. I'm sorry I pushed past you like that, but . . ."

"No problem," said Susie. "I was just in here during the alert. I'm on my way home."

She reached up for her silver-colored raincoat on the back of the door, and Andy watched her, feeling that if Susie just went out of his life now he would never recover. "Will I see you again?" he asked desperately.

"Sure," replied Susie, laughing. "I'll get Matt to invite you over for supper, okay?"

After she left, to Andy the room seemed huge and utterly empty.

"Made a new friend?" asked Fiona, watching him.

"Mr. Seidel's her uncle," replied Andy. "Isn't she nice?"

"Oh, my. She must be Sam's daughter. She should have told me who she was."

A few minutes later the door opened and Simeon Halstead came in and gave Fiona a quick smile. After their experience with Mr. Garvey, it seemed to Fiona that she and Dr. Halstead had known each other for years.

"Well, that was an exciting little episode, wasn't it?" he said to her. He didn't wait for a reply, starting to talk to

Andy. Then he examined him carefully while Fiona watched him, thinking about how he'd dealt with Mr. Garvey and wondering where Garvey was now. Had they kept their word, or had they arrested him and taken him off to the police station in handcuffs?

"Andy needs to come into the hospital, Mrs. Markle," said Simeon finally. "I'm very concerned about what happened this morning, on top of that episode of blindness, and I found a couple of problems with his reflexes and visual fields that bother me."

"Can you tell yet what the problem is?" asked Fiona, feeling her heart contract again.

"No. That's why I want him to come in. For tests. All the ones I was telling you about the other day." His voice was quite different from the last time he'd seen Andy, and she could now hear a genuine sympathy in it. Again the tiniest flicker of a smile crossed his face, and Fiona had a feeling that there was a whole lot going on behind that severe face. Simeon Halstead certainly wasn't the heartless robot she'd previously imagined.

"Okay . . ." Fiona thought quickly. "I'll go home and get pajamas and a toothbrush and stuff for him," she said. "We live only about ten minutes away."

"No, you don't need to do that," said Simeon. "We'll give him a hospital johnny to wear. The nurses and residents are going to be asking him a lot of questions. Stick around for that, and you'll get a much better idea of what's going on."

Fiona felt a kind of annoyance, as if he had in some way usurped her right to make decisions about things that concerned Andy. Sure, he could make the medical decisions, that was fine with her, but somehow this was over the line. But it wasn't worth arguing about.

"Okay," she said. "I'll stick around." She put her hand protectively on Andy's shoulder. "So what happened to Mr. Garvey?"

"They had to tranquilize him in the E.R.," replied Simeon, his face showing no expression. "He's being admitted right now to the acute psych facility."

"Do you think they'll press charges against him? I mean the hospital?"

Simeon shook his head. "I don't know. I hope not. It's up to Marshall Prince, our administrator. I told him it wouldn't do anybody any good, and it certainly wouldn't improve the hospital's reputation with our parishioners."

"What happened to the gun?"

"What gun? Nobody saw a gun, except you and me, and we're not saying anything about it, right?" He patted his trouser pocket. "I'll see you both upstairs in about an hour."

All Andy could think of was Susie, the way she looked, the way she had smiled at him, and the way she moved when she walked. He couldn't believe how in the space of a few minutes she had taken over his entire life, all his thoughts and feelings.

He wanted to walk up to his room, but that idea was firmly vetoed by the E.R. nurse, so they waited until someone from the transportation department came to trundle him along the long corridors. Every female, every candy striper they passed looked a bit like Susie until they came up close. They paused at the elevator, then rattled into it while the other passengers crowded to one side and silently watched him. Finally they stopped at the desk on the neuro floor, where Fiona gave the secretary the sheaf of papers from the E.R.

Ten minutes later Andy, now naked except for his shorts under a shapeless thin white cotton johnny, was installed in his new bed. It smelled clean, the sheets were thin over a firm mattress. His mother left him to go down to the accounts department.

Andy kept looking at the door, willing it to open and admit Susie. He imagined how she'd enter the room, first putting her head around the door and smiling at him, then coming in, and he'd open his arms and she'd walk over to the bed and put her arms around his neck . . . But the door stayed closed. He turned to check out the green-painted oxygen valves and the shiny suction fixtures behind the head of the bed, then experimented with the electric controls of the bed. He soon got tired of that and lay back and thought about Susie some more. He raised his arms and sniffed his armpits through the loose sleeves of the johnny and wondered what she would smell like. What a contrast she made with the girls in his school; most of them thought about nothing but sex and threw themselves at whoever happened to be popular at the time, the footballers in football season or him and the other top players when it was baseball. Would Susie come to his ball games? How would his mother like her?

He thought about having Susie meet his friends at school and how he would smash any of them who said anything or made jokes about her afterward, or even if they looked at her without the proper respect. He looked at his hands. His fists had clenched, just from his thinking about it. Not that he'd need to worry, he realized. The guys would be so jealous of him they wouldn't know what to do with themselves.

And then he thought, What am I doing here? He felt just fine. His head didn't hurt, and he didn't feel dizzy or anything, although there was something weird about his eyes ... Suddenly all he wanted to do was to get out of the hospital and go home. Lying in bed in the middle of the day like this was just ridiculous. He swung his legs over the side of the bed and wondered if the nurses would yell at him if they caught him walking over to the window.

He heard the sound of footsteps and talking in the corridor. They came to a halt outside his door. Andy heard some conversation, some laughter, and then the door opened and in came the resident team, two young men in O.R. greens and a very tall, thin young woman with a long face, straight wet-looking hair, and a curvy back. She was wearing a white coat that hung off her body like off a clothes rack at T. J. Maxx.

The men introduced themselves and told him their names, which Andy instantly forgot.

"And this is Dr. Emily DuPlessis, our junior resident, Andy," said the older of the two men, who had short dark hair and a quiet, authoritative manner. He nodded at the young woman, and Andy wondered why she couldn't tell him her own name, as the other two had.

"You'll be seeing more of her than us. Okay, Andy?" He looked hard at Andy as if he were committing both his name and his appearance to memory.

"I'll be back to do an H and P after we finish rounds," said Dr. DuPlessis to Andy in a flat, unsmiling voice. As he watched her follow the others out of the room, Andy thought she looked like a tired sandhill crane. He wondered what an H and P was. He hoped it wasn't the examination that Kevin had talked about when he had his appendix out. He'd gone on and on about that afterward, about the four doctors who kept coming back and sticking their fingers up his butt. He said it still hurt weeks later.

Andy was thinking about Susie again when his mother returned. She had hardly sat down when the door opened again and a middle-aged man with a purplish nose came in. He was wearing an ill-fitting, rumpled-looking suit and a loose, flowery tie. Andy noticed that his shirt had old-fashioned long collar points.

"Markle?" asked the man in a gruff, almost hoarse voice.

"Yes?" said Fiona.

The man came into the room and closed the door behind him. "I'm Sam Seidel," he said to Fiona, then turned to Andy. "Dr. Seidel to you, kid."

Andy looked at him in disbelief. This old, weird-looking guy was Susie's father?

He sat down in the other chair, facing Andy, his legs spread out. "Marty asked me to look in," he said to Fiona, watching her closely with his big, watery-looking eyes.

Fiona, listening to his tone and seeing the expression in his eyes, got the feeling that however disheveled he might look, Sam Seidel was pretty smart and didn't miss much.

"So what's up?" he asked.

Fiona told him.

"Well, Andy's in good hands," he said. "I know Dr. Halstead pretty well. They say he's about the best in the business."

There was something about his voice that Fiona couldn't quite make out, as if Sam respected Halstead but didn't particularly like him. That rang a bell with Fiona, because that was about how she felt.

Sam stood up, reached into his back pocket, and finally came out with his wallet. He rummaged around in it, then pulled out a card. "Here," he said to Fiona. "If Dr. Halstead wants to talk to me, the number's right there. That goes for you too."

He moved toward the door. "See ya," he said without turning around.

Shortly after that, a young attendant with a ponytail held back by a rubber band came in, pushing a wheelchair. After checking the name on Andy's wristband, he glanced at a folded printout he was carrying. "Chest and skull x-rays and CAT scan for you, young man," he said cheerfully. "Hop in."

"I'd rather walk," said Andy, eyeing the wheelchair.

"Sorry. You have to go in this here limousine. Orders from the president himself." He winked at Fiona.

Andy sighed loudly, got out of bed, put on a hospital robe over his johnny, sat down in the wheelchair, and raised his feet while the attendant put down the hinged footrests.

Fiona, feeling that Andy was not in any immediate danger now, stood up. "I have to go back to school," she announced. "I'll be back a bit after three."

Andy grinned at her, so obviously glad that she was returning later that she leaned over and gave him a hug. On the way out she wondered what was happening to Mr. Garvey and what they were doing to him. The poor man, she thought, losing his son like that. She thought about Andy, looking so healthy, and shivered.

Fiona got back to school during the lunch break and found Wilma in her room, sitting at the desk eating a sandwich.

"How's Andy?" asked Wilma, her mouth full of pastrami.

"Okay. They're doing a bunch of tests . . ."

"Tests, tests," said Wilma. "That's all you hear about nowadays. Why do those guys bother to go to medical school if they can't make a diagnosis without getting all these tests?"

"It's a really wild place, that hospital," said Fiona. She told Wilma about the confrontation between Garvey and Simeon Halstead.

"Jesus," breathed Wilma, looking wide-eyed at Fiona. "You could've got yourself killed."

"You should have seen him," said Fiona in an awed voice. "I mean Dr. Halstead. I've never seen anybody so cool in my life. I tell you, if I ever needed someone in a real emergency, he'd be the one."

"Who knows?" said Wilma. "Maybe he gets a gun stuck in his ribs every day and he's used to it. But it's nice that you've got somebody like that taking care of Andy," she went on. "Here." She pushed half the sandwich across the desk. "I kept this for you."

"Thanks," said Fiona. "I'm not hungry. Not after this morning."

"You gotta eat, baby." Wilma's big eyes were anxious; her own metabolism went the opposite way—when life got tough, she ate.

The door opened and a couple of other teachers came in. Everybody had heard what happened, and before the bell rang a steady stream of people had come in—teachers, administrators, and kids. Fiona got a lot of hugs, a lot of support. Marty appeared and said to her, "I've got a sub lined up for you for this afternoon, if you need to be with Andy."

"No, thanks, Marty," she replied. "I'm better off here than sitting around at the hospital. I'll go back there after school."

After the bell rang and the students were in and settled down, Fiona tried to put everything else out of her mind. "Okay," she said. "Today we're going to do something new and very exciting." When she had their undivided attention, she continued, "We are going to talk about love, passion, lust, hate, and murder."

One could have heard a pin drop.

She went on, "Have any of you ever heard the name Cesare Borgia?"

Chapter 10

After leaving Andy, Susie Seidel hurried down the corridor toward the E.R. exit. She was late, but when she saw her friend Donna Mariani behind the desk, she stopped long enough to ask her what had happened.

"Some guy who was mad at Dr. Halstead because his kid died here," replied Donna with a shrug. "They finally took him over to P5. So now we're all backed up with a bunch of patients who're all pissed because they were locked in their rooms and kept waiting."

"I spent the time with one of his patients, in room seven," said Susie. "A really nice kid. Andy Markle."

Something in her expression, or the way Susie said Andy's name made Donna stare at her for a second. "He's only fourteen," she said. "Isn't he a bit young for you?"

"Right," replied Susie. "It's a pity, because he's a really sexy kid, in case you didn't notice."

Leaving the emergency room, Susie tied the belt of her raincoat and walked over to the staff parking area, feeling a warmth and a kind of excitement when she remembered the way Andy had looked at her. Susie knew the effect she had on males, and she recognized the signs. Then, after wondering briefly what was the matter with him that he should be Dr. Halstead's patient, she got in her car and promptly forgot about him.

Susie lived at home with her father and brother in a big old whitewashed colonial-style house in Brighton Woods, a suburb of New Coventry. Feeling tired and grubby, she went up the wide, carpeted stairs, looking forward to a shower and change out of her uniform, which smelled of things she didn't even want to think about. She'd been excused from her school classes to do a paper on child care and had been helping out on the pediatric floor; it was a messy business.

The door of her bedroom was open, and her younger brother, Matt, was there with a friend of his, both on their knees in front of the dresser. The bottom drawer was pulled open, and they were giggling, holding up various flimsy articles of her underwear. She stopped in shock for a second, then walked quietly into the room until she was right behind them. Then, at the top of her voice, she screamed, "Matt!"

The two boys leaped up as if they'd been plugged into a wall socket.

"Get out!" she yelled at them. "Get out of here! And don't either of you ever come back in this room or I'll break your damn necks. That goes for you too, Alan. I'm surprised at you. What's your mother going to say when I tell her? Go on, beat it, get out!"

Her heart beating fast, she pushed the boys out and slammed the door behind them. She could hear them running down the stairs, and a moment later they passed by her window on their bicycles. Feeling suddenly exhausted, she sat down on the bed and took off her shoes. She still had all her homework to do.

After a shower and a change into fresh underwear and a blouse and jeans, she felt better. At least she wouldn't have to make lunch for the boys. They would go to Alan's house and be very nice to his mother, trying to make points in case Susie did rat on them. She grinned. They probably knew better. And her father wouldn't be home until around six, as usual.

In the kitchen she found a piece of foil-wrapped chicken and a can of Fresca in the refrigerator, made a piece of toast, and sat at the counter for a quick lunch before going back to school.

When her father, Sam, came home it was almost seven. "You're late," said Susie, although she'd said that so often it sounded more like a greeting. "Did you have a good day?"

"Yeah, okay," he answered.

"You've got a few calls," she went on, "and one of your patients called a couple of times. Andy Markle." She grinned at her dad. "But he wasn't calling you. He was calling me."

Early the next morning, Simeon called Dr. Desmond Rosenfeld, the senior psychiatrist who had taken Ted Garvey on as his patient, to find out how Ted was doing.

"Ah, yes, Dr. Halstead," said Rosenfeld. "I'd like to talk to you in person about Mr. Garvey. When would you have a few minutes?"

They arranged to meet in the doctors' lounge at ten that morning, when Simeon would be between cases.

Simeon was in the habit of doing early rounds before going to the operating room. The hospital bylaws specified that physicians were to visit their patients at least once a day, and Simeon obeyed that rule to the letter. He never came without his retinue of residents and the three students presently on his service, Edwina Cole, Terry Matson, and Nina Muldrew.

When they came into Andy's room, he was still half asleep.

"Hi," said Dr. Halstead, looking at the foot of the bed, the chart, anywhere except at Andy. "Everything coming along all right?"

"Yes," Andy replied, rubbing his eyes.

"Any new test results?" Simeon asked the chief resident, who passed the question to the intern, Dr. DuPlessis. She said, "Not yet. He has blood tests, X-rays, CAT scan scheduled for today."

"Good," replied Dr. Halstead. "We can discuss them after rounds. First, I want to show you something interesting here."

He asked Andy to sit up and look straight ahead of him. Andy did so, and the residents and students crowded around. It wasn't every day that Dr. Simeon Halstead did this kind of demonstration. "Okay, Andy. Now, without moving your head, look up at the ceiling."

Without meaning to, Andy tilted his head back to look up.

"Let's try that again," said Dr. Halstead. "This time don't move your head."

Andy tried, but he found that he couldn't look up without moving his head. He hadn't noticed that before, and it scared him.

Simeon turned to the others. "That's called Parinaud's sign," he told them. "Have any of you heard of it?"

The residents all had, apparently, but the chief resident was the only one who had actually seen it before. None of the students had ever heard of it.

"And what does it signify?" Simeon looked at the residents.

"Raised intracranial pressure?" suggested Dr. DuPlessis.

Simeon nodded. "Yes. In a specific area. We'll talk about it some more outside," he said.

He nodded at Andy and led the way out. Andy could hear the faint murmur of voices outside his door, but he couldn't hear what they were saying. Maybe his mom was right when she said he'd deafened himself with rock music. Then fear gradually expanded inside his head as the low murmur of voices continued. He was going to die, he was sure of it, and that was why these doctors had gone outside to talk about him.

On the other side of the door, Simeon stood with the residents and students gathered around him. "We were talking about Parinaud's sign," he said. "Now that's a most interesting diagnostic test, and it can tell you things that a CAT scan or an MRI can't. It's like an early warning system that tells you when trouble is on the way and when it's gone."

Edwina was listening intently to him. "If the patient can't raise his eyes above the horizontal," she asked, "does Parinaud's sign mean there's pressure from a tumor inside the brain?"

Simeon nodded. "It's not proof," he said, "but it's very suggestive. Another fact that's not generally known, even among neurologists and neurosurgeons, is that once it appears, Parinaud's sign is permanent. That is, unless there's a total and complete cure. And of course that doesn't happen too often."

"How do you spell *Parinaud*?" asked Nina.

"Look it up," replied Simeon. "You'll find it somewhere between *paralysis* and *parturition*. Now let's go over to X-ray and take a look at those scans."

*   *   *

Soon after Simeon and his team left, there was a knock on Andy's door, and a young black man stuck his head inside, rolled his eyes at Andy, then pushed a wheelchair into the room.

"I'm Henry," he told Andy, sticking out his hand to shake Andy's. "And I'm the Al Unser of the transportation unit. You need to go somewhere, I'll get you there the fastest. Right now we're going to X-ray, you and me . . ." While he talked, Henry motioned Andy into the wheel-chair, then strapped him in. Out in the corridor, he said, "Gentlemen, start your engines!" and they were off, starting with a wheelie as Henry tipped the vehicle back on its rear wheels. Then he hurtled through the corridors, up and down the elevators, wending his way with smooth accuracy, just like Andy going through a crowd of pedestrians on his blades. "Keep your eyes peeled for speed traps and the police," warned Henry, and he'd no sooner said that when they heard a voice behind him. "Hey, you!" Henry knew he was in trouble and had to resist the temptation to go into high gear and disappear around the next corner. He stopped and saw one of the junior hospital administrators coming up behind them at a trot, making angry gestures at him. "Hey, you, what's your name? You're operating that chair in a dangerous manner."

"Sorry, sir, I can't stop to talk," replied Henry. "This here is an emergency, and they told me to get him over to X-ray as quick as I could."

The administrator was not impressed. He wrote Henry's name down and told him that he would be reported and that meanwhile he was to transport his patients in a safer fashion.

"You need a radar detector," Andy told Henry after the administrator left. Henry was glum, and they continued the trip in silence, at the modest pace he used when trans-porting geriatric passengers.

The radiology doctor was also a black man. He was tall, looked like an athlete, and had a smile that showed a lot of very white teeth. The label on his badge said Dr. Frank Grant, Radiology.

"My name's Frank," he said, putting out his hand. Andy shook it.

"Ever been here before?" asked Frank.

"No," replied Andy, looking around. "It looks like a space center."

"Would you like to see the control room?"

Andy nodded, although he didn't think he would understand much about this high technology. He got out of the wheelchair and followed Dr. Grant. The control room was dark, with a big window that looked into another room. A couple of white-coated people sat at consoles facing the window.

"You know how X-rays work, right?" asked Frank, then grinned at Andy's expression. "Well, you can think of them as very penetrating light rays," he said. "And the different tissues in the body partially block them. Dense tissues like bone block them the most, of course, but different parts of the brain have different densities, so they show up as dark or gray shadows on the X-ray film." He looked at Andy, who nodded. "The CAT scan sends X-ray beams in from different angles, and a computer puts the information together to make a very clear image of the brain. It's like looking at slices of the brain . . . Here, take a look at this." Frank pressed some buttons on the console, and a colored oval image of the top of a brain showed up on the screen. He adjusted the controls, and every five seconds a new picture appeared of the same brain, each time at a slightly lower level. He stopped at one of them and pointed at a little red spot near the center that Andy wouldn't even have noticed. "That's what we were looking for in this patient," he said. "It's a little aneurysm at the base of the brain, like a bulge in a blood vessel."

"Is that what I have?" asked Andy, interested.

"We don't know," replied Frank. "That's why you're here, so we can find out. You're going to be in that room there . . ." He pointed through the window into a room with a raised table in the center, attached to what looked like a body-size tunnel passing through the center of a huge cream-painted metal doughnut.

"They'll put you on that table," Frank went on. "Then the stretcher part moves, and you slide up until your head and shoulders are inside that tunnel. We'll talk to you while all this is happening, and all you have to do is lie real still. You'll hear some noises, like humming and some clattering, but you'll only be in there for a couple of minutes."

Andy felt a bit nervous, but it was all over very quickly, and within a few minutes he was on his way back to his room. A few minutes later, Dr. DuPlessis, the birdlike intern, came in to see him between tests, did a complete history and physical, then sat on the edge of his bed and chatted with him.

"Is Dr. Halstead like that with everybody?" Andy asked her, referring to Simeon's early-morning visit.

"Oh, that's just the way he is. Don't worry about it. He's the best neurosurgeon in this hospital, and he's, well, sort of obsessive about his patients. He doesn't look as if he cares about them, but he's actually thinking about them all the time. You just have to get used to him."

"Does he talk to *you*? What's he like?"

"Yes, he talks to us, but not much. He's all business. I guess he's just not very interested in human relations."

"Do you know a candy striper called Susie Seidel?"

Emily DuPlessis stared at him. "I don't know *any* candy stripers. Why?"

"I just wondered. She came into my room when they had that intruder alert in the emergency room."

Dr. DuPlessis said, "If she knows you're here, she'll probably stop by, don't you think?" She got up, looking even more like a tired bird, with her short dark hair, long neck, and curved back. Andy wondered why she had that bleak, expressionless look on her face. Maybe she'd caught it from Dr. Halstead.

"I'd better go back to work," she said, smiling, but it was clear that she would rather stay there and chat with him. "Now, you be good. I'll see you later when we do evening rounds, okay?"

At ten o'clock, Simeon came out of the operating room into the doctors' lounge wearing his O.R. greens. Dr. Desmond Rosenfeld, Garvey's psychiatrist, was already there, waiting for him in a quiet corner of the room, and Simeon went over to join him. Rosenfeld, tall and white-haired, stood up when he saw Simeon approach. "I've been talking a lot to Ted Garvey since we admitted him yesterday," he said without preamble. "He says he hates you because you killed his son." He watched Simeon over his half-glasses. "In fact, it turns out that his anger has a different cause."

They sat down, Simeon making himself comfortable in a wide leather chair opposite Rosenfeld. He stretched his long legs out in front of him, one ankle across the other. "I'm glad," he said.

"His anger appears to stem principally from a lack of communication between you and the Garvey family," said Rosenfeld, trying not to sound critical. "He told me about how he waited to hear from you after the surgery, how his and his wife's calls to your office were rerouted to the residents . . ."

"He was told ahead of time that that would happen," said Simeon, unflustered. "My job, as I see it, is to diagnose and, when necessary, to operate. I deliberately leave as much direct contact with patients as I can to the residents and their family doctors."

Desmond Rosenfeld was well aware of this, as were most of the physicians at the medical center. He also knew that Halstead's reputation was such that his modus operandi was tolerated, although in anyone else it would have been viewed as arrogant and irresponsible. But Halstead was known to put all his energy into his work, often spending hours in the labs and radiology department trying to figure out complex diagnoses and developing special procedures for individual cases, often with unexpectedly good results. As one physician put it, Simeon's interpersonal shortcomings were offset by the brilliance of his work.

Rosenfeld, a year from retirement and overawed by no one, looked at Simeon with a grandfatherly seriousness. "I think I know the reasons for your attitude," he said, "and I'm sure that none of us here wants to see you burn out." He took off his glasses and rubbed the lenses vigorously with a handkerchief. "On the other hand, Dr. Halstead, that same attitude almost got you killed yesterday."

"Risks of the trade, I guess," said Simeon, shrugging.

"There's nothing wrong with taking risks, as long as they're necessary," said Rosenfeld. "But I'm not sure the ones you're taking are necessary." He seemed to be searching for words, and Simeon watched him, wondering what he was going to say.

"Dr. Halstead, I think you may be underestimating the strength of the patients' and their relatives' reactions to your attitude," said Rosenfeld finally. "They're not all like Ted Garvey, of course, but I assure you that many of these people resent your distance, your ... I guess one could call it social detachment, coldness, whatever. I would like to suggest to you that you try to spend a little more time getting to know your patients personally. I'm aware that you know about the medical and technical aspects of your cases, maybe more than any other physician in this center. But it's not fatal to have personal contact with your patients. I've been doing that all my professional life, and I'm still alive."

Simeon nodded. "Thank you," he said. "I will certainly think very carefully about what you've said."

Rosenfeld stood up. "In my opinion, Dr. Halstead, right now you are in a high-risk situation. Not only from lawsuits, but also from being seriously injured by distraught patients or relatives. But if you start to take a more personal interest in your patients, if you can learn to see them as people rather than merely cases, I believe that both you and they will gain enormously by it. And in addition, you'll have the new experience of becoming a real physician rather than just a technician."

He nodded briefly, then went off, a slightly stooped but decisive figure.

"Dr. Halstead?" A nurse popped her head around the door. "Your patient's on the table."

Simeon sat there for a few moments longer, thinking very hard about Desmond Rosenfeld's words. Rosenfeld was one of the few psychiatrists for whom he had any respect, and his reproof stung. *You'll have the new experience of becoming a real physician rather than just a technician* ...

Simeon stood up and put everything out of his head except the patient he was about to operate on.

After discussing Cesare Borgia with her class, and using his eventful life to illustrate the struggle for power by the popes in Renaissance Italy, Fiona went to pick up Wilma at the gym, and they both went to the hospital.

When they got to Andy's room, Wilma gave him a tight, enveloping hug. "Last week we put your name in for Connecticut Junior Athlete of the Year," she told him. "So get well quickly and don't embarrass us."

Andy grinned with pleasure. He'd heard rumors, but that was all. He didn't know quite what to say, but stammered, "That's great, Wilma. Thanks."

"We're real proud of you, kid," she said, ruffling his hair.

"Kevin came to my room after class," said Fiona. "I think he misses you. He says hi and asked when you were getting out."

"When is he coming here?"

"Tomorrow. He has baseball practice today." Fiona didn't want to dwell on that topic, so she went on. "How was your day?" She fixed her eyes on Andy and did her best to sound unconcerned. "have you had any headaches or . . . anything?"

Andy shook his head. "I'm fine," he said. "I just want to get out of here."

"It shouldn't take too long," replied Fiona. "What tests did they do today?"

"A whole bunch," he said. "They did a CAT scan," he went on, suddenly brightening up. "It was very interesting. There was this doctor who told me how it worked. He took me into the control room and showed me. Do you know it takes tens of millions of computer calculations before you can get an actual picture?"

Fiona tried to look suitably impressed. "Did they tell you what it showed?"

Andy shook his head.

At that moment there was a knock on the door and Dr. Halstead came in, alone. "Hi," he said, looking from Fiona to Andy and Wilma. He seemed uncomfortable. Fiona introduced Wilma, then realized that this was the first time he'd appeared without his usual retinue of students and residents.

"I don't really have much to tell you yet," he confessed after Fiona asked if there was any news. "Tomorrow most of the test results should be in." He turned to Andy. "I hear from Dr. Grant that you had a good time down at the CAT scanner."

Andy nodded, not knowing what to say.

There was a brief pause, then Simeon turned back to Fiona. "You remember our friend from yesterday, Mr. Garvey? Well, I talked to his doctor this morning, and he seems to be doing well."

"I'm glad," said Fiona. "I've been thinking about him. He seemed like a very unhappy man."

"I've been thinking about him too," said Simeon. "Well, I guess I'll be on my way. Oh, and if you hear from my old friend Dr. Sam Seidel, tell him I'll be in touch with him as soon as we have the results."

He nodded in a friendly way at Wilma and left.

After Simeon had gone, the three of them looked at each other.

"I like him," said Wilma in a very definitive voice. "There's something about him that's ... Well, he's not a bit slick or suave. And like you said, Fiona, I'd want him around if there was a real bad emergency."

Fiona nodded and smiled at Andy. "I'm glad he's taking care of you."

"Me too. Am I an emergency, Mom?"

"I guess you were for a little while yesterday. Not now, though." She came over and hugged Andy again.

They stayed until the dinner trolley came. Fiona didn't particularly like the look of the food, a hamburger with mashed potatoes and peas, but Andy seemed quite happy with it.

Coming out of the underground parking lot, Wilma, who had been quiet for a while, said to Fiona, "I think that Dr. Halstead is rather taken with you."

"Oh, come on, Wilma," replied Fiona, rather sharply. "Don't be silly. Anybody could see the guy was working hard just to be polite."

Wilma didn't pursue the matter. Fiona dropped her off at the school to pick up her car, and then she went on home. The place felt big, cold, and deserted without Andy. Although she wasn't hungry, she made herself a quick salad with tuna and artichoke hearts out of a jar, then went upstairs to change out of her work clothes. In the bedroom she looked at herself in the long mirror. Wilma was right; her clothes did look a bit shabby and certainly didn't do much for her appearance. She straightened her shoulders and pulled her hair up to sit in a great curly red mass at the top of her head. She stared at herself, thinking about what Wilma had said about Simeon Halstead. In a way, she was getting to like him, too.

After his mother left, Andy felt tired and settled down for a nap. He didn't hear the door open and didn't see Susie Seidel come in. She stood by the bed for a second, then started to tiptoe out. Andy opened one eye, then leaped up as she was going out the door.

"Susie!" he shouted, and, startled, she turned around.

"What's the matter?" she asked. "Why are you yelling like that?"

"I'm sorry," he said, embarrassed. "I guess I was asleep . . . I didn't want to miss you."

She grinned, closed the door, and came and sat on the edge of his bed. She didn't touch him, but Andy could feel the heat of her body on his legs and could smell the faint, sweet perfume that she was wearing. He was in ecstasy. Also he couldn't think of a single thing to say to her.

She looked at him mischievously and flicked a strand of hair out of her face. "So you called my house again last night?" she said. "My dad thought there must be an emergency."

Andy blushed and was mad at himself for it. "I just . . . well, it wasn't that late, only about nine, I guess. Anyway, your dad said it was long past your bedtime, and so I thought . . ."

It was Susie's turn to blush. "My dad never said that! He wouldn't . . ."

She saw Andy grinning and realized that he was teasing her. She laughed, even though he had got the better of her.

"Well, actually I've been hoping you might come by today and say hello." Again Andy blushed, putting his head down so that she wouldn't notice.

Susie did notice, of course, and being a young woman of some experience, figured out exactly what was going on. She remembered the little flash of interest she'd felt in him

down in the emergency room; there was something about
that boy, she reflected, something about his quiet manner,
about the way he looked, vulnerable but poised. And he
was very sexy indeed, for his age—tall, well built, with good
muscles and a wonderfully smooth skin. But it was just as
clear that he was completely innocent. Matt had told her
how popular he was at school, and for some reason that
made a difference to Susie. She could feel a tentative, spec-
ulative interest stirring somewhere inside her.

She smiled at him and put her hand lightly on the sheet
over his leg, below the knee, in what seemed a perfectly
normal, friendly gesture. It was strange, she thought, to feel
in complete control of this kind of situation, and it gave
her a good feeling, even though Andy was so young.

Andy tensed, as she expected, and he sat up quickly to
hide the uncontrollable erection that had been threatening
ever since she sat down so near to him. They both felt the
throb of sexual energy hit them.

Susie stood up immediately. "I have to go now," she
said. "How long are you going to be in here?"

"I don't know," he replied. He could feel the sweat on
his face. "I have some more tests tomorrow, Dr. Du-
Plessis said."

"My dad's coming in to see you later," she said.

"How about you?" asked Andy. He was feeling excited,
scared, and ready to explode. "Will you come back?"

"Tomorrow," she said. "When I go off duty." She
grinned and said, just to tease him, "Maybe."

And then she was gone. Andy sniffed the air. He could
just smell her perfume, and he hoped the scent would last
till she came back. He slid down in the bed until he could
feel the warm place where she'd been sitting. He held on
to himself for a little while but didn't dare do anything
more in case someone came in and caught him.

Chapter 11

Before leaving for school the next morning, Fiona called Andy's room, but there was no answer, so she figured he'd already started on his tests. When she came into her class-room, there was a stillness, a watchfulness about her eleventh graders that surprised her, until she turned to the chalkboard, where she saw, written in large yellow letters, each word below the other, FIONA SUCKS DICK.

She took a deep breath and turned to look over the class. She knew them well and could narrow the likely culprits down to two or three of her students.

"Marlon," she said, pointing at one rather shambling youth at the back of the class. "Come out here, please."

Marlon started to bluster immediately. "I didn't do that," he said. "I swear."

Fiona wiggled her index finger at him to come up, and reluctantly he did so.

"Marlon," she said when he was standing uncomfortably in front of her, shuffling from one foot to the other, "Marlon, do you think what's written on that board shows proper respect for me?"

Marlon hung his head. "No," he said, "it doesn't. But I didn't do it. Really ..." He raised his eyes to Fiona.

"Marlon, there's no need to defend yourself until you've been accused," she said, "and I'm not accusing you." She looked beyond Marlon at the class, and her voice rose slightly. "I do not appreciate being called *Fiona* by my students," she went on sternly. Then her gaze moved back to the unhappy Marlon, and she paused. "Now, Marlon," she said in her calmest voice, "please erase *Fiona* and write in *Mrs. Markle.*"

Marlon's jaw dropped. He hesitated for a second, looked at the board, then said, "But Mrs. Markle . . ."

"Do it, Marlon." When Fiona used that tone, people obeyed, and Marlon went hastily over to the chalkboard and did as she had told him, while the other kids giggled nervously, not knowing quite how to take all of this.

"Very good, Marlon," she said approvingly when he had finished. "Thank you. You may return to your seat."

The class seemed embarrassed to have the inscription remaining on the board, facing them, and slowly they realized that somehow, without any accusations or display of anger, Mrs. Markle had gotten the better of all of them. As she usually did.

"Now," she said, "let's talk about your test papers from last week . . ."

At the end of the class, one of the kids went up and, without comment, wiped the board clean.

Later in the day, after classes were over, Fiona was coming out of the library with an armful of books and a sheaf of computer printouts, and she met Marty Seidel, who happened to be passing. He held the door open for her.

"I heard how you dealt with the message on your chalkboard," he said, smiling.

"I can't understand why they did that," replied Fiona, straight-faced. "I don't even know anyone called Dick."

Marty laughed. "I'm glad," he said with a sidelong glance at her. "Anyway, I thought you handled the situation very skillfully."

"I wish I could handle the rest of my life so well," replied Fiona ruefully. "I never had a chance to apologize to you about last Saturday."

"No problem. No problem at all." Marty hesitated. "After I left, I felt that maybe I should have stayed . . . Does Victor pull that kind of stuff often?"

"No. Most of the time he's away, but sometimes when he has a long layover he drinks a lot. Never on the job, though. You know how strict the airlines are about that."

"You could always get an injunction," said Marty. "That way he'd be allowed to come to your house only at specific times, if at all." He glanced at the load Fiona was carrying. "Here, let me carry some of those books for you."

"No, thanks. I'm used to being an academic beast of burden," she replied. "It's part of the job. As for the injunction . . ." Fiona thought about it. "If he does that again, I'll mention the possibility to him," she said. "But right now I'm trying to be as nonconfrontational as possible. I know how he'd react, and ultimately it would be bad for Andy. Victor can be very mean when he wants to, and an injunction would make him go off the deep end."

"How's Andy doing?" asked Marty. "I was going to stop by the hospital, but then I figured he'd only be in for a day or two. Sam says he's doing fine."

"He was getting a bunch of tests this morning, and hopefully some of the results should be ready later today," said Fiona, feeling a constriction around her heart at the thought. "Actually I'm on my way there now."

"Good luck, Fiona," said Marty, putting all the sincerity he felt into his voice. "I'll be thinking about you. About both of you."

At about ten o'clock that morning, Simeon had finished helping the residents do a case and was back in his office, thinking about Andy. At this point he already realized that he had a clearer idea about the anatomy of the inside of Andy's brain than about who the boy was, but that, he reflected, was how he usually liked it. Again Desmond Rosenfeld's words came to him. *Become a real physician, rather than just a technician* . . . But somehow, even before the psychiatrist had spoken to him, he'd felt a glimmer of personal interest in Andy, partly because he was an athlete, but more because of something very likeable and understated about his personality. And there was a kind of buzz about him—everybody in the hospital seemed to know about Andy Markle; that morning, one of the women in the gift shop had stopped him to ask how Andy was doing. Her granddaughter was in the same class at school and had made her promise to find out. And of course that incident with Garvey had brought him into much closer contact with the boy's mother than he normally would have been. Fiona. That must be a Scottish name, he thought. A very attractive woman, too. And with plenty of personality and brains. He remembered how firmly she had stood up to him. Parents didn't usually do that—they were nearly always intimidated by him. He was intimidating on purpose; from then on the parents would rely on the nurses and residents to give them whatever information they wanted.

A small red light lit up on his phone console, and a moment later his secretary put the call through. It was Elisabeth. She didn't often call him at work.

"I just wondered if you'd like to come home for lunch today," she said. "I got some Scottish smoked salmon from the Barrys, and I thought you might enjoy it."

"I'd love it," said Simeon, thinking rapidly. "But I can't leave right now. Sorry."

"That's all right," replied Elisabeth. "The salmon'll keep."

Slowly Simeon put down the phone. This invitation was very unlike Elisabeth; in fact, he couldn't remember her ever asking him to come home for lunch, although from time to time he had done so. Like last week ... Recollecting the nuances of her voice, he realized there was something disturbing about the whole thing.

He finished what he was doing, then stood up. "I'll be on my pager," he told his secretary, then left the building and walked over to the parking lot.

His mouth was set as he turned onto the I-95 connector. If, as he suspected, Elisabeth had called merely to be sure that he wouldn't be coming home unexpectedly, it was time that he knew the truth. That goddamned Nick ... Simeon couldn't understand why the man couldn't keep his hands off other people's wives. Wasn't the exciting and glamorous Sandra enough for him? Pushing those thoughts out of his head, he took the fourth exit out of town. Occasional blue glimpses of the sound showed between the trees as he drove along, but he didn't notice them. What if he was wrong? What if it had been a genuine invitation to come home for lunch? How would he explain his presence now? One way or the other, he thought, it wasn't going to make much difference to his relationship with her. Simeon turned off the highway, then down the quiet, tree-lined Shore Lane.

His heart jumped with angry anticipation as he came round the corner into his own driveway and saw that, sure enough, his instincts had been correct. Nick Barry's gray, gold-trimmed Lexus was parked outside, in front of the garage.

A wave of rage hit him. He switched off the motor and sat there for a few moments, trying to decide what to do. The thought of Nick Barry, that treacherous bastard, and what he was at this moment doing inside his house . . .

Simeon got out of the car in one quick move, leaving the door open, and walked rapidly across the grass to the side of the house toward the three steps that led up to the long deck. Unless they were busy eating smoked salmon, thought Simeon, they would be in the master bedroom. At the top of the steps he stopped abruptly when he heard a sound coming from somewhere in front of him, around the corner. It was half giggle and half laugh, with a throatiness he'd never heard before, although he immediately recognized Elisabeth's voice. He was about to step forward, then he heard another voice saying, "Oh, my God, do that again, it feels so . . . o . . . good."

Simeon peered round the corner. The French doors were open, and the breeze was billowing the gauzy white curtains. He moved forward a little, just enough so he could see inside. On her knees by the bed, *their* bed, was Elisabeth, her hands stretched out in front of her, massaging the well-oiled body of someone lying face down on the bed. At first Simeon couldn't see who it was, and he was about to step forward and march in when the person sat up, and to his total astonishment he recognized the sumptuous figure of Sandra Barry. Elisabeth took one of Sandra's breasts in her mouth and played with the other, while Sandra did something to Elisabeth with her hands, something he couldn't see, and after a few moments Elisabeth put her head back and made that same, low, throaty noise again. Then Sandra lay down on the bed, her skin glistening with the oil, legs apart, her curly head nearest the window Simeon was looking through, her feet up on the pillows. Elisabeth started to work on Sandra's belly again, slowly, rhythmically, her strong, muscular hands slowly working up to her breasts, gently massaging the nipples under the palms of both hands. Sandra bucked and pushed until there were moments when her pelvis came up right off the bed, the black triangle of her pubic hair at the apex of the arch. Then she said something Simeon didn't hear, and Elisabeth got to her feet, bent down, and pushed her head deep between Sandra's legs, then turned and moved her own shapely rump until it was over Sandra's upturned face. Using both hands, she pulled herself open. For a second, Simeon saw Elisabeth's bright pink slash, then Sandra's sharp, darker pink tongue came up to it.

Shocked out of his mind, his mouth sagging with astonishment, Simeon watched Elisabeth throw back her head and moan as Sandra started to work on her. He turned and went quietly back to his car and, shaking, drove away.

Part Two

Part Two

Chapter 12

In an angry, confused daze, Simeon drove back to New Coventry, fighting a growing sense of failure and inadequacy. Had all that happened because he was so uninteresting, so sexless? Was it his own deficiencies that had forced Elisabeth to turn for sexual satisfaction to another person? But why a woman? Maybe she'd been inclined that way all the time, and he hadn't seen it. He thought back to the last time the two of them had had sex together. It was several weeks ago, and, he reflected, that wasn't normal for a start. Maybe he'd gotten used to her chilly presence lying beside him in bed ... No. He hadn't. There was always that tension, a kind of formality. They both kept their emotional distance and were very careful not to offend or upset each other. And that time, for once, Elisabeth had initiated it. They'd come back from a party, where she had drunk quite a bit, and after they'd gone to bed she suddenly turned to him and pulled herself on top of him. She didn't kiss him, he recalled, just put her head over his shoulder while she fumbled with his pajamas and then with him, and after he was inside her she had sat up and worked on him with a kind of fury, looking not at him but above him, straight ahead of her. In retrospect, he knew that even then she'd been thinking about someone else.

Back on I-95, Simeon felt his tension relaxing a little as he approached New Coventry and the medical center. In his mind now, the hospital was a haven, more like a home to him than the place where he'd left Elisabeth and Sandra. At the hospital he was in control, he was respected, he did a good job, people did what he told them, things were generally predictable, and overall he had a sense of rightness about his place and his function there.

His secretary had put all of Andy Markle's test results on his desk, and he gave her a quick, grateful smile. At least somewhere in this world things were on track.

He always liked to examine all the scans and X-ray films himself before reading the radiologist's report, for two reasons. First, his impressions were not skewed by the report, and second, when he compared his own findings, he usually learned something from the expert opinions of the people whose job it was to read them. Because he took so much time and care, he occasionally found something the radiologists had missed. He flipped the first set of X-rays up on the long viewing box at the side of his desk, went over to turn off the room lights, then sat down at his desk, swinging the chair around so he was directly facing the hard white glow of the viewing boxes. For the next hour and a half, he pored over the X-rays, stared at the CAT scan sections, and from time to time used a large magnifying glass to examine certain portions of the scans.

Then he put them all back in their buff envelopes and called the office of Dr. Frank Grant, the radiologist.

"Sure, come on over," said Frank.

The two men went into the viewing room and discussed the films in detail, then Simeon walked back to his office. While he was working on Andy Markle's diagnosis, he'd been able to put all thoughts of Elisabeth away, but now, as he waited for the elevator, it all came back to him in a rush. The image of Elisabeth, in an attitude of sexual abandon that she had never shared with him, was etched painfully in his mind. Again the question came to him: What had he done wrong that she had to seek sexual satisfaction elsewhere?

In the elevator was Paula Cairns, a surgeon who was reaching international prominence for her work on blood clotting, and they smiled at each other. Simeon knew that Paula had a great relationship going with the head of one of the important university research labs, and all of a sudden a sensation of being alone, really alone, came to him in a way he'd never felt before. His mind scanned through his circle of friends and acquaintances, and he realized that there was nobody he could talk to about this, even if he wanted to. All his real friends had moved away—Richard,

Bob ... For a moment he thought about Richard Posner, his best man, who at this time must be en route to take up that big job in D.C. But he knew what Richard would tell him: We warned you, Simeon ... Then he'd say, Get out of it, Simeon, get out of it *now,* leave her. As if it could be that easy. He thought about Nick Barry, and wondered if Nick knew about Sandra's involvement with Elisabeth. Maybe all three of them were in it together ... Suddenly Simeon felt a vast distance between himself and them, as if he were on a space shuttle receding from the earth faster than the speed of sound.

Returning to his office, he pulled himself back to the job at hand and immediately felt a different kind of worry. He looked at his watch; Fiona Markle would probably be up in Andy's room, and he wanted to talk with her alone.

He called through to the nursing station and spoke to Mandy Pullen, the floor secretary.

A few moments later Mandy walked along the corridor to Andy's room and knocked on the door. "Dr. Halstead would like to see you," she told Fiona. "Yes, now. Let me tell you how to get to his office ..."

Feeling as if she'd been summoned to see the principal, Fiona went down to the floor where the attending doctors had their offices. Outside the door of Simeon's office, Fiona took a deep breath, squared her shoulders, and went in.

"Go on in, Mrs. Markle," said the secretary, pointing to the door of the inner office. "He's expecting you."

Simeon stood up when Fiona walked in.

The office was large, with a lot of diplomas on the wall behind the desk, a bookcase, and a set of filing cabinets to her left. A large, multisectioned X-ray viewing box covered a good part of the wall to her right, and several films were hanging on it.

She looked at his face to see if it was bad or good news coming up, but she couldn't tell from his expression. His face was as impassive as that first time she'd seen him, and he was talking to his group of students in the emergency room.

"Well, we've completed the tests on Andy," he said. "I'm afraid we're dealing with a major problem. If you come over here I'll be able to show you ..." He went over to the viewing box and Fiona joined him. Every muscle in her body was trembling.

"Here, this cross-section shows the base of the brain," he said, pointing to a small, dark-shadowed mass in the middle of the scan. "You see that white part right underneath it? That's the optic chiasma, where the nerves from the eyes join and then cross over before going into the back of the brain."

Fiona nodded. "That's why Andy was having problems with his eyes," Simeon went on. "That dark area was pressing down on the chiasma, so it affected both eyes."

"What is that dark area?" she asked, feeling as if she'd just told her executioner to go ahead, cut her head off.

"It's a tumor," he replied steadily, and Fiona put a hand up to her heart.

"Is it malignant?" she heard herself ask.

"I don't know, Mrs. Markle," he said. "We're going to have to take a piece of it and look at it under a microscope. Then we'll know for sure."

Fiona went back to the chair and sat down heavily. "Dr. Halstead," she said, "I know you've been in this business a long time, and I feel sure you have a pretty good idea whether it's benign or malignant now, before you do any biopsy."

"I'm not going to guess, Mrs. Markle," he said, but there was a new gentleness in his voice. "I'm going to schedule his surgery for the day after tomorrow, if that's all right with you. At that time I'll try to remove the tumor, and we'll get a biopsy at the same time. I don't usually operate on Saturdays, but I don't want to keep this hanging over the weekend. I'm sorry I can't do it sooner, but I have other cases I just can't postpone."

Simeon, impressed with the way Fiona was dealing with this situation, wondered how Elisabeth would have reacted if it had been her child in such dire trouble. She would probably have just told him to take care of it.

"I'm going back to Andy," said Fiona, standing up. "What shall I tell him?"

Simeon stood up, also. "You won't have to tell him anything," he said. "I'm coming with you."

Chapter 13

As soon as the last class for the day was over, Kevin Woviotis ran to his locker, put on his backpack, sat on the floor to pull on his new rollerblades, and headed down the corridor toward the exit. Students were forbidden to use blades inside the school building, but Kevin was in a hurry to get to the hospital. Although he wouldn't have admitted it to anyone, he didn't feel complete without Andy around to talk to and fool around with, and he was also feeling anxious about what was happening to his best friend. He'd gone into Mrs. Markle's room after class to ask her, but she was talking with a student, so he didn't wait. He zipped past a couple of kids, missing them by inches, then at the door he braked hard, leaving a black streak on the smooth linoleum floor. A moment later, he was outside, slipping in and out between groups of kids walking to the buses, then he was through the gate, across Chestnut Street, hopping onto the median. He waited for a car to go by, crossed the lane and jumped onto the sidewalk, his body bent forward for balance, and he was off, going fast down the gentle slope for almost a mile into the center of town. Kevin felt good; the breeze was strong on his face, and he loved the feeling of power and speed as he flashed past the poor old pedestrians doomed to advance only by the slow, boring process of putting one foot in front of the other. At the junction with Elm Street, where the hospital was, he wheeled sharply left and crossed against the traffic, looking this way and that, wending his way between the slow trucks and cars and taxis. A truck driver leaned out of his window and yelled something as Kevin sped in front of him, and Kevin flipped him a relaxed finger without even looking around.

Outside the hospital's main entrance, Kevin took off his blades, put on his sneakers from his backpack, and went in. Ever since having his appendix out there, Kevin had had a weird feeling about the hospital. He knew the place, but it didn't know him. He felt that the woman at the desk should have recognized him, because it was only a few months since he'd been in, but he didn't recognize her either.

When he was a patient, he'd been on the seventh floor, the surgical unit, and he repressed an urge to press the button for that floor. It would have been fun to go in and visit, but all the patients he knew would have gone home by now, and the staff would probably be different too. The fifth floor, where Andy was, seemed almost the same; the corridors were the same color, the nurses' station was in the same place, but somehow it was very different. It *smelled* different. He knew the number of Andy's room, so he didn't stop at the desk but marched straight on. He wasn't challenged, so they probably figured he was a medical student or a doctor. Yeah, maybe.

He tapped on the door of Andy's room, suddenly feeling less sure of himself. Maybe the nurses and doctors were in there doing things to him ... He opened the door a crack, saw that Andy was alone, playing with his GameBoy. He walked in and thankfully closed the door behind him, feeling as if he'd successfully made his way through a mine field.

They exchanged a high five, both of them glad and relieved to see each other. Kevin sat down on the edge of the bed.

"What are they doing to you?" he asked. "Are they going to cut your brain open or anything?" He grinned. "Of course, they'd have to find it first."

"Just tests," said Andy. He switched off his GameBoy. "Do you know what a CAT scan is?"

Kevin didn't, and Andy explained it as best he could.

"My dad says he's sorry, by the way," said Kevin. "He told your mom he thought you weren't concentrating when you struck out last Saturday."

Andy said nothing. His vision had gone strange again a couple of times since coming into the hospital and it scared him. He wondered if he'd be able to play again on the team.

"Did your mom tell you what the kids wrote on her board?" asked Kevin.

Andy shook his head, and Kevin told him the story. Andy was furious. "I bet that was Marlon Rozinsky," he said. "I'll break his fucking head when I get out of here."

"It wasn't him," said Kevin. "It was his buddy, that asshole Ray Morris. A couple of the kids beat him up already, so don't worry about it."

"You beat him up?"

Kevin shrugged.

"I got a new girlfriend," said Andy, feeling a little self-conscious. "A candy striper here. Her name's Susie."

"Oh, yeah?" said Kevin, disbelieving. "What does she look like?"

"Terrific," replied Andy. "Pretty and smart. Not like those dumb girls at school."

"Have you done anything with her?"

"Yeah, sure. Here in the hospital? Are you kidding?"

"Well, I would. When I had my appendix out, there was this nurse, a blonde, and let me tell you, she was all over me. I could have had her anytime."

"Sure. I remember coming to see you then. You were holding on to your belly and moaning. All that nurse ever did for you was bring you a bowl to barf into."

Kevin contemplated his friend for a few moments. "You're bullshitting me, right, about the candy striper?"

"No, I'm not," said Andy seriously. "Maybe she'll come in when you're here. Then you can see for yourself."

"She got any friends?" Kevin put his hand ostentatiously on his crotch. "Did you tell her you have this horny buddy who's the main hot cock around school?"

"So who's playing instead of me this Saturday?" asked Andy, wanting to change the subject. He'd have to be careful about the friends he introduced to Susie. He didn't want her to get the wrong impression about him.

"Some kid called Ben something. He's a sophomore. Plays shortstop, like you did. Like you do," he corrected himself, looking guiltily at Andy.

"What else is happening?"

"You missed a test. It was a killer, you're lucky. Like, where did the Renaissance start, and who started it, and what made Savonarola so important, stuff like that."

"Do you remember that picture they showed us about when he was executed? Where they built a long platform right in the middle of Florence and made the poor guy go up a ladder so they could hang him, and underneath was this big fire they were going to burn him in ..."

"Yeah," said Kevin, grinning. "I was telling my dad about that picture, and he said that we should start doing the same thing to criminals right here in New Coventry, and it would soon become a crime-free city, like Singapore. He said if he could get the franchise, he'd rent the stadium for it and we'll all get rich selling tickets."

"Did you get your new blades?"

"Yeah. Wanna see them?" Kevin delved into his backpack and pulled them out.

Andy admired them, spinning the free-turning wheels with one finger.

"These ones have brakes on both feet." Kevin pointed out the hard rubber pads that projected up from the toes. "I just about broke my neck the first time I used them."

At that moment the door opened. Andy was hoping it would be Susie, but it was his mother, with Dr. Halstead right behind her.

"Hi, Kevin," said Fiona, smiling. "Would you mind leaving us for a little while? We need to talk to Andy."

"Sure. I was going home anyway, Mrs. Markle," said Kevin, standing up. He put the rollerblades back in his backpack. "See ya," he said to Andy, and was gone.

Fiona came over to give Andy a quick little kiss. He could feel the tension emanating from his mother, and that made him tighten up. He looked at her, feeling instinctively that there was some bad news coming up.

"Did your dad call?" Fiona asked him.

Andy shook his head.

"He said he'll be in later today."

They looked at each other for a moment, both thinking about Victor's long history of broken promises.

Dr. Halstead sat in the chair by the bed and began to tell him about the biopsy they were going to do. When he started to mention needles and "pieces of tissue," Andy unconsciously switched his understanding off. He was listening, hearing the words, making a sincere effort to pay attention and look intelligent, but another part of his mind started to think about Kevin and how they usually went home together from school. Kevin was always behind, trying desperately to keep up with Andy, who just happened to be faster on blades. They'd go up to Foreman Street where Kevin lived, then Kevin would put up his hand to say good-bye, wheel across the street, and be gone . . .

Then, while Dr. Halstead was still talking about the operation and how they would fix and stain the specimen and look at it under a special kind of microscope, Andy's mind switched irresistibly back to Susie. Since her last visit, his feelings for her had changed, intensified, and now he wondered if at last he was going to do *it* with her. Wow! The thought seemed to explode inside his head.

"So we've scheduled the procedure for Saturday," he heard. "Is there anything you don't understand about what I said, Andy, or do you have any other questions?"

Andy shook his head and said no, although if he'd been asked to repeat what Dr. Halstead had said to him, he wouldn't have been sure of a single word.

"I'll leave the two of you together then," said Dr. Halstead awkwardly, looking from Andy to Fiona. It struck Fiona that his manner was at odds with his severe professionalism. When he was talking business, he was totally in control of the situation and the people involved, but now that the focus had changed and he'd gone back to being a human being, he seemed less sure of himself, almost lost, and for no reason she could identify, Fiona felt a growing sympathy for him as a person. Somewhere inside the aura of the famous Dr. Halstead, she could sense a different Simeon, a man who seemed to be hurting. She'd seen many kids with that expression coming to talk to her after school, kids whose parents were fighting or breaking up, and she felt an instinctive desire to ask him, to find a way of getting him to ease up enough so he could tell her about it.

Andy watched; now that nobody was trying to explain stuff to him, he didn't miss anything. He could see that his mother was getting to like Dr. Halstead a whole lot, and he seemed to like her too, but it was in a hesitant kind of way, and he was far too stiff and formal to show it.

It was strange, he thought. Dr. Halstead was obviously a very important man who told other people what to do and made big decisions all the time. But underneath all that, he seemed to be struggling with something. Maybe he should take off his white coat, thought Andy. Then he'd be just like anybody else and would be able to relax, maybe even laugh and joke around a bit.

At that moment the door opened and Victor came in, looking very dapper in his airline uniform with three gold stripes on the sleeves.

Fiona introduced him to Dr. Halstead, and the two men shook hands. Victor stared appraisingly at Simeon's tall and athletic figure. Fiona's heart sank; she could see that Victor's macho instincts were in overdrive today.

"So what's the matter with my boy here?" he asked Simeon, going over and ruffling Andy's hair in a protective manner. "Something you can fix, I assume."

"We don't know exactly yet," said Simeon. "We've done a number of tests . . ."

"Why do you guys always say 'we' when you mean 'I'?" interrupted Victor, with that aggressive smile that Fiona had learned to hate. "Or is that the *royal* 'we' like the Queen of England uses?"

Simeon's calm expression reminded Fiona of when they were locked in the room with Ted Garvey.

"It's not that, Mr. Markle," he said. "Nowadays, taking care of someone is often a team effort. 'We' includes our team of residents, the radiologists, and anesthesiologists . . ."

"Lots and lots of -ologists, huh, doc?" Victor was smiling broadly now. "All that talent assembled just to take care of my kid here. We're honored, I'm sure. Right, Andy?"

Andy lay back in bed, his face immobile. He said nothing, just watched his mother.

"Right," said Simeon crisply, and he seemed to stand up straighter, if that were possible. A look had come over his face that made even Victor pause. "I've told Mrs. Markle everything I know about Andy's case so far," he said. "I'm sure she'll be happy to repeat it to you."

He went to the door, turned for a second, and to Andy's

total astonishment, winked at him. Neither of his parents saw it, and Andy had a sudden, totally unexpected feeling of camaraderie with Dr. Halstead. The guy really was human, and even more surprising, Andy thought, he actually seemed to like him.

" 'I'm sure you'll be happy to repeat it to me,' " mimicked Victor as soon as the door had closed. "Listen, Fiona, I've been investigating that guy, and he's got a real bad rep. Apparently he was screwing some girl technician in his lab, and . . ."

"Victor," interrupted Fiona, "I don't want to hear about it. I don't care what the man does in his spare time. He's supposed to be the best doctor for this kind of problem in this city, maybe in the entire country. He's taking very good care of Andy, and I don't think you should try to undermine our confidence in him."

"He's taking care of him for *now*," said Victor darkly. "I'm going to think about it and decide whether he's going to keep on taking care of him."

Fiona felt her cheeks go pink. "It's not your decision, Victor," she said. "It's mine, and I'm going to make it. In fact, I have made it."

Victor's smile was unpleasant, and once again Fiona wondered how on earth she could ever have loved this man, lived with him for all those years, and had a child with him.

"We'll see about that," said Victor. He went to the door and turned with his hand on the knob. "Hey, it was great to see you, Andy," he said. "We'll make sure you get taken care of properly, okay, fella?"

Fiona had brought Andy's homework assignment with her, but now she decided to leave it in her bag; at this point it didn't seem particularly important. She took a deep breath; the tension from Victor's appearance had left her muscles weak. If she'd been a smoker, she thought, she would surely have a cigarette now.

"So what did Kevin have to tell you?" she asked, trying to make her voice sound normal.

"Oh, what was happening at school, stuff like that," replied Andy, relieved that his father was gone. "He's got a new pair of blades." He had already started thinking about

Susie again. It was like a refuge, thinking about her; everything else he could think about was either scary or sad.

A few minutes later there was a knock on the door, and Sam Seidel appeared, dressed as sloppily as ever.

"Hi, kids," he said. "What's up?" He rubbed the side of his big nose.

"You should be telling *us,*" retorted Fiona. "Dr. Halstead said he was going to call you."

"Yeah." Sam paused, wondering how much Andy knew about his condition and whether it was a good idea to talk to Fiona in his presence. "He did. He's going to take a look inside Andy's head on Saturday." He looked at Fiona and raised his eyebrows questioningly. "Is that what his residents told you?"

"He was here a little while ago," said Fiona. "He told us about the biopsy. Actually he told Andy, and I listened."

"*He* told you? He came here? Himself?" Sam was astonished. He grinned. "Usually the residents do all that face-to-face stuff for him. I had a patient Halstead operated on about a year ago, and she didn't even recognize him when she came in for her follow-up visit. The only time he'd seen her was when she was already asleep on the table."

Again Fiona felt that Sam was not exactly a fan of Simeon Halstead's but was being careful not to say anything derogatory about him. She looked at his rumpled figure, coarse features, and quick, calculating eyes, and realized that Sam knew exactly what he was doing, although she couldn't figure out what or why.

"Maybe Dr. Halstead cut away so much of that woman's brain she couldn't recognize *anybody,*" said Andy unexpectedly.

Fiona laughed nervously, and Sam, amused, made a noise like a partially blocked drain.

"Sam," asked Fiona, "could I talk to you later today? I have a couple of questions . . ."

"Sure. Call me this evening. My home number's on the card I gave you. Do you still have it?"

"Of course." She smiled to herself. Sam obviously thought that since she was a woman, she probably had a tendency to lose things. And he probably figured that she couldn't understand anything complicated or medical either. But somehow Fiona was unable to feel resentful of Sam; he was one of those guys who just didn't get it, and maybe even knew that he didn't get it, but it obviously didn't bother him, and nothing she could say or do would make any real difference.

Sam coughed, then said to Andy, "I hear my Susie's been in to see you."

"Yes," replied Andy, looking down. "She's a really neat person."

"She said something like that about you, too," replied Sam, and he grinned over at Fiona, showing his irregular, yellowish teeth. She wondered if he smoked cigars; he had that kind of a mouth. She was surprised that in spite of everything, she found herself liking Sam Seidel.

Sam looked at his watch. "Well, I'd better get back to the office." Then he looked thoughtfully at Andy. "Hang in there, kid," he said.

Chapter 14

After leaving Andy's room, and feeling the heaviness settle again around his heart, Simeon went back to his office to pick up messages, then headed for the parking lot. And now, he told himself grimly as he drove carefully out of the lot into the Elm Street traffic, he was going to have a showdown with Elisabeth, and he was already convinced that it would end badly.

His mind was full of her, of their marriage. Now, for the first time he recalled exactly the cautious but emphatic words of Bob and Richard and even some of his less close friends before his wedding. They had all had lunch with Elisabeth and him, and she had then gone off to do some shopping. "Don't rush into something you're not totally sure about, Simeon," Bob Kleinfeld had said worriedly. "How well do you really know Elisabeth? Are you quite sure she's the right one for you?" asked Richard Posner. Simeon remembered Richard's unusually serious expression. At the time he'd thought that his two old buddies just didn't want their old friendship to break up, although at the time they themselves were already both married. It even occurred to him that they might be jealous. *How well do you really know her?* That, in retrospect, had been the most telling of his friends' cautionary comments. Simeon felt his ears redden. Had Bob and Richard figured her out? if so, why hadn't they said anything to him?

With self-deprecating honesty, he told himself that he was trying to shift the blame away from himself. She'd never been as interested in the physical part of their relationship as he had, but that didn't necessarily mean she was a lesbian, for God's sake. He didn't turn her on, he'd known that almost from the beginning, but he'd thought things would improve, because he loved her so much. But that turned out to be wishful thinking. Things had got worse rather than better, and over the months Elisabeth would make more and more effort to avoid any sexual contact. She had been pretty clever about it, he thought, trying not to feel bitter. None of the "I have a headache, dear," routine. Nothing as banal as that for Elisabeth. No, what she did was to give the impression that with true love, you didn't need all that touchy-feely stuff. That was trivial, she implied, meaningless, a surface coating that could actually damage the strong feelings below. So, as love was in the soul rather than the body, overt affection was something that serious people would automatically avoid.

About three months into the marriage, they had had their first serious conflict. They'd been celebrating his first major grant for the brain tumor research project, and about the same time Elisabeth had been taken on by a New York gallery. She had gone down to the city to supervise the placement of three large sculptures that had been trucked in from New Coventry. It was all very exciting, and to celebrate, they decided to have a great dinner somewhere in New York, sleep over at the Plaza, and drive back to New Coventry the next morning, a Saturday.

Elisabeth wanted to go to Elaine's.

"I want to spend the time with *you*," protested Simeon. "I don't want to worry about how close our table is to Siberia. And I'd rather go where the food is good and where we can hear ourselves speak. I don't want to be looking up all the time to see people like Liza Minnelli parading around like prize pigs at a state fair."

Elisabeth conceded the point, and they went instead to Caravelle, but she wasn't happy about it. By then, Elisabeth had already developed an unmistakable but difficult-to-pin-down technique of making her displeasure felt. Not very forthcoming at the best of times, she would retreat, always politely, and always in a way that she could totally deny.

"Of course I'm not withdrawn, Simeon," she said, elevating her charming and perfectly shaped eyebrows. They had been eating in what Simeon considered an oppressive silence for several minutes, and he had remarked on it. "I'm just enjoying this delicious pheasant," she went on, her expression innocent and wide-eyed. "You can't expect me to come up with silly chatter all the time, can you?" She put her hand lightly on his arm for a moment and smiled her cat smile, knowing, tasting her power. When she wanted to, Elisabeth could be unanswerable.

He reddened. Did she really think that all he expected and wanted from her was silly chatter? But he knew he'd sound silly and ill-natured if he started to argue the point. In his frustration he stabbed viciously at his rack of lamb, squirting some of the delicious sauce onto the snow-white tablecloth.

Later, they walked through the Plaza lobby, where Elisabeth admired everything from jewelry to leather coats, then went up to their penthouse suite, sat behind the big picture window, and silently looked down at the spectacular view of the park. Simeon opened a bottle of Roederer Cristal, and she drank it carelessly, without comment. By the time they went to bed, he had drunk too much and was simmering with anger and frustration, mostly because he couldn't find any way to lessen the chilly distance between them.

She wore a long white silk gown. He lay there beside her in the huge bed, naked as usual, although in the past she had several times urged him to wear pajamas, or shorts, at the very least. They had left the curtains open, and the lights from the city made slowly moving patterns on the ceiling.

They lay there, both of them, eyes open.

Trying to defuse the tension, he turned on his side and put a hand out, felt the lapel of her gown and slipped inside it to hold her breast. He felt her whole body tighten up.

"I'm sorry, Elisabeth," he said, without knowing quite what he was sorry for.

"No need," she said. The coldness in her voice wiped out all his efforts at conciliation. He pulled his hand roughly out of her robe and got up on one elbow.

"What the hell is the matter with you?" he asked, keeping his voice down, but the fury in his tone was unmistakable. "Here we are, supposed to be celebrating our successes, but instead you've decided to go your ice-maiden routine. Again. Why can't you be just *human*? We're married, for heaven's sake! Why the hell did you marry me? Why didn't you marry God, and go into a nunnery, if you wanted a relationship without physical contact?"

"Oh, Simeon, you're just confusing love with lust. Again," rejoined Elisabeth in the calm, clinical voice he hated so much. And now he thought he could detect a mocking component in her tone. "I know that sex is much more important for men, and you guys get very restive if you don't get enough of it. But when I've had a long day, like today, I just want to be allowed to go to sleep in peace, if you don't mind."

And with that she turned on her side, away from Simeon.

"I *DO* mind, goddammit," said Simeon through clenched teeth. The unaccustomed amount of alcohol had released something in his head, and although he recognized it, he couldn't do anything to prevent it. "You're my *wife,* if that means anything to you!" Even as he spoke the words, he could hear how foolish and petty they sounded.

The white, silk-clad back didn't move, and after a couple of seconds of silence, a sudden surge of anger hit him and he caught her shoulder, pulled her onto her back, and pushed away the lapels to expose her breasts.

She looked at him impassively, and that made him want to strike her hard, slap her face, anything to get a response, any kind of human response, anger, joy, it didn't matter what."

"You want to fuck me?" she asked, with that same infuriating calm. "Go ahead."

He took her with a rage, a pounding fury. It was over in moments, and while he was still on top of her, she said, in a voice that chilled him to the soul, "Are you done?"

After that awful night, they had sex rarely, and when it did happen, it was usually initiated by Elisabeth, without warning. Simeon's work was taking up most of his time, and he felt little desire to go home in the evenings. His colleagues saw him gradually transformed from a witty, enthusiastic, energetic man with a lively sense of humor to a somber, remote clinician, respected for his skill but intimidating and aloof. Some thought it was arrogance brought about by his professional success, but others saw the sadness around his eyes, and could sense the unhappiness that beset him.

And now, one way or another, he thought as he turned off the freeway, now it's all coming to a close.

As he came around the corner into his driveway, he pushed the button to open the garage door. The garage was empty, and he felt a strange feeling of relief. Her car wasn't in the driveway, so she wasn't home.

He pulled in and went into the house. It was still, quiet. Sitting on top of the silver tray they used for the mail, he saw an envelope addressed to him, and it took him a few moments to recognize the writing. It was Elisabeth's.

"Dear Simeon," he read. "I thought it would save a lot of anger and ill-considered words if you were to *see* who I am now. That is why I arranged your visit here earlier today by inviting you for lunch. Simeon, you are a very predictable man.

"I have taken my things and will not be back. If for any reason you need to get in touch with me, I have taken a post office box here, number 42441. Elisabeth."

Chapter 15

Victor Markle was a first officer for one of the major airlines, and although he hadn't given up on his goal of gaining a captain's magic fourth stripe, everybody else who knew him professionally had. The brotherhood of commercial pilots is very close; they all go through the same selection process, training, and tests, and thus have a keen appreciation of each other's ability and overall competence. Victor was thought of as a skillful enough pilot; nothing had ever gone wrong on a flight because of his negligence or lack of ability, and his annual evaluations were satisfactory, if unenthusiastic. He loved flying and owned a one-third share in a twin-engine Cessna that he kept at the Groton airport and used as often as he could. The airline's chief pilot, a distinguished older man who had earned a chestful of Vietnam medals, told a senior colleague, off the record, what he thought about Victor. "It boils down to character," he said. "He's selfish, not a team player. It's nothing I could make an adverse report about, but, for instance, I wouldn't have wanted Markle in my squadron in 'Nam."

So the invisible grading system of his brethren had marked Victor for failure as surely as if they'd put a bloody cross on his forehead, although on paper he could not be distinguished from dozens of other pilots who did have a bright and successful future.

Victor left the hospital feeling tense and angry, as he usually did after spending even a short time with Fiona, but that was, as much as anything, because of his frustration with her. Goddamn bitch, he thought. She thinks she knows everything, even about medical matters that I know a lot more about. And Victor felt that that was his turf. His mind went back to the pre-med courses that he'd taken as a student in Miami. Although to his great chagrin he hadn't got into med school, he'd stayed interested, had a couple of doctor friends, and overall felt he had a pretty good insight into what was what in the medical world. And when Andy had a cold, or whatever, he'd always been able to diagnose him, tell Fiona what medication to give, that kind of thing. So now he felt he'd been left out of the loop; just because she had custody of Andy didn't mean that he wasn't his father anymore. And after all, it was really stupid and deliberately offensive of Fiona to ignore the specialized knowledge that he possessed.

Later that afternoon, Victor called Andy's number at the hospital.

It took a couple of rings before Andy picked up. "Hi, Dad," he said. "Dr. Seidel's here. Can I call you back?"

"Who's Dr. Seidel?"

Andy explained, feeling embarrassed because Sam was there listening to him.

An idea struck Victor. "Can I speak to him for a second?"

Andy passed the phone to Sam.

"I'd like your advice, Dr. Seidel," said Victor in his most respectful tone. "May I call you this evening?"

"Sure," said Sam. He gave Victor his home number. "Don't call after ten," he went on, "or you'll get my daughter or my answering machine."

That evening, after a dinner of canned ravioli and Italian sausage that he put together in the kitchen of the high-rise apartment he'd rented on the outskirts of town, Victor called Sam. After asking a couple of general questions, he said, "Dr. Seidel, what do you honestly think about Dr. Halstead? Do you think Andy's in good hands?" Victor deliberately said the words in a tone of serious doubt.

Sam, sitting at his desk in his home office, raised his eyebrows, as usual wondering how he could turn this conversation to his benefit. He hesitated. "Yes ... he's pretty well thought of and very capable ... But quite honestly, between you and me, Mr. Markle, I'm not sure I'd want him looking after my kid."

"Why is that?"

"He's not ... Well, it's important for patients of any age to feel some kind of rapport with their doctor. Halstead's not an easy guy to get along with. He doesn't like to talk to his patients ..."

"Frankly, I disliked him on sight," said Victor. "Something about his attitude, I suppose. Who else is there at the medical center? I'd certainly like a second opinion on Andy's case, for a start."

"You want one here in New Coventry?" Sam was flipping his Rolodex as he spoke. "I know the head of the department. Cadwaller's his name, Felix Cadwaller. He's a nice guy, and very competent."

"Maybe it would be better to get one from out of town," said Victor. "You know what these guys are like when they work in the same institution. Cadwaller might not want to contradict one of his own colleagues."

"I don't think that would be a problem in this case," said Sam, briskly rubbing the side of his nose and grinning to himself. He knew that Felix Cadwaller was no friend of Dr. Halstead's, and if there was any possible cause for disagreement with diagnosis or surgery, Cadwaller would take full advantage of it. Sam had heard that Felix Cadwaller had leaked information to the local media about the harassment incident with Simeon's laboratory technician. And Sam had reasons of his own for encouraging Victor to call for a second opinion.

He gave Cadwaller's office phone number to Victor, who said he'd call first thing in the morning.

When Sam put the phone down, his daughter, Susie, called to him from the adjoining room.

"Was that about Andy?" she asked.

Sam stood up and went to join her. "Yeah," he said. "His father wants a second opinion for Andy."

"Oh?" Susie was surprised. "I don't know why. Everybody at the hospital says that Dr. Halstead's the best." She sucked on the tip of her left index finger. "Who did you get?"

"Dr. Cadwaller."

Susie shrugged. "I thought he just did research." She took the finger out of her mouth and examined it. "Donna

Mariani told me those two guys hate each other," she went on, looking hard at her father.

"Don't worry, hon," said Sam, smiling at her. "I'll make sure Andy gets taken care of."

"Dad, are you up to something?" demanded Susie, looking closely at Sam, her hands on her hips.

"Of course not," he replied. "Now I'm going upstairs to do some paperwork."

Next morning, Felix Cadwaller was in his lab early. And he was annoyed; his grant coordinator was sick, so he was having to collate all the different parts of a grant application himself. He went over to the file cabinet. At around five feet eight, Cadwaller was tubby, square-faced, intense, with a bristly graying crew cut. He moved fast, with sudden, jerky movements, as if he were activated by a clockwork motor.

The telephone rang, loud in the small office. He picked it up.

"Cadwaller."

"Sir, my name is Victor Markle. My son, Andy, is a patient there in the medical center, and I'd be very grateful if you would take a look at him."

"Sure, I'll be happy to. But I don't make the appointments. Would you call my clinical secretary? The direct line is 543-2212 unless you're in the hospital. How did you get this number?"

"Dr. Sam Seidel. He suggested I call you."

Cadwaller wrote Sam's name on the pad beside the phone. "Oh, yes ... well in that case, Mr. . . . ."

"Markle. Victor Markle." Victor spelled his surname out for him.

"Yes, well ... Okay, where is your son?"

"On the fifth floor. Room 504."

"Got it. Does he have a staff physician?"

"Yes. Dr. Halstead."

Cadwaller blinked. "If he already has a staff specialist taking care of him," he said cautiously, "why would you want to consult another one?"

"Well, to tell you the truth, Dr. Cadwaller," said Victor in a confidential tone, "it seems that my son has a very serious problem, and I'm not really convinced that it's being dealt with in the best possible way. I should tell you that I have a fair amount of medical knowledge myself."

"Dr. Halstead has a reputation as a very capable surgeon," said Cadwaller, pushing the office door closed with his foot. "I suppose you're aware of that."

"I'm sure you're right," said Victor, picking up on the carefully bland way Cadwaller had spoken, "but I'd still very much like to have a second opinion."

"Yes, of course," said Cadwaller. "I'll stop by and see your son later this afternoon. Have you mentioned this to Dr. Halstead?"

"No, I haven't," said Victor.

"I'll give him a call," said Cadwaller, smiling with grim satisfaction. "Don't worry about it. We consult on each other's cases all the time."

"Great. I really appreciate your taking the time."

"My pleasure. I'll call you when I've had a chance to go over the scans and test results and to see him. Give me a number where I can reach you."

After Victor hung up, Cadwaller sat at his desk for a moment. This consult would probably not add up to much, but it might be an opportunity ... and an opportunity to get at Simeon Halstead was one thing he never let pass. As always when he thought about Halstead, an image of his sister, Ann, his beloved sister, came to him with extraordinary clarity, although she had been dead for more than five years.

They had been residents together, Simeon and Felix, on the neurosurgical service at Bellevue Hospital in New York, and although Felix was chief resident and a year ahead of Simeon in the program, they were very good friends. People called them the Bobbsey twins because they were so often together, although they didn't look a bit alike. Once they even had their picture in the hospital bulletin giving blood together for a Red Cross blood drive. Felix, already with a rep as a politician and general fixer, had arranged for both of them to go to the Bahamas for a diving weekend. Felix's sister, Ann, was going along too. Simeon had already met her briefly a couple of times; she was taller than Felix, slender, good-looking, but with a pale, tired look that Simeon interpreted at the time as rather aloof and distant.

Felix was a scuba fanatic who took every possible opportunity to dive, even in the polluted and chilly waters off the New Jersey coast, whereas Simeon, although competent enough, dove only maybe four or five times a year.

At the last moment a major emergency arose at the hospital, and Felix was unable to leave. Simeon, who had left a couple of hours earlier, was already at the airport when Felix reached him by phone and told him to go on ahead and he would follow the next day.

They had arranged to meet Ann at the gate, and she was there, dressed in blue shorts and a sleeveless shirt, a duffel bag at her feet. Simeon was shocked by her appearance. She looked pale and shaken, and her eyes were puffy and red-rimmed. She seemed glad to see Simeon, who explained why Felix wasn't there.

"Are you all right?" asked Simeon, concerned. "You look as if you've got the flu or something."

Ann shook her head. "I'm okay," she said. When she tried to smile, small premature wrinkles showed at the corners of her eyes.

On the first leg of the flight, to Miami, they sat together. Ann put her seat back and tried to doze, but every couple of minutes she'd start awake, her eyes would open wide as if she were seeing something she didn't want to see, then she'd close them again.

"Would you like to play Scrabble?" asked Simeon after she seemed to have given up the attempt to sleep. "I have a portable set."

"Okay."

They played for a while, but Ann didn't seem to be able to concentrate, and they arrived in Miami before the game was finished.

On the small plane going over to Eleuthera, Simeon tried to entertain her by telling stories about the Bahamian pirates that preyed on Spanish ships in the eighteenth century, but she was getting more and more shaky. Simeon was worried that she might fall apart before they got to the island.

The air was hot and humid when they got off the plane, and Ann clung to Simeon's arm all the way through the slow line of immigration, baggage claim, and customs, where their scuba gear was examined with sullen suspicion before being passed.

An old yellow taxi took them to their hotel, and Ann seemed to be feeling better. After they were shown to their adjoining rooms and Simeon was putting away his clothes, he heard the sound of sobbing from next door. He stopped still, wondering what he should do, then went into the corridor, stood outside her door for a moment, knocked softly, then turned the knob on the unlocked door and went in.

Ann was lying face down on the bed, her whole body shaking with the sobs she was trying vainly to control.

Simeon sat down on the edge of the bed and put a hand on her shoulder. Ann grabbed the pillow and buried her face deeper into it.

"Stay right there," he told her quietly, although she had shown no signs of doing anything else. "I'll be right back."

When he came back, it was with a quart bottle of Wild Turkey in his hand, together with a smaller bottle of whiskey sour mix and two glasses.

He took them into the bathroom, and a minute later he stood by the bed holding out a full glass to her.

"Okay, kid," he said. "Sit up and take your medicine."

Ann turned around, an expression of such despair on her face that Simeon was truly concerned. He wondered if her misery was the result of some unhappy love affair or perhaps some insoluble family problem.

She sat up and held out her hand, not looking at Simeon.

"Would you like something to eat?" he asked. She hadn't touched the lunch served on the flight to Miami.

She shook her head and drank greedily.

"Another, please, Simeon."

Simeon filled her glass again, not sure if it was the right thing to do, but he figured that at least it would act as an anesthetic.

"When did Felix say he was coming?"

"Same flight tomorrow. That's what he's planning, anyway. Unless some other problem turns up at the hospital, of course."

Simeon watched Ann; he was uncommitted at that time, and although she was certainly attractive enough in a physical sense, for some reason she didn't turn him on. Not even a little bit. It was as if she'd put up an emotional barbed-wire fence around herself, a kind of de-sexing aura of distance and separateness, not aimed particularly at him but at the entire human race.

"I hope his plane crashes," she said.

Simeon's mouth opened slightly with astonishment.

"Only the good die young," he replied. He couldn't think of anything more appropriate to say.

"If that's true, he'll live forever," she said.

Simeon looked at her, hoping to see a smile that would show she was joking, but her expression was hard.

Neither of them said anything for a while, and Ann downed her third large whiskey sour. A queasy foreboding invaded Simeon's spirit, and his own drink was doing nothing to improve it. Ann, on the other hand, was now sitting up, ramrod-straight, her eyes glittering with an unusual intensity.

"I thought you and Felix got along pretty well," he ventured finally. "Or were you just kidding about the plane crashing?"

"Yeah, we got along," replied Ann. She laughed, a high-pitched, shaky laugh that sent a new pulse of anxiety through Simeon. "We've always got along," she went on. "Ever since we were kids, it seems now."

"You want to sit out on the balcony?" asked Simeon, glancing through the picture window. It was getting dark quickly, and the lights were coming on in the harbor below them. To the east, far over the water, a faint glow suffused the sky.

Ann stood up, Simeon opened the glass door, and they went out and sat in the white-painted cast-iron chairs facing out over the water.

"It's so quiet here." Ann looked around anxiously. Her head jerked in quick, birdlike movements. After Manhattan, the silence here was certainly intense, and Simeon was enjoying it as much as the warm, moist, unpolluted air. Even though she'd had a lot to drink, Ann still looked wound up so tight she might explode. She stood up, went back into the room, and turned on the radio full blast, then came back, leaving the glass door open.

She almost fell when she sat down, and some of her drink spilled on her dress. She stared at Simeon with sad, calculating eyes.

"Did you know that Felix is eight years older than me?" she asked him.

It sounded more like a statement than a question, and there didn't seem to be any urgent need to answer, so there was silence for a while. It was dark now, and the dome of the moon was starting to come up over the horizon, sharp-edged and startlingly bright, throwing a luminous silver sheen that spread across the water toward them. Simeon sighed quietly, wishing he'd brought a girlfriend to share the beauty of this scene; Ann's presence beside him was supplying only a harsh, tense, and discordant note. He wanted to turn the radio off and enjoy the peace and tranquillity of the scene, but after another glance at Ann's rigid profile, he decided not to. He sighed quietly, wishing that Felix had come with them. If Ann had some kind of bone to pick with her brother, they could have fought it out without involving him.

Simeon was starting to feel hungry. "If you don't want to go the restaurant," he said, "I'm sure we can get room service. Would you like anything?"

"Go ahead," she said. "I'm not hungry. I'd like another drink, though."

Her voice was slurring, and there was no question in Simeon's mind that she had already had more than enough.

"How about a Coke or something?" he asked. "There's a dispenser at the end of the hallway."

"Are you telling me I've had too much of this stuff?" she asked, holding up her empty glass and looking at it.

"Probably yes," he ventured. "Especially on an empty stomach."

Ann laughed, inappropriately loudly. "An empty stomach," she said. "That's what I have, no question. Okay, why don't we go down to the restaurant? I'll have a glass of wine while you eat."

There were very few diners in the restaurant, and they

got a table near the windows, overlooking the quiet dock, the still boats lit by rickety yellow lights.

At the last moment Ann decided to have some pea soup, and Simeon ordered crayfish, cooked Bahamian style with butter and herbs.

"I had an abortion," said Ann suddenly. "Two days ago."

"I'm sorry," said Simeon lamely. He wished that Ann wouldn't speak so loudly. "I mean, I'm sure that it was the right thing for you, but it must have been awful all the same."

"Felix was the father," said Ann in the same obstinate tones.

"Oh, Jesus," breathed Simeon. He took a deep breath. "Look, Ann, I don't think you should be telling me this. Whatever it is, it's between you and Felix, and I'm sorry, but I don't want to hear any more about it, okay?"

"He started with me on my twelfth birthday," she went on, quite oblivious. "He's had sex with me almost every day since then, except when he was away at school or on call, stuff like that."

"Are you telling me he raped you? Again and again?" asked Simeon disbelievingly. As soon as he said the words, he regretted them, because the last thing he wanted was to hear more about it.

"Oh, no. Actually I liked it—for a while, anyway. Felix was nice enough with me, and I didn't have to bother with other boys like the other girls did, with all that emotional stuff, heartbreaks and disappointments and so on. It was actually okay, or seemed to be, for a long time. I don't know how our parents never found out, but that's beside the point."

Simeon stared at her. Ann's soup arrived, and Simeon only hoped she would wait until the waiter had gone before continuing her story, which she seemed determined to tell him.

The waiter poured the wine and Simeon tasted it, but he was so upset and distracted that it could have seen club soda for all he knew.

"It went on for all that time," said Ann, shaking her head. "Eleven years . . ." She stared over Simeon's shoulder into the distance. "And it may sound strange to you, but most of that time I felt pretty okay about it. There was a kind of safety about being with him. He was always very protective of me. Our parents didn't like each other and fought a whole lot, and so when he was holding me close to him it was like a defense, a protection against them, against everything out there, and I felt there was at least one person who really loved me . . ."

"So what happened?" By now, Simeon was reluctantly sucked in to the story, fascinated in a weird kind of way. Visions of Felix came to him, Felix playing tennis, in the operating room, teaching students . . . He shook his head. And all that time, during all the things the two of them had done, all that time Felix had been living with this guilty, nasty secret. Simeon's instinct was to get up, go to the desk, and find the first flight home. But then he figured he'd waited a long time for this vacation, so he'd just stick it out until Sunday evening, have a good time, and leave the two of them to their own devices. Back in New York, of course, that would be the end of his friendship with Felix. Simeon's whole being revolted against what these two were doing.

"What happened?" repeated Ann. "As I said, it was more or less cool until a couple of months ago when I got pregnant, and suddenly it hit me what I was doing. IN-CEST. A dirty word I'd never even used before, and now it was shouting out at me from everywhere, from the people I passed in the street, from the shops and subway entrances. And what had happened, what I'd done, made me unfit for any normal relationship with a man. Any man. Any person. Ever. Simeon, can you imagine what that feels like?"

Ann's knuckles were white with tension. Simeon noticed a thin gold ring with a small green stone on her middle finger. She turned it around and around.

Simeon said, "To be perfectly truthful, Ann, no, I cannot imagine what that feels like."

"Well, it feels like being the most hateful and loathsome person that ever existed in the whole history of mankind. And that horrible person is me! Me!" Ann thumped her chest with her clenched fist. "You know, Simeon, Felix and I had even talked about the possibility before, if anything happened ... Felix used condoms most of the time, but sometimes he forgot, and he didn't want me to go on the pill because he said they could eventually cause cancer."

Ann took a deep breath and shook her head as if she were trying to remember the content of a nightmare. "So when I got pregnant, Felix said I had to get an abortion. I was scared, terrified, actually, and said okay, Felix, whatever you say, but after that it hit me more and more that everything in my life was going wrong, and it was already at the point when it could not be straightened out again, not ever."

Ann grabbed the wine bottle and filled up her glass. Her hand was shaking, and some of the wine spilled out of the glass onto the white linen tablecloth. Simeon picked up the salt shaker, covered the stain with salt, and rubbed it in with his finger.

"Where did you have it done?" he asked.

"The Lower Manhattan Women's Center," she replied.

"I know a couple of the people there," he murmured. "I guess they have a pretty good rep."

His discomfort and embarrassment were turning into a strong desire to get the hell out of there and away from this situation and this woman. In a way he felt sympathy for her, but surely a lot of her problems were at least partly of her own making. At the same time, Simeon could feel his anger against Felix growing. That despicable bastard ... And what would he say to him when Felix got off the plane tomorrow evening, wearing that phony politician's smile of his?

"Who was your doc at the Women's Center?" he asked, wondering if it was anyone he knew.

"A woman called Olga something," replied Ann. "A big blond woman. I don't remember, Simeon. I don't *want* to remember."

"Olga Petrikov?"

"Right. It's a small world, huh?" Ann was looking into space, as if her replies were about another life, one that no longer belonged to her. "Felix said this trip was to make up for all of that, for everything. He said, 'Then you can just forget about it.' That's what he said, as God's my witness."

"So what are you going to do now?" Simeon glanced at his watch. He felt very tired, all of a sudden, and he wanted to go to bed and sleep. But now for some reason he was having difficulty believing all of Ann's story. He couldn't really see Felix involved in something like this.

"I don't know. I feel really desperate ... You see, Simeon, there's nothing I can do. It's all done. Like Omar Khayyám said, 'The moving finger writes; and having writ, nor all your piety nor wit ...' "

" 'Shall lure it back to cancel half a line, nor all your tears wash out a word of it.' " Rather somberly, Simeon finished the verse for her.

"You looked at your watch," said Ann. "Let's go."

Simeon signed the bill and they went back upstairs. At her door, he was about to leave her when she turned to him, her eyes full of tears. "Simeon," she said, "I'm going to ask you a big favor. Would you please sleep with me tonight?"

Simeon, astonished, was opening his mouth to refuse, when she said, "Not to have sex with me, Simeon, that's not what I meant. I just need to feel a human body next to me, one that isn't Felix ... And I like you, you're a very kind person. Please, Simeon. You see, I'm really scared that I'm going to lose my mind."

Chapter 16

Against his better judgment, and feeling a little nettled about being thought of as "safe," Simeon followed Ann into her room, which suddenly took on a different and threatening aspect.

Ann turned her back to him. "Please, Simeon, unzip me."

The zipper reached from Ann's midback all the way to her lower back, and as he reached the bottom she gave a little shake. A quite unexpected and dangerous feeling arose in him, which he was able to suppress instantly, but it was followed by a strong urge to get away from this woman, to get the hell out of this room.

"I'm going back to my room," he said, but when Ann turned and he saw her anguished expression, he felt enough compassion to add, "To brush my teeth."

It was late and the corridor was deserted. Feeling as if the Furies were in hot pursuit, Simeon opened the door, locked it behind him, went into the tiny bathroom, and brushed his teeth, mostly to give himself some time to think.

His head was still clouded by the whiskey sours and the wine, and he could feel competing emotions struggling inside him, compassion for her versus distaste for who she was and what she had done, as well as other urges that surfaced only because the alcohol had liberated in him a recognition of his own thoughts—thoughts he didn't wish ever to surface.

It was a warm night. Standing naked and ready for bed at his window, he could see the bright moonlight etching out black shadows of trees and buildings and suffusing the rest of the view with a glowing white light that Simeon didn't remember ever seeing before.

On impulse, he turned and picked up the phone. The more he thought about it, the crazier Ann's story seemed, and he needed some confirmation. After a delay, he got the Manhattan number he wanted.

Then he dialed it. "Olga? This is Simeon."

There was a wild yell from the other end. "Goddamn you, Simeon! Where are you? Where have you been?"

Simeon smiled. In med school, Olga had been his partner in the anatomy lab; she was a big, rawboned, very smart woman with a deep laugh and a great sense of humor. At that time she was living with a pathologist, a quiet-seeming young woman who turned out to be just as boisterous and funny as Olga. The three of them used to go out together occasionally. One time they'd gone to a very formal, very stuffy party at Simeon's boss's house, where Olga and her friend Bernice had scandalized everyone by pretending to be a small part of Simeon's harem.

Simeon asked if she remembered performing an abortion on an Ann Cadwaller two days before.

"I remember the name yes," said Olga. "A girlfriend?"

"No. I just wanted to be sure." A thought struck him, and he asked Olga a couple of questions and made a request that surprised her but that she agreed to. Then, anxious to change the subject, he asked, "Are you still with Bernice?"

"Of course. We don't fuck around like you heterosexuals do. When are you coming to have dinner with us?"

"Soon. Listen, I'll call you when I get back to New York. Give Bernice a hug from me."

Several minutes later, there was a knock on the door of Simeon's room. Simeon grabbed a robe and stood behind the door. "Who is it?" he asked unnecessarily.

"It's me, Simeon, as you know perfectly well. Open the door, please."

Simeon hesitated for a moment, turned the lights on, then opened the door. Ann, wearing a white terry-cloth robe over red silk pajamas, marched right past him and got into the bed. She slid over to the right side, watching him. She seemed all tensed up and about ready to weep again, and Simeon's heart sank. He was out of his depth with all this, and short of going to sleep next door in her room or sleeping on the beach, his options were limited.

"Simeon, it's very late. Come to bed. I won't bother you." She smiled. "And to reassure you, the doc at the clinic said I shouldn't have sex for at least a week."

Simeon, who hadn't brought pajamas because he always slept nude, tied the belt of his robe and came slowly toward the bed. He was so tired he couldn't see straight, and he fell on top of the bed, closed his eyes, and went to sleep. The last thing he remembered was Ann moving closer to him and positioning her body warmly against his. It didn't feel so bad.

It must have been around four in the morning when Simeon woke up suddenly. The light was still on, and he could feel Ann's body right up next to him, tense but moving gently and rhythmically against him. He could tell she wasn't asleep, because of the way she was breathing. His robe seemed to have ridden up and was bunched around his waist, and he could feel her pubic hair moving scratchily against his thigh.

He turned on his right side and put his other hand out. It landed on her full right breast, and her nipple was erect and hard as a raisin. At his touch, Ann moaned and bucked hard against him. Against his will, he felt his own desire rising like the mercury in a thermometer. In the space of a few seconds he told himself to get out of bed, take a cold shower, sleep on the couch, go for a walk, but under no circumstances should he do any more than he'd already done with a participant in an incestuous relationship. At the same time he began to wonder to what extent Felix had been the prime mover. This Ann was something else, with a sexual aura and energy that many men would find irresistible. Even a brother, maybe.

Now Ann's fingers were busily undoing the belt of his robe, and Simeon knew that it was now or never; if he was going to back out, he had to do it in the next ten seconds. As soon as she'd untied the belt, Ann caught his hand, pulled it gently off her breast, and guided it down between her legs.

Maybe it was because she was so excessively wet, or because he suddenly thought of Felix doing the same thing, but a feeling of revulsion struck Simeon so strongly that he pulled his hand away and jumped out of the bed.

"You told me you just wanted somebody to lie beside you," he said, breathing hard. "I'm going to sleep on the couch."

"Come back," said Ann. "Please, Simeon!" There was a desperation in her voice that made Simeon hesitate.

Shaking, he went over to the brocade-covered couch and flung himself down on it. Wide awake, he could hear Ann moving and groaning on the bed. The sounds reached a crescendo and then there was silence. Her breathing became regular and deep, with little intermittent snorts. Simeon didn't go to sleep for another hour. He was turning it all over in his mind, but he couldn't really get a clear picture.

When he woke up, feeling stiff and annoyed, it was because the sun was coming up and the sunlight coming through the big windows was shining on his face with a crystal brightness. He sat up and looked over at the bed. It was empty. At that moment the telephone rang. It was Ann, calmly asking if he was ready to go down for breakfast. He looked at his watch. The dive boat was supposed to leave from the hotel dock in just over half an hour.

"We'll have to hurry," he said.

"I checked on the boat already," she said. "They're fixing something on one of the motors and they'll call us when they're ready."

Simeon put down the phone with a feeling of anxiety and puzzlement. Ann's voice was calm enough, apparently quite free of the tension and panic of the evening before, but there were other vibrations that made him feel very uneasy. Was this woman crazy? If she was crazy, was it because of what had happened to her? In spite of the fact that he wasn't looking forward to seeing Felix, he was glad that her brother would soon be here to take her off his hands.

He picked up the bag that held all his scuba gear, the regulator, mask, fins, octopus, all the paraphernalia he would need, and lugged it down to the restaurant with him.

Ann was looking surprisingly good; now that her face

wasn't puffy or her eyes bloodshot, she was striking without being particularly beautiful. Dressed in a bright red tied shirt and short white shorts, she had great legs and a good figure, better than when she had no clothes on. Looking at her, Simeon remembered the little network of stretch marks on the top of both her breasts, and again he wondered if she had more history than she admitted to, even though she was still only in her early twenties.

She made no mention of the night before, and chatted about other places she'd gone scuba diving with Felix—the Great Barrier Reef, Hawaii, the Red Sea, all over. There was no question, Ann was a pro.

They were finishing their breakfast of sliced mangoes, papaya, coffee, toast, and orange juice when a white-coated waiter came over to the table.

"The dive boat is ready when you are, gent and lady." He grinned and pointed out the window. "They waitin' for you."

They looked out at the boat, a white, low-draft fiberglass vessel with a high blue canvas awning. It was bobbing up and down at the dock in the wake of a large boat that was just passing on its way out of the harbor. Simeon noted the two big outboards tilted up at the stern, half a dozen scuba tanks fastened to a central rack with canvas straps, and a couple of black and yellow wet suits hanging from a metal rack behind the tanks. A long radio antenna whipped from one side to the other as the vessel rocked in the big boat's wake.

"Ready?" Ann was looking at him with a smile, just an upcurling of the corners of her mouth.

"Sure." He picked up his bag, and they both went out through a glass door directly onto the gray wooden planks of the dock.

The crew, both tall, slim black men, watched them approach. One, wearing a yellow shirt, had one foot on the dock and the other on the boat, obviously enjoying the game of keeping his balance. When Ann and Simeon came up, he held out his hand for their bags. The other, a lanky man with several missing teeth and startling green eyes, smiled broadly at them. "Welcome to you both," he said in a deep, resonant voice. He extended a hand to Ann and helped her on board. He was the captain, he told them, and his name was Leon Marryatt. After asking them how much diving they had done recently, he asked to see their diving certificates, then they cast off and purred gently through the harbor. Once past the low boulder-built jetty, Leon opened up the throttles and they were off, bow up in the air, a high mound of water bubbling and foaming at the stern, heading for the reefs. After about thirty minutes the reef showed up as a white line of surf on the horizon.

Ann and Simeon sat on the built-in seats at the side of the boat, both busy checking and putting together their diving equipment. Ann seemed relaxed and content now, as if something had happened to resolve her problems, or she had come to some internal peace about them, although to Simeon they seemed far too big to deal with overnight.

"I've been here before," said Ann. "Why don't I lead?"

"Fine with me," Simeon answered.

Leon told them that the best diving was on the inside of the reef, where the water had a maximum depth of seventy feet. In any case, he said, the water was too rough to venture out into the open sea.

"You'll stay together, right?" he asked Simeon. In the way of Bahamian men, he invariably addressed Simeon and ignored Ann.

"Of course," replied Simeon. Ann nodded.

"Visibility's down to about twenty-five feet," Leon went on. "We had a storm last week, stirred everything up. There's a wreck down there in fifty feet, a freighter that almost made it through the inner channel, but not quite. That was back in 1982." Leon's voice was deep and rich, with educated British overtones.

He brought the boat around in a wide semicircle, cut the engine, and dropped anchor. They were less than a quarter mile from the reef and could hear the booming of the surf, pounding on the ocean side. "The wreck's about seventy yards toward the reef," Leon told Simeon. "And when you're there, don't put your hands in any dark holes. There's a couple of big morays down inside, so keep your eyes open."

Seconds later they were in the water. As always, Simeon was filled with a sense of having entered another world as they swam down through the hazy green depths. It was unlike anything else in his experience, floating down in a silent, submarine forest through a door as magical as any in the Arabian Nights. It was silent, vast, mysterious, with everything happening in timeless slow motion.

Ann led, and as Leon had warned them, the visibility was not the best. Simeon stuck close to her, watching the oscillating line of rising bubbles coming every few seconds from her mouthpiece.

She headed for the wreck. Simeon checked his compass; his normally good sense of direction went totally out of whack under water. A ledge of coral, projecting from the still distant reef, appeared, and they swam toward it, dazzled by the multicolored beauty of the coral and its inhabitants.

Ann turned, her hair waving like blond seaweed, and pointed. The wreck appeared suddenly. It seemed only a few yards away, a greenish shape lying on the sandy bottom, stanchions and rigging festooned with barnacles. Angelfish with gossamer fins, silvery, yellow-striped goatfish, and little schools of yellowtail jack meandered above the sloping metal deck. Simeon knew that distance and depth perception were altered in the water, and it took longer than he expected to reach the wreck.

Ann stopped, adjusted her buoyancy to neutral, unclipped the flashlight from her belt, and pointed forward with it. Simeon unclipped his own flashlight and swam slowly with her closer to the wreck. It was much larger now than it had seemed, and its encrusted sides loomed high above him like a massive wall. A row of empty portholes ran along the side of the vessel, but they were too small to get through.

Trying to ignore visions of huge moray eels with snapping jaws, Simeon followed Ann up the side of the wreck until they came to the deck. A huge fish with glistening brown scales came suddenly into view just above them, and Simeon took a moment to recognize it as a grouper and not a shark. His heart beating fast, he watched as it swam idly past them, its eyes watching them with mild curiosity.

Ann paid no attention. She swam to a large open hatch in the deck and waved to Simeon to go on in ahead of her.

He gripped the flashlight tight, switched it on, and very cautiously made his way down through the hole into the dark, murky interior of the ship. Festoons of electric cables hung down from the ceiling, and sponges, gorgonian sea fans, and encrusting corals grew like tumors on the rusting metal. A school of tiny silversides, alarmed by the light, flashed, wheeled, and disappeared ahead of him. What must have once been a light fixture hung at an angle from the ceiling, all jagged and lumpy with marine growths and barnacles of various kinds. Fascinated, Simeon moved slowly forward, passed into another compartment, then looked around to see how Ann was doing.

There was no light behind him, nothing. She had disappeared.

Chapter 17

Thinking that Ann had stayed outside the wreck for some reason, but anxious about her all the same, Simeon retraced his way back between the decks toward the open hatch where he had left her. As he was cautiously ascending toward the pale green square of light, he suddenly found that he wasn't moving forward. It took him several seconds to realize that his air tank had become caught in the hanging leash of the overhead electric cables.

He thought for a moment, then moved back to free the tank, but the cables just moved back with him. He rocked backward, put his feet on the hatch coaming and pushed himself backward, but of course he couldn't see, and after several minutes of trying to maneuver his way to freedom, he realized that he was firmly stuck. His breathing was coming fast and irregular, and he was aware that if he didn't pull himself together quickly he would die there. He made a huge effort to control his breathing, then looked at his pressure gauge. Six hundred pounds of pressure remained from the initial twenty-one hundred. They had spent more time examining the reef than he had realized. Now he was about fifty feet down, with about eight minutes' worth of air remaining in his tank, a little less than he'd expected. He stretched his hand behind him and felt around. The two-inch-thick cables were entangled above and below the tank, and he knew there was no way his knife could cut through them. And where was Ann? Had she just gone off and abandoned him? He wanted to shout, but of course he knew that no useful sound would get outside his mask.

Still feeling the threat of panic in his chest, Simeon forced himself to calm down. For five minutes he tried to ease the cable free, pushing with his feet against the jagged edge of the deck to get some leverage. The cables swayed, but didn't release their grip.

His air pressure gauge was now hovering around two hundred psi, enough for an emergency ascent, but first he had to free himself, and there was only one thing he could do. Moving as cautiously as possible, and trying to remember the drill he'd been taught during scuba training, he ripped open the Velcro closure of his buoyancy vest and was just able to slide out of it. He next jettisoned his weight belt, and still attached by the air hose to his regulator but now free of the cables, he took several deep breaths, then spat out the regulator mouthpiece and started to go up, remembering to exhale all the way up so his lungs wouldn't burst from the internal pressure. It seemed to take forever to reach the surface. When his head emerged, he coughed and spluttered and shouted from the pain in his chest. All he could see was the choppy water around him. Then he became aware of the roaring surf crashing on the rocky coral reef only a hundred yards away. A few moments later he realized that he was moving quickly toward the channel. The tide was receding, and he was being sucked out to the open sea.

He turned around to look for the boat and glimpsed it for just a moment, far behind him. He raised one arm and waved it up and down, but he realized that they were probably too far away to see him, even if they were looking. He was getting chilled now, and he tried to swim toward the boat, but the current was far too fast for him to make any headway. He decided to save his strength and rely on the buoyancy of his wet suit, watching helplessly as the rocks and the surf came closer. He knew that in that turmoil of sharp coral and high waves he wouldn't stand a chance.

Back on the boat, Leon was getting anxious because his clients' time was up and they weren't back. He scanned the area around the site of the wreck with his binoculars, and by a lucky chance happened to glance over toward the reef. For just a moment he saw a black speck. It disappeared, and he was about to look elsewhere when it reappeared and he realized that it was one of his divers. There was no time to pull up the anchor. "Let it go!" he shouted to his mate, jumping to start one engine. He spun the wheel around and opened the throttle wide, and while they raced toward the channel his crewman started the other outboard. Within a minute they had reached approximately the spot where Leon had sighted the diver, but now they couldn't see him. The boat rocked violently in the fast-flowing, turbulent current; this was a very dangerous place when the tide was running, and Leon knew it. He pushed away the urge to head back to safety and tried to keep the boat from getting swamped.

"There! Port side!" The mate was pointing, but for a few moments Leon couldn't see anything. A wave broke over the bow, and the whole boat shivered and lurched. Leon was scared to cut the motors because he'd lose control and the boat would be swamped and overturned for sure. Then he saw Simeon's head in the water, just a few feet away. Another wave came and he disappeared again. The mate, risking his own life, leaned over the gunwale, a boat hook in his hand, and managed to hook onto Simeon's belt.

They dragged him on board, then Leon turned the boat around and pushed the throttles fully open. With both engines going flat out, they were able to make headway against the racing current. For several minutes Simeon lay on the deck gasping, then he struggled back to the rear of the boat, still coughing and spluttering.

"Ann!" he gasped. "Where is she?"

"We haven't seen her," shouted Leon, who was already thinking of all the inquiries and reports he would have to file if he lost one of his divers. "Wasn't she with you?"

"Go back to where the wreck is!"

"I'm doing my best," said Leon.

Once they were out of the grasp of the current, Leon headed back to the site of the wreck. The water was relatively calm there, but there was no sign of Ann. The mate called for help on the radio, and within an hour three other boats had joined the search.

After almost two hours of cruising to and fro in the vicinity of the wreck, Leon said they were running short of fuel and would have to return to the harbor.

"Sweet Jesus," thought Simeon to himself, sitting miserably in the stern, holding on to his last vision of Ann as the boat raced back to Governor's Harbour, "what am I going to tell Felix?"

That evening Simeon met the plane. When he told Felix what had happened, Felix completely lost it.

"How could you let that happen?" he screamed, standing in the middle of the airport lobby. Completely beside himself, he swung furiously at Simeon, who avoided the blow and grasped Felix's wrist hard enough to hurt.

Felix eventually calmed down, but in his irrational fury he blamed Simeon for the accident. Ann's body was found washed up on the reef the next day, and although the coroner's verdict was accidental death, Simeon was certain that she had committed suicide.

Simeon returned to New York the next day, as planned. He had offered to stay on the island and help Felix with the arrangements, but Felix remained violently angry with him and said he never wanted to see or hear from him again, although since they were on the same neurosurgical service that didn't make too much sense.

But from that time on, Felix was Simeon's avowed enemy. He did everything he could to give his junior a hard time, and three years later, a year after Simeon joined the staff of New Coventry Medical Center, Felix, who had a good research job at the National Institutes of Health in Bethesda, Maryland, applied for the job as chairman of the department at NCMC, although he almost passed it up because Simeon was there. Felix got the job. Once there, his contact with Simeon was slight, but he never missed an opportunity to damage him. And now, with this young patient of his, Andy Markle, Felix wondered if he might have another chance to avenge his beloved sister's death.

Chapter 18

Kevin had lent Andy a new game, an electronic pinball machine, for his GameBoy, and Andy was well on his way to a score of one million when Dr. Felix Cadwaller came into his room with his retinue of nurses and residents.

Andy wasn't feeling great, although he'd reported no problems when Simeon and his team had stopped in earlier. In fact, his eyes had blurred several times and he'd felt dizzy after that. He didn't know why he hadn't told Dr. Halstead; maybe he was so used to saying "Okay" when someone asked how he was, that he'd just said it automatically.

Andy hated to give up the pinball game when it was going so well, but this new doctor looked very important, so he switched it off.

"I'm Dr. Felix Cadwaller," said the one who seemed to be the boss, a thickset man with a square face and a gray crew cut. He smiled in a friendly way. In spite of his gray hair, he still looked quite young. "Your dad asked me to take a look at you," he went on, coming up to the bed. "We call that giving a second opinion."

Andy said nothing, wondering why his mother hadn't mentioned it to him. Was Dad trying to pull something against her again?

Dr. Cadwaller sat down at the end of the bed and asked him the same questioned that everybody else had been asking, then examined him in the same way too, the same lights shining into his eyes, all the same stuff. But there was something different about this new doctor. He explained things more and was a lot more friendly. Andy grinned to himself. Dr. Halstead was too distant, this Dr. Cadwaller was too friendly. On the whole, Andy preferred

Dr. Halstead because he was real and didn't try to impress him with what a nice guy he was.

It was soon over. Dr. Cadwaller told Andy he was going to review his chart and the test results, then they all left. Andy started up the GameBoy again, but it didn't go well this time; his electronic ball kept falling down between the paddles and ending the game.

The door opened, and in came Susie, looking bright and cheerful as a spring daisy.

She came over and kissed Andy on the forehead, a light, teasing, happy-to-see-you-kid kiss. "So what's up?" she asked.

Andy told her about Dr. Cadwaller's visit. "Does he know you're supposed to have surgery tomorrow?" she asked.

"I don't know," replied Andy, eating Susie up with his eyes. "He didn't ask."

Susie's big eyes were troubled. "Did he say anything else?"

"Nope. He was going to look at the chart and tests and stuff. He said my father asked him to check me out. I don't know why."

"He wanted a second opinion, I guess," said Susie, shrugging. "My dad said there's more than one way of dealing with this kind of problem, and it's a good idea to look at all the ways before settling on one."

An aide came in, pushing a stainless steel cart with a water jug and other paraphernalia. "Andy Markle?" he asked. He was a slender young man with a tiny black ponytail. He looked from Susie to Andy.

Andy nodded.

"My name's Anthony, and I'm going to shave your head," said the aide, after checking Andy's wristband.

"All of it?" asked Andy. Suddenly, for the first time, he felt afraid.

"Yep. You're gonna look as if you play basketball for the Knicks."

"The Celtics," said Andy.

"Under the circumstances," said the aide loftily, "you can play for any team you wish. We'll start at the occipital area, then go over the vertex . . ."

"What's that?"

"Oh, that means the top of the head."

"You a med student?" asked Susie.

"Next year," said the aide, surprised but pleased. "How did you know?"

"It figures," said Susie pertly. "Whenever a kid uses a complicated word for a simple thing, he's usually a med student or going to law school." She stood up.

"Are you leaving?" asked Andy.

Susie looked at him. He had too much pride to ask her to stay while he was getting his head shaved, but she could tell he was scared and would really appreciate her presence. She checked her watch. "Okay," she said. "I don't go on for another ten minutes. And anyway . . ." She nodded at the aide. ". . . somebody should be here to keep an eye on this kid."

The aide started by putting a towel round Andy's shoulders, just like a barber; then, using an electric clipper, he started at the back and went up over the top to the hairline at the front. Andy's hair was fairly long, and it felt strange and scary to see the long strands of red-blond hair falling silently around him.

Susie took his hand in her small, soft one, and Andy concentrated on that until the aide was done. Anthony collected the hair, put it in a plastic Ziploc bag, and gave it to Andy.

"I don't want it," he said, looking at the bag.

"Your mother might," replied the aide. "Anyway, the rule is that you get the hair." He collected his tools and left, smiling at Susie.

"How do I look?" asked Andy. He tried to sound as if it didn't matter to him. His head felt cold.

"Different," said Susie, after examining him critically. "But okay." She took back her hand. "Now I have to go," she said. "See you later."

Kevin stopped in for a short time during the lunch hour and was visibly impressed by Andy's shaved head. That evening, almost at the end of visiting hours, he and a group of half a dozen of Andy's school friends came to the hospital and talked the charge nurse into letting them into

Andy's room. She laughed, then gave her permission, but warned them not to make too much noise.

They filed in, said hello politely to Fiona, who looked at them with astonishment, and gathered around the bed, grinning rather self-consciously at Andy, who started to laugh.

Looking at the boys, Fiona couldn't prevent the tears from coming to her eyes. All of them, including Kevin, had had their heads shaved.

After reviewing the charts and documents concerning Andy Markle, Felix Cadwaller went back to his office in the medical school building, sat down, and thought for a few moments. Then he called Simeon.

"I've just seen your patient Andy Markle in consultation, at the request of his father," he said brusquely. "What are you planning to do for him?"

"Before we discuss that," replied Simeon coolly, "I think we have a slight jurisdictional problem here. Andy lives with his mother, and according to the information I have, Mrs. Markle has full custody of him. The husband, I believe, has only limited visitation rights." He paused for a moment, feeling his ancient anger and disgust at Cadwaller rising again. "The point I'm making is that I don't believe Mr. Markle has any right to ask you or anybody else to consult on his son."

"That's just a legalism," said Cadwaller dismissively. "In any case, I *have* seen him, so there isn't much point in discussing whether I should or I shouldn't. So, if I may repeat the question, what are you planning to do for the boy?"

"It's not just a legalism," said Simeon carefully. "What I am saying, and you're forcing me to put it more bluntly, is that you had no right to examine Andy Markle. His father has no authority to ask you for a consultation."

"What the hell are you talking about?" Cadwaller's face was red. "May I remind you that as chairman of this department I have the right to examine any patient on the neurosurgical service and, if necessary, to take over their care."

"Do you have the hospital bylaws handy?" asked Simeon. "You will find on page fourteen, section eight, I think the second paragraph, the following words: 'in the event of physical or mental disability of any physician, or when strong grounds for suspecting mismanagement exist, the chairman of any clinical department may, at his discretion, direct or take over the treatment of any patient in that clinical department.' Is that the *right* you were referring to?"

Cadwaller paused. He knew all about Simeon's phenomenal memory, and he knew that his quote from the bylaws was word-for-word correct.

"I have no doubt that Mr. Markle's request to me was with his wife's agreement," he said. "Which would make it perfectly legal, right?"

"Why don't we find out?" said Simeon. "If that is what happened, I'll be happy to discuss the case with you."

"I'll be happy to call her," said Cadwaller.

"*I'll* call her," said Simeon, not giving an inch. "And I'll get back to you."

Cadwaller, furious that he hadn't taken the elementary precaution of finding out if Andy's father had the authority to ask him for a consultation, hung up. He stared for a moment at the photo of his sister, Ann, on his desk, then checked the phone book and dialed Sam Seidel's office.

"Hi, Dr. Seidel?" he said. "This is Felix Cadwaller. I saw your patient Andy Markle as requested by his dad, but I've run into a bit of a problem. Maybe you can help me out. Can you tell me if Mrs. Markle knew about this request?"

Sam grinned to himself. Things were working out more or less as he expected. "I don't think so," he said. "But I don't suppose she would object."

"Would you mind confirming that with her? I'd really appreciate it."

"Sure. I'll call her, then I'll get back to you, okay?" Sam looked up. Gloria was mouthing something at him, but he waved her away.

He looked at his watch. Fiona should be home by now, unless she was at the hospital. He tried Andy's room first, and she answered the phone. "Small problem, Fiona," he said in his gravelly voice. "Victor asked one of the other surgeons at the Center, a Dr. Cadwaller, for a second opinion, and we need your okay on that."

"Andy told me. Why?" Fiona put her hand on Andy's shoulder. "This is none of Victor's business, and he knows it. Why do we need a second opinion? Isn't Dr. Halstead's sufficient?"

"In a complicated situation like this," said Sam, "it doesn't hurt to have another input. Dr. Cadwaller is the head of the neurosurgical service, and personally I think it's a good idea."

There was a brief silence. Fiona smiled at Andy. There was no sense in getting him upset. "Okay, Dr. Seidel, if you think so . . ."

"Good. Actually, he's seen Andy already, this afternoon. This'll just make it legal, if you know what I mean."

"They're still going ahead with the surgery tomorrow?"

"I suppose so. I don't expect that there would be any disagreement on that score."

Fiona was getting unnerved. "Will someone let us know?"

"Sure. I just needed your okay so that Dr. Cadwaller can talk to Dr. Halstead."

Fiona took a deep breath. It was bad enough that Andy was facing surgery, without getting involved in this kind of hospital politicking. "You have it. My okay. Will somebody let me know what they decide?"

"Sure. I know it's confusing, Fiona, but it's in Andy's best interest, okay?"

Sam's next call was to Simeon Halstead, who listened to him in silence. "Both Mrs. Markle and her husband would be more comfortable with a second opinion," said Sam. "I've talked to both of them, and they agree."

Simeon shrugged. "That's all right with me," he said. "As long as it's Mrs. Markle's wish, I'll be happy to discuss the case with Dr. Cadwaller."

Gloria came in again as Sam hung up. "You have patients waiting," she said.

"Okay, okay, I'm coming," he replied. "And when I'm done, I want to call Vargas in Puerto Vallarta."

Chapter 19

Talking to Simeon had set Felix Cadwaller to thinking again about his sister, Ann. Even now, after all this time, and even though he'd seen and identified her body, he couldn't quite believe that she was dead. When the phone rang and Simeon told him coldly that he had Mrs. Markle's permission to go ahead with his consultation, Cadwaller, still looking at her photo on his desk, said, "Good. I've already seen the patient, as you know. Why don't you come over here and we can discuss his diagnosis and management."

"No. I'll meet you in the X-ray department," replied Simeon. "We can go over all the films there."

Felix's jaw clenched. Simeon was the hardest-headed man he'd ever met, but that didn't make any difference to him. Just hearing that voice, Felix could feel his ever-simmering anger bubbling up to the surface again. Sooner or later, somehow, he was going to destroy that bastard, ruin him professionally and any other way he could. Only then would he feel that Ann's death had been avenged, although it still wouldn't bring her back to him.

"Okay," he said. "Ten minutes."

Simeon hung up, and thought about it. He had no illusions about Felix's intentions, and knew that he wouldn't hesitate to use a patient to hurt him if he could, but on the other hand he didn't see how Felix could use Andy Markle for that, because he was primarily a researcher, didn't do much operating, and was not known for his clinical ability. Simeon knew himself to be a much better surgeon than Felix was, and there weren't any loopholes in Andy Markle's case. All the necessary tests had been done, there were no slips in the workup, no errors in his plan of action.

But all that didn't help Andy, he thought. Poor kid. Simeon's experience told him that the tumor was most likely malignant, and judging from its location, it would not be easy to deal with. Simeon had seen many such cases, but for some reason Andy struck him as very different. After his talk with Dr. Rosenfeld, Garvey's psychiatrist, he had made a deliberate effort to spend more time with his patients, and of course with the Garvey episode, he'd gotten to know Andy's mother. For a moment he dwelt on Fiona; he could sense something intriguing about her, something fiery and exciting under the surface, hidden by her anxiety about Andy. He remembered watching her out of the corner of his eye while Ted Garvey was waving his gun at them in the emergency room. She hadn't panicked, she'd stayed calm and self-possessed. Aside from being very attractive, Fiona Markle was without question a woman of character, he reflected, a person who deserved ... what exactly? He grinned. More than she was getting, maybe. Like him.

But there was something very appealing about the boy himself, he reflected. Andy was an interesting kid, a good athlete, from what he'd heard, and personally very likable. The nurses on the neuro floor all adored him. His mind went back to Andy's mother, and he thought about how she looked and what a tough time she must be having. A broken marriage, a vengeful ex-husband, a demanding job, her only child with a probably fatal brain tumor ... It all made his own problems seem petty and small, and his heart went out to her.

Felix Cadwaller was already in the radiology department when Simeon got there, and all the films and scans were up on the fluorescent screens. Frank Grant was there, much taller than the stubby Felix, and they were discussing the scans, one by one. For a moment it irrationally annoyed Simeon that they should be discussing his patient.

"Hi, Dr. Halstead," said Frank, seeing Simeon approach. He sounded guarded; he knew how unusual it was for Halstead and Cadwaller to be working on a case together.

"Hi, Frank. Felix." Simeon nodded with easy confidence at Cadwaller. "Did you find anything that Frank and I missed?"

"Not so far." Cadwaller eyed Simeon. "But then, we haven't gone over everything yet, have we, Frank?"

They discussed all the films in detail.

"Pretty clear," said Cadwaller after they had narrowed the crucial films down to half a dozen. "I'd say what we're dealing with is down there at the base of the third ventricle." He pointed at the screen with his finger. "Frank, can you zoom that up for us, please? Here ... it's pressing on the optic chiasma and that's what's giving the kid his intermittent visual symptoms. My guess is that it's an astrocytoma, malignant, of course, or one of the variant ..."

"Right. It could be a number of things," interrupted Simeon. "But *exactly* what it is, we won't know until we see it in the O.R. and do a biopsy."

"I was only making a provisional ..."

"No point in doing that, Felix," said Simeon. "When we know, we know, and until then there's no dividends from guesswork."

Felix flushed with annoyance. Simeon had just quoted one of the favorite sayings of their former chief at Bellevue.

"You have him scheduled for tomorrow?" he asked Simeon.

"Seven-thirty."

"What are you planning to do?"

"I'll use a posterior approach, get at the tumor from underneath the brain, and try to remove it. If I can't, I'll do a biopsy, debulk the tumor, then we'll talk to the oncologists."

Cadwaller stared at Simeon for a moment, then spoke very deliberately, in a tone calculated to make Frank Grant remember the comment if the subject ever came up at a later date. "Do you know that we're setting up a double-blind research project on pediatric brain tumors, right here at the center?" he said. "This kid would be a perfect candidate for this study."

Simeon shook his head decisively. "Yes, I've heard about your project, and no, I don't want Andy Markle to be in it. I know about these studies; I worked on one when I was in London. It's just a matter of ringing the changes on a bunch of different types of radiation and chemotherapy.

It's not a real way of treating patients, just a way of getting research funds. Right?"

Cadwaller's mouth had become a straight and furious line even before Simeon stopped talking. "Not so, Simeon." He tried to keep his voice at a conversational level. "We're trying out a new dosage regimen that has been very promising in computer simulations . . ."

"You did say it's a double-blind study, didn't you?" asked Simeon.

"Yes, I did."

"Which means that some of those kids with tumors won't get any treatment at all? Just simulated treatment?"

"Well, as you very well know, Simeon, that's the only way to prove that a new form of treatment is effective, by comparing it with what happens when treatment is withheld. Or at least, to show statistically that its effectiveness is significantly better than what was being done before."

"I suppose to a researcher that makes sense," said Simeon. "But I want Andy Markle to get the treatment that's the very best for him. I'm not about to sacrifice him for the sake of a bunch of statistics and a couple of research papers."

"Well, after the study's over, he'd get the most appropriate treatment, of course," said Cadwaller, who knew that showing his anger wouldn't help his cause. "The whole thing is funded by the Institute of Neurological Diseases, so the treatment wouldn't cost the Markles a penny."

He was sounding defensive now, and Frank watched and listened to the two of them, storing their words for later retelling to his colleagues.

Simeon's voice got colder, if that was possible. "You're seriously asking me to recommend that to my patient? That he undergo a maybe treatment with a maybe chance of improvement, with a fifty-fifty chance of receiving no treatment at all?" Simeon stared at Cadwaller. "Are you serious?" His tone took on a hard emphasis. *"No way."*

"Then I assume you have a better treatment to offer him. If you do, I'd love to hear what it is." Cadwaller stepped back from the viewing boxes, his expression sarcastic.

"Right now we're whistling in the wind," said Simeon.

"Tomorrow in the O.R. we'll know what we're dealing with, and we can make a decision then."

"Yes. I assume you know that both the Markle parents have requested that I take part in the operative procedure tomorrow? Sam Seidel, their general practitioner, reported that to me on their behalf earlier this afternoon."

"No, I didn't know." Simeon wondered what Cadwaller was up to; he thought it unlikely that such a suggestion would have come originally from the Markles, especially Fiona, or even from Sam Seidel. "I'll certainly talk to them about it."

"I can bring a couple of my residents to give us a hand, if you like," Cadwaller went on.

"Thanks," said Simeon, "but I think my team and I can handle this. Of course, if *you* feel it's necessary to come along and *assist,* it's okay with me."

"I'll be there, Simeon," said Cadwaller, turning to leave. "I'm really looking forward to this case." His tone set off alarm bells in Simeon's head, and he knew there would be trouble if Cadwaller could find a way to make it.

For a moment, Simeon looked at his onetime friend, and a vision of Cadwaller's abused sister and the haunted expression on her face before her suicide rose up in front of him. He had to turn away to hide his revulsion at the man who had caused it. Felix stumped out of the radiology department, and an old medical dictum came into Simeon's mind: "First, take care of the patient." Now, he knew, that wise and altruistic saying had been replaced by "First, cover your ass. Then if there's any time left, take care of the patient." Well, with Andy Markle he was doing both. As for Felix, sooner or later, he'd get him in a vulnerable position. And then . . . Simeon looked down for a second at his clenched fists. He left the radiology department and went back toward his office, thinking it might be a good idea, he thought, to have a little chat with Dr. Sam Seidel.

Back behind his desk, he called Sam and didn't waste any time. "What's this about the Markles wanting Dr. Cadwaller in the O.R. tomorrow while we're operating on Andy?" he asked. "Was that your idea?"

"Actually, yeah, I figured it would probably be good for you if Cadwaller was there," said Sam, who had been expecting the call. "That Victor Markle,' he went on, "he's a pain in the butt, difficult to deal with, and he also carries a grudge, according to someone who knows him well."

"I don't see why . . ."

"Because if there's any kind of problem," said Sam, sitting back at his desk and sucking on an unlit cigar, "Victor's the kind of guy who would sue you at the drop of a hat. And as you probably know, the malpractice lawyers we have in this town don't give a shit if they have a case or not; they sue, regardless, because it's cheaper for the insurers to settle than to go to court."

"Well, I would have preferred to make the decision on that," said Simeon. "And Dr. Cadwaller would not be the person I'd choose to assist me."

"Well, he's head of the department, so we figured he'd be able to give you the most useful support," Sam went on smoothly. He grinned up at Gloria and gently pushed her hand away from him. Their last patient had gone, and she was hot for a little extracurricular activity.

"Okay," said Simeon. He didn't trust Sam, but he couldn't figure what he was up to. "I'll give you a call tomorrow when we're done and tell you what we found."

"Thanks." Sam hung up. He turned to Gloria. "Let's try Puerto Vallarta again," he said. The evening before, they'd tried for an hour to get a line, but without success.

This time they got through immediately.

"Good to hear you," said Dr. Vargas. "I was hoping you'd call."

"Why, what's up, Antonio?"

"You remember that woman you sent us, Carla Locarno? She certainly had been taking too many vitamins, but that wasn't why she was yellow."

"Oh, yeah? So what was it?"

"Hepatitis."

"Oh, shit. Well, you can take care of that, right? No big deal."

"I just wanted you to know. Actually it was Paolo Mendez who diagnosed her."

"Who?"

"Paolo Mendez. I told you about him a couple of weeks ago. He's the new doc who joined the clinic a few months back. Paolo's an M.D., and pretty good, I guess, but I'm a bit worried about him. He's into all kinds of herbals and diet and meditation philosophy and all that. Anyway, like I told him, that's fine, that's okay for his dad, who's a shaman down in El Tuito, but this clinic's different. We're here to make money, and there isn't much money in herbs."

"So?"

"I told him to follow our protocol, you know, every patient to get all the tests and X-rays and injection treatments, but he's resisting. He's quiet and very polite, but he needs what you call an attitude adjustment."

Sam looked at the clock, looked at Gloria, and shrugged.

"Well, just tell him. Lay down the law. You're signing his paycheck, so you call the shots, right?"

"Okay, I'll try again. But we need him, and we didn't have any other applicants, so I'm a bit stuck. Meanwhile, do you have any more patients for us?"

"Maybe," said Sam. "I'm trying to get you a kid with a brain tumor. They're going ahead with the standard treatments, but those never work anyway, so if they don't kill the kid off, I'm going to suggest they send him down to you."

"Great. That would really help. Get some photos of him now, if you can."

"Why?"

"For the before and after shots for the brochure. Except that the 'after' one gets taken first."

Sam grinned.

"How old is the kid?"

"Fourteen."

"Great." Vargas was beginning to sound excited. "People love to hear about sick kids who get better, especially if they're from the U.S. Nobody cares about a sick Guatemalan child, but an American child . . . I mean a *North* American child, that's different. The story gets in all the newspapers, *Time, 60 Minutes,* you name it, then everybody with that disease packs their bags for Puerto Vallarta, the new center of healing. Get me this kid, Sam, and with the right kind of publicity, it could make all the difference in the world to how the clinic does."

"Yeah, right." Sam shook his head and grinned at Gloria,

who was listening in on the other phone. He and Vargas had had this kind of conversation before. "Everything you say is true, except this kid isn't going to get better. Listen, Antonio, I know you're totally *lleno de mierda*, but I love ya. And I'm working hard to get the kid down there, but it won't happen right away. Maybe two, three months, maybe more, I don't know. But we'll get him there, believe me."

Chapter 20

Up in Andy's room, Fiona talked and laughed with him about school, about how his team had lost their last baseball game, about everything she could think of, but underneath, all she wanted to do was grab him up and snatch him out of the hospital, anything rather than let him submit to this awful surgery. She couldn't bear to look at his bald scalp, and she visualized him on the operating table, with the surgeons cutting into the back of his head, removing part of his skull to expose his brain . . .

And there were still too many unanswered questions. She and Wilma had spent hours in the school library, which had computer links with Yale and other major libraries, and now she knew a whole lot about astrocytomas. She was reaching for the phone to call Simeon's office, to find out if she could talk to him, when the phone rang.

"Mrs. Markle? Hi, this is Simeon Halstead. I'd like to talk to you about Andy, about the surgery tomorrow, and hopefully answer any questions you might have. I'll be talking to Andy later. Would you like to come over to my office? You know where it is."

"Yes, I would," replied Fiona. She felt more relieved than she had expected, maybe because Simeon Halstead was now sharing the responsibility with her. "I'll be there in just a couple of minutes, okay?"

She checked the big canvas-and-leather bag she always carried with her. The list of questions she'd prepared was there on the front page of her notebook. For important things, Fiona was very well organized.

Simeon stood when she came into his office and pulled up a chair for her. Trying not to look too shaken, she sat down and put the notebook on her lap.

"Good," said Simeon, watching her. "I'm glad you wrote down your questions. Now, if it's okay with you, I'll just tell you where we are with Andy, what we're planning for tomorrow, and the treatment possibilities after the surgery. Then if you have questions I haven't covered, you can shoot them at me."

"Okay." She looked hard at him, then smiled. "Thank you for doing this," she said. "I remember Mr. Garvey said you usually left this part of the job to the residents."

Simeon sat back in his chair. "Not anymore," he said. He was astonished at how comfortable he felt, having got close to Andy and Fiona. He smiled at her. "Quite honestly, I'm happy that I've got to know you both as people, not just as a patient and his mother."

Fiona, pleased in a way that she couldn't quite fathom, adjusted her skirt and folded her hands in her lap. "I'm happy about that too," she said, and she meant it. "Now tell me about Andy."

"I'm not quite sure how to do this," he confessed. Then, still watching her, he seemed to make up his mind. "Fiona," he said, "I'm going to give you a choice. I can give you the standard spiel, which will give you an accurate but sanitized account of Andy's problem and the options. Either that or I can truly level with you. It's your choice, but I'm warning you that if you're feeling fragile or need comfort at this point, you should choose version one."

Fiona thought for a moment. At this moment she certainly was feeling fragile and in need of comfort, but it was more important to know what was really going on. "Tell it to me the way it is," she said. "Comfort is fine, and yes, I like it, but not if it's unrealistic."

"Okay. Good. I've already told you I think Andy has a tumor."

"How about Dr. Cadwaller?" asked Fiona, checking the list of questions on her notepad. "Does he think so too?"

"Yes, he does. He'll probably report back to you or your husband later this evening."

"Former husband," said Fiona firmly. "And I must tell you that Victor and I do not see eye to eye concerning Andy and his care here. I'm more than happy with the way you're taking care of him." She paused for a second. "And it might interest you to know that Andy really likes you."

Simeon looked mildly astonished, and Fiona, watching him, felt that either he didn't expect to be liked or, more likely, he never even thought about it.

"Good. It's very positive for a patient to have confidence in his surgeon," he replied.

That's not what I said, thought Fiona. I said he *likes* you. And what's more, I can tell you're not used to this kind of conversation.

"From my experience, and from the scans and other tests," Simeon went on, "I believe there's a strong possibility that we're dealing with a malignant situation."

Fiona's hands became tight fists, and her nails dug into the palms of her hands. "What exactly does that mean?" she asked, although she already had a pretty good idea.

"Well, the difference is that benign tumors usually just push the surrounding structures out of the way, but malignant tumors tend to invade the surrounding tissues," he said.

He watched her to see how much he needed to explain. "In other words," he went on, "when you're dealing with a benign brain tumor, you can often remove it, then the structures it was pressing on can go back to normal function once the pressure is off."

"And with a malignant one?"

"The malignant tumors are frequently invasive. For instance, if it's close to the nerves from the eyes it will be more likely to infiltrate those nerves . . ." He hesitated for a second. "You can see that if we had any hope of completely removing such a tumor, we would also have to remove those nerves."

"What you're saying is that Andy would be left blind. Totally and forever." Fiona spoke quietly, but she felt caught up on a wave of something that was part fear, part a sense that everything in her life, in Andy's life, was getting hopelessly and insanely out of control. "But then he'd be cured, right? If you took it all out? It wouldn't come back? Could you be sure about that?" Jesus God, she thought, don't let him ask me to make that decision. She could already see Andy, his eyes rolled up so that only the whites were showing, tapping tentatively around him with a long white stick . . .

"No, I couldn't guarantee that," said Simeon. "Even with that kind of extensive surgery the statistics on tumors in this location are not good."

"So what are we supposed to do?" asked Fiona, unable to keep the desperation out of her voice.

"We can't make any final decisions until I've actually seen the tumor," said Simeon gently. "But at this time the alternatives are total removal of the tumor or chemotherapy and maybe radiotherapy."

Fiona could feel that she wasn't taking it in, but there was one other thing she had to know. "Can't the malignant kinds of tumors also travel to different places, like into the liver and lungs? Meta . . . something?"

"Metastasize. Yes, they can, but it's not likely with this kind of tumor. No, I don't expect that'll be the most difficult problem here."

"What do you think that will be?" Fiona heard herself speaking, as if she were far above the room, looking down at Simeon and herself.

"As I said," said Simeon gently, "there is a good chance that some important structures in and around his brain may already have been invaded by the tumor."

Fiona stared at the list of questions she had so carefully prepared, but now the letters and words were blurring together and she couldn't make them out. Anyway, they didn't seem too important at this point—like how long would it take for his hair to grow back? How long before he could go back to school? Would he be able to play baseball again?

Simeon told her about chemotherapy and radiotherapy, listing the possible benefits and also the dangers and complications, which ranged from brain damage to protracted vomiting and damage to normal tissues in the vicinity of the tumor.

She decided provisionally not to go that route, and after more discussion Fiona stood up, shaking. "Thank you, Dr. Halstead," she said, but she had trouble getting her words out.

Simeon came from behind the desk, hesitated for a moment, then took a deep breath and made a decision. He put out his arms and held her, gently, and with infinite compassion. It had been a long time since Fiona had been held like that, and she felt the comfort and warmth of him through his white coat. She wanted to put her own arms around him and allow herself to break down, to hold on to him and weep until she was drained of every last tear, but instead she gave a little return hug, stood back, sniffed, and looked in her vast satchel for a tissue. He took one out from the dispenser on his desk and gave it to her.

"We'll be starting at seven-thirty," he said. "Andy'll come down to the O.R. suite maybe forty-five minutes before that. We'll give him medication to make him drowsy so he won't worry about things too much, and afterward he won't even remember what happened."

The intercom buzzed. "Your students are out here," said the secretary's voice.

"Tell them to meet me up on the neuro floor in five minutes," he replied. "In Andy Markle's room."

Chapter 21

The three students, Terry Matson, Edwina Cole, and Nina Muldrew, trooped into Andy's room.

"Hi, Andy," said Edwina. She grinned at him. Andy liked her; she'd spent a whole lot of her spare time visiting with him, and he knew her better than almost anybody at the hospital.

Terry Matson came over and critically examined Andy's shaved head. "Not a bad job," he said. "How does it feel?"

"Cold," said Andy. "And weird. I feel sorry for bald people." He put his hand on the back of his head and felt his scalp. It didn't feel as if it really belonged to him. All three of the students laughed at his comment. To Andy, the laughter sounded a bit forced.

"How's your vision?" asked Nina Muldrew. "Any more problems?"

Andy shook his head. 'I'm fine," he said.

Edwina Cole, who seemed the most focused of the three of them, asked if the residents had talked to him about what would be happening tomorrow.

"No. My mom says Dr. Halstead's coming by to do that."

Edwina glanced at the other two, and Andy thought they all looked a bit surprised.

"Well, I'm on call tonight," said Edwina. "I'll stop by to see if you have any more questions."

Andy could feel an underlying tension in the group. He'd gotten to know them pretty well in the short time he'd been in the hospital and had developed a good rapport with them.

Edwina asked Andy to sit up and look straight ahead of him. Then she asked him to keep his head still and look up. What was it Dr. Halstead had said about Parinaud's sign? Once it appears, it won't ever go away, unless there's a complete cure.

"Why can't I look up?" asked Andy. It always made him nervous when they did that test.

Edwina was trying to explain when the door opened and Simeon came in, carrying a large tan X-ray envelope. The students straightened up.

He grinned at Andy. "I'll come back to talk to you in about fifteen minutes," he said. "And meanwhile," he went on, addressing the students, "we're going outside to look at some films."

They followed him to the viewing room, and after they had all examined Andy's films and discussed the diagnosis, Simeon said, "Okay, we have a pretty good idea of what the problem is here. So what do you think we should do?"

Edwina spoke first. Maybe it was because she worked in Simeon's lab and knew him better than the others, but she felt she could say things the other two might not have dared to voice. "We just did rounds with Dr. Caleb Winter," she said. "He says that one of the dangerous compulsions that surgeons can have is to *do* something. Cut. Anything."

Simeon nodded. "It's true, Edwina. That's our job. But of course we try to limit our cutting to situations that require it."

"Do you think we could make a case here for doing nothing?" asked Terry Matson, who was hoping to become a psychiatrist. "The tests tell us pretty conclusively that it's a malignant situation, and it's in a critical location. There's some evidence that the trauma of surgery can speed up a malignant process. Why not just leave him alone? It's a fatal condition, so why make him go through all that surgery and everything when there's no real hope of cure?"

Terry glanced at the softhearted Nina Muldrew, who had become very attached to Andy and was particularly distressed about his condition. She nodded her agreement, not trusting herself to speak.

"Well, for one thing," answered Simeon reasonably, "at this point we don't know for sure what we're dealing with. Second, depending on the cell type, such a tumor isn't necessarily fatal. Third, removal of the tumor, if we can do it, should result in a cure. So it's pretty clear that although the statistics are not encouraging, we can't just sit back and let his tumor destroy him."

"Dr. Halstead," said Edwina. "I always thought that with specialization, patients with different diseases were sent to the people best suited to deal with them. Judging from the statistics, Andy Markle and others with his kind of problem shouldn't be surgical patients, because surgery doesn't give them even a fifty-fifty chance of survival."

Terry and Nina looked openmouthed at Edwina. Even though she was a little older than they were and had an advanced degree in microbiology, this wasn't the kind of question medical students usually asked their professors—or were likely to get away with.

"So who do you think has a better chance of curing him, then?" Simeon stared at Edwina. He liked challenges from students, and although he always gave them a hard time, he admired Edwina's courage. But he didn't let her answer on her own; he tried to pin her down by giving her choices. "Are we talking about the oncologists? Or radiotherapists? Who else? Maybe hypnotists? Homeopaths? Or perhaps Christian Scientists?"

"No, Dr. Halstead," said Edwina. She wasn't going to be intimidated. "Right now we're talking about a basically hopeless situation, where everybody's going through the moves, diagnosis, surgery, treatment, although nobody really expects any good results, let alone a cure." She stared challengingly at Simeon. "Sir," she went on, "almost a year ago, up in your lab, you were telling us about your research project to target tumors of this kind. It was a wonderful idea, and I was so excited that all I wanted was to be a part of it. So I signed up to do my thesis with you—I couldn't wait to get started, to work on a program that would deal with what had been an insoluble problem." Edwina paused. "But nothing happened. You were never in the lab, and nobody there had any idea what they were supposed to be doing. But if we'd all worked on it, Dr. Halstead, right now we might be figuring out doses of a tumor-destroying system that would *cure* Andy, instead of just going through a bunch of standard moves, basically the same moves that neurosurgeons have made for years, that are painful, damaging, and ultimately useless."

The two other students moved instinctively away from her, not wanting to be anywhere near the focus of Dr. Halstead's anger. Even Edwina felt she'd gone too far. "I'm sorry, Dr. Halstead," she said. "But you can see I feel very strongly about this. Andy . . ." She stopped, bracing herself for the thunderbolt.

It never came.

"Let's talk for a moment about the natural history of these tumors," said Simeon calmly, as if Edwina hadn't said anything.

Edwina flushed. She would rather have had him yell at her than simply ignore her comments, as he was doing now. She resisted an angry urge to walk out of the room.

Simeon was talking, in his quiet voice, almost as if he were talking to himself. "Very often in this type of case, there's a pause, a remission, that lasts on average about five months after the first appearance of symptoms and after surgery," he said. "Then something, we don't know what, activates the tumor again, and it's all over in a matter of weeks."

They talked about the possible factors that might be involved in that process.

"Maybe it doesn't really stop growing," suggested Terry. "Maybe it just grows slowly for a while, then something triggers the fast rate of growth again."

Simeon nodded approvingly. "That seems to be the current thinking," he said. "It's certainly true for some types of malignant tumor. But of course it's hard to know for sure when it's happening inside the skull, because usually we get only one look at it."

After some more discussion, Simeon ended the session because he had to go back to talk with Andy about his operation. He turned to Edwina. "After we finish the operation tomorrow, Miss Cole, I'd like a few minutes of your time." He spoke politely, as always, but there was something in his tone that chilled her. "In my lab, please, after we're done."

Edwina nodded glumly. "Yes, sir." This wasn't the first time she'd got herself in trouble with the medical center faculty because of her outspokenness. And this time it was clear that she'd picked the wrong person. Dr. Simeon Halstead had quite a fearsome reputation, and she knew that by daring to challenge him she was taking her career in her hands.

Chapter 22

Andy was feeling the tension. It was affecting everybody—the nurses, the residents and students, his mother, Kevin and the other kids—and he knew that it was related to his approaching surgery. Even Kevin was talking to him now in a strange way. He didn't laugh at things the way he normally did, or else he laughed too long and seemed uncomfortable and didn't stay very long. He hated the hospital, he said, but Andy remembered when Kevin had had his appendix out, and he didn't seem to hate it then.

Andy figured they all knew better than he did what was going to happen to him, and he was feeling more and more scared. He didn't know how he'd be after the operation, but he was sure that if he couldn't run and play and fool around with them anymore, his friends would feel he was a drag to have around, and he'd lose them. It all seemed weird; he felt that if somehow he could just change the channel and get himself back to reality, everything would be okay. He remembered that kid who used to live down the road, a girl, who, his mother told him afterward, had a brain tumor. She had been away from school for two weeks, and nobody had even noticed her absence until the day she came back to school wearing a big bandanna thing around her head because all her hair was gone. She looked weird and geeky, with a long white neck, and she walked very slowly and a little unsteadily, usually by herself, and she never smiled. And then she started to get thinner and her eyes seemed to get bigger and darker and more sunken until one day she stopped coming to school at all, and a couple of weeks later Mr. Seidel assembled the school to tell everyone that one of their schoolmates had died, and it took Andy, Kevin, and their friends a while to figure out who he was talking about.

Andy looked up when Simeon came in and stood by his bed. From where Andy was, Simeon looked a mile high.

"It's weird, huh, having your head shaved?"

Andy nodded and touched the back of his scalp.

Simeon nodded. "I had mine shaved once too, when I was about your age," he said. "But not all of it. I was on my bike, coming down a hill too fast, and there was a sharp turn at the bottom, but I kept on straight ahead. I had a big cut on the back of my head, and they shaved most of my hair off before sewing me up. It looked a lot worse than yours."

Simeon pulled a chair up by the bed and sat down.

"You're our first case tomorrow," he said.

"What are you doing to do?" Andy was feeling really scared now; his mouth was dry, and the palms of his hands were sweating.

"First we're going to take a look inside," said Simeon. "Through the back of your head. There's this little lump of tissue that's been pressing on your eye nerves. We have to find out what that lump is and figure out what to do about it."

"Can you take it out?"

"I hope so. If not, we'll take a piece of it to look at under the microscope and hopefully do a tissue culture."

"What's that?"

"Tissue culture means growing the cells in the laboratory, so that we can see if different medications can work against them."

At the back of his mind, Simeon was thinking that even the tissue culture might be a problem. For this type of tumor, it wasn't easy, and he was wondering if his lab would be able to set it up in time. Otherwise he could probably get it done by the neuropathology lab, but as that was under Felix Cadwaller's control, there might be problems.

"When will I be able to play baseball again? And go back to school?"

"You should be able to go back to school in a week or two," replied Simeon. "As for baseball ... that's hard to tell. Maybe a couple of months ... But by that time, the season'll be over." Simeon could see that his answer had not satisfied Andy. "It'll depend on how quickly your reflexes and your vision come back," he went on. "There's millions of nerves and reflexes that go into action and synchronize before you can hit a ball that's coming at you at fifty miles an hour. Any kind of surgery inside your head is liable to jangle those mechanisms up for a while."

"But after that while, I'll be back to normal, right?"

"Sure," said Simeon. He smiled. "Of course."

After leaving Andy, he wondered if he'd given him the wrong answer. If he'd been older, Simeon would have been more frank with him, but it was obvious that Andy was scared, and Simeon didn't know how he would handle a straight account of the probable outcome. He realized now that he simply didn't know how to talk about serious problems to kids of Andy's age. It was all very well, he thought, deciding to change the way he dealt with his patients, spend more time and be straight and honest with them, but it was something he'd avoided for so long he didn't really know how to do it.

Who could he ask who knew about kids? Fiona came to mind, of course, but he hesitated; such questions might seem odd to her. Maybe Sam Seidel; he had a teenage daughter. He thought about that for a moment. No, not Sam. Fiona ... His mind slipped back to her. After all, she dealt with teenage kids all the time at school, so she could be a good resource. The idea set a train of thought going in his head.

When Simeon had a case at seven-thirty, that meant that five minutes before the appointed time, the patient was to be on the table, positioned, anesthetized, with all the equipment and personnel ready to go.

The residents had been up for hours already and had done rounds. Emily DuPlessis, the intern, in a rare moment of humor, had baptized them the Dawn Patrol.

Andy had been given his preop medication, 5 milligrams of Valium by mouth, at six-fifteen, and he was feeling sleepy and flushed. The neuro nurses and aides on duty that morning, workers who sent patients down to the operating room every day and thought nothing of it, had all managed to come into Andy's room to spend a few moments and say a few cheerful words to him.

When the stretcher came clattering down the corridor for him, it was driven by Andy's old friend Henry, the transportation orderly. On this occasion he suppressed his Grand Prix instincts and very gently helped the nurses lift Andy onto the stretcher.

Andy was dimly aware of doors opening, closing, fluorescent ceiling lights flicking past, voices talking high above him; then the stretcher stopped in the waiting area outside the operating rooms. People bustled around, a young woman in greens checked his wristband and put his metal chart in a rack marked "Room Six."

"Stay cool, dude," Henry told him, and vanished.

A few minutes later, two green-clothed people with masks and paper bootees pushed the stretcher into the O.R. The main operating lights were off, but the ceiling was almost entirely covered with fluorescent lights, and they were bright enough to make Andy scrunch up his eyes.

"Hi, Andy. Remember me? Gabe Pinero?" The voice coming from behind Andy's head belonged to Dr. Gabriel Pinero, one of the senior anesthesiologists. He'd visited Andy in his room the evening before and told him how they were going to put him to sleep. Dr. Pinero was in greens, wearing a mask and cap. Andy would never have recognized him, not even from his voice.

Gabe did his job efficiently and fast, and before Andy realized anything was happening, his eyes rolled up and he was out. It took the combined efforts of the three residents to position Andy correctly, in a three-quarter supine position with his head tilted to a forty-five-degree angle.

"Why don't they use the sitting position anymore?" asked Edwina Cole. This was the first case of this type she'd seen, and she had been reading up about it.

"Too much risk of air embolism," replied Ben Foreman, the senior resident. "Push that roll further up in his axilla, Edwina ... When the head is up above the heart, the venous pressure is less than atmospheric, so if a vein is accidentally opened during the procedure, air gets sucked in,

and obviously that can be fatal. Now, help me adjust the
Mayfield . . ."

Very gently, they placed Andy's shaved head in the Mayfield head holder, a system of adjustable tongs that would
keep the head securely fixed during the operation.

Simeon came into the room. He had a way of appearing
without anyone actually seeing the doors open or him walking up.

Everybody replied to his quiet "Good morning," but
they didn't stop what they were doing. Simeon went over
to check the video setup and the Zeiss Contraves microin-
strumentation equipment. The parts that would be in the
operative field were inside a sterile cover. "Pat, we'll be
using the variable focal length system," he told the scrub
tech, who nodded.

"That's how we've got it set up for you, Dr. Halstead,"
he replied.

"Has anyone seen Dr. Cadwaller yet?"

No one had.

After making sure that the positioning was just the way
he wanted it, Simeon marked out the incision with a skin
pen. Then, when everything was ready, he went through
the double doors into the scrub room.

A few moments later Felix Cadwaller came in, accompanied by Tim Morris, his senior resident. Both men were
dressed in green scrubs, and Tim looked uncomfortable.

"I'm bringing Tim in with us," announced Cadwaller
over the noise of the water spraying in three sinks. "He's
one of our best . . ."

"No," said Simeon. "We have all the personnel we need,
and I've gone over the procedure in detail with my team.
Thanks all the same." He turned and grinned at Tim, who
had worked on Simeon's team the year before. "Nothing
personal, Tim."

"No problem, Dr. Halstead," mumbled Tim. "Is it okay
if I stay and watch for a while?" He respected Simeon a
lot and didn't appreciate being used as a pawn in a power
play by Dr. Cadwaller. Also, it was a rare treat for residents
not on his team to be allowed to watch Simeon operate.

"Sure."

Cadwaller went to the next sink and slammed the faucet

open with his knee. "I see you're not using the sitting position," he said after glancing through the big window into the operating room. "Any particular reason?"

"I get better results this way," replied Simeon calmly. This wasn't the time to tell Cadwaller that the sitting position was considered obsolete for this type of operation. But he could feel the tension rising. There were enough problems doing a delicate case of this kind without the additional stress of having a hostile person in the operating room, especially one who wasn't up to date on technique.

Because of his seniority, Cadwaller took the position of first assistant, obviously an unusual situation for him. And as Simeon well knew, the tasks of first assistant were quite different from those of the operating surgeon in charge of the case. He wondered when Cadwaller had last assisted.

After gowning up, Simeon took up his position on the right of Andy's head, and Cadwaller walked around the table. Ben Foreman, Simeon's senior resident, stood in the cramped space on Cadwaller's right.

"Check the video," said Simeon. Ben switched it on. The large screen above them lit up. Ben put his gloved finger in front of the tiny fiberoptic camera, and a huge color image of it appeared on the screen. Simeon nodded, and Ben switched it off.

Simeon looked over at Gabriel Pinero. All he could see was his big, wet-looking, pouchy eyes in the slit between his mask and cap. Pinero nodded. "We're all set here, Simeon," he said. "Pressure's fine, all's well."

Simeon felt relieved that Gabe was working with him. Pinero was very expert and had a reputation for being unflappable even in the face of the direst emergency.

"Skin knife." Simeon held out his hand and took the scalpel. He made the roughly semicircular incision in one quick sweep, and Cadwaller and Ben had to scramble to catch the bleeding points with the cautery. Used to demanding the most meticulous and precise work from his assistants, Simeon was instantly aware that Cadwaller's technique left something to be desired; he was holding the cautery to the bleeding points just a second longer than the brief moment of contact that was needed, and as a result the tissues around the blood vessels were being charred.

Ben glanced at Simeon, who said nothing. Ben hoped that maybe once they got inside the skull Cadwaller would settle down to do the tasks that were more familiar to him.

Once the scalp flap had been raised and secured, Simeon asked for the Midas, a new type of high-speed drill that had recently replaced the old system, in which burr-holes were drilled through the skill and the piece of skull removed by cutting between the holes with a flexible Gigli saw.

It took just a minute. The high-pitched whine was followed by a jet cloud of powdered bone as the bit cut through the bone like a hot knife through butter.

With great care, Simeon picked up the dura, the thin, tough membrane that lay just within the skull, separating it from the pink underlying brain tissue. Using the needlelike electrocautery, he coagulated the tiny blood vessels that coursed through the dura at the point where they would have to be cut.

Simeon spoke to Ben. "We have to be particularly careful with the brain retraction in the next phase, Ben," he said. Ben nodded. He didn't have to be told, and he had the feeling that Simeon had actually been talking for Cadwaller's benefit.

"Why is that?" asked Edwina, looking over Simeon's shoulder. She wasn't scrubbed and didn't actually have to be there, but like the others she took every opportunity to watch Simeon operate. And this was a very special case for all of them.

"Because if you press on the brain with the retractors more than very, very gently it will lose function," replied Simeon. "And if one pressed too hard on this particular part of the brain, Miss Cole," he went on, "what do you think might happen?"

"Problems with balance," said Edwina, thinking fast.

"Right, if you compressed the cerebellum," said Simeon, who didn't stop working while he talked. "What else?"

"Problems with vision, I suppose," said Edwina. "The back of the brain contains the visual cortex."

"Correct. Blindness, hemianopsia ..." Simeon stopped speaking for a moment while he gently lifted the dura and started to open it. Cadwaller was holding one edge with a pair of small forceps while Simeon carefully cut the membranous dura.

There was a sudden crash behind the anesthesiologist. The circulating nurse had tripped over one of the shielded cables and dropped a metal basin on the floor. Simeon didn't even blink, but Cadwaller made a small startled movement, tearing the dura under the edge of the skull. A small blood vessel started to pump into the wound. Ben held his breath. This was potentially a bad complication; they couldn't see exactly where the bleeding was coming from, and if it wasn't stopped within seconds, it could rapidly turn into a major problem. He wondered how Simeon would deal with it. Trying to clamp a tiny blood vessel when you couldn't see it was no easy task.

"Midas," said Simeon calmly. He picked up the drill and cut out an additional small piece of the skull around the place where the bleeding was occurring. Once he'd done that, it was easy to find and stop the bleeding with the electrocautery.

"That was brilliant," said Cadwaller, with reluctant admiration when the bleeding had stopped.

"Yes, it was. Dr. Cadwaller, would you put down the forceps and take a step back, please?"

Cadwaller, surprised, did as he was requested, thinking that Simeon was about to reposition some of the equipment.

"Ben, take Dr. Cadwaller's place, please."

"What ...!" The visible part of Cadwaller's face suddenly went red. "I'm assisting here at the request of the family," he spluttered. "You can't have the damned impertinence to ..."

"Dr. Cadwaller, I'll be happy to discuss my decision with you later," interrupted Simeon. "I'm doing this in the interests of the safety of this patient."

There was total silence in the operating room. Everybody knew that there was no love lost between Simeon and Felix Cadwaller, but to eject Cadwaller, the chief of the department from an operation was a shocking move that no one could have foreseen.

"Ben, pick up the edge of the dura."

With a scared glance at Cadwaller, Ben murmured, "Excuse me, sir," then stepped in front of him to take his place. He picked up the forceps and did as Simeon requested.

For a good half minute, Cadwaller stood there, breathing heavily, obviously beside himself with fury but not knowing what to do about it.

"Dr. Halstead, I'd like you to come to my office when this operation is over," he said finally, then turned on his heel and strode out without waiting for Simeon's reply.

"Right, Ben," said Simeon, after Cadwaller had left. He was apparently unflustered, but he could feel his heart beating fast. "We've wasted enough time already. Let's get on with this."

An hour later, the operation was proceeding smoothly. Simeon and Ben had worked together many times, and they had fallen into the steady rhythm that accompanies the most efficient surgery. The underside of the brain had been carefully raised, and using the video probe, they could now see the tumor, a grayish mass that seemed about the size and shape of a cherry.

"You see where it's pressing on the optic chiasma?" asked Simeon. He glanced around to see if Edwina was watching. Tim Morris, Cadwaller's resident, had left quietly very soon after his boss. "That's why he was having visual symptoms," he went on. "On the two occasions when he went suddenly blind there must have been small hemorrhages inside the tumor."

"What are you going to do now?" asked Edwina, after watching Simeon carefully remove a small piece of the tumor for a biopsy. She was thinking about Andy and what a nice kid he was. One could never tell who was going to get what in this life. It was all a matter of chance, and Andy was one of the unlucky ones.

"We're going to try to remove it," said Simeon.

Ben looked up. "*All* of it?" he asked.

"We'll try," said Simeon, although he knew that the chances of being able to do that were less than slender.

It seemed like five hours, but in fact it was only two by the time Simeon had isolated the greater part of the tumor. Then he stepped back from the table. "We have a major problem here," he said, to no one in particular.

Ben said nothing; he just hoped it wasn't something he'd done.

At that moment the pathologist came in to report on the biopsy. "It's malignant," he said. "Looks like an astrocytoma. That's about all we can tell you until we get the permanent sections."

"Thanks," said Simeon. "That's about what we expected."

He turned back to the screen and pointed with the tiny forceps he was holding. "Do you see, Ben? The tumor's invading the tissues around it, here, and also on in the midline, on the optic chiasma."

Edwina, standing behind Simeon, felt her eyes pricking. She knew what that meant.

But Simeon hadn't given up. "We're going to use the CO_2 laser," he told the scrub tech. Gabriel Pinero raised his head, and the tension in the room took a quantum leap. That meant that Simeon was going to try to dissect the tumor off the optic nerves using the laser; that would be a hair-raising procedure, with absolutely no room for even the slightest error.

"Keep the saline streaming onto the chiasma," Simeon was telling Ben. "That'll protect it from the beam."

Ben nodded, but he could feel himself starting to sweat. It was a big responsibility to know that the preservation of Andy's sight was now partly in his hands.

The silence in the operating room was palpable and oppressive. Simeon was going to try to separate the tumor from the underlying nerves using the laser beam, a job that needed the highest degree of skill and control and carried a very high risk. Ben knew that few neurosurgeons would even attempt it.

The tech handed Simeon the laser probe, tethered by its cable, and Simeon rolled it in his hand for a moment, getting the feel of it.

"Don't anybody drop anything on the floor for the next half an hour, okay?" Simeon grinned at the circulator, who blushed under her mask.

Then he got down to work. Ben, tense as a bowstring, kept up the slow stream of saline over the optic chiasma and prayed that nothing would go wrong. And Simeon, gently, ever so gently, lifted up the edge of the tumor, pressed the button, and a narrow red beam flashed out and vaporized the tissue at the exact point where it was pressing on the nerves. He repeated the procedure, patiently, precisely, again and again, until the tumor seemed to be freeing up, and then he ran into a knot of blood vessels that took forever to dissect, and behind it there was more tumor. Fifteen minutes later, Simeon straightened up, the sweat running down the inside of his mask.

"I can't get it out," he said, and a kind of sigh escaped from everyone in the operating room. "It's invading the brain tissue and extending posteriorly. I'm going to debulk as much of it as I can." Without a change of expression, he turned to Pat. "The COUSA, please."

Pat silently passed him the COUSA probe, and in a second a high whine indicated that it was liquefying the accessible tumor tissue with ultrasonic waves, and Ben, wielding a tiny suction tube, instantly removed the fluidized cancerous tissue from the operative field.

Behind Simeon, Edwina, like everybody else in the room, felt a profound sadness envelop her. She knew that Andy would be okay for a few months. He would be free of symptoms because the bulk of the tumor had been removed. But sooner or later the tumor would come back. And when it did, there was nothing more that could be done, and the outcome would inevitably be fatal.

Chapter 23

Felix Cadwaller strode down the corridor after being ejected from the operating room. He stopped outside the O.R. waiting room and stood still for a moment, tense with fury, waiting for his heart to slow down. Andy's parents would be in there, he knew, or at least one of them.

He went in. Fiona and Victor were both sitting in the back. Victor was watching the wall-mounted television, and Fiona was trying to correct papers. When she saw Cadwaller approaching, she stood up immediately, as did Victor a moment later.

"Is Andy all right?" asked Fiona, surprised to see Cadwaller.

"Dr. Halstead's working on him," said Cadwaller. "So far, everything seems to be going well."

"I thought you were going to be staying there during the operation," said Victor, his eyes narrowing suspiciously.

"No, no. I just wanted to be there long enough to get Dr. Halstead started," said Cadwaller. "He has a team of very capable residents who'll assist him during the remainder of the case."

"I understand the early stage of the case is often the most difficult part," said Victor, nodding gravely, in a voice that suggested he was thoroughly familiar with every aspect of neurosurgical operations.

Cadwaller nodded back. This was going to be easier than he'd expected. "Right. Now what I want to discuss briefly with you is what will need to be done after the surgery's over. My feeling is that unless Dr. Halstead can remove the tumor entirely, which in my opinion is most unlikely ..." Cadwaller hesitated.

"Yes?" said Victor.

"I don't know if Dr. Halstead told you about the clinical trials that we have recently set up here in this hospital," replied Cadwaller.

Victor shook his head. Fiona watched and listened. There was something about this Dr. Cadwaller that she instinctively mistrusted. Maybe his smile was too quick, his attitude too friendly. Whatever it was, he didn't seem quite genuine.

"No, he didn't say anything about clinical trials to us," said Victor. "Is that something he should have mentioned?" Again the suspicion leaped into his eyes.

Cadwaller hesitated for exactly the right length of time. "Well, if Dr. Halstead didn't mention it, he didn't, and no doubt he has reasons of his own not to. Of course, there are other methods of dealing with such tumors, but it does seems a pity that he should reject the very latest ..."

"Tell me about it," said Victor. "I mean, tell us about it." His eyes were gleaming. "If there's something Halstead should have told us before the operation that could have helped Andy, and he didn't tell us, I'll have that son of a bitch's ass ..."

Fiona grabbed his arm hard, and Victor glanced at her angrily, but he did shut up.

Cadwaller smiled understandingly. "No, of course not. He probably considered it a minor omission, but at this point I might as well tell you about the clinical trial. You probably have heard that New Coventry Medical Center is one of the designated hub hospitals where new neurosurgical techniques and methodologies are tested out. In the last several months, we've started ..."

"I hope you're not talking about experimental drugs or procedures," said Fiona. "Because we're not interested in anything that hasn't been already tried and tested."

Cadwaller was used to dealing with comments of this kind. He waved his hand dismissively. "I'm sure that at this point we are all aware ..." He glanced at Victor, including him as if he were a colleague, "... that the treatment for brain tumors in children is very often ... unsatisfactory."

"Dr. Halstead explained that last night," said Fiona. "He was very frank about it and laid it on the line."

"Good. I insist that the doctors on my staff pay attention

to their patients' families," went on Cadwaller earnestly. "But in order to try to reverse the bad results everybody's been getting, the National Institute of Neurology recently decided to award us a large grant to work on a protocol that would offer some hope to young people with brain tumors of this kind."

"That sounds tailor-made for Andy," said Victor. "Why the hell didn't Dr. Halstead mention it to us?"

"Well, I suggest you ask him about it," said Cadwaller smoothly. "It might turn out to be the only thing that could help Andy. And now, if you'll excuse me, I have to go. I have other patients to take care of."

"Of course," said Victor. "We appreciate your stopping by. And thanks a lot for the information."

Cadwaller hurried out, feeling that he'd perhaps accomplished something. Maybe not, but every little thing counted, in the long run.

Back in the operating room, when the case was almost over, Edwina slipped out. Ten minutes later, Simeon turned to the circulator. "Tell the relatives in the waiting room that we're done, that Andy's okay, and that I'll come and talk to them in a little while."

Edwina went glumly up to Simeon's lab in the research tower.

"Well, hello, stranger!" Denis Popham looked up from his desk. "We haven't seen much of you around here."

The other tech, Sonia Goldenberg, a white-coated, plump blonde with a rather sulky expression, turned her head when Edwina came in, smiled briefly, then went back to the book she was reading.

"I'm supposed to meet with Dr. Halstead here," said Edwina. She looked at her watch. "He's just finishing a case, and he should be here soon. So what's happening up here in the research nerve center of the world?" Edwina sat down at the wooden desk that had been assigned to her but that she rarely used.

"The usual," replied Denis. Edwina couldn't quite figure his accent; born in Canada, Denis had gone with his parents to live for a few years in Melbourne, Australia; then when he was sixteen they had moved again, to Birmingham, England. Denis's accent now defied anything but the most erudite analysis. "You know how it is," he said, smiling weakly. "Every day fighting off the TV news reporters, the medical press wanting to hear the latest news about our research, paparazzi hiding in the closets to take photos . . ."

Sonia giggled. Just about anything Denis said made her giggle. Edwina wondered if it was the accent rather than what he was saying.

"How I wish," sighed Edwina. "Did you hear about the boy Dr. Halstead was operating on today?"

"Yes." Denis looked over at Sonia, who nodded too. "Everybody in the whole hospital seems to be talking about it. What's so interesting about him?"

"I'm not sure. Andy's a real nice kid, and I guess the nurses talk about him a lot. Also he seems to have become a kind of football between Dr. Halstead and Dr. Cadwaller. God, I hate that," she said with sudden intensity. "I'd no idea that doctors would ever use patients in such a way."

"What sort of way?" Sonia put down her book and came over to join them. Edwina had long ago noticed that Sonia never left Denis untended for very long.

"I suppose it's the same in any business," said Edwina. "People are competitive, jealous, even hate each other . . ."

"You mean like Dr. Halstead and Dr. Cadwaller?" asked Sonia. "Dr. Cadwaller certainly used Pamela Evans to try to get Dr. Halstead in trouble. Pamela was before your time, Edwina, so I don't know if you heard of her. She worked here as a tech, in this lab."

"I heard rumors, that's all. What happened?"

Denis made a face at Sonia. "We promised not to discuss this," he said, but she shook her blond head back at him.

"We can tell Edwina, surely," she said. "Seeing as how she works here in the lab with us."

Denis shrugged, and Sonia sat forward on the edge of her chair. "Pamela was really bad news," she said. "Of course, she had good references, and a degree from Cornell. She was certainly smart . . ." Sonia made a face, as if *smart* were a synonym for *halitosis*.

"She liked men," said Denis, a little smugly.

"She especially liked Dr. Halstead," said Sonia. "That was after she'd had an unsuccessful crack at Denis here."

Denis looked up at the ceiling.

"So what happened?" Edwina looked at her watch again. "Maybe you should save it and tell me later. Dr. Halstead should be here any second."

Sonia glanced at the door. "I think he just hates coming here," she said. "Ever since that woman ... Anyway, Pamela's best friend Nicole was one of Dr. Cadwaller's techs. They were always together, lunch in the cafeteria, walks on the campus. Sometimes I even wondered if ..."

"Stick to the facts," said Denis.

"Anyway, Pamela was always after Dr. Halstead; she had some sort of fixation about him ..." Sonia shook her head. "She'd wear dresses you wouldn't believe ..."

"The kind where just one little sneeze would have popped her tits right out of her dress," said Denis.

"Denis!" said Sonia, shocked. "Please! Actually, it's true," she went on to Edwina in a confidential tone. "And she had big ones. That girl did just about everything except actually pull his clothes off and rape him."

"Did he like it?"

"He didn't even notice!" said Denis and Sonia together. They both laughed.

"I suppose he must have, at some point," said Edwina. "I mean, noticed."

"Yes. He did, eventually. Okay, Sonia, you tell her."

Sonia adjusted her skirt with a fussy movement. "Well, one morning, when Pamela was sitting at that microscope over there ..."

"Boy, was she hot that day!" Denis laughed.

"Then Dr. Halstead came in. You know how he is, very proper, in that laundered white coat and everything ..." Sonia made a low whistle of retrospective amazement. "Anyway, he walked over to where Pamela is sitting, and looked over her shoulder. She turned around and put her elbow in his crotch. Gently. But she held it there."

"I still can't believe she had the nerve to do that," said Denis.

"Pamela thought Dr. Halstead was just being shy, up till

then, and all she had to do was make her interest a bit more obvious."

"So what did he do?"

"Well, he didn't do anything for about a second, then he sort of jumped back. I think he was so surprised he didn't know what to say for a minute. Then he said in that scary voice he sometimes uses: 'Miss Evans, please come into my office.' "

"We thought he was going to take her and screw her right there on his desk," said Denis.

"Denis! We certainly did not! What's got into you today?" said Sonia, irritated at Denis's uncharacteristic crudeness. "Of course we didn't think that. We could hear the way he was talking to her. His voice. It was as cold as . . . as . . ."

"Charity?" suggested Denis.

"His voice made charity sound like a heat wave," said Sonia. "And after a few minutes she came out, and she was crying."

Just as Sonia stopped speaking, the door opened and Simeon came in. He seemed very relaxed.

"Good," he said, looking at them. "I'm glad you're all here." He turned to Edwina. "First, I want to talk to you."

Edwina felt her stomach turning upside down as he led the way into his office and closed the door. He pointed to the chair, and she remembered the expression on his face when she'd challenged him about Andy Markle's treatment. Oh, well, she thought sadly, if worst comes to worst, I can always go back to Boston and finish my Ph.D.

"First," said Simeon, "I want you to know that I've been thinking a lot about what you said yesterday about Andy Markle."

Here it comes, thought Edwina. Okay, I was totally out of line, he's heard I've done the same kind of thing in other clinics, and they've decided that my impertinence is a hindrance to their teaching program and I'm a bad influence on the other students . . .

"You were entirely correct," said Simeon, and Edwina thought she must have heard him wrong. "At the time, your comments were not easy to accept, because of course we surgeons feel not only that we're very skilled but that we're doing the very best that anyone can do for our patients."

Edwina looked at the floor and didn't see the wry smile on his face.

"I'm sorry, Dr. Halstead," she said, "I know I was out of line. I didn't mean to make my point quite so strongly."

"No, don't be sorry. I'm glad you did. I'm going to be perfectly frank with you. When you've spent years doing something well, and doing it again and again, it's easy to get tunnel vision and think that your way is the only correct way of doing things. We surgeons are particularly prone to that way of thinking, as you may have noticed." This time, Edwina did see his rather tentative little grin. "What you did, Edwina, was remind me that present treatment of most kinds of brain tumors is basically useless. We've always known that, of course, but you brought it home."

Edwina looked up. Simeon was sitting on the corner of the small desk, looking very thoughtful.

"Maybe it's because I've had a different kind of training," she ventured. "As a microbiologist I look at things differently. Not better," she added. "Just differently."

"Actually, it's your training that interests me as much as anything."

Edwina smiled but took no offense.

"I've been thinking very hard about a lot of things recently," he said. Simeon straightened up and went to sit behind the desk. He looked at Edwina and she could feel his intensity and commitment. "Here I am, working in one of the world's most celebrated medical centers," he said. "We have some of the most brilliant people in the world working just down the corridor from us or across the street. Look at Caleb Winter, or Paula Cairns . . ." He sat back in his chair and put his hands on the desktop. Edwina looked at them; they were long-fingered, sensitive, well cared for, real surgeon's hands. "Now these two are making real strides in their fields. But in this department, nothing's happening. We just operate and do our work in the same old way, as if time had stopped." Simeon stopped and looked at her, astonished at himself for being so frank.

"But you're in a different field," objected Edwina. "As

a neurosurgeon, you need extraordinary skills, beyond the normal acceptable range of competence."

"Even if that's true," he said, "there's only one reason to be working in a center like this, and that's to make major advances in whatever field you happen to be in. Otherwise I could be working in ... I don't know, New London, or any such medical backwater—operating, making money, doing a good enough job, and at the end of it, seeing most of my patients die."

Simeon stood up, and for the first time Edwina got a real feel for the energy and power pent up inside this man. "I've come to a conclusion," he said. "I'm going to change what I do, and how I do it."

Edwina moved in her chair. She felt uncomfortable that somebody as important as Simeon Halstead should be unburdening himself like this to her, a mere medical student. But she was a few years older than most of her colleagues and had given up a successful career to start a new one in medicine, so she wasn't just a callow kid fresh from the Ivy League like many of her classmates.

"So what are you going to do, Dr. Halstead?" She grinned at him. "Become a microbiologist?"

Simeon laughed. "Not exactly." He sat down again and leaned forward over the desk. There was a tautness, an intensity about him that almost scared Edwina. He said, "As of right now, I am going to concentrate all my time and energy into that anti-tumor protocol I'd started work on and that you were doing your thesis on. In my opinion it's still the best bet for making a real advance in the treatment of pediatric brain tumors. And I'm going to need your help to make it happen."

"You're going to spend *all* your time on it?" asked Edwina, astonished. "What about your practice? What about ... Well, I don't know, what about the other things in your life?"

"As of today," continued Simeon, "I'll be seeing no new patients, and except for the ones presently in the hospital, I'm transferring them to other associates. I won't operate anymore, and I plan to take a leave of absence from teaching. I am *determined* to do this and make it work."

"How long do you think it's going to take?"

"I don't know," replied Simeon frankly. "Six months, a year, who knows?" He looked at Edwina and smiled. "But I'll make sure that you get your M.D. thesis out of it, and in good time. That is, if you're still interested."

"Of course I'm interested," said Edwina. "This is the best news I've heard for ... since I started med school. You'll find me as full of enthusiasm as you, and I'll work just as hard."

"Good," said Simeon. "We have a lot of work to do, just getting the show on the road again."

Edwina stood up. "Dr. Halstead, may I ask you a question?"

"Go ahead."

"Does this decision you've made have anything to do with Andy Markle?"

Simeon nodded briefly, thinking about Andy and Fiona. "Yes," he said. "It does. But he certainly wasn't the only factor. In any case, I don't expect our work can have any impact on his survival. We won't have time." He hesitated, and looked at Edwina. "Of course, I wish we could."

Edwina pursed her lips. "How long do we have?"

"How long does Andy have? Maybe six months, maybe a little more, but not much."

"I honestly don't see how we could do all that in six months," said Edwina, shaking her head. "Even the animal testing will take months and months, and then if we need FDA approval, that takes forever."

"Exactly. It would be great if we could, but it's not realistic to even consider him in the equation."

"I agree," said Edwina, who was familiar with the kind of problems that occurred in even the simplest research projects. And this one was far from simple.

"Now, Edwina," said Simeon, sitting back. "With your research experience, you know that nowadays most projects have to follow certain well-defined protocols and procedures, set up by government and foundation bureaucrats. As I'm sure you know, most of these rules are a sheer waste of time, just steps that have to be followed because those people say so. Right?"

Edwina nodded, wondering what he was getting at.

"Well," said Simeon, his face breaking out into the big-

gest smile she'd ever seen on it, "we're going to put this
project straight onto the fast track. So don't be surprised if
we break a few of those rules on the way."

"That's fine with me," said Edwina. "I won't slow you
down."

"I didn't think you would," said Simeon. "And now let's
go back there and tell Denis and Sonia about it."

Walking back into the lab, Simeon was acutely aware
that his project might go nowhere and that he'd need a lot
of new money for equipment and supplies. He certainly
couldn't depend on the big granting agencies, with their
procedural rules and regulations. He'd be needing other
kinds of help too. A vision of Felix Cadwaller's furious face
came to him. Maybe he, Simeon, should have handled that
situation in the operating room with more finesse . . . No,
he told himself. An enemy is an enemy, and Felix Cadwaller would never be anything else to him.

Chapter 24

As soon as he'd finished talking to Denis and Sonia, Simeon hurried back to the neuro intensive care unit. Ben Foreman looked up from writing orders in the chart. "I'll go talk to the family as soon as I've finished this," he told Simeon.

"No, I'm going to talk to them," said Simeon.

Ben's eyebrows went up, and he nodded okay but said nothing, wondering what had come over Dr. Halstead. All of a sudden he was paying all kinds of attention to the patients and their families. Ben didn't dwell on it; he had too many other things to think about. He made a list in his head of the postop routine. Andy was still unconscious from the anesthetic, so special precautions had to be taken while transporting him. Also Ben had to make sure that Andy's intracranial pressure didn't go up, that he was placed in the correct head-up position in his bed in the NICU, and that he was hooked up properly to the cardiac and other monitoring equipment.

Gabe Pinero walked alongside the stretcher with Ben. The endotracheal tube was still in Andy's windpipe; he wasn't breathing on his own yet, so Gabe was inflating his lungs at regular intervals by compressing a portable respirator bag.

The double doors of the NICU opened in front of them.

"Bed five," said the charge nurse. "Jasmine Wu's the nurse."

"Good." Gabe glanced at Ben. They both knew Jasmine, a tiny young Asian woman who was generally considered the best nurse in the unit.

Jasmine was waiting for them at the foot of the bed, with an orderly standing by to help lift Andy.

"Respirator?" she asked Gabe as her small fingers adjusted the monitoring wires on Andy's chest. "We're all ready."

"No. He's just beginning to breathe on his own, so I'll stay here and ventilate him for a while. Let's get some blood gases on him, though, while we're waiting."

"Gabe," said Ben, once everything had settled down and Andy was breathing spontaneously again, "if ever I need an anesthetic, I want you to give it, okay?"

"I hope you never need one," replied Gabe very seriously, not taking his eyes off the monitor. "I can tell you, nobody's ever going to give *me* one."

"Oh, yeah? How come?"

"Maybe I've been in this business too long," said Gabe. "But when I croak, I want to do it at home, in my bed, with my family around me, and not in some ICU with a tube down my throat so I can't even say good-bye to them."

Ben stared, astonished at Gabe's vehemence.

"Pass me the little syringe," Gabe said. "I'm going to deflate his balloon."

Gabe watched Andy's breathing pattern for a couple of minutes, waiting to remove the endotracheal tube until he was quite certain he wouldn't have to put it back in. Andy's respirations were steady and regular. "Okay, out it comes," said Gabe once he was ready. He gently grasped the end that protruded from Andy's mouth and pulled it out. Jasmine was ready with a piece of gauze to clean up the mucus that came out with it. Andy gagged, coughed, went red in the face, then quieted down. Gabe, confident in his own judgment, went over to check another patient.

Ben stayed for another minute.

"I'll be on my pager," he told Jasmine after making a final check to make sure the venous and arterial lines were open.

"He'll be all right," said Jasmine in her calm, bell-like voice. Ben went off, knowing that he was leaving Andy in good hands.

Out of curiosity, and because he had several things to discuss with Simeon, Ben went into the waiting room. Simeon was there, talking with Andy's parents, whom Ben had met a couple of times. Even before he came up, Ben noticed that the husband, Victor, was standing in a hostile position, arms crossed in front of his chest, leaning slightly backward, feet apart.

Simeon turned when Ben came in. "Everything okay?" he asked him. Simeon's face was drawn; he wasn't used to giving bad news to relatives.

"Andy's looking good," replied Ben.

"I was telling the Markles what we found," said Simeon in an unusually quiet voice.

"And I was asking why the tumor wasn't all removed," said Victor. Victor's aggressiveness was never far from the surface, and now he couldn't suppress it. "That makes it a death sentence, doesn't it?" Victor's eyes moved from Simeon to Ben and back.

Ben took a small step back. He certainly wasn't going to get into this one. He smiled grimly to himself. Simeon Halstead was finding out what it was like to talk to the relatives, but Ben hoped that this experience wouldn't make him change his mind and go back to his old ways.

"It often happens that such tumors involve parts of the brain we can't safely remove," said Simeon patiently. "As it is, there's a very good chance that Andy can look forward to several more months of happy existence."

"If Dr. Cadwaller had been there throughout the operation, as we had requested," said Victor, "would you *then* have been able to remove all the tumor?"

Ben gave a little snort of derision, which he quickly converted to a cough when both Simeon and Victor stared at him.

"I don't think so," said Simeon.

"But with that level of assistance," persisted Victor, "I'm not saying anything against your residents, but wouldn't you have had a better chance of removing all of that tumor if you'd had the assistance of the best-qualified neurosurgeon in this hospital?"

"I don't think so," repeated Simeon.

"When can we see Andy?" asked Fiona, embarrassed and anxious to change the direction of this discussion.

"You can see him anytime the nurses aren't working on

him," said Simeon. "But just for a minute at a time, at first, anyway. I'll take you into the unit now if you like."

They all followed Simeon back along the corridor to the NICU. Ben, walking fast beside him, noticed something different about Simeon: Normally he was precise, unhurried, calm, but now there was an eagerness about him, a quickness, as if he were in a hurry to be getting on with something.

Ben told him briefly about some of the other cases on their service, and asked for his opinion about an elderly man who's come in with a subdural hematoma and hadn't done well since his surgery. Answering Ben's questions, Simeon knew he would sorely miss this clinical contact. But he knew that he couldn't do both the research and his clinical work adequately, and in any case he'd already made up his mind.

The four of them gathered around the foot of Andy's bed. His eyes were closed, and his eyelids and upper cheeks were puffy and bluish-looking below the bandage that went around his head like a turban. Fiona, feeling that her heart was about to burst, went up, leaned over, and kissed him very gently on the little strip of forehead that was still visible.

Gabe had returned and was putting his equipment together before leaving; Simeon introduced him to Victor and Fiona. Gabe shook hands and escaped. He didn't want to be drawn into a conversation with relatives, particularly where there was going to be a bad ending.

Victor stood next to Fiona. In the last couple of days they had worked out a kind of temporary truce between them. Fiona considered it would be hurtful and ultimately bad for Andy if his father were totally excluded from the decision-making process where it concerned their son. But it wasn't easy. Victor ignored the fact that Fiona had custody and that legally he had no say in these matters. He also had other things on his mind, other agendas; he was tired of living by himself, even tired of the succession of stewardesses and other transient women in his life.

And as he stood there, looking at his son, a plan was forming in Victor's mind. He looked at Fiona out of the corner of his eye; he'd somehow have to convince her, and if he was able to do that, they would come together again. They would have to, or his plan would have no benefit for him.

Jasmine Wu appeared, tiny and charming. Victor stood up a little straighter and watched as she expertly injected intravenous medications into Andy's plastic IV tubing. As an airline pilot, Victor had easy access to all kind of women, and he had long ago found that Asians were his favorite. Less aggressive than American women, they seemed to enjoy taking care of him, and he liked the uncomplaining way they accepted orders and criticisms, and when it became necessary to administer punishments, their humiliated submissiveness made him feel very male and potent. He wanted to read Jasmine's nameplate so he could call her, but her back was turned.

Andy was still asleep, so Fiona and Victor left. On the way out of the NICU, Fiona glanced into the different booths. The patients looked so white-faced, so *sick*. She felt guilty that she was able to walk out of there under her own power.

"You want to go out for dinner tonight?" Victor asked as they stood on the steps outside the hospital.

"No, thanks," replied Fiona. For a second she considered inviting him back home, but decided not to. There was no point. She was divorced from him and happy about it. She also knew that Victor would seize on any little concession and try to parlay it into the next step toward moving back in. No way, José. No more, Vic-tor.

So Victor found himself walking along Elm Street in the opposite direction from Fiona. To his right was the huge white concrete expanse of the hospital, beyond that the big medical school research tower, a modern blue and white building that towered over its less exalted neighbors. Victor waited at the traffic lights where Elm joined Haven, then crossed, trying to work out the various steps of his plan.

On Haven he turned right, past the storefronts, bars, and a green-canopied restaurant next to the entrance of West-brook House, an impressive name for the less than impressive eight-story apartment building where he lived.

In the lobby, he looked at his watch. It was one o'clock. He felt hungry and was tempted to go over to the McDonald's across the street for a Big Mac, but he had more important things to do first.

In his rented apartment, he sniffed again at the faint but displeasing smell of mold, compounded with the odor of the spray he'd been using to kill cockroaches. Well, he thought, if things work out right, I won't be staying here much longer. Fiona would soon realize that he was doing her a favor by coming back; no woman could enjoy living alone like that, not for long.

He checked a number in his address book and dialed it. Within a few moments he was talking first to Gloria, then to Dr. Sam Seidel.

"How's it going?" asked Sam. "How's Andy?"

"Okay for now," replied Victor and told him what Simeon Halstead had said about Andy's tumor. "Listen, Sam, there's a couple things that are really bothering me about this here," he went on. "Can I come over and talk to you?"

Sam sighed, and looked at the typed schedule in front of him. "I got a busy afternoon here, Vic," he said. "Hold on a minute."

Victor heard his muffled voice talking to someone, presumably his secretary, then he came on again. "Five," said Sam. "Five o'clock, okay? We're on the ground floor. Ring the doorbell, and we'll let you in."

"Five o'clock," said Victor. "See you then."

Chapter 25

About ten minutes before two o'clock that afternoon, when Simeon had scheduled a meeting to go over the project plans, Edwina Cole walked into the lab. She immediately sensed a new atmosphere there: The lab looked and smelled as if it had just been cleaned, the covers were off the instruments, all of them were turned on, and Denis Popham, resplendent in a symbolically new white coat, was methodically checking the function of each one. Sonia Goldenberg, looking unusually lively and excited, was going through a list of reagents, comparing it with her stock and checking expiration dates.

"Hi, guys," said Edwina.

Denis turned around. "Hi, Edwina. Look, we're getting everything ready. And all my equipment seems to be in pretty good shape." He sounded faintly surprised as he looked back at the row of instruments.

"Huh!" said Sonia, looking up. "Boasting again, Denis!"

Denis looked puzzled, then his face reddened. "That was not funny," he said sternly to Sonia.

"Yes it was, actually," grinned Edwina. "I came early because you never told me the end of the story."

"What story?" asked Sonia.

"About Pamela Evans. She's put her elbow in his groin, Dr. Halstead had just given her a talking-to in his office, and she'd come out crying."

"Oh, yes." Denis looked at Edwina for a moment. "There isn't much more to tell. After that she behaved perfectly, did her job, and we didn't think anything more about it. Then we heard that she'd accused him of sexual harassment . . ."

"We read about it in the *Register,*" put in Sonia angrily.

"So we went to talk to Dr. Cadwaller, the head of the department."

"Go on."

"Well, we told him that it wasn't true, that Pamela had come on to Dr. Halstead, that she was harassing him. We told him the whole story, about the way she dressed and everything. Anyway, he was very polite, said we might be required to make statements at some time in the future, but basically he told us it wasn't our problem, and we should mind our own business or we'd be in trouble too."

"Wow! Didn't you tell me that Pamela's friend worked for Dr. Cadwaller?"

"Right, Nicole. Apparently they had cooked up this story together, Pamela and her friend, and took it to Dr. Cadwaller."

"Then what?"

Denis looked downcast. "I think that's when we screwed up. We wrote a letter to the dean of the faculty, and we were called in and told that although no further action was being taken against Dr. Halstead, there were certain things about the situation that we didn't know about. Like Dr Cadwaller, he told us more or less to shut up or we'd be out looking for jobs."

"He made us *promise* to shut up," said Sonia, tossing her short curls.

"And so we did," said Denis, shrugging. "Under pressure. What we should have done was talk to the reporter at the *Register,* because there was never any follow-up story, any retraction, or any conclusion. Pamela got another job somewhere else, but it left everybody, except us, of course, wondering what had really happened."

"Why didn't he do anything? I mean Dr. Halstead?"

Denis sighed. "He was very busy . . And I don't think he even cared that much. He knew he hadn't done anything wrong, and that was enough for him."

"I'm sure Dr. Halstead would have done something to defend himself if they'd taken it any further," said Sonia. "But they didn't, so he didn't."

At that moment, Simeon was getting out of the elevator and heading for his lab, feeling more pumped up than he could remember. He'd made an appointment to see Felix

Cadwaller the next day to tell him that he was taking a six-month clinical leave of absence, maybe longer, in order to work in the lab full time.

Everybody was in the lab, as he'd requested. Denis, one of whose ancestors must surely have been a butler, stood up.

"Good," said Simeon, looking quickly around and noting the changes. He grinned at Edwina. "Glad you could join us, Edwina," he said. "Now," he went on, "what I want to do right now is go over the main goals of this project, split it up into its different parts, and assign the different parts among us."

"From each according to his abilities," murmured Denis, "to each according to his needs."

Sonia made a face and gave him a hard nudge in the ribs.

"You're exactly right, Denis," said Simeon, smiling. "Although I don't suppose that's what Karl Marx had in mind. Now, let's get on with this. Our stated goal is as follows: to develop an effective method of treating malignant brain tumors, specifically astrocytomas." Simeon looked at his little team and again wondered if he wasn't biting off more than he could chew. "I needn't remind you that millions of dollars have been spent trying to achieve this," he said. "Hundreds of people in medical centers all over the world have worked on the problem, basically without making any major difference to the overall miserable outlook in this disease."

"What is the state of the art right now," Dr. Halstead?" asked Edwina.

"The current treatment, once the diagnosis has been established and surgery has not totally removed the tumor, is external beam radiation and chemotherapy, either singly or as a combination. This may slow the progression of the tumor, but only temporarily."

"That's no different from the treatment of ten or twenty years ago, is it?" asked Edwina.

"Well, there have been some improvements in radiotherapy, and a few new chemotherapeutic agents have surfaced, but basically, yes, it's the same deal." Simeon grinned at Edwina. "I'm assuming you're asking these questions for the benefit of Denis and Sonia. You know what I'm talking about." He paused for a moment. "The problem with chemotherapy is that it's highly toxic and affects all the cells in the patient's body to a greater or lesser degree."

"That's why their hair falls out?" asked Sonia.

"Exactly. Hair follicles are destroyed by chemotherapy in the same way as the cancer cells are killed. And that's only the visible part. Lots of other normal cells are killed, such as white cells in the blood. And radiotherapy has major disadvantages too; it kills a lot of normal brain cells, reducing the patient's intellectual capacity, accuracy of reflexes, and so on."

Edwina thought about the zombielike kids she'd seen wandering around the neuro outpatient clinic and felt glad that Andy's parents had decided against both chemo and radiotherapy.

"I always think of chemotherapy in terms of a china shop," Simeon went on. "Imagine one single defective set of plates in among all the dozens of rows and stacks of perfectly good china. Chemotherapy is like sending a guy in there with a sledgehammer. He doesn't know the difference between a good plate and a defective one. Sure, he eventually gets rid of the defective plates, but in doing so he has to smash all the other ones too."

Edwina nodded, wincing at this very visual metaphor.

Sonia was getting restless. "So what are *we* going to do?" She pointed at the equipment on the benches. "All that stuff isn't radiotherapy, and it isn't chemotherapy either."

"Right. What we have to do first is identify and mark the cancer cells. Like painting the defective plates in the china shop so that when you shine an infrared light, only the bad ones glow. Then the guy with the sledgehammer can see exactly what he needs to smash and can spare the rest."

"So how will we do that? I mean, how can we identify the cancer cells?" Denis, who had a degree in chemistry, had been working on various cellular proteins, but he didn't know exactly how his expertise was going to fit into the overall project.

"By certain of their characteristics," replied Simeon. "Now I want you to think for a moment about hard-boiled eggs."

Denis's mouth opened very slightly, and Sonia stared at Simeon, but Edwina, who had an idea of what was coming, just grinned.

"Albumen is the main protein of egg white," Simeon went on, smiling at their expressions. "It's a transparent, viscous, slightly yellowish material in its normal state, but when it's gets heated, it gets damaged, or 'denatured.' That's when it turns white and hard. In other words, it's a heat-coagulable protein. There are others besides albumen. The point of this is that if a protein in a cell is coagulated by heat, that means the death of the cell."

"So that's why I've been looking for proteins that coagulate at different temperatures," said Denis.

"Right. Another key factor is that tumor cells have a different metabolism from normal cells. They can use certain amino acids the normal cells can't use, and so ..." Simeon banged his fist gently on the table to emphasize his point, "we want the tumor cells to take up these amino acids and form heat-sensitive proteins so we can destroy them."

"By heating up the brain ..." Edwina said.

"Just the part you want to heat," said Simeon. "The part with the tumor. And we do it by sending in several narrowly focused beams of microwave radiation from different locations around the head, so that the beams intersect where the tumor is."

"Sounds easy," said Sonia. "How come everybody isn't doing this?"

"Because it's *not* easy, and also because nowadays everybody's attention is focused on radiation and chemotherapy."

Sonia was blinking, and Simeon realized he had to get back to basics or he would lose part of his audience. "There are two main problems we have to solve," he said. He held up one finger. "First, we have to develop a microwave technique that doesn't damage the normal brain. That's going to be my job, and Sonia's going to help me. Second, we have to develop a protein or amino acid that only the tumor cells will take up and metabolize, and that will make them coagulate at a lower temperature. That's going to be the job of the Cole-Popham team." Simeon nodded at Edwina and Denis. "Right now, the coagulation temperature of tumor cells is almost the same as that of normal cells, too close to use to destroy them. We have to increase that margin by at least 1.5 degrees Celsius before we have a safe technique."

"That's it?" asked Edwina, smiling.

"That's it."

"We have a lot to do."

"We can do it."

"Right on!"

Simeon grinned. "What I'd like you to do first, Edwina, is go over the recent literature on hypercoagulable proteins. When you've done that, the person to talk to is Dr. Win Park in the biophysics department. This isn't exactly his field, but he's very smart and knows a lot about the kind of problems you're going to run into. Here's his number." Simeon wrote it on the lower left corner of the chalkboard. "I've already spoken to him, so he'll be expecting your call. Let's get together here tomorrow, same time, and we can go over what you've found."

He looked at the clock. "I have patients to see," he said. "I'll be back in an hour. Meanwhile, Sonia, pull all the manufacturers' specs for the microwave equipment and call them to see if they have anything new that we haven't heard about, particularly if they've been able to miniaturize the units, because we're going to be working for a while with rats. Our own specs are on the computer."

As the door closed behind him, Edwina, Denis, and Sonia joined in an ecstatic triple high five across the small table.

"If this works," said Denis excitedly, "Dr. Halstead'll be in line for a Nobel prize."

"And if it doesn't work," said Edwina the realist, "we could be all in such deep shit that it'll take the rest of our lives to climb out of it."

There was an astonished pause, then Edwina continued, "We're maybe in trouble even if it *does* work. You guys told me how Cadwaller tried to screw Dr. Halstead through Pamela Evans. I have a powerful feeling that he ain't done with our fearless leader yet."

Chapter 26

Later that afternoon, before leaving to see Sam Seidel, Victor checked with his dispatcher, as per his airline's standing instructions. He found that he was scheduled for a flight next morning to Atlanta and on to Dallas and was to report at the Providence terminal office at six. That would have been seven o'clock if he'd been a captain, thought Victor. It was the copilot's job to file the flight plan, get the weather reports, and carry out the pre-flight physical checks of the aircraft. That always took time, particularly if he found something wrong. And Victor, the picky pilot, as he was known to the ground crew, usually did. Well, it wouldn't be long now; his promotion review was coming up in a month, his third since becoming eligible. Everything was in place: He had all the necessary flying hours, his instrument rating was up to date, he'd passed his medical exam and completed all the new equipment courses. Victor briefly considered asking his supervisor for time off for Andy's illness, but decided not to. There wasn't anything he could do in New Coventry anyway, he realized, and furthermore he hated hospitals. He'd be better off on the job. Plus he had a lady friend in Dallas he hadn't seen for five weeks.

Sam Seidel's office was in a two-story building near a small shopping mall, not the best part of town, although not the worst either. Sam's neighbors were an H&R Block franchisee on one side and on the other, a lawyer who, according to the rustic wooden signpost outside the office, specialized in defending DWI cases.

Victor rang the bell as instructed. A crackly female voice replied from a small speaker above the door. "Yes?"

Victor announced himself and pushed the door when he heard the buzzer.

"Sorry about that," said Sam, appearing in the short corridor with Gloria behind him. "This is a tough neighborhood, and there's always somebody out there looking for drugs. I get broken into two, three times a year, right, Gloria?"

Gloria nodded and smiled below her jet-black bouffant hairdo.

"Coffee?" she asked Victor. This guy looks good, she thought, big, healthy-looking, with good clothes and expensive shoes, probably Italian, nice soft leather, not something he bought in this area. Shoes were always what she checked out first on a guy.

"So what can I do for you?" asked Sam, shaking Victor's hand.

Victor glanced at Gloria.

"Don't worry about her," said Sam. "Everything that happens in this office, Gloria knows about it."

"I'd like to talk to you alone," said Victor.

Gloria wasn't at all put out. "Did you say yes to coffee?" she asked Victor, who said no thanks.

Sam shrugged and went into his office, closing the door after Victor. The office felt very small and close, with a single curtained window and cheap wooden paneling covering the walls. Victor noted a faint but penetrating aroma of air freshener. There was the usual desk, a filing cabinet, and on the wall opposite the window, a touristy painting of Jerusalem as seen from a nearby hill. Sam's medical diploma hung, slightly askew, on the wall behind the high black leather desk chair.

"Sam, I'm concerned about what's happening with Andy," said Victor, sitting down. "I mean the kind of care that he's getting."

"I spoke to Dr. Halstead and Dr. Cadwaller both this morning after the surgery," said Sam, a grave expression on his face. "I'm sorry. Really. Andy's a real nice kid."

"Right. Yes, he is." Victor paused to let his grief at Andy's bad prognosis show on his face. "Remember when I talked to Felix Cadwaller?"

"Yeah."

"Well, he told me—and I'm quite sure of it—that he was going to assist Halstead during the operation. Now, doesn't that mean that he's going to be physically present *the whole time*? I mean, that he's going to help him do the entire case?"

Sam shrugged one shoulder noncommittally. "I guess. If that's what he told you . . ."

"Cadwaller told me, 'Look, if it'll make you and Mrs. Markle feel better to have the department chairman keeping an eye on things, I'll be happy to assist Dr. Halstead.' That's what he said, in those exact words."

"You saw him afterward, right? In the waiting room? Why didn't you ask him then?"

"It wasn't afterward. When he came in, the case had hardly started. And it wasn't the right moment to ask. Fiona likes Halstead and would have got mad if I'd said anything. Anyway, I didn't think about it until later." Victor leaned forward. "This is what I'm wondering, Sam. Could Doc Halstead have done something really bad, something really incompetent or maybe dangerous, something that would have made Cadwaller walk out of the operating room in disgust?"

Sam looked startled. "I doubt it. If something like that had happened, he'd have mentioned it or let you know somehow."

Victor shook his head emphatically. "No way. You know how those guys stick together." He grinned. "You should know, you're one of them."

"Yeah. You could be right, I suppose . . ."

"There was another thing, Sam. He was telling us about a clinical trial . . ."

"Who was?"

"Cadwaller. When he came into the waiting room. Anyway, he said he was the head of a whole big clinical trial funded by some big government agency and aimed specifically at kids with tumors like Andy's. He also indicated that Halstead knew all about the trial, although he never mentioned it to us."

Sam sat back and looked at Victor. He rubbed the side of his nose. Things were coming along just the way he wanted.

Victor wasn't finished. "You know, Sam," he said, "I'll

be honest with you, and I can tell you without boasting that I'm a pretty good judge of people. Goes with the job of being an airline captain, I suppose. Anyway, I can tell you this. From the very first time I set eyes on Dr. Simeon Halstead, I could feel there was something secretive, underhanded, maybe, or even *dishonest* about him. I hate to say that about somebody I hardly know, but don't forget there was that business about his lab tech, the one he was sexually harassing, and that would seem to support what I'm saying. Of course, I didn't know about that at the time, or I can tell you Andy would certainly have gone to see some other surgeon."

"Halstead's pretty well thought of as a surgeon," murmured Sam.

"My position," said Victor, "is this. First, Halstead didn't give us the full info about the various different ways Andy could have been taken care of. Second, we hired Dr. Cadwaller to give us a second opinion and also to help Halstead make the correct decisions during surgery. That didn't happen, and I have no idea why." Victor stared challengingly at Sam. "Do you? Did they say anything to you that could have explained it?"

Sam shook his head. "No. And I'm not sure how much that really matters. What matters is how Andy . . ."

"I know how you guys stick together," said Victor. "Don't try to bullshit me."

Sam had difficulty suppressing a grin.

"It's not that," he said. "I'll ask them what happened, if you like."

Victor made a decision. "I'm going to talk to a malpractice attorney," he said.

"Doesn't your ex-wife have custody of Andy?" asked Sam. "Have you talked to her about it?"

"Andy's my son," said Victor, "and I need to take care of his interests. How the legalities are handled will be up to the lawyers, not me."

"So what did Dr. Halstead tell you about Andy's prognosis?" asked Sam.

"Six months," replied Halstead. "I can't believe that in this day and age, with all the medical miracles we hear about all the time, they can condemn a fourteen-year-old boy to death like that."

"The thing is, Victor, that with this type of tumor ..." Sam shook his head sadly, "*scientific* medicine doesn't really have anything very encouraging to offer at this time."

Victor rose nicely to the bait. In fact he almost leaped out of the water to get at it. "Scientific medicine?" he asked. "What do you mean by that? Is there any other kind?"

"Well, I'm thinking of, you know, modern medicine, all that scientific stuff that we've had pumped into our minds for the last fifty years. The fact is ..." Sam leaned forward and tapped a finger on the glass top of his desk, "with all the millions, actually *billions* of dollars spent on cancer care during that time, I'm talking about since the forties, the end of the war, did you know that the survival statistics for cancer are no better now than they were then? In fact, they're worse. More people are getting cancer and more people are dying of it. I hate to tell you this, Victor, but the only real difference between then and now ..." Sam's voice rose, betraying his indignation at his own profession. "... is that if you happen to get struck by cancer now, it'll cost you one hell of a lot more, but the treatment won't do you any more good than it did fifty years ago."

"Jesus." Victor was shocked. "Is that really true? In all that time, and with all that money ..." His face went red. "Then where does all that bullshit about 'winning the war against cancer' come from? What happened to all that money?"

"Ask the American Cancer Society," said Sam. "You may have a little trouble finding their top executives, but if they're not lunching at the Four Seasons their limos are taking them out to the golf course, and if they're not there, then they're probably out on their yachts in the Bahamas."

"Goddamn," said Victor, really furious to hear this. He had been very active as one of his airline's fundraisers for the ACS, but he had simply assumed that it was the dedicated and socially responsible organization that its ads represented. He'd never thought of asking tough questions about the actual results they were getting. "I'll make it a point to find out about that."

Sam raised both his hands in a pacific gesture. "There's no need to get excited, already," he said. "That's life. Those guys, they're doing the best they can. For themselves. Anyway, that's not what we were talking about."

"Right . . . Andy. I'm thinking about him. Is there any real alternative to scientific medicine? Anything that actually does get good results?"

"Victor, when I was in med school scientific medicine was all they taught us. It was the answer to everything. And of course we believed it, because every day we were hearing about new miracle drugs, heart transplants, what have you. Nobody ever taught us about all the dozens of other ways of taking care of sick people. Except in passing, and that was only to say it was all a load of shit." Sam swiped at a fly on his desk and missed. "The thing is, these alternative medicines have been used effectively for centuries. All over the world—Greece, Europe, South America—they're still making progress, finding real cures, although you never see it reported on *Dateline,* and you won't read about it in *Time* magazine."

Victor said nothing for a few moments. He hadn't been expecting to hear anything like this, certainly not from a regular M.D.-type doctor. But what Sam was saying certainly made sense, and it fed into Victor's deep distrust of organized medicine.

"So is anybody outside of scientific medicine doing anything about brain tumors?" he asked.

Sam settled back in his chair, ignoring the fly taunting him from the desktop. "Well, actually, yes," he said slowly. "There's this place I know of in Mexico . . ."

Ten minutes later Victor stood up to leave.

"You said you were going to see a malpractice attorney," said Sam. "Do you know one?"

"I don't," replied Victor. "But I know some people . . ."

"Then this is the guy you should talk to," said Sam. He wrote a name and a telephone number on a scrap of paper and passed it to Victor. "Haiman Gold," he said. "He's the best around here. Tell him I sent you. In fact," he went on, rubbing the side of his nose, "I'll call him for you right now, to give him an idea of what this is all about."

Chapter 27

Twenty minutes later, Victor stopped outside an office building near the center of New Coventry. Haiman Gold, Jr., the son of the firm's founder, had told Sam that if the matter was urgent he could see Victor right away.

It wasn't exactly what Victor had expected. The building on Cedar Street seemed run-down, and the glass door to the outside was so dirty that Victor could hardly see through it. He took the tiny elevator to the eighth floor and, following the directions on the wall opposite the elevator, turned right and walked down a long, grubby, carpeted corridor all the way to the end, where a black sign on the frosted glass indicated that he had arrived at the offices of Gold, Reilly, and O'Connell.

Mr. Gold's own office didn't look too prosperous either, but Victor quickly found that the man knew his business. Haiman Gold, Jr., was somewhere in his early forties, heavy-looking but not fat, and there was a generally shiny look about him—bald dome, shiny black hair at the sides, shiny well-fed cheeks and nose, and well-polished shoes. He wore a big ruby class ring on the third finger of his white, veinless right hand. After they had shaken hands and sat down, Haiman Gold, Jr., pulled a blank yellow legal pad in front of him and picked up a thick Mont Blanc pen in his right hand. His manner was brisk; it was clear that he didn't have time to waste, especially since the first consultation was, by rule of the firm, free.

"Let me first tell you something about medical malpractice, Mr. Markle," he said, settling behind his desk. His eyes went a little glassy, and Victor figured that he'd come out with his spiel a thousand times.

"First," he said, raising his index finger, "simply getting

a bad result from surgery or medical treatment does not necessarily constitute medical malpractice. Second ..." A second pale finger joined the first, "... a doctor must have made a significant error, or have omitted, through carelessness or ignorance, some medical or surgical treatment or test that other doctors, capable and similarly trained, would have considered important and essential." Mr. Gold's eyes wandered to the clock on his desk, then went back to Victor. "And of course, in order to prove that, Mr. Markle, you'd have to hire a doctor to testify for you *against* whatever doctor you consider committed malpractice. That's not very difficult these days," he went on, "but we always mention it."

Mr. Gold paused and gazed at Victor with his shiny eyes. "Do you still think you have a case, Mr. Markle?" he asked.

"I understand what you said," replied Victor carefully. "Whether or not I have a case is for you to decide. Let me tell you why I'm here."

Gold nodded, and Victor told him his story, finishing up with his request for a second opinion from Dr. Cadwaller and his failure to assist during the operation.

Gold raised his head. "Did you have a contract with Dr. Cadwaller?"

"A verbal one, I guess. I don't know the legal rules for that, but he told me he would be there *during the operation* to 'keep an eye on things for me.'"

Gold wrote, in a big, flamboyant style right across the page, without margins.

"Any witnesses? With Dr. Cadwaller?"

"No. The first time was on the phone, then just the two of us in his office."

"Did he make any notes?"

"Yes. As we talked."

Gold raised his head again. "Is it Dr. Cadwaller who you think committed malpractice?"

"No. It's Dr. Halstead, for the reasons I told you. He didn't mention, let alone discuss, the clinical trials to me or my wife—my former wife, that is—and Dr. Cadwaller seemed to think it might offer a better chance of success than surgery."

"You said your 'former wife.' "

"Yes. Fiona."

"You have joint custody of your son?"

"No. She has. That's because . . ."

"If you don't have at least joint custody," interrupted Gold in a tired voice, "you can't legally do anything on his behalf." He put down his pen. "Have you discussed this matter with Mrs. Markle?"

"Sure," lied Victor. "She'll go along. She's not anxious to sue the doc, of course," he went on, seeing the unconvinced look that had appeared in Gold's eye. "But if it's clear that there's a case . . . Like I said, she'll go along."

Gold got up. "Well, okay, but before we can go any further, I'll need her signature to confirm that you're both acting as a legal unit on behalf of your son in this matter."

"No problem," said Victor confidently. "Actually we're well along in the process of getting back together. So if you can give me the forms, I'll just have her sign them."

"Okay," said Gold briskly. "I'll give them to you on the way out. Meanwhile, if you think that there has been *criminal negligence* on the part of any of the physicians taking care of your son, you would need to get in touch with the state's Child Welfare Department. I can give you that number . . ."

"No, thanks. I just want to know if we have a case here or not, then I can make some decisions."

Gold thought about that for a few seconds. He knew that New Coventry Medical Center had lost several recent, well-publicized malpractice suits, and both NCMC and their insurers would almost certainly try to settle another major suit out of court, assuming that the case had at least an appearance of merit.

The personalities that Markle had mentioned also intrigued Gold. As a malpractice attorney with several contacts within the hospital itself, he knew of the antagonism between Halstead and Cadwaller. If he could pit the two of them against each other, it might turn a nothing case into one worth fighting, even if only for the publicity.

"Hard to tell at this point," replied Gold. "But if you can document what you just told me, and maybe add some meat to the story, I'd say there's a reasonable chance."

"Good," said Victor. "Is there anything else I should be doing?"

"Yeah. Write up everything you told me, everything the doctors and nurses say or do with your son, all treatments, medications, comments, everything you and your wife can think of. Keep a notebook, make sure the date's marked on everything, and try to have witnesses. Write down their names. For instance, 'night nurse' isn't enough; you gotta have the name. I know that isn't always easy, but if you could get, say, one of the nurses on your side, it would make a huge difference."

Victor nodded, thinking about Jasmine Wu, the pretty Asian nurse who had taken care of Andy in the ICU, and he knew just how to mix this kind of business with pleasure.

Gabe Pinero flitted like a moth around Andy for the rest of the day, checking IVs, monitoring pressures and cardiac output. By late afternoon, he figured everything was stable, and it was okay to send Andy over to the stepdown unit. Things weren't as hectic there, and Fiona would be able to stay with him all the time.

Simeon had come in several times to see his patient.

"He's having a bit of a problem looking upward," Gabe told Simeon after examining him. "But I don't expect it'll last more than a few days." Simeon nodded noncommittally, surprised that Gabe didn't know about Parinaud's sign.

Andy, seeming very shaken, lay immobile in his bed. Normally he couldn't keep still for five seconds at a time, but now, although he was apparently awake, he just lay there, his eyes open most of the time, staring in front of him. His face was almost as white as his around-the-head dressing.

"Can I get you anything, sweetheart?" Fiona asked him several times, leaning over him and speaking very softly. "Some water? Juice?" For her, the worst part of it was feeling so helpless. Andy was hurting, it was clear, and she could sense that things were happening inside his head that were disturbing him, but he didn't complain, and there wasn't anything she could do. They had given him a little gadget that he could press if the pain in his head got bad. It automatically squirted some pain medication into his veins. Andy hardly used it.

"No, thanks," he told his mother. Even to him, his voice sounded strange and metallic, as if he were speaking from somewhere inside the spaceship *Enterprise.* Earlier Andy had shaken his head to say no when a nurse asked him if his IVs were hurting, but that one experience quickly taught him not to move his head if he could possibly avoid doing so.

It all felt so weird. He found it difficult to open his eyes, because they were so puffy, and it was hard work keeping them open. And when he looked at things, like somebody walking past his bed, or at the big white lamp fixture over the doorway, it would look okay for a second, and then it would start to move and sway and change its shape until he had to look somewhere else. When he looked back at it, it was a lamp again, but the same thing would happen all over again within seconds.

It was just as bad, in a different way, if he kept his eyes closed. Actually it was worse, because then it felt as if he were at sea in a small boat, sinking into huge troughs and climbing dizzily up the sides of vertical waves. And that made him feel as if he were going to throw up, so he'd open his eyes and things would stop swaying. He knew his mother was there, even when he couldn't see her; she would come in and out of his field of vision. He knew it was her face, her movements, although sometimes he didn't recognize the way she looked, because her face was big and oval and pale, and it would slowly get all distorted and her mouth slipped all round the side of her face and then down into her chest. He recognized her voice, of course, but even when she didn't say anything, he still knew who she was. Maybe it was the smell of her perfume, but he didn't think so, because ever since he woke up there had been a bad smell in his nose, a sweet, chemical smell that he didn't recognize, and nothing seemed to make it go away. And his nose felt all hot and clogged and hurting from the tube they'd had in it. It was very sensitive now, and when the nurse wiped it with a Kleenex it felt as if she was scraping it with a piece of sandpaper.

"I need to pee." He tried not to move when he spoke.

The nurse appeared with a urinal, which she pushed under the sheets and between his legs. Embarrassed, he pulled it up and fitted himself into its mouth. Luckily he was wearing a gown and not pajamas. It took almost a minute for him to start the flow; he'd never peed in this position before, and it felt as if he were peeing straight into the bed.

Even when he drank water through the straw, it felt strange. His lips seemed fat and numb, and the straw was like a big pipe with pieces missing from its circumference.

After a while, he found that the worst thing of all was that he couldn't keep his mind on any single thing for more than a second or two. For instance, he'd think about Kevin, and the image of him would come up all right, but immediately it disintegrated into a big red and green blob that changed its shape and grew smaller blobs on the surface, and then he couldn't remember who or what he'd been thinking about in the first place.

When that happened he closed his eyes and tried to sleep and then the weird roller-coaster feeling would come back. So he opened his eyes again, and tried to be patient, and wait until things improved. Dr. Halstead had told him before the operation that he'd probably feel rotten for a day or so, and although they would give him medicine to make it less uncomfortable, basically the message was that he'd have to tough it out for a while.

And then he coughed. Suddenly. He didn't have a second's warning, and his whole head felt as if it had exploded. The pain hit him so hard that he moaned, and he could feel the tears come rolling down his cheeks. Fiona came over instantly and put a cool hand on his brow, just below the bandage. It was the sweetest touch Andy had ever felt, and he wanted her to keep her hand there forever.

Time passed. Half of it was occupied by bad dreams, the other half by an unstable and equally bad reality. Lights went on and off. His IV stopped working for a little while, but after Fiona drew the nurse's attention to it, they got it going again, and that hurt. The hand he could see best, his left one, was all puffed up, strapped with tape to a board, his fingers curled around the end. He didn't recognize it, even when he straightened out his fingers to prove they were his.

His father came in at some point during the evening and patted him on the shoulder and said, "Hang in there, old buddy," or something like that, but Andy's mind drifted off, and when he looked again, his father was standing next to his mother saying in an urgent kind of voice, "Fiona, I need to talk to you about Andy," and his mother replied in that guarded voice she used only with him, "Not now, Victor, this isn't the moment, okay?" Andy closed his eyes tight, certain that his father was going to tell her that he was dying, that Dr. Halstead had told him so, privately . . .

Much later, there was a subdued clattering noise and somebody came in and set up a low collapsible cot over by the window to his left, then somebody else brought in a pillow for her. His mother came and kissed him on the forehead, then lay down on the cot with all her clothes on, but he knew that she wasn't asleep, because of the way she breathed and because she kept turning her head to look at him.

It's strange stuff, Fiona was thinking as she lay watching Andy, that maternal instinct. Every fiber of her body was geared right now to him, to protecting him . . . but from what? Her job as mother-protector had in an essential way been taken over by Simeon Halstead, by the hospital, by the whole system, and right now she was just an onlooker, unable to do anything real for him. Lying on her cot in the semidarkness, Fiona had a sudden recollection of a news video she'd seen a few years back, when Andy was about five. It was from Helsinki, or Copenhagen, one of the Nordic countries. A small boy had somehow got through the railing of the polar bear enclosure and had trotted down to the edge of the pool to get a better look at the animals. Before anyone could come to his rescue, a large bear with matted yellow fur came up, sniffed at the child, knocked him down, put one foot on him, then pulled him to pieces and ate him, raising its big pointed head from time to time to look up, expressionless and bloody-jawed, at the spectators screaming from behind the fence. That poor mother. Fiona remembered how she and her friends who also had kids had talked about nothing else for weeks. Some of them

had been so angry with the mother, they said she deserved
how she felt, she'd been so careless with her child ...

Was what had happened to Andy something *she* had
been careless about? Why hadn't she taken Andy to see a
doctor earlier, when he first started to have problems? In
retrospect, it was obvious that something was the matter
when he couldn't hit a ball he normally would have sent
into the next county ... Before the operation, Fiona had
taken books out of the library, called a nurse friend at
Yale–New Haven Hospital, researched everything she
could find about brain tumors in children, but a lot of the
terminology was unfamiliar to her, and much of the literature assumed medical training and was too difficult for her
to understand. Still, she'd been able to get a pretty good
idea of what it was all about. There was such a sense of
unreality about these papers, with their neat rows and col-
umns of mortality statistics, each number reflecting a child,
each with his own unrecorded aura of suffering, of agonized
family and friends. Like Ted Garvey. No wonder Simeon
tried not to get involved; Fiona tried to imagine how she
would feel, with an unending succession of dying children
in her care.

But he *had* got himself involved—maybe not intentionally,
but it had happened. She sensed it, felt his new warmth, his
intensity, his caring, even in the way he stood, by the amount
of time he was spending with Andy and the way he looked
at him. And yes, by the way he looked at her, too.

Andy stirred, and she sat up. His head turned slightly,
but he didn't wake up. Fiona watched him, feeling her heart
pounding, then she lay quietly down again.

It was strange how Simeon's presence seemed to be everywhere, around the unit, the hospital. She knew that the
nurses were taking especially good care of Andy, partly
because they were all very professional, and of course they
liked him a lot, but also because he was Dr. Halstead's
patient and they jealously felt a part of his team, sharing
the spirit of meticulous responsibility and attention to every
detail that he had developed in them over the years.

The next day wasn't much better for Andy, except that
he could open his eyes a bit more, but when Dr. Halstead

asked him, he still couldn't look up, and when he tried, he saw double. It was still as difficult when he wanted to pee, although they tried to help by swinging his legs out over the edge of the bed, but they wouldn't let him get out of the bed to do it.

Andy was getting to appreciate Dr. Halstead more and more. He came several times a day, talked very quietly to him, which was a relief, because he'd found that loud noises hurt, not in his ears, but somewhere inside his head. Andy couldn't believe that even the noise of a squeaky wheelchair going past his bed could hurt, but it did. He remembered one night a few months ago when he and Kevin went over to a friend's house to check out a new stereo system when his parents weren't home. They turned the speakers up so loud the neighbors complained and the police eventually came. His ears hadn't hurt even then, although they did buzz for a couple of days and for a week after that he had trouble hearing what people were saying.

There was something else that he liked about Dr. Halstead. He didn't lie, and if he said something, that was how it was. Even his presence reassured Andy, and he knew that if something really bad happened to him Dr. Halstead would be able to take care of it.

Andy became aware that his mother had started to feel the same way about Dr. Halstead. He knew how tough all this was for her—worse in some ways than for him. The first day, Fiona hardly moved from his room; she had brought her big satchel full of papers to correct and stuff to read, but it was difficult for her to concentrate, and she didn't get much done. However, she did quickly get to know the nurses, and on Andy's second day there, she even took over the unit phone for a couple of hours when the secretary had to go home early because of some domestic emergency.

She noticed that it was always something of an event when Dr. Halstead came into the unit; a kind of generalized quiver seemed to go through everyone, and they all straightened up and went about their business with renewed energy, keeping one eye on him. As the head nurse told Fiona, he never used to come in without his team of residents, and he *never* spent this much time with a patient.

"We don't know what's come over him," she said. "But it's making everybody feel good."

Victor was another matter. Although he was very polite when Dr. Halstead was there, after he'd gone he made grumbly, disapproving noises under his breath and mumbled things to Fiona that Andy didn't hear.

Simeon, who spent a lot of time in the unit that day, was very aware of Victor's antipathy, although of course he didn't show it, especially to Victor. Once Simeon came in just as Victor was leaving and noticed that Victor was looking red-faced and flustered. Jasmine Wu was with Andy; she'd stopped by to see how he was doing. She looked angry, and when she came out with Simeon a couple of minutes later, he asked her what was the matter.

"That Markle man," she said. "He *propositioned* me. Right there, with his son lying sick in bed. What a pig! How did a nice kid like Andy get a father like that?"

After that, Victor's visits to the hospital were infrequent and brief.

Late on the second evening, after the unit lights had been dimmed and most of the patients had been bedded down for the night, Andy was asleep, and Fiona was sitting in the easy chair by his bed, when she saw the unit door open. Dr. Halstead's silhouette appeared, then he came quietly over toward her.

"I'm glad you're still here," he said. "I'd like to talk to you. Do you feel comfortable leaving Andy for a few minutes?"

Fiona got up to check on Andy. He was still asleep, the corner of his mouth drooping a little. Very gently she wiped a little saliva off his chin.

She nodded at Simeon and tiptoed out behind him. The lights in the corridor were bright, and she blinked.

"You look as if you could use a cup of coffee," he said, looking carefully at her. "The cafeteria's two floors down, right below us, and it's still open."

Without waiting for a yes or a no, he went to the door to the emergency stairway and held it open. Fiona passed under his outstretched arm and they went down the four half-flights, their footsteps resounding in the concrete stairwell. She was so tired and unsteady that she was glad to hold on to the metal railing.

The cafeteria was almost deserted. A surgical team of five, three men and two women, all in greens, were lining up silently with their trays. Fiona thought she'd never seen a group of people who all looked so desperately tired.

"Do you want anything to eat?" asked Simeon.

"A cup of coffee will be just fine, thanks," she said.

"It won't keep you awake?"

"Nothing keeps me awake," replied Fiona. "Especially tonight. Unless Andy moves, of course, and then I'm wide awake."

Simeon went to a table next to the dark windows, pulled out a chair for Fiona and sat down.

"He's doing nicely," he said.

"For now."

"Right."

There was a brief silence while Fiona stirred in a pink package of Sweet'n Low.

"We got the final pathology report back this afternoon," he said, and Fiona felt her whole body tighten up. This was going to be bad news, she was sure of it.

"It's what we expected, I'm afraid," Simeon went on, his eyes on Fiona.

"An astrocytoma?"

"Yes. An astrocytoma." He looked faintly surprised that Fiona knew the term.

"Can you tell me exactly what that is?" Fiona's fingers gripped the edge of the table, and her knuckles were white. "I've looked it up, but I can't understand the terminology."

"Yes." Simeon put his hands on the table too, fingers extended. "Astrocytes are normal supporting cells between the nerve cells in the brain," he started, watching Fiona's face for signs that she wasn't understanding him. "They're called astrocytes because they have a lot of filaments that stick out, and somebody long ago had the notion that they looked like stars . . ."

"From *astra,* Latin for a star. I'm with you so far," said Fiona, listening intently. "Go on."

"Good. An astrocytoma is a tumor composed of astrocytes that have gone wrong," he went on. "Normally there's a mechanism that tells the cells when to stop growing, but when that mechanism breaks down they keep on growing to form a tumor, a lump that takes up space that's needed for the brain. And of course, it's a closed space in there, inside the skull, and there isn't any room for expansion."

"So the brain is compressed."

"Yes. But that part we were able to deal with. The worst problem is that the area of the brain near the tumor is also *invaded*. That's because the astrocytes normally exist between the brain cells, so when they become malignant it's easy for them to infiltrate the adjoining normal parts of the brain."

"I remember that's what you told me after the surgery," said Fiona. "But aside from what you did to remove most of the tumor, what can you do?" Fiona was shocked to hear how desperate her voice sounded.

"That's really what I wanted to talk to you about," he said. "As you know, at the present time, the overall outlook for this kind of situation is not good. The tumor will grow back, whether or not we put him through radiotherapy or chemotherapy."

Fiona waited for him to go on. He paused, watching her.

"When I was doing research in London a few years ago, the team I was working with came up with some promising results," he said. "This morning I called Dr. Bannister, who's the head of that team, hoping that maybe they could suggest something, but he told me that unfortunately their work had fizzled out."

Fiona had the feeling that Simeon was struggling to say something but was having trouble getting around to it. Again he paused, then took a deep breath. "I don't want to raise your hopes unduly," he said. Then as Fiona watched him, he threw caution to the winds. "I'm working on a completely new method of curing these tumors," he said. "It's too complicated to tell you the details now, and it will probably take longer than . . . but I just wanted you to know."

"How long?"

Simeon shook his head, astonished at himself that he'd even mentioned this to her. Why make her feel that there was maybe some hope for Andy when he knew there wasn't? But he had to let her know that he was working on the problem, doing something, *trying* . . .

"I honestly don't know. A realistic estimate might be a year, maybe more."

"That's too long," replied Fiona immediately. "I mean, by the time you have it ready, it'll be too late for Andy."

"Fiona," said Simeon, his voice so intense that mentally her eyebrows raised in surprise. "I want you to know that as of yesterday, I am going to devote my total energies to developing this process. I'm not seeing any new patients and I'm phasing out the ones I have. I have a modern laboratory, and a first-class team working with me on this protocol. I want to get this process working, in time for Andy. I can't promise that, of course, but I can tell you that I'll move heaven and earth, and any other place in between, to do it."

Without stopping to think about what she was doing, Fiona jumped up, went around the table, and hugged Simeon as tightly as she could. He stood up, feeling something he could not have put into words, and put his arms around her with an instinctively protective gesture, rather awkwardly but gently stroking her back, and Fiona could feel her tears, all those long-suppressed tears, starting to stream down her face.

Chapter 28

Simeon escorted Fiona back to Andy's room. Although they were both tired, by common unspoken consent they went back up the way they had come, walking up the emergency stairway instead of taking the elevator. He walked alongside her on the broad concrete steps, in a silence that for both of them was crowded with all kinds of thoughts and unexpected feelings. When they reached the neuro floor, Simeon stopped, looked at her, then put his hand on her arm and held it there for a moment. He opened the door, and without a word they went their different ways down the silent corridor, Simeon heading toward the elevator and his lab and Fiona back to the stepdown unit, trying to sort out all that he'd told her and all that she was feeling. It seemed extraordinary that he should suddenly decide to start in again on his research project now. Was he just whistling in the wind about that? Or trying to impress her? No. Fiona was sure about that. She smiled to herself. He wasn't the kind of person who would try to impress anyone; he didn't need to. As she came up to the double doors of the stepdown unit the full force of Andy's illness hit her again. Was it right of Dr. Halstead to give her even that little bit of hope for him? Was it realistic? It had to be, she thought, or he wouldn't have even mentioned it. But hope was scary stuff, and Fiona wasn't sure if she dared indulge in it. Because if it didn't work out ... It was going to be bad enough without such additional heartbreak. Fiona remembered the young student who had died of a brain tumor not so long ago. She remembered her drawn face, the slow, wobbly walk, how she'd lost weight from day to day ... Was there an epidemic going on? Until then, she'd never known anybody who had a brain tumor, and all of a sudden there were two. But, as her mother used to say, things ran in threes, so where was the third one? Maybe that was Mr. Garvey's child, the one who died. Her mind was rambling on, unfocused, trying at the same time to avoid and to confront the topic of Andy's tumor.

She stood outside the unit for a few moments, gathering her thoughts and trying to suppress her disturbing new feelings about Simeon Halstead. Independent as she was, Fiona had felt a kind of relieved joy from Simeon's support. It was the emotional equivalent of getting into a hot tub after being chilled for hours. For years ... Had she ever had emotional support from Victor? Even when they were first married? At that time he was more concerned with the ups and downs of his own career. When things weren't going well for him, when he was having difficulties with his job, she was supposed to drop whatever she was doing, ignore whatever else might be on her mind, and listen to his problems, discuss ways of overcoming them, and make him feel better. And of course she was more than happy to do that. At that time, it made her feel like a woman, a nurturer, the kind of wife and helpmate that she wanted to be.

But he didn't reciprocate. A year after they were married, the Connecticut school system was having across-the-board cutbacks in the teaching staff. She was pregnant with Andy at the time and found herself in danger of losing her job. Fiona tried to talk to Victor about it, but he was trying to lose weight for his flight physical and was being increasingly short-tempered and abrupt with her. The once charming and attentive Victor had developed the habit of cutting her off in midsentence when she talked about things he didn't want to discuss. Fiona recalled the conversation exactly when she finally insisted on talking to him about the school situation. They were in the kitchen of their home, he'd just come back from a trip, she was feeling shaky and sick, and when she started to tell him, he interrupted to ask what there was for dinner.

Fiona got mad. "Damn it, Victor, I'm throwing up every morning, I may lose my job, and all you can think of to say is 'What's for dinner?'!"

He stared at her. "So? You can always find another job, can't you?"

Fiona put away her thoughts about Victor, opened the door to the unit, and went in. Everything was quiet. The nurse behind the desk smiled at her. They had all heard about how she'd stepped into the breach and manned the phones earlier in the day. In Andy's cubicle she found Victor sitting in the easy chair next to Andy's bed, and she felt a sudden jolt of uncomfortable surprise, although of course he had a perfect right to be there. All of a sudden she felt that he was a total stranger, further out of her life than he'd ever been.

Victor stood up quietly when she came in. "He's asleep," he whispered. "Here, d'you want to sit down?"

Fiona stared at him in the semidarkness. This didn't sound like the Victor she knew and didn't like. She sat down, and he pulled up a chair.

"I came in just after you left," he said. "The nurse said you'd gone off with Dr. Halstead." He smiled, and his white teeth showed. "I'm jealous."

"Nothing to be jealous about," she replied. "And in any case, I'd like to remind you that we're not . . ."

". . . married anymore," said Victor, mimicking her, but his words were without the sharp edge of sarcasm she expected.

"Just what I was going to say," said Fiona. "I notice you never lost the habit of interrupting."

Andy stirred and moaned. Fiona went over to him and stroked his forehead very gently, and after a minute he went back to sleep.

"Let's talk outside," said Victor. "Then we won't risk waking him up."

He took her arm, and Fiona had a serious urge to shake his hand off as she would shake a spider off her sleeve, but she didn't want to make a scene here. She waited until they were outside the unit.

But Victor was on his best behavior. Sounding concerned and sympathetic, he asked what Dr. Halstead had told her about Andy.

"He's doing okay," replied Fiona. "For now." She didn't want to go into any details or tell Victor about the research that Simeon was undertaking.

"How's work?" asked Victor. "Are they giving you a hard time at school?"

"Not at all," replied Fiona.

"Who's taking your classes?"

"Subs."

"Yeah. I guess Marty would be very helpful."

"He is. And so is everybody else." Fiona's friends had gathered around; she had a support group that Victor could only envy. "A lot of them have kids of their own, of course, so they understand."

"And they're glad it's you and Andy, not them and their kids," said Victor.

"I don't think so," replied Fiona, surprised that Victor's sarcastic words weren't bothering her in the least. "I'd do the same for any of them."

Victor stared at her. There was something different about Fiona's attitude, something new going on with her, and it gave him a strange sense of discomfort. "Have you talked to Sam Seidel?" he asked after a pause.

"Yes. He came in today to see how Andy was doing." She grinned. "He was supposed to be the go-between, the translator for Dr. Halstead."

"So?"

"Well, I guess Dr. Halstead's been doing his own translating," said Fiona, and Victor got that uncomfortable feeling again. "As I said, Sam looked in, but he didn't tell me anything I didn't know already."

"At least he found Dr. Cadwaller for us," said Victor.

"Yes, well, I'm not sure how good an idea that was," said Fiona. "Cadwaller confused me. Quite honestly, I'd rather get just one story from one person I trust."

"Even if it's incomplete? Or wrong?"

"Wrong? What are you talking about?" Fiona's voice rose, and the nurse at the desk ten feet away looked up from her book. "Look, Victor," she went on in a quieter tone, "in a situation like this, you have to put your faith in the person you've entrusted to take care of your son. And they say Dr. Halstead's the best here, maybe anywhere. So please, don't make it any more difficult than it already is."

"Okay," said Victor. "But let me tell you this. This afternoon I went to see a medical malpractice attorney. He's supposed to be the best around. I told him the whole story, and he said ..." Victor emphasized by pointing his finger at her, "He said that we had a case, no question, and it was his opinion that Halstead had been seriously neglectful. And we owe it to Andy to follow that up, right?" He stared at Fiona, swelling with righteous indignation at Dr. Halstead. "The only thing is that as Andy's legal guardian you have to agree ..."

Fiona was about to interrupt, but he didn't allow her to do that.

"All we need is your signature on one single piece of paper," Victor went on. "That's all. And of course, unless there's a clear-cut case, the attorney won't do anything, won't pursue it. So really it's your duty as a mother to do it, for Andy's sake. And there's no downside risk, no expenses for us ..."

"No way," said Fiona.

"Just think about it," urged Victor. "There's no possible harm, and maybe we can do some good here—maybe not for Andy, but for other kids in the same kind of trouble."

Fiona wanted to hit him. "Didn't you hear me?" she asked. *"No way!"* The nurse looked up again. Fiona took a deep breath and went back into the cubicle to check on Andy. He was still sleeping soundly, and his color looked better, even in the dim light.

"I think I'll go home," she told Victor more calmly when she came out. "He looks okay, and I'm so tired I could drop."

"Would you like me to drive you? I could bring you back here in the morning, early."

"No, Victor." The coldness in her voice was unmistakable, even to Victor.

He put a hand on her arm. "You know, Fiona," he said in a quiet, earnest voice, "Maybe, with Andy being sick and everything, we should think about trying to repair things between us. You and me. For his sake, and because quite honestly, I still ..."

"No, Victor." Fiona cut him off. She got rid of his hand with a quick movement. He's just the same old Victor, she thought, still as transparent as ever. And he still doesn't realize that I'm not quite as stupid as he thinks.

"I've learned a lot since we were separated, Fiona," he went on, his voice pleading, "and I promise ..."

"We're not separated, Victor," said Fiona, trying hard to keep what she was feeling out of her voice. "We're divorced. And the reasons why we're divorced are still very obviously present and unchanged. And now, as I said, I'm going home."

Chapter 29

"Dr. Cadwaller's expecting you, Dr. Halstead," said Joy Grieve, Cadwaller's secretary. She was an attractive woman in her mid-thirties, and she smiled up at him. "He called just a minute ago to say he was running a few minutes late."

Simeon nodded. He had been expecting something like that. He looked at the little carriage clock on the secretary's desk. It showed that he was exactly on time.

"No problem," he said, turning back to the door. "Page me when he gets back."

"He won't be long, Dr. Halstead," said Joy, alarmed. "Just a few moments. Wouldn't you like to wait in his office? Can I get you a cup of coffee?"

Simeon grinned. Even the secretaries got into this power playacting. Because Dr. Cadwaller was the department chairman and Simeon was visiting *his* office, Joy Grieve felt that Simeon should wait for him, not the other way around.

"Three minutes," he said, looking at his watch.

"Coffee?"

"Yes, thanks. Milk, no sugar."

She stood up and went over to the coffee machine in the corner. Simeon, watching her, wondered about the persistent gossip that Cadwaller was having an intense personal relationship with her.

She came back with a full cup, balancing it on a matching saucer.

"Thanks." said Simeon, taking it. He looked at the flowery pattern. "Nice china."

"Rockingham," she answered, sitting down at her desk. "Dr. Cadwaller brought it back from London, England on his last trip."

"Certainly beats my office set," he replied. "Mine's Styrofoam. From Newark, New Jersey."

Joy Grieve stared at him for a moment. She'd just won her little battle, and as long as he stayed there until Dr. Cadwaller appeared, she didn't care what he said or what he drank out of.

The door opened and Cadwaller came bustling in, his white coat tight around his thickset body. Although his hair was now gray, it still had the same short, bristly look, and he had the same aura of restless energy about him that he'd had as a resident.

"Sorry to keep you waiting," he said to Simeon, then turned to his secretary. "Take any calls for me, Joy, please. Simeon, come on in."

Simeon put his cup and saucer down on the secretary's desk and followed Cadwaller, again feeling that familiar surge of dislike and contempt for him.

Cadwaller's office was large, as befitted his importance, but the view from the double window was marred by a new administrative and legal building whose blank brick walls were only a few feet away. The decor was plain, matter-of-fact New England, with a heavy dark oak desk. Cadwaller's diplomas hung in impressive array behind the desk, and around the walls were various framed photos, all of Cadwaller with different people—group shots, a big black-and-white press photo of Cadwaller receiving the Harvey Cushing Award, Cadwaller several years younger, on a boat in scuba gear.

"Well?" snapped Cadwaller. "What do you want?"

He stared over his desk at Simeon, thinking about his recent humiliation by this man in the operating room, about Ann . . .

"I'm taking a clinical leave of absence," replied Simeon. "I want to concentrate on my research for a while."

Cadwaller's eyebrows went up. "What research?" If there was a faint sneer in his voice, Simeon paid no attention.

"Some work I started in London, at Queen Square," he said. "If it works, it'll be a system for destroying brain tumors, specifically astrocytomas."

Cadwaller smiled. "An admirable goal," he said. "And

what makes you think you can accomplish this when others who have spent their entire lives thinking and working with this kind of problem, haven't been able to?"

" 'Hope springs eternal in the human breast,' " quoted Simeon.

"Pope wasn't referring to neurosurgical research," retorted Cadwaller. "For that you need a lot more than hope. You need experience, talent, and in addition it's essential that you have an encyclopedic knowledge of everything that's happening in the field."

Simeon nodded. "Right. Thanks for reminding me."

"Does that mean that you're abandoning your clinical practice?" Cadwaller stared. He could hardly believe that Simeon, who had worked long and hard to establish himself in this brutally competitive field, would, on a whim, give up his hard-earned place.

"For a while. Only until I've completed this job."

"I don't know," said Cadwaller, drumming his fingers on the edge of the desk. "This is very unusual and irregular. You said you were *taking* a leave of absence?"

"Yes."

"Such leaves are not given automatically," said Cadwaller. "You'll have to apply for one and state the reasons. And quite honestly, I can't guarantee that a leave would be granted, in which case you would have to resign your appointment."

"Is there a form to fill out?"

"Joy can give you one on your way out," he said, nodding at the door of his secretary's office.

" 'Joy cometh in the morning,' " said Simeon, who for some reason was feeling a new kind of lightness in his life. He shook his head. "It's amazing the stuff you read in the Bible, of all places, isn't it?" he went on, watching Cadwaller with a malicious grin. "And it's probably not always true, I mean about Joy, I don't suppose."

Cadwaller took a deep, furious breath, and his face turned a blotchy red. He stood up. "I wouldn't know. Was there anything else you wanted to see me about?"

Simeon wasn't at all sure why he was baiting Cadwaller, and he felt annoyed at himself that he had let his antipathy and dislike show. It certainly didn't make much sense at this time.

But Cadwaller, by instinct more aggressive than Simeon, was so eager to return the attack that he let himself get petty. "Interesting that you should be giving up everything to work on astrocytomas, Simeon," he said. This time he made no effort to disguise the sneer. "That boy Andy Markle must have made a very profound impression on you. Unless, of course, it was his mother?"

"Both, actually," said Simeon, thinking that one day he would strangle Felix Cadwaller with his bare hands. It would take patience, but he'd get him, one way or another, sooner or later. Simeon had plenty of patience, and timing was everything.

In the outer office, Joy gave Simeon copies of the leave-of-absence request forms. She seemed uncomfortable with him, and after the door had closed behind him, she stood up and walked into Cadwaller's office without knocking.

Chapter 30

News of Simeon's insult to Felix Cadwaller in the operating room traveled around the hospital in less time than it takes a Benihana chef to slice a steak, and Cadwaller was meeting sly smiles and even the occasional jibe in the corridor and staff rooms.

Caleb Winter, his highly respected surgical colleague, stopped him outside the library. "You're going to have to keep better control of your troops, Felix," he said very seriously. Winter knew perfectly well that Cadwaller was a less talented surgeon than Simeon Halstead, but he also knew that departmental discipline had to be maintained or else anarchy would ensue. "We academics have a hard enough time trying to maintain some restraint over our private-practice colleagues," he said. "If the members of our own staff feel that they can throw us out of the operating rooms, we might as well pack our bags and abandon the whole clinical field to them."

Squirming with rage and embarrassment at being criticized by such an august colleague, Felix returned to his office even more determined to repair his own tarnished image. And at the same time he would teach Simeon Halstead a lesson he'd never forget. Cadwaller was already considering different ways to accomplish that goal.

Aside from teaching and his other departmental responsibilities, Cadwaller's main interest was in research. His kind of work didn't depend on brilliant inspiration; instead it consisted of administering different combinations of known chemotherapy agents with varying doses of radiation in an effort to treat malignant brain tumors, hoping that one particular combination might work better than the others. As Paula Cairns, one of the center's internationally known researchers, put it rather succinctly, Cadwaller's research was like opening unlabeled boxes, hundreds upon hundreds of them, one after the other, in the faint hope that one of them might contain a million dollars.

But Cadwaller made a good living at it. He was a skilled preparer of grant applications, which he presented with colored three-dimensional charts and statistical analyses, and he knew exactly how to impress the site visit teams that trekked out to New Coventry every few months to review his progress. He had cultivated important friends who were able to add their weighty opinions in his support, and by now his department had achieved enough self-sustaining momentum and the big drug companies had already invested enough money in him that things would really have to fall apart for him to lose his high position in the clinical research establishment.

Cadwaller worked on his present project until late that night, using a computer to calculate graded dosage schedules for the new clinical trial that he'd wanted Andy Markle to join. In a different part of his mind, he considered a variety of options he could use in his battle against Simeon Halstead. And it would be a battle to the death, he knew that. But he felt confident that he had all the weapons he would need. As chairman of the department, he could instigate a review of all Halstead's patients, check out the records with a fine-tooth comb. He knew that such a measure would turn up errors in the cases of any surgeon on earth, but he would have to find some very good reason to order it. After giving the question serious thought, he realized it wasn't a good idea. The same kind of move might one day be made against him, and Cadwaller didn't have to check his own records to know that if that happened, he would fare less well than Simeon Halstead.

Another possibility was to load Halstead up with committee work to the point that he wouldn't have time for anything else, but committee places had already been assigned for the year, and anyway that couldn't ever amount to more than a minor annoyance to Halstead.

It didn't take long for Cadwaller to dismiss those possibilities and, with the instinct for the jugular that chairmen of medical departments quickly develop, to realize that Halstead's weakness would be in the research project he'd talked about. Cadwaller was certain about that, because he knew Simeon was at heart a clinician, an operating surgeon, not a researcher. Even though Halstead might have an occasional bright idea, his lack of experience and aptitude would eventually bring him down. And most important, Cadwaller knew that Halstead didn't have the network of helpful contacts in industry and government that he and all serious research pros took such care to develop. So Cadwaller decided to follow the advice of Rabelais: "Give the man enough rope and let him hang himself." Cadwaller would help by making a good noose, and that would give him great pleasure. It would have his initials on it, just so that everybody would know that he, Felix Cadwaller, wasn't a man to fool around with. And when that happened, he thought grimly, it would go a long way toward avenging Ann's death.

Part Three

Part Three

Chapter 31

Andy's postoperative recovery was fast, and five days after his operation he was home, a bit shaky, still unable to look upward, but otherwise feeling okay. Contrary to his anxieties, Kevin and his other friends stuck with him, although he felt that he didn't have the same quickness and accuracy of movement. He took a couple of spills on his blades, not serious ones but enough to make Fiona put them firmly away. "You can just walk for a while," she told him. "Just like the rest of us."

Four months after Andy's operation, well into the school summer vacation, Simeon Halstead's lab was in full swing, taut with the sustained activity of his crew.

"I never thought he'd turn out to be such a slave driver," complained Sonia Goldenberg during one of Simeon's rare absences. "What a change! For months we never saw him, and now he's in here eighteen hours a day. It's not easy to get used to this. I liked it better the way it was."

"No, you didn't," replied Denis Popham, hard at work with a three-dimensional computer model of a globulin molecule. He didn't look around. "You remember the day we restarted this project? Well, that very morning you'd said that if there wasn't some action soon you were going to go out and find another job. Remember?"

"Well, maybe I did ..." Sonia stood close behind him, and Denis could feel the warmth of her breasts on the back of his shoulders. He wiggled a bit, and she pressed into him. "Denis, did you see our new microwave collimator? It can beam the microwave radiation almost like a laser. One percent energy loss at eight inches."

"That's enough energy to bore a hole right through those rats' brains," said Denis. "You guys are going to give a whole new meaning to the expression 'in one ear and out the other.' "

"You don't understand," Sonia went on in a superior voice. "You have to pick a point on the power-duration curve. At a given power setting, the actual amount of microwave energy you put in depends on how long you apply it."

"For heaven's sake, Sonia, don't be so simpleminded." Denis did something at the keyboard and a new set of colored molecules appeared on the screen. "That's not all. How about variables like different transmission rates through white and gray matter, or power attenuation because of the heat removed by the circulation? Or are you planning to stop the circulation in the brain while you do your microwaving?" Denis laughed. "That's a great idea, actually, and you'd certainly have a better fix on how much rise in temperature you could expect at any given point. The only problem would be that your patient would finish up dead, heh heh."

"That's not funny," snapped Sonia. "You think you're so smart. Leave me alone. Go play with your silly proteins."

The outside door opened and Simeon came back into the lab, followed by Edwina Cole. Denis didn't look around, but his eyebrows went up. They seemed to be arguing about something, and Denis, having been brought up in the rigidly stratified British system, could hardly conceive of a student like Edwina having the temerity to talk back to a professor, especially one of Simeon Halstead's stature.

Simeon walked through the lab into the little office with Edwina close behind. She closed the door, and Simeon went behind the desk, opened a drawer and pulled out an official-looking letter from Dr. Franz Leibowitz, dean of students at the medical school.

"Here," he said, passing it over to Edwina. "This is a copy. Did you get yours yet?"

Edwina barely scanned it, because she knew the contents already. She had received the letter that morning, informing her that her recent attendance record at classes, demonstrations, and clinics had been unsatisfactory and asking her to explain the reasons for this. Also, she was to correct these deficiencies immediately or further action would be taken.

Attached was a Xerox copy of her attendance record for the last three months. The form showed a remarkable number of blank spaces.

"Yes, I did," said Edwina, after glancing at the letter. "And I already told them. I said that I was so involved with my thesis research I wouldn't be able to attend all the classes. I missed some of Dr. Cadwaller's clinics. I bet he's the one who's making the fuss."

"But you've hardly been to any classes at all," objected Simeon, tapping the attendance record. He noticed that Edwina was looking very tense, with dark rings around her eyes. He stared at her. "How much sleep are you getting?" he asked.

She grinned tiredly. Edwina was normally a striking-looking young woman, tall, with a decisive bearing, but now her features were sharpened by exhaustion.

"Not much. Most of the time I'm here, as you know, but I've been trying to keep up with my assigned reading . . ." A tear suddenly appeared on her lower eyelid and, annoyed, she brushed it away. "The thing is, Dr. Halstead, we're really getting somewhere with the hypercoagulable proteins, and I've got so caught up in it . . . I can't stop. I work until I can't see straight, or else my mind shuts down . . . and I see these darned protein and amino-acid molecules floating around in my dreams . . ."

"That's great," said Simeon unexpectedly.

Edwina wasn't expecting sympathy, or to be told she had to slow down, but nevertheless she was surprised.

"It's a kind of euphoria," he said. "It's exhilarating, exciting, and totally exhausting. All the best researchers get it from time to time. You live the work, sleep it, dream it . . . And that can be the best, the most productive time in your life, if you're lucky enough to be involved in a first-rate project. So you won't get any sympathy from me, Edwina Cole, only a kind of envy . . ."

The phone rang and Simeon picked it up. "Yes, Dr. Leibowitz," said Simeon, looking over the desk at Edwina. He picked up a pen and made a notation on a yellow pad. "Five o'clock Friday, your office. Sure. Yes, I'll tell Miss Cole."

He put the phone down. "You have a meeting with Dean

Leibowitz scheduled for Friday, as you heard," he said. "It's apparently to discuss your ... academic problems." He paused. "Look, Edwina, I'll write you a note explaining your absences, but you really have to get to more of your classes."

"That's my problem," said Edwina stubbornly. "It's my life, and I'm making the choices."

About half an hour later, after Edwina had gone back into the lab, the phone rang again. This time it was Sam Seidel, with his gruff Bronx accent.

"I'd like to talk to you," he said to Simeon.

"What about?"

"A bunch of things. Andy Markle. His dad. His mom. Stuff like that."

"You want to come to my office?"

"Nah. Let's go for a drink somewhere. I'm tired of meetings and conferences in people's offices."

Simeon thought about that. He knew Sam fairly well, but didn't particularly like him. "I'm pretty busy ..."

"Yeah. You think I'm just sitting here with my fist up my ass? We're *all* busy."

Simeon grinned and thought he heard the faint sound of a female laugh at Sam's end of the phone.

"Okay. How about the Four Seasons lounge? Nine tonight?"

"That's sort of late ... But okay, I'll see you then."

Chapter 32

At eight forty-five that evening, Simeon, tired but elated, locked the door of his lab and walked down the dimly lit corridor on the twelfth floor of the research tower. The curving corridor went all around the building, the big windows on the outside affording a view of the city that changed with every few steps. Now he could see only a few dim lights below; the rain pattered against the windows and the wind shook them. Clouds enveloped the tower and the lights disappeared. Simeon hoped it wouldn't be too foggy on the way home.

It was strange, not seeing patients, not operating, and he still wasn't used to it. He calculated that most of his life had been taken up with patients, surgery, clinics, teaching ... let's see, he thought, med school from age twenty to twenty-four, internship, residency for four years, research fellowship in London for a year, then here at NCMC. Wow. That was almost half his life, doing the same kinds of things, seeing the same kinds of patients, dealing with the same kinds of technical problems in the operating room. A man has to change his point of view from time to time to stay awake, to stay alive, he thought. He pushed the heavy door open and walked into the underground parking garage. And that's exactly what I'm doing, he thought. I'm changing my life.

He drove up the ramp, and as soon as he hit the street, fat raindrops from the summer storm smacked into the windshield so suddenly that for a moment he couldn't see anything. Even at full speed, the windshield wipers could hardly cope with the torrents swirling and pouring down in front of him. He tried to remember if there was a canopy over the entrance of the Four Seasons.

It took Simeon about seven minutes to get through the flooding streets to the Four Seasons lounge. Cars were moving slowly in the opposite direction, their bow waves washing up against his car. He passed a stranded van, axle-deep at the side of the road, blinkers on but fading.

The Four Seasons was a new place in town, part of an attempt to refurbish the inner city. As he pulled up under the wide canopy, the rain stopped as if by magic. Simeon wondered how much the city had given up in taxes and bribes to get the Four Seasons to open this place.

Inside it was modern, comfortable, well lit. A three-piece band, apparently local talent, was playing at the end of the foyer, next to a long grand piano framed by two large potted palms. A noisy fountain next to them almost drowned out their sound. Simeon looked around. Sam wasn't there, so he wandered over to where the band was playing and stood next to them, his fingers itching. As a student in Boston, he'd made some money and drunk a lot of beer playing piano two or three times a week in a restaurant-bar called the Old Grotto just off Cambridge Square.

Now the band was playing "The Girl from Ipanema," and the leader, a tall, lanky kid with long hair, grinned over his sax at Simeon, who pointed at the piano and raised his eyebrows. The kid hesitated for a second, then nodded, and Simeon opened the piano, pulled back the bench and sat down, found the key they were playing in, and finished the piece with them.

The three kids stared at him; within seconds they'd been able to tell that he was a really good player, out of their class.

"Do you guys know "Satin Doll"?" he asked them. They did. After that, Simeon led them into "All Blues," a Miles Davis piece, then Sam appeared at the door. Simeon finished the piece, stood up, and closed the piano.

"Thanks for letting me join you, guys," he told the trio. "I really enjoyed that."

"Any time," said the leader. "Really."

Sam was at the bar, already hunched over a drink. Close up, he looked older and untidier than Simeon remembered.

He sat down on Sam's left.

"You sure tinkle those ivories good," said Sam. "If

things don't work out for you at the hospital, you could get a job here."

"Yeah, I could have made a living at it," replied Simeon, looking back at the group. "A few years back. Now I'm out of practice and behind the times."

The bartender came up, a large, comfortable-looking woman in a tight black dress with pearls.

"Double Macallan, straight up, please," said Simeon.

"I hear you're a lab doc these days," said Sam when Simeon's drink was on the counter in front of him. He looked over at Simeon curiously, as if he were trying to figure out why he would give up a prestigious clinical practice and start doing drudge work in a *lab,* for God's sake.

"Yep, that's what I'm doing," said Simeon. "For now. What's it to you, anyway?"

"They say you're setting out to cure brain cancer. In six months." Sam's grin showed his irregular, yellowish teeth. He raised his glass. "Cheers. And the best of luck."

Simeon took a sip of his single malt. "So what did you want to talk about?"

"I'm worried about Andy Markle," said Sam. "He's doing okay, but he has a death sentence hanging over him, and it's having a bad effect on all of them. Him, Fiona, even Victor." Sam glanced sideways at Simeon. "That's her ex, in case you didn't remember his name."

"What did you expect?" Simeon glanced around the bar. It was almost deserted; the rain must have kept people home. He listened for sounds of the weather, but the place was too insulated to tell if it was day or night, let alone if it was raining. "Isn't that something you deal with every day, Sam?" he asked. "The social effects of illness? I thought that was what family medicine was all about."

"I want him to go to a place in Mexico," said Sam. He banged his glass on the wide counter. Florence, the bartender, was watching professional wrestling on the television at the other end of the bar. She turned her head, then came over to refill his glass. "I know it's not conventional medicine," Sam went on, "but they've had some successes down there."

Simeon stared at him. "Successes? With brain tumors? Astrocytomas? What kind of successes?"

"The guy who's running the cancer program there is a Dr. Paolo Mendez. He's an M.D., did his training at Georgetown before going back to Mexico. His father's a faith healer in a place called El Tuito. Anyway, this guy Paolo is something else. He set up a program there and he's had cures. Several of them."

"El Tuito? That sounds more like a bird sanctuary than a clinic."

"Yeah, very funny. The clinic's outside Puerto Vallarta."

Simeon gave a short, disbelieving laugh. "Faith healing, huh? Eat the right mushrooms and you can hallucinate that you've been cured? And if you give those mushrooms to the docs . . ." Simeon tried to keep some of the skepticism out of his voice. ". . . they'll believe it too. Why are you telling me about this?"

"Because we need your okay. Fiona Markle won't hardly let Andy go to the toilet without your say-so." Sam's bulbous nose seemed to get redder, and he rubbed the side of it with vigor. He half turned to face Simeon, holding his drink almost at eye level between them. "I think she's got a thing for you," he went on, watching Simeon carefully.

"Nice lady, Mrs. Markle," said Simeon. "I like her a lot. The answer on Mexico is no. No way." Simon looked as if he were about to add to that, but he didn't.

"Dr. Mendez is coming up here in a few days," said Sam. "The doc I was just telling you about. I'd like you to meet him."

"Listen, Sam," said Simeon. He caught Florence's eye and nodded. "You're a smart guy. Don't give me this bullshit about miracle cures, because I know you don't believe them any more than I do. I've heard them all, and I've seen some of the results. It's all a mixture of hypnosis and mumbo jumbo, with a sprinkling of diet and herbs thrown in. Sam . . ." He waited while Florence poured out two measures of malt whiskey into his glass. "Sam, don't make me mad. You know as well as I do that those kind of 'cures' are just a cynical way of exploiting frightened and dying people."

"Right. I agree. Up to a point." Sam wasn't a bit put out by Simeon's opinion. "Did you ever go to Lourdes,

France?" He didn't wait for an answer. "We went there, the last trip Ruth and me took."

"Ruth?"

"My wife. You never met her. She died two years ago. Anyway, at Lourdes, their collection of crutches would make a bonfire that would reach all the way up to heaven. Downtown, they have shops that sell nothing but crutches, and they do a land office business. They sell them to the people going up to the chapel, because it's steep and most of those people ain't walked that far in years. Then the cripples get caught up in all the ecstasy stuff and throw their crutches away. But they have to buy a new pair when they get back to town, because they still need them." Sam looked into the distance, thinking about Ruth.

"I'm not talking about Lourdes," said Simeon. "What I'm talking about is selling hope to the hopeless. It's the most cynical and despicable traffic I've ever heard of. It makes your average drug baron look like Mother Teresa. At least the druggies who buy their stuff know what they're getting into."

"Would you talk to Paolo Mendez? Just talk to him?"

Simeon put his drink down with a bang, and Florence started to move toward him until he shook his head at her. "Look, Sam, I have to deal with enough ordinary, conventional M.D.-type charlatans and other assorted bozos around here, without needing to go looking for a Mexican one."

"Which brings up the subject of Felix Cadwaller," said Sam. "He's gunning for you."

"Tell me something I don't know," replied Simeon. He looked at his watch.

"Okay ... Did you know that Victor Markle has consulted a malpractice attorney here in town, and Cadwaller is giving him some under-the-table assistance?"

That got Simeon's attention. "On what grounds?"

"Oh, that you didn't give him and Fiona Markle info about alternative ways of dealing with Andy's tumor, that you refused the assistance of Cadwaller in the operating room, although they'd hired him to do that. There's probably a couple of other things they'll dig up. You know how those lawyers are."

"He's wasting his time and his money," said Simeon. "I've been around the block a couple of times with this malpractice stuff. He doesn't have a leg to stand on."

"As the judge said to the amputee's attorney," murmured Sam.

"What?"

"Doesn't matter. The thing is, Simeon, that Victor's heard about Paolo Mendez and the clinic. Now, if you advise Fiona, who has legal custody of Andy, not to go to Mexico, she won't do it. She tells me that she trusts your judgment completely. But if the case ever came to court, and it also came out that Dr. Mendez really has something to offer to patients like Andy, your insurance company and this medical center would be in the hole for a lot of millions of dollars. And of course Victor'll ask for punitive damages, and as that's not covered by insurance, that might leave you with ... with not much more than that very nice raw silk jacket you're wearing." Sam put his hand up to feel the texture of the lapel. "Where did you get it?"

Simeon pushed Sam's hand away.

"You don't just happen to own this Mexican clinic, do you?" he asked.

Sam shrugged. "Let's get back to basics," he said. "Honestly, what do you have to offer Andy Markle that's any better?"

"Answer my question," said Simeon.

"Yeah, I have a part share in the clinic. So what? I'd still want Andy to go there even if I didn't. You were going to tell me what you're going to do with Andy that's so much better."

"I don't have anything better," said Simeon. "*Nobody* does. This medical center's as good as any in the world. We've done the surgical part of the procedure just the way we're supposed to. We have a tissue diagnosis, I debulked the tumor, removed all I could of it, and that should keep him around for several additional months." Simeon put his hands on the counter in front of him. "Then I called some of my old buddies in London, thinking they might have something to offer, but their project bit the dust a year ago. And we haven't tried radiation yet, or chemotherapy ..."

Sam kept looking at Simeon, but didn't say anything.

There was a long pause.

"I know what you're saying," said Simeon in a quiet voice. "And it's true. That's one of the reasons I've given up my clinical practice, so that I can work on something that hopefully might work a bit better."

"You know, Simeon," said Sam, looking angry for the first time, "you're the one who's full of shit. You know how much money's been spent on cancer research in the last twenty years? How many billions? Of course you do. And up there in your little lab, you think you're going to find the cure? Wise up, fella. You can kid the Markles maybe, I suppose you've already kidded the people you get your research money from, but don't kid yourself. Or me. I'm sure you'll make a heroic effort, work all day and all night, but you aren't going to do any better than the thousands of researchers who've had great ideas before you. And a couple months down the road, maybe less, I'm going to watch Andy Markle die, while you try to save what's left of your career from the lawyers. And from Felix Cadwaller."

Simeon rolled the drink in his glass and watched it swill around the bottom.

"Same again, gents?" asked Florence.

Simultaneously the two men shook their heads.

"Sam," said Simeon after a while, "I know you. And I want to ask you one simple question: Did you set this whole thing up, with Cadwaller, Victor Markle and his malpractice attorney, the Mexican clinic—all that just to make a few bucks?"

Sam pursed his lips and thought. "Yeah," he said.

Simeon's fists tightened, and he could already feel the bones of Sam's big nose crunching under his blow.

"At first that was the idea," Sam went on. "The clinic badly needs this kind of business. But ... I guess now I have a different insight. Andy is a real nice kid, and Fiona's a sweetheart. So, yes, there's a bit of everything here. Greed and altruism. But now I really think Paolo could be onto something. Don't ask me to prove it; it's not my field. That's why I want you to meet him."

Sam eyed Simeon warily. "And don't even think about

bopping me one. I was a wrestling champ in college, and I could still break you in half with one hand."

"You're a fat, out-of-shape old fraud," said Simeon. "You couldn't break a breadstick in half without your oxygen tank."

Sam heaved himself off the stool. "Paolo's coming up next week," he said. "I'll give you a call."

Chapter 33

It had stopped raining when Simeon left the Four Seasons, but the water was still pouring off the entranceway canopy as he waited for his car. The air was warm, humid, and not at all cleared by the storm. Across the street, people were emerging from and disappearing down the steps to the Red Hot Pepper, a basement restaurant popular with the college crowd. Young couples walked by, hand in hand, laughing, flipping back the hoods of their still-wet raincoats. Evidently the rain had only just stopped.

Simeon, normally comfortable in his own privacy and self-containment, was feeling very alone now. The thought of going home to his empty house didn't make him feel any better, and for a moment he considered going back to the lab, doing some work, then going to sleep on the couch. But then he remembered his two double Macallans—or was it three?—and decided that although he was by no means drunk, he wouldn't get anything worthwhile done. And anyway, Edwina would probably be planning on sleeping on the couch, as she often did.

"Your car, sir," said the doorman, handing him the keys and at the same time dexterously accepting Simeon's tip in his white-gloved hand.

Simeon got into his car and drove slowly out, waiting for a few pedestrians to pass on the sidewalk in front of him. Everybody seemed so cheerful. There were lots of summer school students, apparently unfazed by their approaching exams, full of the boisterous joy of youth. One young man walked unsteadily on the curb in front of Simeon's car, trying to drink beer out of a can as he went. Simeon saw a long brown fizzy stream trickle down the front of his coat, to the screaming delight of two girls walking behind him.

Away from the center of town, the streets were quiet and
still wet. The car hit a puddle and sprayed muddy water over
the sidewalk, so he slowed down to avoid splashing the few
pedestrians wending their way through the mist-shrouded
streets. The rain came again in bursts that lasted only a minute or two, and after a few sharp turns from one small street
to another in the warehouse area down by the railroad station, he crossed the bridge over the rain-glistened tracks and
then drove up onto the curving ramp to the interstate.

I-95 was crowded and the traffic was slow, nose to tail,
and although the distance to his exit was only a few miles,
the trip took almost an hour. Orange barrels were out in
force, and the roadway was down to a single lane for much
of the way. He left his mind in neutral, thinking about
whatever came around.

"I think she's got a thing for you." Fiona. "She won't do
anything without your say-so." Simeon didn't trust Sam
very far, but there was no reason for him to invent that.

When he got home, Simeon checked his answering machine. There were several calls, but only the last of them
interested him. Fiona Markle had called and asked him to
call back. He did so.

"Fiona?"

"Oh, Simeon." She sounded happy to hear his voice.
"Thank you for calling back. It's nothing urgent, Andy's
okay. It's ... I wondered if you would like to come and
have dinner with us tomorrow ..." She hesitated. "Of
course, with Mrs. Halstead—that is, if ..."

"I'd love to come," replied Simeon. "If it's okay that I
come alone. Elisabeth and I are separated."

"Of course." Fiona tried to hide the satisfaction in her
voice.

"Tell me where and what time."

When Fiona put the phone down, she turned to face
Wilma, who stood grinning at her from the kitchen doorway. "You were right," said Fiona.

"As usual," replied Wilma. "Aren't you glad now we got
you some clothes?"

Next day, although he was busy as usual with the lab and
a number of other matters, at the back of Simeon's mind

was the cheerful thought that he was going to have dinner with Fiona and Andy. He tried to figure out what would be a nice thing to bring them. Flowers would not be appropriate, a bottle of wine was okay but rather banal. In the late afternoon he went to the big new video store on Stamford and bought a cassette for Andy—*The Best of Professional Baseball*. Fiona was more difficult; finally he went into a bookstore and saw a big illustrated volume on the Italian Renaissance. She'd mentioned once that she was teaching that period and loved it, so he bought the book, because everything else he could think of was either too personal or not personal enough.

Six-thirty, she'd said. At six-twenty, Simeon passed the house for the first time, noted its neat lawn and bright geranium border. He drove around the quiet neighborhood for ten minutes, then parked outside on the stroke of six-thirty.

Andy opened the door. His hair was completely regrown, although it was a slightly different color, darker, than before it had been shaved. He seemed pleased to see Simeon; by now they considered each other friends, without going quite so far as being buddies.

Simeon gave Andy a quick, unobtrusive once-over. It was now just over sixteen weeks since his operation, and he looked good. His last checkup at the hospital had been two weeks ago, and at that time Simeon had found no signs of recurrence of the tumor, although Parinaud's sign was still silently but ominously present. Now, Andy seemed to have grown taller; he was slim but didn't look as if he'd lost any weight; his arm and neck muscles looked as strong as before. He was a good-looking kid; Simeon wondered if he'd kept up with Susie Seidel.

"How's it going?" he asked.

"Okay. Can I get on my blades again? Mom says no way unless you say it's okay."

"Let's talk to her about it," said Simeon, coming in. He was carrying a bag with his gifts plus a bottle of Sauvignon Blanc he'd picked up on the way. He got an instant feeling of cheerfulness and comfort when he stepped inside the house. Fiona called out from the kitchen, and he followed Andy there.

She looked stunning. She'd had her hair done earlier in the day, and it was up in a great curly mass on top of her head, showing the graceful curve of her neck and with little ringlets coming down over her ears. A very elegant pale blue cashmere turtleneck showed off her figure and contrasted with her green eyes, and a dark blue skirt over sheer lighter blue stockings and blue leather shoes with a little gold chain across the top completed a very pretty picture indeed.

Simeon, caught unaware, just stared for a second, then said, "Hi."

"I'm late," she said, slightly flustered by his expression. "As usual. One of my kids came to see me after school. She was very upset. She'd just found out that she'd been adopted, and nobody could tell her who her real parents were."

"Interesting," said Simeon, putting his package down on the counter. "The same thing happened to me. When I was twelve."

Fiona turned around, a wooden spoon in her hand, her face the picture of astonishment. "You? Really?"

"Sure. It was a surprise, but not fatal."

"Did you get counseling? How did you handle it?"

Simeon grinned, and Fiona noticed how the smile transformed his face. "No, no counseling. It felt strange for a while, as if I'd been . . . uprooted. But when you're twelve, you're amazingly adaptable. Life went on."

"Didn't you ever want to find out who they were? Your real parents?"

"For a while. I used to wonder about them, why they'd had to give up their kid, and if I had any brothers and sisters that I didn't know about. Then when I was in med school I started to wonder if I had any defective genes, stuff like that. But there's a big paranoid component to the med school experience anyway."

Simeon took the cassette out of the bag and gave it to Andy. "I haven't seen this video," he said. "But the guy at the store said it was pretty good."

Andy squinted at the label. "Thanks," he said. "I'll go watch it now." He grinned at Simeon. "How about me getting back on my blades?"

Simeon had been thinking about it. He knew that Andy's reflexes were as good as before his operation and that the risks were therefore unchanged. "Do you wear a helmet?" he asked.

"Yes. Well, most of the time." Andy glanced at his mother, who shook her head at him.

"Okay," said Simeon. "If your mother agrees, I think it's reasonable as long as you wear your protective gear. You're a sensible person; if you start getting any dizziness or you can't see, or if any other problems show up, the deal's off, right?"

Andy's face broke into a big grin. "Deal," he said. "Okay, Mom?"

"If it's okay with Dr. Halstead, it's okay with me—and dinner's in five minutes," Fiona called after his retreating figure.

"Can I do anything?" asked Simeon.

"No, thanks. I hope you like salmon." She turned around and pushed a corkscrew curl of hair out of her face with her forearm.

"I love it," he answered. "Actually I like just about everything except summer squash."

"Good. This is with a dill sauce and new potatoes ..."

"We're in luck. I brought white wine, just on a hunch." He looked around. "Do you have anything to open the bottle with?"

Fiona pointed at a drawer, and a moment later Simeon had poured out two glasses and put one on the counter next to Fiona.

"Cheers," he said.

She raised her glass. "I'm very glad you could come," she said simply.

The dinner was delicious. Simeon told them stories about pranks he and his friends had got up to when they were medical students, then they went into the living room and Simeon spotted the upright piano in the corner. After Andy went to bed, they talked about him, about the progress Simeon was making in the research, about travel, about the Uffizi Gallery in Florence, which he'd last visited a few days before it was bombed by terrorists.

"That's one place I've always wanted to visit," said

Fiona. "It's ridiculous—my primary interest is in the Renaissance, and I've never even been to Italy."

They talked about Florence for a while; Simeon had visited the little-known home of Giorgio Vasari, the architect who'd designed the Uffizi. Fiona opened the book he had brought, at a page that showed Luca Della Robbia's stupendous marble panels in the cathedral.

"I really love this book. Thank you so much, Simeon," she said, after leafing through it. "To see it in reality must be stupendous."

Fiona's eyes were shining, and Simeon smiled at her enthusiasm. He couldn't remember when he'd felt so much at ease with anyone.

"Do you play?" he asked, standing up and going over to the piano.

"I used to, a bit," replied Fiona. "But my real instrument's the guitar." She pointed at the case. "I haven't played for a long time, so I'm totally out of practice. And I used to sing, a little." She remembered how impressed Victor had been by her musical ability before they were married, but he'd never paid any attention since then.

Simeon sat down and ran his fingers over the keys, a light arpeggio from the bottom to the top and back again.

"Wow," said Fiona, impressed by his technique.

He started to play a quiet, rather fanciful interpretation of "Misty." He grinned up at her. "I used to play for Elisabeth, but the last time I did that she fell asleep."

He played "Over the Rainbow," and she sang it softly with him. Fiona had a slightly husky, strong voice; it reminded Simeon of Reba McIntyre.

"It's funny," he said, impressed that she remembered all the words, "I can remember the music to hundreds of songs, but I don't know the words to a single one of them."

"I get a feeling that this isn't the only kind of music you play," said Fiona.

For answer, Simeon hitched up the cuffs of his jacket and launched into a piece that she quickly recognized as a Schubert Impromptu.

"That used to be my showoff piece," he said, after finishing with a flourish. "You probably noticed I left out the hard section in the middle. I didn't want to embarrass myself."

Fiona resisted a strong urge to put out her arms and hug him; she'd done that before, in the hospital cafeteria, and she remembered the moment very clearly, but she didn't feel it would be right now, not in her home.

About nine-thirty, Simeon looked at his watch and stood up to leave. "This was the nicest evening I've had in a long time," he said at the door. "Thank you." He put out both hands and touched both her cheeks with his fingertips for a moment, then turned and walked to his car.

Fiona went back inside, feeling a deep pleasure about the evening but also more than a tinge of restlessness. That night her bed felt very empty.

Chapter 34

On the way home Simeon thought about Fiona and what a very attractive and interesting woman she was. It felt so easy being with her, so uncomplicated—such a contrast to being with Elisabeth. Fiona was funny, quick, direct, spoke her mind and seemed to expect him to do the same. Simeon hadn't had to watch what he was saying, hadn't needed to preview his comments for their potential to offend. And he enjoyed getting to know Andy at home; altogether it gave him a glimpse of the kind of life he would have liked to have himself. That made him think about Elisabeth, the willfully barren Elisabeth, and he felt guilty because of his thoughts about Fiona, as if he'd been caught doing something dishonorable.

And that made him think about Sam, Svengali Sam Seidel, who had been quietly trying to persuade Fiona to take Andy to his Mexican clinic. Simeon had avoided saying anything to Fiona about it, but Sam was surely the most persistent man he'd ever met. He was renowned throughout New Coventry as a man to whom dollars were sacred, so Simeon's instinctive reaction to him was simply to follow the money trail, knowing that was where Sam's motives would be found.

Off the freeway there was virtually no traffic on the roads, although a lot of leaves had been blown down by the recent gale and the pavement was slippery. A couple of times when he slowed at intersections, he felt the faint vibrations of the anti-skid braking system against his foot. Small wet leaves dropped from time to time on the windshield and collected on the front of the hood. Then the rain started again in earnest.

There were lights on at the house, and Simeon stiffened

when he saw the car parked near the door, away from the garage.

He pressed the button for the automatic opener and drove in, his mind going at full speed.

He got out of the car and ran across the gravel forecourt, past the parked car. Lightning flashed over the sound, again and again, and the thunder rolled and rumbled, getting closer. He opened the front door and went in.

In the living room, sitting on the floor in the lotus position, at a right angle to the door, so that she was in profile as he entered, was Elisabeth.

He stopped in the doorway and said nothing. He stood there, legs slightly apart, watching her, thinking that Elisabeth must have second sight to reappear just when she could cause the most mischief. He tried to put his warm feelings about Fiona out of his mind and concentrate on Elisabeth, names as for a medieval British queen coming to his mind: Elisabeth the Faithless, Elisabeth the Cold, but finally, inevitably, Elisabeth, his wife.

She was wearing a simple long black gown of plain chiffon, and to Simeon's ironic eye it made her look like a carefully prepared *penitente*. He wondered how long it had taken her to choose the outfit. Elisabeth's theater was overdone, but with style.

"Am I interrupting a meditation or anything?" he asked. When he spoke, he felt the dryness in his mouth. Elisabeth didn't move. When she had her attention fixed on something, she ignored irrelevancies. She usually didn't even hear them.

"May I come back?" she asked, looking not at Simeon but at the wall directly in front of her.

Simeon came slowly forward and stopped a few feet away.

"Why?" he asked.

Elisabeth stood up in one graceful, balletlike move and turned to face him. "Because this is my home," she said. "And I am guilty. I haven't been taking care of it, or of you. Also, I don't have anywhere else to go."

Nothing was said for a few moments, while Simeon thought about the situation. He wondered what had happened with Sandra; had Elisabeth been living with her? Had the two of them had a falling-out?

"Are you planning to stay?" Simeon asked eventually. His tone was cool, curious.

"Yes."

Simeon stared at her. So often Elisabeth's words had ambiguous overtones, even in a definite pronouncement, as now, as if she knew there were far too many variables to make any kind of firm statement about the future.

"Is that yes, or maybe?"

"Yes."

Was she agreeing with his 'maybe' or repeating her previous affirmation? He couldn't tell, and there was no point asking. Elisabeth was watching him with her great big dark eyes, and slowly, hesitantly, she held out her arms and stepped forward until she was standing right up against him. They stood there, facing each other, immobile, barely touching, she high on the balls of her feet. He could smell her, that very faint and always exciting body odor that she had, quite innocent of commercial perfume, a natural compound of body warmth and musk, and enclosed somewhere in there, an olfactory pledge of intimacy, of love, of truth, and sincerity—a firm, unwavering promise of all the things that Elisabeth couldn't deliver. Simeon wondered if it was her odor that had turned Sandra Barry on to her. Now he could feel a physical, electrical tension between the two of them that hadn't been there for a long time, and he couldn't tell whether it was entirely sexual or part of the drama of her return.

"I've missed you," she said.

"I missed you too, for a while," replied Simeon. "But I think I got over it."

Elisabeth stared at him. "It's going to be different now," she murmured. "Very different."

Simeon nodded, thinking about Fiona, the warmth of her personality, her laughter, and the sound of her voice singing next to him at the piano.

Elisabeth's theatrical instincts demanded that the proper formalities be observed.

"I can't just return without a complete explanation," she

said softly. "It would be like denying that anything had happened."

"Not necessary," said Simeon briskly. "I don't really want to know all the sordid details, thank you."

"Dearest Simeon," she said, putting a hand on his forearm. "Nowadays people talk to each other about their problems."

"My main problem right now is that I need a drink," replied Simeon. He walked over to the bar at the far end of the living room. "How about you?"

He half turned. She hadn't moved, and was watching him.

"No, thanks, Simeon," she said. Her voice was quiet, controlled, and sad. Once again, he couldn't tell how much of this was acting and how much was real.

He poured himself a small drink, realizing that he didn't really want one. It was a difficult situation, but he couldn't turn her out into the street.

"So what went wrong? With Sandra?" He walked back to the center of the room.

"That wasn't my real lifestyle," answered Elisabeth, shaking her head. She shrugged dismissively. "I guess I'm not truly into women after all. If I were, I wouldn't be back here, would I?"

"You certainly fooled me, that afternoon you put on your little show," said Simeon.

"Things do change, you know," said Elisabeth.

"Did you bring your clothes and stuff back?"

"I left them in the car. Most of them. I wasn't sure if you wanted me back."

Simeon put his glass down. "I'll help you bring them in." He tried to keep his voice neutral. "You can use the guest bedroom."

Late the next afternoon, Simeon called to thank Fiona for dinner, and when he heard her voice on the phone, all his feelings for her came to life again.

"I had fun last night," she said. "I can't tell you how much I enjoyed it."

"I loved your singing," he said. "And on top of it all you're a great cook. That salmon was out of this world."

Simeon cleared his throat and felt his heart contracting, but he had to tell her. "Elisabeth came back last night," he said. "Actually she was there when I got home."

"Oh." There was a silence. Then Fiona said, in a strange voice, "Will she be staying?"

"I don't know, Fiona. Elisabeth is not a very predictable woman."

"Do you *want* her to stay?" Fiona knew she was getting right out of line here, but she couldn't prevent herself from asking.

Simeon retreated. "At this point she has a right to stay," he said.

There was a long silence, broken by Simeon. "I'm seeing Andy in a couple of weeks," he said. "Will you be coming with him?"

"I suppose so," she replied, annoyed at the slight tremor she heard in her own voice. "I always have up to now."

The conversation ended, and Fiona put the phone down, feeling very shaken, and startled to realize how much emotional capital she had invested in Simeon Halstead.

Two nights later, Simeon was wakened around four in the morning by a movement beside him. Elisabeth had crept into bed next to him. She lay there silently, without moving.

Simeon turned onto his back and waited for a few moments.

"If you don't like your present accommodations, Miss," he said finally, "tell them at the office in the morning. I'm only the caretaker here."

"They told me you were the man to see," replied Elisabeth. Her voice was husky with tension, but she made an effort to be light. "They said you know how to take care of everybody." A moment later she put her hand on his thigh, and Simeon realized that she was naked.

"That's true," replied Simeon, suddenly feeling angry. "I take good care of everybody except myself."

"*I'm* here to take care of you," she replied softly. "I told you things were going to change."

After several minutes of silence, Simeon asked her a

question he'd been turning over in his mind for some time. "How was it, with a woman?"

Elisabeth made a small movement with her shoulders. "Okay," she said. "Up to a point."

"Was it love? Or just sex?"

"Let's talk about something else," she said. She sounded uncomfortable. "I'd rather just forget about it."

He smiled up at the ceiling, enjoying her discomfort. "Nowadays people talk to each other about their problems," he said, mimicking her. "Or so I heard."

"I don't know what to tell you," replied Elisabeth.

Simeon got up on one elbow and stared at her. The only light was coming from the bathroom, through the cracked-open door, and it made Elisabeth look unusually soft and vulnerable. "Look," he said, a little steel coming into his voice, "I have a right to hear all about it. Everything. The whole story. Okay?"

"I love it when you're so masterful," she said, turning her head a fraction to look at him. The highlights in her eyes glinted.

She'd changed, there was no doubt about that. She seemed softer, less brittle, less ready to pick a fight, but that ironic touch was still there. Maybe Sandra had done her some good.

"Okay . . . Let me see if I can put it all into words. The first inkling I had of anything at all was that time we had dinner with the Barrys at the yacht club—you remember, about eight months ago?"

"No, I don't."

"You were being horrible. You had a patient you were worried about, and you didn't talk or listen to anything anybody was saying. It wasn't just then. You'd been awful for days, months. Anyway, there was hardly anybody at the club that night because there was a storm. You remember the French door blew open and a whole lot of glasses and plates got broken?"

"Yes. I remember that. Sort of." Simeon did have a vague recollection of that evening, but he had indeed been preoccupied. He remembered very clearly who the patient was, a young woman with temporal lobe epilepsy that he'd operated on. She'd had a very stormy postop course, although she eventually recovered.

"We'd all ordered coffee, then we went off to the ladies' room."

"Sandra and you."

"You remember?"

"Not really. But if you and *Nick* had gone off to the ladies' room, I'm sure I'd have remembered that."

Elisabeth sighed quietly. "Anyway, on the way, Sandra took my arm—you know how she always likes to be physically close—she's a very touchy woman. Once we got inside the ladies' room, I suppose I was bitching about you, anyway, while I was sitting doing my makeup, she came up behind me and put her arms around me and kissed me on the back of the neck ... It was a strange feeling, gave me goose bumps, and then she put her hands on my breasts, very gently, just for a few seconds."

"Didn't that feel weird? A woman doing that?"

"Yes it did ... No, not really; it was more of a surprise. Then there was a wave of something ... Not like what I've felt with you, but something different, and quite new. Yes, it was exciting. I didn't really respond then, I don't think, not externally, but later she told me I did. Not obviously, but she said she could feel it."

"Weren't you worried somebody'd see you?"

"There was nobody else there. But I was shaking all the way back to the table. I looked at you and wondered if you noticed anything. Silly me."

"Then what?"

"Well, we all went home, and you went to sleep. I stayed awake a long time. You snored. All I could think about was Sandra, and I was having all kinds of fantasies ... Honestly, Simeon, I'd never had an experience like that in my life, although women have occasionally made passes at me. The difference was that this time I felt I'd actually participated. Then next morning Sandra called and invited me over for coffee, and I went. She was so nice when I got there, so loving ... She was funny, paid a lot of attention to me. I suppose it was flattering, but my God, she is one seductive woman ..."

Simeon shook his head. "I don't get it, Elisabeth. It

seems a long way to go from a normal friendship with somebody of the same sex. For instance, there are guys I enjoy being with, you know, whose company I really like. But the idea of . . ." Simeon made a face in the darkness. "Tell me how it happened."

"Well, Sandra had sort of laid the groundwork the night before, so I knew I wasn't just coming over for coffee. I didn't know what was going to happen, but I felt all excited and shivery in anticipation. She'd bought a whole lot of clothes, some really nice things, and she said, 'Help me decide what I'm going to keep.' "

Simon could feel something stirring, but he tried to keep his voice casual. "So then what happened?"

Elisabeth's eyes turned toward him. "Simeon, do you find this exciting? I mean, hearing me tell you this?"

"Well, it's certainly different. Yes, I suppose I do." He turned toward Elisabeth and tucked himself firmly against her hip. Her hand strayed toward him again.

"Well, she had all this stuff, all these new clothes laid out on the bed . . . on *one* side of the bed. It's a king-size, like this one." She smiled at him. "So she stripped down to her bra and panties . . . I tell you, Simeon Halstead, that girl has a body . . . Well of course, I don't need to tell you, you've seen it. Didn't she turn you on? I mean that time when you were standing watching out there on the deck?"

"No, not that time," answered Simeon in just the right tone of voice, and she pinched him hard.

"Where was I? Right, bra and panties. Lacy stuff. You know I don't usually buy that kind of thing myself, but on her it was dynamite."

"And then?"

"Well, she tried on a couple of things and modeled them for me, and for some reason that was exciting. She was totally focused on me . . ."

"I know how you like that," said Simeon.

"It is nice, just occasionally, if somebody pays attention to one," Elisabeth admitted. "My, my, this is really turning you on."

Simeon didn't answer.

"So then she'd put on this two-piece beach suit. It was very flowery, very sexy, and really well cut. Then she took it off and came over to me. I was sitting on the bench with my back to her dressing table ... She was so hot I could feel the glow. All she did was take my hands and put them on her breasts."

Elisabeth paused. "I'd never done that in my life before. I mean, held another woman's breasts like that ... It felt wonderful. Really. I couldn't believe it. Firm, exciting ... And then she undressed me. She was so gentle, so ... sure. And then we lay on the bed together. On the part that didn't have clothes all over it."

It seemed strange to Simeon that he should be reacting in this way about his wife's seduction, and by a *woman,* at that. Would he have listened to all this if the seducer had been a man? If it had been Nick Barry instead of Sandra? Would he have even let her back into the house? He didn't think so, but he couldn't figure out why.

"I love it that you have a cock, Simeon," said Elisabeth, smiling at him in the semidarkness and holding on to it. "I have truly missed it."

"Did you use a dildo with her?"

"No. She has one, she said, but she never used it with me."

"So how was it?" asked Simeon, still curious about lesbian techniques. "How ... well, aside from what I saw, and that was only for a second, how do you get it on with a woman?"

"It's mostly touching and feeling," said Elisabeth softly. "Here, there, and everywhere, with everything you can touch or feel with."

"It looked like a bit more than a little gentle touching to me," said Simeon.

Elisabeth took his hand and placed it at the top of her pubic area. "What's this bone called?" she asked. "That part you can feel, that sticks forward?"

"The pubic bone," he answered. "There's one on each side and they join in the middle at the pubic symphysis."

"Whatever," said Elisabeth. "Sandra would get on top of me and start working that bone against my clitoris," she went on. "And I would kiss her, and play with her breasts ... When you come like that, it feels exciting, different, but quite honestly it's not anything like as wonderful as having this great ... big ... cock all the way inside me." She sat up, pushed a leg over him, and slid over so that she was straddling him, and he pushed himself inside her, thrust upward, feeling as if it were the first time he'd ever been inside her, the first time he'd made love with her.

He came quickly, excited and tantalized by thoughts and visions of Sandra doing this to Elisabeth, holding her breasts, feeling her move, coming with her.

"I love you," said Elisabeth a minute later, snuggling against him. Simeon knew that she didn't say things she didn't mean, and he fancied he heard a new depth and a new meaning in what she had just said.

"Yes," he replied in a neutral tone, but he wasn't thinking about Elisabeth, because his thoughts had turned to Fiona, and he could almost feel her body lying there next to him.

Elisabeth turned her back to him with a contented, feline little sound and soon went to sleep, but Simeon lay awake for a long time, listening to the distant sounds of traffic and the regular, mournful booming sound of the foghorn half a mile away on Old Coventry Point. He felt uncomfortable with Elisabeth lying there next to him; his sense of oneness, his sense of partnership that he had worked hard to establish with her, was gone. He had remained entirely faithful to her since their marriage, but he didn't feel at all righteous about it; he had just followed his instincts and upbringing. Maybe if he'd acted differently, he thought, if he'd been a more interesting and attentive husband, she wouldn't have needed to go looking for all that outside excitement. But there was no question that his feelings for her had changed; now he felt detached, distanced, as if he were a third person, coolly viewing their relationship from a safe distance. He turned his head to glance at her, sleeping peacefully, her mouth slightly open, as if she were smiling at something ... He shrugged to himself and turned on his other side. Certainly he had loved her, and of course he didn't want her to come to any harm, and he would do whatever was necessary to protect her. I'll give it one more try, he said to himself. But if she starts any more of her capers, that's it.

But as if his unconscious mind had taken on the task of explaining his feelings to him, when he finally went to sleep it wasn't Elisabeth he dreamed about.

Chapter 35

The next morning, Simeon woke up as usual at a quarter to six and lay there for a moment, very still, feeling a slight shock when he realized that Elisabeth was there, still naked, beside him. She had pushed back the bedclothes and most of her body was exposed, her fine breasts rising and falling gently with her breathing. He got up quietly, astonished at how unmoved he was by the sight of her.

The rain had stopped sometime during the night, and there was a stillness, a kind of breathless post-storm exhaustion about the countryside as he drove along the expressway. A quarter-mile to his left, beyond the trees and buildings, was Route 1, the ancient Boston Road that had been supplanted as a main artery when I-95 was built, and beyond it he caught glimpses of the blue-gray sound. The traffic thickened with trucks and cars as sleepy, ill-tempered commuters headed for New Conventry, drinking coffee out of nonspill mugs and already doing business on their car phones. The air had been clear enough when he left his house, but now he could smell the chemicals in it, and by the time he went down the ramp to the underground parking lot beneath the research building, the industrial haze was already established, softening the outlines of the tall buildings, killing the more distant colors into different misty shades of gray. It was going to be another sticky, sweltery summer day.

There were a few cars already in the underground parking area, and Simeon walked over to the elevator, his footsteps echoing in the cavernous chamber. A couple of minutes later he unlocked the door to his lab, opened it, and walked in.

"Who's that?" He heard a startled female voice from the far end, but he couldn't see anything.

"It's me, Edwina. Simeon. And the top o' the mornin' to you."

There was no sound for a few minutes, then Edwina appeared from the back of the lab, sleepy, shiny-faced, her hair straggly, wearing a loose olive-green T-shirt several sizes too big for her. It came down to less than mid-thigh, showing most of her strong, shapely legs. Even now, tired and sleepy, her body revealed youth and strength and tightness in every movement she made.

"Hi, Dr. Halstead," she said, pushing a lock of hair out of her face. She pointed to her lab area. "We're making progress here."

"Good. Would you like a cup of coffee?" Simeon went over to the machine and in a few seconds had poured the old coffee out of the glass container, refilled the reservoir, and placed a pre-packed measure of ground coffee in the tray. "It'll be ready 4.8 minutes from now."

"Thanks ... I'm going for a shower. I'll be back in 6.2 minutes. Milk, please, and a little sugar." She grinned at him. When Edwina smiled, it transformed her tired, rather immobile features and made her look young, alert, and sensuous. No wonder Sonia watched Denis so carefully, he thought, although it was clear enough that Edwina wasn't interested in Denis.

She went back for a little flowery bag with her toilet things, slung some clothes over her arm, and went off down the corridor, her bare feet making no noise on the floor.

When she came back, coffee was ready, and Edwina was transformed. Even with her hair still wet and with dark strands sticking to her forehead and face, she had a strong, competent beauty. A passionate woman, too, from the looks of her, thought Simeon, looking at her wide, laughing mouth. Some guy would wind up with a real handful there; he'd need to be able to do a lot of things well to keep up with her.

"Would you like to go over your data?" he asked.

"Sure. But we can't access a lot of the new stuff I was doing yesterday, because I didn't put it into the main program yet," she replied. "It'll take me about ten minutes to put it in, okay?"

Simeon went over to Denis's area, meticulously neat as always. His equipment, notebooks, and backup tapes were all carefully put away, always in the same place.

The day before, a shipment of three experimental microwave probes had come in, and Simeon hadn't had a chance to check them. He picked them up and examined them with a hand lens. They were tiny, beautifully crafted instruments, and came with a custom-made mechanism for fixing the probes to the skulls of the experimental rats. They had been manufactured in Singapore and had cost a lot of money. Simeon shook his head. Before placing the order, Denis had contacted three American companies that made similar equipment, but none of them could match the price. As soon as Simeon had shown interest in the purchase, one of the Singaporeans' technical reps had come up from New York to discuss the equipment. Not one of the American companies had even called them back.

Denis came in, accompanied by Sonia. The two of them lived together in a high-rise apartment complex that belonged to the university, and today Denis's face was glum and Sonia was looking tight-lipped and angry.

Simeon spent an hour with Denis going over the bench checks that he'd done on the tiny probes. The basic idea was to aim three microwave beams at a single cancerous point in the brain, each probe being positioned at a different location on the circumference of the skull. At the point where the beams intersected, the amount of heat produced would be three times that produced by a single beam, enough to coagulate the cancer cells, which had been previously been treated with hypercoagulable protein. It was the high-tech equivalent of the boxer's blow to the solar plexus, to be followed by the microwave Sunday Punch.

"We're ready to start on our rodents," said Denis. "Our computer simulation says it's going to work the way we thought it would." Denis was looking upset, and from time to time he would look over at Sonia.

"Are you guys all right?" asked Simeon in a quiet voice, inaudible across the room. "You and Sonia?"

"Not really, sir." Denis seemed of two minds about saying anything more, then he went on. "She thinks that I'm having some kind of a fling with Edwina," he said. "But that's nonsense. I swear it. Anyway, as I told her again and again, it's not me she's interested in. I mean Edwina."

"Women are hard to convince," said Simeon.

"Yes, sir. I have the rats ordered from the animal facility. They're available when we need them."

"How about the pathology?" In order to prove the effectiveness of the technique, sections of the rats' brains would be examined to show how much heat damage had occurred along the paths of the microwave beams. The goal, of course, was that damage would occur only at the point where the beams intersected.

"We have a problem," said Denis. He opened a drawer under the bench and pulled out an envelope. "I got this yesterday in the interdepartmental mail."

Simeon took out the letter. "Dear Mr. Popham," he read, "Further to our provisional agreement with Dr. Simeon Halstead to review and report on thermal injury patterns on rat brain slices originating from your laboratory, due to the pressure of other departmental work we will be unable to carry out this assignment. Sincerely, Ralph Baum, Director, New Conventry Medical Center Laboratory Pathological Services."

"What's this?" asked Simeon. "Dr. Baum agreed to do all of that for us weeks ago. Provisional agreement, nothing. We had a commitment from him."

"Did you notice to whom a copy of the letter was sent, Dr. Halstead?"

"Yes." Simeon couldn't help smiling at Denis's formal language. At the bottom of the letter was "Cc: Dr. Felix Cadwaller, Chief, Neurosurgical Service."

"He'd have got a copy anyway," said Simeon, but he too wondered if Cadwaller had had anything to do with the pathology department's sudden inability to process the rat brain sections.

"I checked several of the commercial labs yesterday afternoon," said Denis. "The best is probably MidWest Path, in Minneapolis, Minnesota. They're a good lab, sir, well established and thoroughly reliable. I've used them on a number of previous occasions."

"Yes, but that's very different from going down the hall to our own pathologists, discussing their techniques and looking over their shoulder at the slides," objected Simeon. "This could be a major setback." In his mind, Simeon calculated the additional time this would take. There would be a delay if MidWest Path had a backlog, and then additional time would be spent in sending specimens through the mails, and then there would be long telephone discussions about the interpretation of data. Simeon had a goal, maybe unrealistically, but a goal nevertheless, of having the system up and working within the next two months. Statistically, Andy Markle had an eighty-five percent chance of not having a recurrence before then, but after six months the statistics mounted inexorably against him.

Denis watched him quietly for a moment. "We're also running out of money, sir," he said.

Chapter 36

Two weeks later, Simon was scheduled to see Andy Markle for a routine follow-up visit, and he made his way up to the fifth floor of the clinic building, looking forward to seeing both Andy and Fiona, although he had not spoken to either of them since he'd told her about Elisabeth's return. He felt tense about being in the same room with her.

"We miss seeing you around, Dr. Halstead," said Cecelia Crawford, the attractive head clinic nurse, when Simeon appeared. She smiled cautiously at him. "So when are you coming back to work with us?"

"Not quite yet, Cecelia," he replied, smiling. "How many patients do we have today?"

"Just two." The clinic was deserted; the general surgery residents had finished an hour before. "Everybody's getting very excited about your research project," she went on. "How is it coming along?" At this point Cecelia was the only clinical person who had any contact with Simeon, so she had to get all the information she could for later retailing to her colleagues.

"We're making headway," said Simeon. "A few problems here and there, but that's how those things go. Where's Andy Markle's chart?"

Cecelia looked uncomfortable. "It'll be a few minutes coming up, Dr. Halstead," she said. "Do you want to see the other patient first?"

Simeon gazed at the nurse for a second. "Where is that chart?" he asked.

"I called for it from records, the usual way," she said. "Apparently somebody in administration has it. Anyway, they're sending it up right away."

Simeon could smell a rat somewhere. "Who in administration, do you know?"

Cecelia wouldn't look at him. "They said it was signed out to Mr. Prince."

Simeon raised his eyebrows. Marshall Prince was the hospital's CEO and administrator, an unlikely person to have any need to see a patient's chart. Unless . . .

Simeon picked up the phone. "Marshall? Simeon Halstead."

"Oh, good. I'm glad you called." Simeon smiled grimly to himself. Marshall didn't sound that glad.

"I'm seeing a patient by the name of Andy Markle here in the clinic," said Simeon. "I need his chart. I believe it was signed out to you."

"Right. It's actually on the way up to you right now," replied Prince. He paused for a moment. "The reason it's here is because it's been subpoenaed. I wanted to have a look at it first."

"Subpoenaed by whom?"

"Hold on a second . . . Here—it's a local attorney by the name of Gold. Haiman Gold. The name on the letterhead is Gold, Reilly, and O'Connell."

"Thanks, Marshall."

"I'd like to discuss this matter with you, Simeon—unofficially, of course. Can you stop by after you finish your clinic?"

"Sure. It shouldn't take too long, maybe half an hour."

Simeon put the phone down slowly. Cecelia watched him, trying to figure out what was going on. She'd heard the word "subpoena" and knew what that meant. Simeon looked shaken. And he felt shaken. To him, the fact that Andy Markle's hospital chart had been subpoenaed meant that someone was considering a malpractice suit against him. It might just be a fishing expedition, but that seemed unlikely. And if someone was instituting a suit, the only person with the legal right to do that, apart from Andy himself, was Fiona Markle, who he knew was Andy's legal custodian.

At that moment, an orderly came in with Andy's chart. Simeon picked it up and looked through it briefly, but of course there was no way to tell whether it had been copied, or whether at this moment somebody might be going through it with a fine-tooth comb trying to find—who knew what they were trying to find? Simeon had enough confidence in his clinical ability and judgment to consider himself relatively fireproof. He glanced through it, checking the residents' handwritten notes. Sometimes an inadvertent written comment by a tired resident could do huge damage, but not here. And he'd taken particular care with this case, thanks to Felix Cadwaller. Simeon had been an expert witness in enough cases to know the kind of thing plaintiff's attorneys liked to find, and in this chart there was nothing anybody could make a case from. He was sure of it. But the thought of Fiona Markle going against him like this made him feel sick.

"Okay, Cecelia," he said, picking up the chart. "Let's get this show on the road."

The first person he saw in the exam room was Fiona. She stood up when he came in. Her smile was friendly enough, he thought, maybe a bit reserved, but that was surely natural, considering the abrupt way he'd terminated their relationship, almost before it had even started. Seeing her standing there, he felt a hard, unexpectedly strong feeling of regret, a sense that he'd stupidly missed the boat with her. In a fraction of a second, as he came into the room, he remembered how they'd laughed, how she'd looked at different moments that evening, and how easy and uncomplicated it had felt being with her. He shook hands, first with Andy, who was sitting on the stretcher, then with her. She seemed quietly happy to see him.

How could she possibly be planning a malpractice suit against him and look at him like that?

His expression and his thoughts changed abruptly. If that was what she was doing, he needed to get into a different mode with her. Watching him, her smile seemed to flutter uncertainly, then her mouth opened slightly in an expression of surprise. She didn't take her eyes off his face.

He turned to face Andy. "So how's it going, tiger?" he asked.

"Good." Andy nodded, his eyes watchful. He liked Simeon and was happy to see him, but he could feel the tension between the doctor and his mother.

"Any problems?"

Andy shook his head. He glanced at his mother.

"If you're ever in court, on the witness stand," Simeon told him, smiling, "and they ask you a question, they'll tell you to answer yes or no."

"We're not in court," said Andy, grinning.

"Of course not," said Simeon. "I was just kidding." He paused, then turned to Fiona. "Anything you've noticed about Andy?" he asked. "Is his appetite good? Sleeping well?"

Fiona, still looking fixedly at Simeon, replied, "He's wonderful. He gets a headache if he runs or jumps, but otherwise ..." She glanced at Andy. "Everything's okay, right, Andy?"

Andy nodded. "Yes, Your Honor," he said very distinctly to his mother, then grinned quickly at Simeon.

Fiona didn't smile.

For the next several minutes Simeon examined Andy very carefully. Then he straightened up and hung the ophthalmoscope back on the stand. "He's doing all right," he said, without looking directly at Fiona. "Everything else seems to be working nicely—reflexes, motor and sensory function. He still can't raise his eyes above the horizontal position, but I expected that." He didn't want to go into any details about the ominous Parinaud's sign beyond the fact that it was still present.

"Am I going to get radiation?" asked Andy. "And chemo ... that medicine? Dr. Cadwaller said that ..."

Fiona interrupted Andy. "Victor insisted that Andy see Dr. Cadwaller," she said. "Last week. Although personally I ..."

"There's no problem," said Simeon, a shade abruptly. He was furious that Cadwaller had seen Andy behind his, Simeon's, back. "I'm happy to discuss Andy's treatment with Dr. Cadwaller, or any other qualified person, if that's what you wish," he said. "But it doesn't help Andy if I don't hear what Cadwaller's opinion is."

Fiona's eyes seemed to be glistening, and her lower lip quivered for a second.

"Look," said Simeon, "if you'd feel more comfortable having Dr. Cadwaller take care of Andy from now on, that's fine with me. I can have his records transferred over today."

"No!" Her answer was more emphatic than she wanted it to sound, and she covered it with a little cough.

There was a brief pause while Simeon tried to figure out what she was up to.

"Then, yes, I'll be happy to talk about radiation and chemotherapy again," he said. "Although when we discussed it before, you felt that the side effects were too severe to consider either modality. That's probably the route we need to take, but we have to sit down and discuss the pros and cons again in some detail." He looked at Fiona. "Will your husband want to join us for that?"

"Victor and I are divorced," said Fiona quietly. "Still."

"Will your ex-husband want to join us to discuss radiation and chemotherapy for Andy?"

"I don't know," replied Fiona in a very low voice.

Simeon nodded. "Please find out. If he does, I'll have my secretary set up an appointment," he said. "For later this week. Okay?"

As they were leaving, Fiona turned to Simeon. "I'd like to talk to you privately, Dr. Halstead," she said, but his expression seemed to drain her self-confidence. "If that's possible."

"Okay, Mrs. Markle," replied Simeon. "Certainly. How about this afternoon? Five o'clock, in my office?"

Simeon walked back down the corridor of the outpatient building toward the elevator, feeling upset and betrayed by Fiona. How could she be so two-faced? Maybe he should have said something about the subpoenaed chart to her . . . He walked along, his footsteps resounding on the hard composition floor. The clinic was in one of the oldest parts of the hospital, scheduled to be demolished in the near future. The administration had been promising that for the last ten years, said the cynics, so that they wouldn't have to put any money into repairs and refurbishings. Everything looked dirty, out of date, and worn out; the white paint on the doors was flaking, the furniture was solid but decrepit. Simeon glanced through the door of the sterilizing room; inside, it looked like something out of a sixties hospital movie.

This whole experience was beginning to make him wonder whether he'd made a monumental mistake by letting his guard down with Andy and Fiona. It might have been easier and safer to continue in the old way, letting the residents take care of the relatives and their emotional support. If he'd done that with the Markles, he wouldn't be in this turmoil now. And then a disturbing thought arose: If he hadn't felt this way about Fiona, would he be doing anything different with Andy—treating him differently? He considered that for a few moments. He didn't think so, but in the old days, when he wasn't personally involved with his patients, that kind of question just didn't arise.

And Fiona and Andy Markle weren't his only problem, he reflected, trying to get the image of her out of his mind as he passed the entrance to the neuropathology department. He caught a glimpse of Cadwaller talking to the director just inside the door. Abandoning his clinical practice wasn't working the way he'd hoped, because it hadn't freed up all of his time for the lab. Too many things were coming up that interfered with his work, and he was getting seriously frustrated. Damn Fiona, he thought angrily, as the image of her came back into his mind. He tried to replace his feelings about her with the usual wary attitude that physicians take when they're expecting a malpractice suit against them, but it wasn't easy. He decided to confront her with it when he saw her later this afternoon.

Marshall Prince's office was at the far end of the administration corridor, and as Simeon walked toward it he thought about the last time he'd been there, the day Ted Garvey had gone berserk. Marshall was a smart and diplomatic man, a loyal and capable administrator who never failed his employers, the hospital board. He could be relied on to put the interests of the hospital first, before those of the people who worked in it or the patients who came there to get help.

Prince's office was large, old-fashioned, with one wall devoted to portraits and photographs of his predecessors in office. They were a grim-looking lot, thought Simeon, glancing at them as he sat down in Marshall's comfortable visitor's chair. But their job had surely not been as stressful as Marshall Prince's.

"I can't find out anything about this subpoena," said Marshall, wasting no time. "All I have is the name of the attorney and the law firm that asked for it. Can you enlighten me?"

"No. I suppose it must have been his mother," answered Simeon, pushing his words out reluctantly. "She has custody of the child."

"We'll find out soon enough, I suppose." He looked at Simeon. "Were there any problems with that case? Anything we should be concerned about? If there was, I should know about it now rather than later."

Simeon shook his head. "No," he replied, "I don't think so. The surgery went well enough, although we weren't able to remove all of his tumor. I saw him upstairs in the clinic a few minutes ago. He's doing well. For now, anyway."

Marshall put his big hands flat on the table. "You know we don't need any more lawsuits against this hospital," he said, and Simeon could see that the flurry of recent litigation had taken its toll on him. "And especially we don't need one involving you. You're like . . . in some ways you are the standard-bearer around here. If they feel they can sue *you* . . . then they can sue anybody in this entire medical center. I'm worried that if that happened we'd have a fresh rash of suits that could pretty well destroy this establishment."

"As far as I know, there's no grounds for any kind of suit," said Simeon steadily. "But Dr. Cadwaller has been involved in the case, on and off. You might want to ask him."

Marshall looked at Simeon oddly. "As it happens, I had a meeting with Dr. Cadwaller earlier today," he said. "At his request." He didn't elaborate.

"What was the name again of that law firm that wanted Andy Markle's chart?" asked Simeon.

"Gold, Reilly, and O'Connell. I had one of my assistants check them out. They do mostly commercial law, but one of the partners is into medical malpractice."

"Do we have a name?"

"Gold. Haiman Gold."

Simeon got up. He knew who would know about Haiman Gold and who would also know if Fiona was initiating a lawsuit. Sam Seidel was that man. And, as he recollected, Sam had actually warned him that something like this might happen.

"I suppose you'd better let your malpractice insurance carrier know about this," said Marshall.

"I'll call them tomorrow," replied Simeon. "Thank you."

Sam was in his office when Simeon called. "Yeah, I know about Haiman Gold," he said. "I was the one who told the Markles to talk to him."

Simeon stared speechlessly at the phone for a second. He could understand that Sam might have done that, in his sly way, but to admit it seemed too outrageous, even for Sam.

"Look," Sam went on. "Victor was going to see a lawyer, one way or the other. I know you, I know Andy, I know everything that's happened. I also know Haiman Gold pretty well. Knew his dad, too. Haiman is a real smart lawyer, but he doesn't like to waste his time. He'll think about this, make some inquiries, talk to a few people, then he'll decide there's nothing there and bag it. And that'll be to your advantage. Victor could easily have gone to see some hungry schlock lawyer who'd be delighted to go after you, even though they'd lose in the end. Simeon, I've done you a favor."

"Sam, with friends like you, I sure don't need any enemies," said Simeon when he got his breath back.

"Oh, you've got your enemies," replied Sam cheerfully. "But I'm not one of them."

"Was ... Mrs. Markle involved in the decision to see Haiman Gold?"

"Hey, I don't know. Victor couldn't legally do it by himself, could he? Anyway I hear that him and Fiona are maybe getting back together."

Simeon's grip tightened on the telephone, but before he could say anything, Sam went on, "By the way, remember I told you about Paolo Mendez? The doc at the Vallarta clinic? He's here in town, staying with some friends, and I'd like to bring him over to your lab sometime next week, if that's okay with you. Hey, I have to run. I'll call you in a couple of days ..."

Chapter 37

At ten minutes before five, Simeon reluctantly left his lab and walked over to the hospital. Fiona was interrupting his work, and he couldn't get over what she was doing. The anger in him had been quietly building up all day. Was she trying to get some kind of revenge because he'd told her that Elisabeth had come back? Maybe she'd got back together with Victor and they'd both cooked it up ... But that morning she'd told him they were still divorced, and her tone didn't suggest that there had been any rapprochement. It just didn't seem like her to be secretly initiating a malpractice suit against him. But what other explanation was there?

He ran up the seven flights of stairs.

"You're not in the best of shape," said Victoria, his secretary, looking him over. "You used to run up those stairs without even hardly raising a sweat."

"That was when I was younger," panted Simeon. "And anyway, I always waited outside for a couple of minutes to get my breath back. Just to impress you."

"Mrs. Markle's here," said Victoria, glancing at the door of his inner office. In a quieter voice she said, "She seems upset."

"Wouldn't you be, if you had a kid with brain cancer?" said Simeon, more sharply than he wanted. Victoria stared at him. With a strange feeling in his chest, he opened the door and walked in.

Fiona stood up quickly when she heard him come in. She seemed more carefully dressed than usual, in a light beige chamois-leather dress. Simeon couldn't tell if it was real or faux chamois; Elisabeth, of course, would have known after one disdainful glance. Anyway, it looked very good on her, he thought, and a wave of pent-up anger swept over him.

"I hope I didn't keep you waiting," he said. He simply could not keep the coldness out of his voice.

"Not at all, Dr. Halstead. I just got here." She gazed at him, obviously taken aback by his tone.

Simeon sat behind his desk, glad of the distance and the barrier it put between him and Fiona. She was certainly a disconcerting person, to say the least.

"So what can I do for you?"

Fiona took a big breath and felt the tears come up into her eyes. Annoyed at herself, she took out a handkerchief and blew her nose.

"I need to talk to you about Andy," she said, completely losing what she had planned to say to him and bringing up the first thing that came into her mind. "I don't think he told you this morning, but he's coaching some of the physically challenged kids at school who want to play baseball." She smiled shakily. "Have you ever seen those kids? They use a light ball as big as a football, and they throw it from just a few feet from the base. That way the game doesn't go faster than their reflexes."

"Tough to throw a knuckleball with one of those, I imagine," said Simeon.

"Yes, I suppose it would be," said Fiona. She could feel a kind of panic invading her. Why was he being so cold to her? She hadn't been sure this morning, but she was sure now. Memories of their evening together flooded back; she'd felt so good about it at the time, but now her happy recollections seemed to have curdled. Maybe he'd just pretended to enjoy himself. Maybe, thinking about it afterward, he'd found that he really didn't like her, and maybe his wife hadn't really come home, he had just said that to get rid of her . . .

Simeon reddened, realizing instantly that his answer had been frivolous and out of place. "I'm sorry," he said. "I know that wasn't funny. How does Andy like being a coach?"

"He likes it a lot," she said. "I don't."

Simeon looked up. "Why?"

"Because I look at him working so hard with these kids

who can barely swing a bat, who mostly can't walk, who can't talk properly, and it makes me think that soon that's how my beautiful Andy is going to be, that's how he's going to look to other people, weird, like he's from another planet, in a few months, for a while before he dies," replied Fiona, her words coming out in a rush. By the time she finished speaking, her voice was so low that Simeon could hardly hear her.

"You wanted to see me for a particular reason, Fiona?" he asked.

"Yes, I did." Again she gazed at him as if she were feeling and saying things that she didn't quite know how to express. "For one thing, I wanted to thank you for being so . . . *kind* isn't the right word, and *supportive* doesn't quite cover it either . . . What I mean is that you've helped Andy and me more than I can possibly tell you. It's not been easy, for either of us, but it's been a lot easier when . . . when we knew that you . . . well, when we knew that you were there for us."

"Yeah, right." His anger at her hypocrisy was coming to a boil, and the sarcasm in his voice was clear. He looked away, and Fiona stared as if he'd slapped her.

Simeon opened his mouth to ask her why she'd had an attorney subpoena Andy's records, but she spoke first.

"Victor's been seeing a lawyer," said Fiona. Her eyes flashed. "A man by the name of Gold, who specializes in medical malpractice. I want you to know that he did that entirely on his own. I had nothing whatever to do with it and only learned about it by accident."

A long, involuntary sigh left Simon. "Andy's in your legal custody, isn't that so?" he asked. "His records were subpoenaed by Gold, and he wouldn't have had the authority to do it without your approval."

"I suppose so. I don't know the legalities, but I'll call them and find out."

"I'm glad it wasn't you, Fiona." Simeon's relief was so clear that Fiona smiled. "Didn't Victor expect you to cooperate? Did he talk to you about it?"

"Yes, he did. More than that, he wanted to move back in with Andy and me," said Fiona with a short laugh. "He had me fooled for a while. I tell you, Simeon, we women are suckers for blarney. And you men ..." She corrected herself. "I'm talking about Victor. When it's in his own interest, he has a sure instinct for saying the right thing to me when I'm down, so that I turn to putty in his hands. Luckily I figured him out some time ago, so I don't do the putty bit anymore." She paused and put her hands together in her lap. "I guess it takes years to figure out any man."

Again she gave Simeon that vivid look that he found so difficult to interpret. The first time she'd done that, he remembered, was after the Garvey incident, when he'd taken her arm as they were leaving the room.

"Two other things I wanted to talk to you about," she went on in a more matter-of-fact voice. "First, how's the research coming along?"

"It's going pretty well," said Simeon. Then he hastily added, "Of course, there's no way yet of telling whether it's going to work, let alone have a functioning system in time to use with Andy, although I want you to know that my team and I are busting our butts to get there."

"The other thing I wanted to talk to you about," said Fiona, "is Sam Seidel."

"He wouldn't like to be called a 'thing,' " said Simeon, feeling a sense of euphoria. "Under that rough and crusty exterior, Sam's a very delicate, easily offended person."

"Yeah, sure," said Fiona. "Sam's about as delicate as a New York garbage truck. Anyway, he's been talking to me about sending Andy to Mexico for treatment. He says that there's a clinic there ..."

"The Maya Clinic? That clinic belongs to him," interjected Simeon.

"I know," said Fiona. She frowned. "He told me. Does that make any difference?"

"I'm sorry," said Simeon. "I never know when to shut up. Go on, please."

"He told me about this doctor called Paolo, Paolo Mendez, who he said has done some extraordinary things with patients like Andy. Sam even brought him over to talk to us."

"He's here? Sam wants to bring him over to the lab. Did Mendez tell you he could cure Andy?" Simeon's voice was sharp.

"No, he didn't. I don't think that's even what they have primarily in mind, although they have had patients whose tumors have regressed. Maybe even been cured. I don't know."

Simeon, very aware of his own prejudices, tried to keep them out of his voice. "And if curing the patient isn't primarily what they have in mind, then what *do* they have primarily in mind?"

"Learning to live. I know that sounds trite, but I don't know enough about it to explain it to you. Sam told me he was bringing Dr. Mendez to see you later this week. I'm sure he'll tell you all about his methods when you see him."

"Learning to live!" Simeon couldn't hide his skepticism. "When you've only got a few months at best . . ." He took a deep breath. "If it were me, Fiona, I think I'd want to learn how to get cured, not how to *live.*"

"Dr. Mendez has a different point of view, I guess," said Fiona, and Simeon felt unaccountably disturbed that she seemed to be defending this Mexican quack's position, although it was clear that she didn't know even approximately what that position was.

Simeon, feeling that silence was his best bet, said nothing.

"So, what do you think, Dr. Halstead? I already told Sam that I wasn't letting Andy go anywhere unless it was okayed by you."

Simeon hesitated. "Fiona, right now I don't know. As I said, Sam's planning to bring Dr. Mendez over to the lab. I'll talk to him and find out if he's for real or if he's just another charlatan trying to make a buck off sick and gullible people. I'll give you a call as soon as I've had a chance to evaluate him."

"Thanks. I really appreciate . . . everything." Fiona's expression said it better, and looking at her, Simeon felt the clouds lifting from his spirit; he couldn't see how he could ever have thought that she'd start a malpractice suit against him—now the mere thought seemed ridiculous.

When Simeon arrived at the lab the next morning, Denis had the books ready, as requested. After they went over the numbers for an hour, it was clear that Denis was right: There was no money left in the kitty. As Simeon readily acknowledged, it was mostly because he hadn't anticipated all the necessary equipment purchases or the high level of ongoing expenditures after the project got under way.

"Your salary and Sonia's are safe, at least," said Simeon.

"Yes, we're very grateful for that," said Denis. "But that alone won't get the project completed, will it, sir?" His face was looking more horselike than ever, with its big nostrils and sad gray eyes.

They were looking at a deficit. Not just a little one, either. Simeon had known what equipment he needed, and in the enthusiasm of the moment he had ordered it all. And now the bills were coming in, and there wasn't enough money to pay them. Already there was a stack of copies of bills, passed on from the medical school purchasing unit, on Denis's desk. Each bill had a red ink stamp on it that said, "INSUFFICIENT BILLING INFORMATION. GRANTEE PLEASE PROVIDE IMMEDIATELY."

"How far in the hole are we, Denis?"

Denis gulped. "Over a hundred thousand, sir. Actually one hundred and eighteen thousand, plus a few."

"Can we return any of the equipment?"

"Some, perhaps. But every instrument is in use. We didn't buy anything we didn't need, and there's nothing major wrong with any of them. Most of the manufacturers give you a fourteen-day grace period to return equipment. After that, they'll send someone out to fix it, or to take care of training or technical problems, but we've had most of the equipment we're using now for well over three months. We're going to have to pay for it somehow."

"Make a list of anything we can return, will you?"

"I've done that, sir. With difficulty we might be able to return about twelve thousand dollars' worth of equipment, but the suppliers will kick up a big fuss, and they'll take it to the university. And anyway, we need it. All of it. The amino-acid analyzer, for instance. If I can't use that, it'll add months to the project."

Simeon thought about it. As a relative newcomer to the research field, he didn't have the experience or the know-how to deal with such emergencies, nor did he have a network of associates who could help him over the hump.

"I'll call Helen Wayland at the National Institute of Neurology," said Simeon. "She's been the case officer on this project. Maybe she can help us out."

"She wasn't very helpful last time we spoke to her," Denis reminded Simeon. "As I'm sure you recall, she even threatened to cut off our funding entirely if we didn't get a quarterly report in to her quickly. *Real pronto* were her actual words, sir, as I recall."

Simeon was thinking hard. Other sources of funding shouldn't be difficult to find; there was plenty of research money around, and the name of New Coventry Medical Center was magical. Look at Cadwaller, with his huge annual budget to support his research, although it wasn't much more than an ongoing clinical crap game. But Cadwaller had been at it a long time, and it had taken him years to latch on to the drug companies that financed his research. Also, Simeon realized, it might not be so easy to get deficit financing—nobody liked to provide funds that had already been spent.

Departmental funds . . . These were under the control of Felix Cadwaller, and there was no point in wasting time even thinking about them.

Pharmaceutical companies. Simeon thought of David Marsh. David was now a senior exec at the Thomson and Thomson Foundation, a grant-giving tax shelter for Thomson and Thomson Pharmaceuticals, one of the biggest corporations in the industry. Simeon had known David when he was a general surgeon in New Coventry. After a number of bad surgical results, he'd lost his confidence and had some kind of a breakdown. Simeon had done his best to help him and talked to some friends who'd found him a job with T&T, and David Marsh was now in the happy position of annually distributing millions to various research projects around the world.

Simeon started to make a list of people to call. But he knew that even if he did find some organization to sponsor his work, it wouldn't cover the present problem. These bills had to be paid within a matter of days or his lab would be shut down without ceremony.

He thought about that some more, then stood up.

"Don't worry about it, Denis," he said. "This is my prob-

lem, and I'll take care of it. What we need to do is press
on with the project, full steam ahead."

"Yes, sir." Denis hesitated, looked as if he were about
to say something, then went back to his bench.

The phone rang. "Dr. Halstead?" asked a pert female
voice. "Yes, sir, please hold for Mr. Rob Lawson, head of
Research Accounts."

Here it comes, thought Simeon. How am I going to get
out of this one?

Rob Lawson sounded like an old man, with a quavery
voice, but he didn't beat around the bush. "There are a
couple of things I need to discuss with you, Dr. Halstead,
in person," he said. "Can you come down to my office?"

"Now?"

"Now."

Simeon thought fast. "No, I can't," he said. "Sorry."

There was a pause. "This matter has to be addressed as
soon as possible, Dr. Halstead," said Lawson. "But if we
can't do it today, we'll do it tomorrow. After lunch?
Around two?"

"Fine. Where are you located?"

Lawson told him. His office was in the accounts building.
Simeon knew where that was, about five minutes' walk on
the other side of the campus, next to the big new legal
building.

Simeon then made a number of phone calls, the last
being to David Marsh at Thomson and Thomson. Marsh
remembered him well, and when Simeon told him he was
looking for research funding, Marsh suggested he come to
visit him in New Jersey, and they set up a time for early
the next week.

Edwina, still in her O.R. greens, came over to ask him a
couple of questions about the project, then, just as he was
settling down to some serious work with the microwave
equipment, the door opened and Sam Seidel came in with
a youngish, slightly disheveled-looking man dressed in a
white open-necked shirt and olive-colored chinos.

Sam put out his hand and said hello to a rather reluctant
Simeon. "I'd like you to meet Dr. Paolo Mendez, from
Puerto Vallarta, Mexico." Sam pronounced it *Mayhico,* in

the Spanish way. "Paolo, this is the famous Dr. Simeon Halstead that I've told you about."

Simeon sighed under his breath and shook hands with Paolo, who had a warm, soft handshake and a smile that was gentle and unaggressive. Not the kind of firm, I'm-as-much-of-a-man-as-you-and-maybe-more handshake that Americans are taught early in life, Simeon thought. It was a change to meet somebody who wasn't trying to impress him.

"Good to meet you," said Simeon.

Paolo nodded, as if he couldn't quite decide what to say. He had a shy, diffident look, with big brown eyes that nevertheless appeared to take in everything that was going on. For a second, there even seemed to be the faintest touch of surreptitious humor in his gaze, but Simeon might have been wrong about that. At any rate, there was only humility in his voice when he spoke.

"Sam has told me many good things about you, sir," he said to Simeon. His voice was soft, musical, but again there were the faintest vibrations of something quite unsubservient, and Simeon sensed a very alert and independent mind tucked away inside this gentle and unsophisticated-looking person.

Edwina was watching Paolo with interest, and Simeon introduced her, then Denis and Sonia.

"Sam, you should have called," said Simeon. "Because right now isn't a good time to show Dr. Mendez around." He turned to Paolo. "How long are you going to be in New Coventry?" he asked.

Sam replied for him. "Just a few days. There's a lot going on back at the Vallarta clinic, and he can't stay away too long—right, Paolo?"

Again Paolo nodded vaguely, as if he understood only in the most general terms what Sam was saying.

"Dr. Halstead's very anxious to talk to you," said Sam, looking from Simeon to Paolo. "Seeing as how you're both working in the same kind of field."

Paolo turned his big eyes from Edwina to Simeon, but said nothing.

Simeon said, "How about Friday? This Friday morning, about eight? Here?"

"That'll be just fine," said Sam. "Will you remember that, Paolo? Friday at eight?"

"You won't need to bring him," said Simeon to Paolo, indicating Sam with a nod of the head.

"I'm his transportation," said Sam.

"You could take a bus," said Simeon, ignoring Sam.

"We're on our way, then," said Sam, going to the door. "See you Friday."

As Simeon worked with Denis on the computer analysis of the microwave probes, it became clear to both of them that the rat might not be the best experimental animal for this particular purpose.

"The brain's just too small," said Denis, rolling his chair away from the computer. He was looking tired and frustrated. "We can't get reliable attenuation data, because the distance from the tip of the probe to the intersecting point is too short." He leaned forward and pressed a couple of buttons on the keyboard. "Look, sir, we're only talking a few millimeters, one and a half centimeters at most. So we can't be too accurate with predictions of drop-off in energy levels when we extrapolate to a human brain."

Simeon nodded thoughtfully. When he was in London, he'd done most of his experimental work with rats, so when he was setting up this series of experiments, he'd naturally assumed that it would work with them. He hadn't expected this particular problem. "We're going to have to make do," he said, after thinking for a few moments. "It's too late to change to any other type of animal, and anyway, the probes were made specifically for this job and we can't buy new ones. If you plug in that new statistical software package, I think we should get what we need. It's a very powerful program, and it should be able to get us the attenuation predictions if we input the parameters directly. It was made to analyze very small differentials, exactly the kind we'll be getting here."

Denis's frown lightened. "Yes, of course . . . I'd forgotten about that stats pack. I'll set it up now. So you think we should go on with the rat experiments, then? They're still scheduled to start tomorrow morning."

"Yes. Where are we doing them? Here?"

"Yes, sir, as you suggested. It would waste a lot of time setting up all our equipment in the animal lab."

"Good. Now I'm going over to see how Edwina and Sonia are doing." He glanced at the two women. They were working at the opposite end of the lab and had their backs turned. "Any messages?" He grinned at Denis. "For either of them?"

Denis blushed. "No, sir, thank you. I don't think either of them has any desire to hear from me."

"Are you and Sonia having problems again?"

"There always seems to be something," said Denis. "And it's getting worse. Aside from this project, all we seem to talk about nowadays is relationships. We used to talk about films, books we'd read, lots of things. I'm so bored with it now that I've stopped saying anything." He paused for a second, watching Simeon. "Even talking less doesn't help, Dr. Halstead, because she just takes up the slack, and the conversations don't get any shorter."

"Did something happen to trigger all this?"

Denis hesitated, and his blush, which had almost gone, reappeared. "She thought I was interested in Edwina," he said. "And, I suppose, I *was* interested, sort of, but nothing serious, you know . . ."

Simeon nodded encouragingly. "She'll get over it," he said. "I mean Sonia. She's devoted to you."

"Yes, sir," said Denis glumly. "Where did you put the stats package?"

"It's in with the new programs," replied Simeon. "Should be on the top."

"Women aren't easy, sir," said Denis, glancing at them.

"No kidding." Simeon stood up and went across the room.

Edwina and Sonia were making good progress, better than he and Denis were doing with their microwave probes.

"We're getting there," said Edwina when he came up. "Take a look at this."

On the screen was a color-coded column of names of amino acids, collected in sequences according to the coagulation temperatures of the proteins they combined into. Most of them had similar characteristics to the ordinary proteins that made up the astrocyte cells, which started to coagulate when exposed to a temperature of 42 degrees Celsius for longer than two minutes. The five proteins at the bottom of the list coagulated at a temperature of 1½ degrees lower than the regular proteins did, and that temperature was theoretically attainable in the tumor tissue using the three microwave probes.

"We've narrowed it down to these five possible candidates," said Edwina. She did something on the keyboard, and the screen flashed up the structure of each of those amino acids in three-dimensional color. "The problem is to get them to combine the way we want them to once they get into the cells," she went on. "We've started to use a DNA template now, and that should pretty well guarantee it."

"That was Edwina's idea," said Sonia.

"Great. What are the coagulation values?"

"Good. Better than good."

"How much incorporation do you expect to get in the tumor tissue culture?" Simeon knew that this was one of the critical factors. How much of the amino acids was taken up by the cancerous tissues, and how much of it was converted into the hypercoagulable protein?

"Enough. Over ninety-five percent." Edwina's smile was full of confidence. "According to our computer simulation, anyway. We'll find out for sure soon."

Chapter 38

First thing next morning, Denis went over to the animal house and came back carrying two wire cages, each containing four white laboratory rats. He put the cages on the teak bench. The rats looked out at their new surroundings with their pink eyes, accepting rather than curious.

Simeon sniffed. "It doesn't matter how clean they are, rats always manage to stink," he said.

"Have you ever worked with bats, Dr. Halstead?" Denis opened one of the cages, put his hand in, and brought it out holding a rat in the approved manner, by the back, one finger on either side of the nape of the neck so that it couldn't bite. "I did, doing some echolocation experiments, when I was in the RAF, at the Farnborough research labs. Now those suckers *really* stink."

"Any animal that ends in *at* stinks," grinned Simeon, taking a syringe and giving the rat a dose of quick-acting intraperitoneal anesthetic. "Rat, polecat, bat . . ."

"Brat," said Denis, thinking of his sister's year-old child.

The rat went limp a few moments later, and they placed it in the previously prepared apparatus, with its head firmly positioned inside the metal ring that held the three microwave probes. These were attached to the computer, and data on the screen gave the precise coordinates of each probe, indicating the focal point where the three beams intersected.

"Low power input for rats one and two, right, sir?" Denis went around to the keyboard.

Simeon nodded. He checked the position of the metal ring, and the numbers flipped on the screen. This particular breed of laboratory rat had remarkable anatomical uniformity, so the complicated positional measurements had to be done only once for the whole batch.

"Power input eight seconds."

Denis typed that in. "Ready when you are, sir."

"Go."

They watched in silence while the microwave radiation beams invisibly and soundlessly passed through the rat's brain. The cumulative dose counters from each probe spun faster than they could follow them, then after exactly eight seconds stopped.

"One down," said Denis. He disconnected the rat from the apparatus and took it, still limp, over to the bench, putting its neck on the metal edge of a guillotine-type paper cutter. He pulled the handle down, and off came the rat's head. Pinching the still-pumping neck, Denis dropped the body into a plastic-lined garbage can, then clipped an identifying tag on one ear before dropping the head into a bottle containing a formalin preservative solution.

The next rat, not quite as docile, managed to get its head around to bite Denis's finger.

Denis was philosophical. "I'm glad it wasn't a *Rattus Norvegicus*," he said, sucking his finger. "Those guys can just about take your effing finger off."

"Here, put on some betadine," said Simeon, pouring some brown solution out of a bottle onto a piece of gauze.

Two hours later the first series of experiments was finished.

"And off go the six little rats to Minneapolis," said Denis after placing the six containers with the heads in a special mailing pouch. He put the pouch on a postal weighing scale. "They seem to have lost a lot of weight this morning."

"Off go the six little rats to Minneapolis," repeated Simeon in a musing tone. "It sounds like the first line of a children's story." Suddenly he thought about children. He wanted a family, but he knew that Elisabeth was not the person he wanted to have the family with.

"When do you think we'll get the results back?" asked Denis, cleaning up the bench.

"I talked to the lab director in Minneapolis a couple of days ago," said Simeon. "He said he'd put them through as fast as possible, but it's not a routine test, and they have to do a special setup, special stains, stuff like that. It may take a while."

"I think the girls are ahead of us," said Denis. "They're all set to test the amino-acid uptake and conversion in tissue-culture." Denis hesitated, his eyes on Simeon. "That's going to cost a lot of money, sir, and we don't have it."

"Right." Simeon sounded distracted. His mind was rushing ahead, thinking of what he had to do before his meeting with Rob Lawson, the university accountant and trying to decide how to pitch his request for funds to David Marsh, the now important vice president for outside research funding at Thomson and Thomson. David had sounded very enthusiastic and didn't see any difficulties. Listening to him, Simeon felt a moment's envy. David had not been the best surgeon in the world and had dropped out because he couldn't stand the strain, but with this job he had certainly landed on his feet. It must be a nice feeling, thought Simeon, to be so generous with millions of dollars of other people's money and to be very well paid for handing it out.

Simeon got that uptight feeling he always experienced when he was forced to think about money. He'd never been good with it; the stuff came and went without his noticing its passage. Elisabeth, who had been born into a much wealthier family than his, was much more focused; she knew about investments, tax-free municipals, IRAs, and such things. They kept their money separate, but she contributed to the household finances only when she sold a piece of her sculpture, and that wasn't often. As a successful neurosurgeon, Simeon had made a lot of money, especially in the last few years, but most of it seemed to disappear to taxes and mortgages and overhead of one kind or another.

"I'm going to my office," he told Denis, but he was feeling restless and decided to take a quick walk first.

It was a clear, calm day, unusual for the second half of July, and the feathery outlines of high cirrus spread across the pale blue sky. Elm Street was busy, as usual. An ambulance siren howled and died as the boxy white vehicle turned the corner, rolled up the ramp, and came to a stop outside the emergency room entrance. Simeon walked past a hot dog stand near the corner of Elm and Broad, tended by a fat young man in a vast, grubby white apron. He was squeezing a wiggly line of yellow mustard onto a hot dog evidently destined for his own consumption.

The lights were changing, and as Simeon sprinted across the street, he was reminded of how much he liked running, so he kept going around the block, then ran back the half-mile to the hospital, slowing to a sedate walk in the corridors until he reached the emergency stairwell and ran up the steps.

"Did you run all the way up?" asked Victoria, his secretary.

Simeon nodded, out of breath.

"Yes. Any messages?"

"Lots." Victoria looked at Simeon, a serious expression on her face. "Dr. Halstead, a lot of your colleagues are mad that you're not seeing new patients," she said. "You're going to lose your entire referral system."

"I'll be back in a few months," he said. "It'll be all right."

Victoria shook her head. She was a smart, attractive middle-aged career medical secretary who knew what was what.

"It doesn't work like that," she said. "There are plenty of other neurosurgeons in this town. If the referring docs don't think you're reliable, or if you just disappear for a while, like you're doing now, they'll send their patients elsewhere. Look at Dr. Moser. He called this morning, and he was really p ..." Victoria blushed momentarily and caught herself. Simeon grinned at her.

"If he was pissed, you can tell me," he said.

"Yes, he was really angry," Victoria went on without missing a beat. "He'd already told his patient that he was sending her to you, because you were the best, and then he had to call her back and tell her you're not seeing new patients. It makes him look silly, and he won't be sending you more patients in a hurry."

"I'm sure you're right," said Simeon. "But there isn't anything I can do about it now."

"Your mail is on your desk," she said, looking oddly at him.

On the top of the pile was a registered letter with a subpoena for the office records of Andy Markle, requesting copies of any other reports, tests, or materials pertaining to the above-mentioned patient. The letter had been signed for by Victoria.

When he came back to the outer office, Victoria was looking very formal. "Dr. Halstead," she said, "I'm resigning, as of two weeks from today. I like the job, and I like you, but now there isn't enough for me to do here, and I need to be busy. I'm sure you understand."

Simeon stared at her for a moment. "Of course, Victoria. I'll pay you to the end of the month, which is, let's see, in three weeks. If you just finish up whatever you're doing, you won't need to come back after Friday. I'll get a temp. And if you need a reference, I'll be happy to give you one. Thank you. You've been a great worker."

Simeon left a few moments later, and Victoria watched the door close behind him. She shook her head and started to get her things together.

Chapter 39

Simeon stopped off at the Charles Schwab discount brokerage office he used occasionally, then went across the street to his bank. He didn't stay long, and from there he headed across the university campus toward the accounts building, where Rob Lawson was waiting for him. Simeon imagined him as an aged, wizened old sorcerer squatting in the center of his musty financial web.

The weather was getting overcast, and a gentle but insistent southerly breeze was bringing in the rank odor of chemicals from the factories of Bridgeport. It was like New York, he thought. You could tell where the wind was blowing from by the flavor of the pollutants it brought. New Jersey's acrid yellow miasma versus the Bronx's toxic brown stink. The morning's cirrus clouds had been replaced by a high stratus, and the sun was now a glowing yellow disk. A few of last year's dead leaves kicked up and rustled in sudden spirals as he left the green sward of the campus, past the new legal building, which was now the de facto center of the university's operations. Well-dressed young men in dark suits walked in and out of the huge glass door; uniformed security men stood respectfully on guard.

The accounts building wasn't nearly as grand. Rob Lawson's office was on the third floor. The entire floor was open plan, with four-foot-high partitions dividing the area into a maze of little offices and alcoves and narrow passageways, with rows of old filing cabinets that Simeon had to squeeze past to get to the part that Lawson inhabited. There it was a little more roomy, but not much.

"Go right in, Dr. Halstead," said the young man at a tiny desk outside Lawson's office.

Almost as Simeon had imagined, Rob Lawson was small,

elderly, and wizened, with a triangular face and a pointed, gnomelike chin. His eyes were bright and watchful behind his half-glasses, and his small hands moved over his papers with purpose and precision. Simeon had a quick impression of a man who had seen just about anything that could come down his particular pike and knew exactly what to do about it, quickly, without muss or fuss.

"Ah, yes," said Lawson. "The famous Dr. Halstead." He grinned and sat back, examining his visitor with interest, then reached over to a side table for a folded spreadsheet printout with faint green stripes across it. He opened it up, looked at it, then glowered accusingly at Simeon over the top of his glasses. "You have one of the smallest outside grants in the entire medical school," he said, "and you're giving us the most trouble."

Simeon crossed his legs and waited.

"The university owes, on your behalf, a lot of money. One hundred and twenty-two thousand and eighteen dollars, to be exact."

Lawson folded the spreadsheet and put it back where he'd got it. Simeon had the feeling that he had all the numbers memorized and hadn't needed to look at the paper at all.

"You don't have that amount in your research account, Doctor," Lawson went on. "Not even close."

Simeon nodded.

"Do you have other research moneys that we can transfer over to that account?" asked Lawson.

"No," said Simeon.

Lawson, beginning to look a little irritated, glanced at the clock. Simeon guessed he was anxious to get back to his other accounts, fat multimillion-dollar projects that functioned like clockwork, shedding without complaint their statutory twenty or more percent to provide the university's share.

"Well, then, doctor," said Lawson, putting his gnarled little hands together, "What do you suggest we do?"

"Can you lend me the money?" asked Simeon.

Lawson seemed to swell up in his chair. "Lend you the money, doctor? Do you think this is Household Finance?"

"I didn't think so," said Simeon. "I was joking. How much did you say it was?"

"One hundred and twenty-two thousand and eighteen dollars exactly," replied Lawson, watching Simeon with his sharp little eyes. His eyes widened when he saw Simeon take a checkbook out of his pocket, lean over the desk, and hold it open with his right hand.

"How shall I make it out?" asked Simeon.

Lawson's mouth opened, but he didn't say anything for a moment.

"Is that ... your own personal money?" he asked.

"Yes," replied Simeon. "How did you say I should make it out?"

"Now just wait a minute," said Lawson, putting both hands on the desk and staring at his visitor, as if Simeon had suddenly grown horns and a tail. "Are you proposing to *loan* this money to your research grant?"

"No," said Simeon, writing. "I incurred the expense, so I'm paying for it."

"I can't believe this," said Lawson, half to himself. Then to Simeon, "Are you paying this out of a trust fund, or ... or an endowment, or what?"

"Out of my standard checking account," said Simeon cheerfully. He passed the check across the desk, but Lawson wouldn't touch it. "I cashed in most of my retirement fund. The teller at the bank thought I'd won the lottery."

"This is insane," muttered Lawson.

"You have a better suggestion?" asked Simeon.

"I don't," said Lawson. "But it doesn't make sense to do it like that ... Wait a minute," he said. "Are you using this to take a tax loss?" His eyes cleared. That would make a lot more sense. If Simeon had sold stock at a loss to get this money, he'd be able to deduct the amount of the loss from that year's income tax.

Simeon shook his head. "No tax loss," he said. "Sorry. Actually, I'm not a bad investor," he went on modestly. "Most of my stocks actually made money."

"Then why ... ? Look, Dr. Halstead," he said. "If you really want to pay this out of your own money, there are ways ..." He looked up at the clock again and sighed. "For example, you could set up your own nonprofit foundation.

There are all kinds of tax laws that will work to your benefit if you do that. You could put together a charitable organization, like a limited partnership dedicated to contributing to certain projects that would be specified by you . . ."

Lawson was sounding like a counselor trying to talk someone out of jumping off a bridge.

"But this way . . ." Lawson flicked the back of his hand at the check on his desk, ". . . this way you're just throwing money away."

"Thanks for the advice," said Simeon. "I appreciate it. But I'd go nuts with foundations and partnerships and financial devices like that. I'd get into worse trouble with them, sooner or later. So this is the way I'm going to do it," he went on, nodding at the check. He grinned at Lawson. "No big deal," he said. "I'll just have to work a bit harder next year."

"If you've really given the matter proper consideration," said Lawson, not happy to be participating in such a crazy transaction, "I'll take your money." He reached forward and took the check. "But what happens now? Do you have more bills coming in? Are you lining up some other financial support?"

"Nothing definite," replied Simeon. "But I have a couple of possibilities."

"Good." Lawson hesitated. "I hope you get them. Look," he said, "I'll personally help you to set up a foundation, if you like. I can explain to you how it works, make sure we send in the necessary IRS and state forms, stuff like that." He raised his hand. "Just think about it, okay? There's no point bankrupting yourself, especially for a project that I've heard isn't . . ." Lawson caught himself, and his wrinkled face reddened for a second. He stood up. "Let me know, Dr. Halstead. I'm here to help you, as Romulus said to the Sabine women." He grinned. "You read Plutarch?"

"A long time ago," said Simeon, smiling back. "But I remember that bit. What Romulus meant, though, was that he was there to help himself. And so he did."

They both laughed.

Lawson walked around his desk and stuck out his hand.

He was even smaller standing up, a little bowlegged, wizened man who nonetheless seemed to expect people to look up to him.

"Thanks for the money," he said. "Can you find your own way out?"

Chapter 40

That Friday, Paolo Mendez appeared, by himself, at the lab as scheduled. Apparently Sam had no desire to see what Simeon was doing in his lab, and so he had dropped Paolo off. Listening to Paolo's soft, hesitant voice, Simeon got the strong impression that Sam and Paolo were not hitting it off too well. Paolo still hardly fit the bill of a medical doctor visiting a world-renowned medical center. With his faded greenish cotton jacket and well-worn chinos, Paolo looked more like someone from the housekeeping department on his day off.

Simeon brought him in, and they chatted for a few moments with Denis and Sonia, who were both too busy to spend more time with him. Edwina wanted to hear more about what he was doing, so Simeon put her in charge of the visitor.

"Bring Dr. Mendez back to the office when you've shown him what we're doing," he told her.

Half an hour later, Simeon realized that Dr. Mendez hadn't reappeared, and he went out into the lab. He found Edwina and Paolo in a corner, deep in an animated discussion.

"When you're ready," said Simeon. They broke off their conversation, and Paolo followed Simeon into his office.

"So where did you go to med school, Dr. Mendez?" he asked his visitor after he sat down.

"The University of Guadalajara," replied Paolo. "And then I spent a year at Georgetown. But ..." When he smiled, Paolo's smooth brown skin and gentle golden-brown eyes gave him an otherworldly, almost ethereal look. "With all regard for those centers of learning, I learned most of what I know from my father."

"He's a physician?"

"Yes, a healer. Like his father and his father's father and forever before that. My mother, too, with her family. She knows more about herbs and plants than anyone in Mexico. Maybe anywhere."

Simeon was interested but unimpressed.

"Would you like a cup of coffee?"

"A glass of water would be very acceptable, Dr. Halstead, if that isn't too much trouble."

Simeon went to the cooler in the lab and came back with a Styrofoam cup full of water.

Paolo stood up to take it, and clutched the cup with both hands, as if it were a treasure. Then he sat gingerly down again.

Simeon watched him. The sun was shining on the back of his curly, almost frizzy dark brown hair, giving the impression of a halo around his head.

"Dr. Halstead, can you tell me why people get cancer?" asked Paolo, looking at Simeon with his serious brown eyes.

Simeon's own eyes opened wide. This was not the kind of question he was used to fielding. "Why? Well, there's a variety of reasons, I suppose. Genes, for one. And ionizing radiation like X-rays causes cancer, then there are certain kinds of chemicals that can start cancers, hormonal imbalances may play a part, for instance, in cancer of the breast. It may be connected with the aging process and is certainly connected to smoking ..." He shrugged. "I'm sure you didn't want a list. What are you really asking?"

Paolo took a sip of water. It was a small act, but Simeon was observing Paolo carefully, and he felt rather than saw that Paolo had focused all his attention on what he was doing, that his hands had appreciated the lightening of the cup as he drank, his lips had felt and registered the light, woody texture of the Styrofoam, and the cool swirl of water had been tracked all around his mouth and throat until it was gone.

Paolo smiled. "It's interesting how our different cultures define words," he said. "To you, a highly intelligent and scientifically trained person, the question Why? means one thing and sets off a series of logical responses ..." Paolo gave a self-deprecating shrug. "To me, it means something different."

Simeon didn't really want to get into this kind of philosophical discussion because he knew that it could go on forever without coming to a useful conclusion. But there was something about this young man that intrigued him.

"So how would you answer your own question, then? Why do people get cancer?"

"I don't have an answer," said Paolo. "That's the magic of certain questions—they set off a train of thoughts and associations rather than prying out an explanation. As for cancers ... Well, as physicians, we see lots of people with cancers, and there are certain things many of them have in common. Like anxiety ..."

"I suppose if you have cancer, you've got a right to be anxious," said Simeon.

"They're anxious *before* they get it," said Paolo. "My father, who is almost eighty years old and still working as hard as when he was twenty, lived in the same community all his life. He could predict who was going to get cancer, sometimes years before it actually hit them. He could tell by looking at them, talking to them, seeing the way they did things."

Simeon nodded. Before specializing in neurosurgery, he'd seen many cancer cases—stomach, intestines, throat, bones, liver. But he'd never known any of his patients well enough or long enough to associate anxiety with cancer. Paolo's idea certainly wasn't scientific, but what he was saying was interesting.

"How about Andy Markle?" he asked. "And how about small children who get various kinds of malignancies? Do you think that's also caused by anxiety?"

Paolo shook his head. "No, although we adults are wrong if we think that children can't suffer from severe anxieties. Anxiety is only one of the causes, and we don't know *how* anxiety does that kind of damage. We are born with cells that know how to grow and when to stop growing. These cells need a certain environment—oxygen, nutrients, hormones, minerals, fluids ... And we have a system of blood vessels and lymphatic vessels to provide that environment." Paolo looked suddenly embarrassed and glanced at Simeon.

"I'm sorry, Dr. Halstead. Of course you know all that better than I do."

"You're taking this argument somewhere, Dr. Mendez. go on. I'm interested."

"When I was at Georgetown," said Paolo, apparently going off on a different track, "I had a patient, a physician about thirty years old. He was severely allergic to certain kinds of nuts and was unlucky enough to eat a cake that had some of these nuts baked into it. He had a severe reaction, almost died, and was left virtually brainless, bedridden and unable to take care of himself."

Again Paolo stopped to take a sip of water. "We're all allergic to certain things," he went on. "It's part of the immune defenses of our body. And we have powerful mechanisms to prevent these substances from getting to our sensitive little cells. But these mechanisms are not infallible. Look at tobacco smoke. It causes cancer. And we can prevent that, if we want to, by avoiding tobacco smoke."

The door opened and Edwina appeared. "We're going to do some coagulation testing tomorrow, Dr. Halstead," she said, with a quick smile at Paolo. "Will you be around?"

"What time?"

"Eight."

"Yes."

Edwina left, closing the door softly behind her.

Paolo looked at the door. "Now *she* won't die of cancer," he said, smiling. "She glows with confidence and ability. You can see how every cell in her body is tuned and functioning smoothly and perfectly." Paolo paused for a second, then said, "On another topic, did you know that people in love hardly ever get cancer? It only comes after love has died."

"If you taught that kind of stuff to American medical students, the faculty would hang you from a tree," said Simeon.

"But everybody knows that, except in the United States," said Paolo very seriously.

Edwina reappeared at the door. "May I listen in?" she asked Simeon.

"Sure. Come in. Pull up a chair." He turned back to

Paolo. "In a way, I agree with some of what you're saying," said Simeon. "But does that knowledge make any real difference to your patients who have cancer?"

"I think so," replied Paolo, including Edwina in the discussion. "We change their cellular environment, get rid of the toxins, the pesticides we all eat, the food products that cause disordered cell growth, and restore a balance where the cells can regain their health."

"Are you talking about avoiding things like animal fats? Did you see that JAMA study that linked eating burned meat, like meat cooked on a grill, and intestinal cancer?"

"Yes, and that's only the top of the iceberg. Or do you say the *tip* of the iceberg?"

"Either. I suppose it depends on where you're standing." Simeon grinned, then tried to remember something Fiona had said. "Mrs. Markle mentioned that you treat people with cancer by teaching them how to live. Or did I get that wrong?"

"It's not just cancer patients," said Paolo. "I don't know when I'm going to die. Nor do you. It could be one heartbeat from now, or fifty years. What we try to teach our patients—all our patients—is to enjoy and appreciate every second of every hour of every day. Most of the time none of us pay real attention to ourselves or to what's around us. We think we have an endless procession of days ahead, so each individual day doesn't have any particular value. The pattern that many of us fall into is to regret what happened yesterday and worry about what's going to happen tomorrow. So today . . . well, it gets lost too. What my father has taught me is to focus, to concentrate *totally* on everything around us, everything we do, and give meaning to every moment. Then we don't have time to think ahead, and thinking ahead is the root source of fear."

Simeon grinned. "I agree with you. And time does get lost." He shook his head. "A couple of years ago I was making a professional resumé for a grant application. And somehow I lost a year. I simply couldn't remember what I'd been doing at that particular time. An entire *year*!"

"My father could tell you what he had for breakfast any day you chose, ever since he was a boy," said Paolo.

"That's amazing," said Simeon. "I always admire people with that kind of memory."

"Yes." Paolo smiled his gentle smile. "But of course, he's had the same breakfast every day since he was a child. Six slices of mango and two glasses of goat's milk."

Edwina, her lips slightly parted, was watching and listening to Paolo, and smiled.

Simeon laughed. "So what kind of success have you had with your treatment?"

"I only mentioned a small part of what we teach our friends and patients. Much of it has to do with other parts of our needs, like silence, comfort, meditation, exercise, and a sense of integration with nature and life on this planet."

"Successes?" Simeon the scientist wanted some statistics from Paolo.

"Yes," said Paolo. "Excuse me. Each day of life," he went on, "if it's happily spent, is a success. That's what we aim for. We don't even think about the cancers."

The sun had moved, and Paolo's hair stood black against the white-painted wall, now without its halo. "But to answer what you really meant by your question, yes, we have had some cures. Not all, of course. Not even many. They might have got better without us. But some . . . Even some that you would have given no hope for."

"How do you like working at the Vallarta clinic, Dr. Mendez?" Simeon was a little puzzled. Paolo's philosophy didn't seem to jibe too well with what he knew about Sam Seidel's.

For the first time, Paolo seemed to waver. He thought about the question. "I'm trying to get them to adopt some of my ideas," he said. Then he smiled, a beautiful, open smile that reflected his attitude as much as his words. "Everything worthwhile takes time, doesn't it, Dr. Halstead?"

Simeon sat for a few moments, thinking, looking at Paolo, evaluating, putting his thoughts together.

"Let me tell you what the situation is with Andy Markle, as I see it," he said. "You probably already know that he has a malignant astrocytoma, located just above the optic chiasma. I operated on him, let's see, a little less than five months ago. I removed most of the tumor, all I could get without causing serious nerve damage. The pathology confirmed the diagnosis, but it didn't look like a particularly fast-growing tumor." Simeon took a deep breath. "I discussed chemotherapy and radiotherapy with them, but neither the boy nor his mother wanted to go that route." He put his hands together on the desk. "What is going to happen here, unless we have some kind of miracle, is that the tumor will grow back and Andy will die sometime in the next few weeks or months. Of course we're trying our best to have a working anti-tumor system developed that might help him in time, but we have to be realistic."

Paolo was watching him with his deep brown eyes. Simeon could almost see the thoughts dancing behind them.

"I've listened carefully to everything you've said, Dr. Mendez," Simeon went on, "and I have to make a recommendation to Mrs. Markle. I honestly don't believe that taking Andy to Mexico would extend his life or be of any other help to him. I don't think you can do anything that will slow the progress of his tumor, let alone cure it, and I don't believe in giving people false hope. That's what I'm going to tell Mrs. Markle, and that's going to be my advice to her."

Paolo stood up slowly. "I understand, Dr. Halstead. In fact, I had predicted your response. All I ask you, sir, is that you think, really think, about our conversation this afternoon. With great respect, I don't believe you heard very much of what I said. Thank you for taking the time to show me your work. I truly hope you get good successes with it."

Edwina stood up, gave Simeon a quick, reproachful look, and went back into the lab.

Simeon and Paolo shook hands, Paolo with his soft and almost feminine handshake, then Simeon showed him out. He had already dismissed him and his crazy ideas from his mind.

Before going back to the lab, he decided to call home, for no particular reason.

It rang several times before she answered it, and when she picked up, Elisabeth had laughter in her voice as if she had just been talking to someone there.

But it was the way she spoke, the way she said the simple

word *hello* that made him put the phone quietly back in its
cradle without saying anything.

He sat there for a while, feeling the last shreds of his
allegiance to her slipping away.

Part Four

Chapter 41

Three weeks later, Victor Markle came back to New Coventry. He had been away almost a week, and had slept in Holiday Inns in Atlanta, Dallas, Denver, and Washington, the last being an unexpected stop when they added the flight to his schedule. What a romantic life he led, he thought sarcastically, so full of exciting travel and adventure. And none of the women he knew had been available in any of those places.

But the worst part of the entire trip had been on the last flight, from Atlanta to Dulles International. It was an add-on flight, one that he legally didn't even have to do. That's what comes of being a nice, agreeable guy, he thought furiously. Damned if he'd ever do that again.

The aircraft had been a Boeing 737, known affectionately to flight crews across the world as the "flying guppy." The captain, Ev Gerard, was an old-timer, a spare, white-haired former C5A jockey, competent, uncompromising, humorless, and said to be next in line to be the company's chief pilot. Victor didn't like flying with him, and the feeling was reciprocated, although Gerard never gave him any indication of that.

When Victor came on board, he found that he knew one of the flight attendants, an attractive young woman by the name of Janine Stewart. Janine and he had spent a night together at the Chicago Hilton about two years before, after a stormy and eventful flight into O'Hare, but neither of them had followed up on that encounter.

Now Victor was feeling very horny after his prolonged celibacy—it had been almost two weeks since he'd spent time with his latest friend in New Coventry. He joked and chatted Janine up while they waited for the passengers to board, and he felt that she was responding nicely—although in fact she was being merely polite and had no intention of starting anything up again. Halfway between Atlanta and Dulles, Janine came onto the flight deck to see if either Ev Gerard or Victor wanted coffee or something to eat. Gerard was having a nap, and Victor was flying the plane. Actually he was doing nothing; the plane was on automatic pilot, and Victor was thinking about how he could make it with Janine. He turned when he heard her come in, and when she stepped close to them behind the seats, Victor playfully slipped his hand between her legs, all the way up. Caught by surprise, Janine yelled and slapped his face hard. Ev Gerard awoke, startled, and saw what was happening. Victor was very embarrassed, mumbled an apology, and nothing more was said until after the flight, when he and Gerard were leaving the aircraft.

"I'm reporting that incident back there in the cockpit, Markle," he said coldly. "I hope they throw the book at you."

So when he arrived home in New Coventry, with all his other problems coming back to him, Victor was not feeling happy. His apartment was hot and stuffy, and after taking a shower, he made a couple of phone calls. But neither of the people he talked to would give him information over the phone, so he changed out of his uniform, put on a shirt and a pair of slacks, and went out into the street. It was already getting hot; the walls of the office buildings radiated heat at him, and a smoky yellow sky veiled the sun.

The offices of Gold, Reilly, and O'Connell were much cooler. Haiman Gold kept him waiting twenty minutes, and when he did come out, he leaned against the doorpost and talked to him as if he were on his way to a more important appointment.

"We can't take this case. I'm sorry, Mr. Markle," he said. "In fact, you've put us in a very bad position. We subpoenaed Dr. Halstead's office and hospital records, everything you suggested, and there wasn't anything we could build a case on. Then we found that you had forged your ex-wife's signature on the release forms. I have to tell you now that if anyone follows up on that, we'll have to make a full disclosure, and then you could find yourself in serious legal trouble."

Victor left, feeling severely shaken. He had been counting on Gold's taking the case and making a whole lot of money out of it; he hadn't realized how much he'd got caught up in the project. In his head, he'd already built his skiing chalet in Colorado, his vacation spot in Bermuda. Damn Fiona, he swore as he came back into the bright sunlight; if she'd been a bit more cooperative, this wouldn't have happened.

Two blocks further down Orange Street, Victor went into a much smaller, much less impressive office building and walked up to the third floor and through a door marked B. D. Investigations.

Mr. Bandra Deshar, a small, dark-skinned man in a wide-shouldered brown suit, stood up deferentially and shook Victor's hand over the top of his crowded desk.

"There isn't much to tell you," he said. "We have a list of visitors to your house during the period you specified, the time they arrived and the time they left. We have the names of most of them ..." He opened a grubby file on his desk and passed over a single sheet of typed paper.

"How do you get their names?" asked Victor, without looking at the list. "You walk up and ask them while they're waiting at the front door?"

"Auto registrations, Mr. Markle," replied Mr. Deshar in his singsong voice. He handed Victor another, smaller piece of paper. "And we have a small balance here, sir, if you'd like to take care of that now."

"A *small* balance," said Victor, examining the paper. He flicked the bill with the back of his hand. "You call this a small balance?"

"We discussed my company's terms before I took on the job, sir," said Mr. Deshar, "and you agreed to them." He sounded tired, as if he had this kind of discussion with every client.

Victor grunted, took out his checkbook and a pen, wrote out a check, and left, after folding the typed list and putting it into an inside pocket.

He didn't look at the paper until he got home.

There weren't that many visitors to Fiona's home. Marty

Seidel, the principal of her school had come by a couple of times but hadn't stayed very long on either occasion. There were a few other people whose names appeared only once, repairmen, delivery people, and such like. But one name stood out among the others, as he had suspected.

"The bastard," said Victor to himself, gritting his teeth and staring at the paper. He crushed it in his hand and threw the ball into the wastepaper basket. "That fucking bastard." Then he laughed.

That same morning, before his scheduled fund-raising trip to Princeton, New Jersey, Simeon sat in his office and thought about David Marsh at Thomson and Thomson. The more he thought, the less enthusiastic he felt. He had never cared much for Marsh personally and hadn't had much respect for him as a surgeon when he was working at New Coventry. In spite of Marsh's enthusiastic invitation, certain facts had come to light that made Simeon wonder if the trip was going to be worth the effort. Yes, it was, he reminded himself. He really had to have that research money, and at this stage he didn't have any options about other sources. Then he had an idea, a laugh bubbled silently up inside him, and he pulled his Rolodex file over to him. The person he wanted to reach had moved, but after a couple of tries, he finally got through. His conversation took only a few minutes, but by the time Simeon was ready to leave, he was feeling a burst of lightheartedness that reminded him of his student days. He drove down to the station and took the metroliner to Trenton; from there, he took a taxi for the fifteen miles or so to Princeton, where the headquarters of the Thomson and Thomson pharmaceutical empire was located.

It was like a university campus, on hundreds of acres, with impressive buildings set in a vast and beautifully tended park, flowers and trees and exotic plants vying with each other to make an impression of culture and prosperity. Through the grubby window of the taxi, Simeon watched this triumph of American business skills and wondered how many billions of pills had to be sold annually to support this breathtaking corporate showplace.

At central reception, Simeon was told that David Marsh's

office was in building three. The attractive receptionist checked to make sure that he was expected and issued him a three-hour pass that she personally clipped to his lapel. Five minutes later a uniformed security guard at building three escorted him up to David's spectacular fifth-floor corner office.

David was rather fatter than Simeon remembered him, his square face a little paler, a little puffier; his well-cut suit made him look a lot more prosperous. The place was New Jersey, but the suit, and the shirt and silk tie, were New York. There was a radiance of contentment and security about David that hadn't been there in his previous life. Simeon remembered the tweedy clothes he used to wear, and the slouching, hangdog look he'd had the last time he'd seen him—five years back, just before he left New Coventry.

"Well, long time no see," said David, smiling at Simeon and putting down his telephone before coming around his huge all-glass desk.

"Nice little place you have here," said Simeon, shaking David's hand and taking in the big windows that looked out over the campus. On the left, beyond the manicured green expanse of grass and trees, was a man-made lake, beyond which fluttered tiny red flags on the corporate golf course. Simeon looked around the office. It was large, with what looked like an Isfahan rug in front of the desk and a long matching glass coffee table, with two white leather easy chairs and a sofa disposed elegantly around it.

"How was the trip?" asked David. "Did you come by train?"

"It was okay . . ." Through the window Simeon could see the corporate limousines coming and going, and he guessed that nowadays David probably didn't travel in anything as plebeian as a public train.

"How's Sarah?" asked Simeon.

"Sarah? Ah . . . actually Sarah and I are no longer together," said David. Simeon wasn't exactly surprised. Sarah was a few years older than David; he had married her in haste after an earlier matrimonial disaster and had spent a year persuading his bride to have tummy tucks, buttock reshaping, and breast implants. It must have been a difficult parting for David, considering how much money he'd invested in her.

"And Elisabeth?"

"She's just fine," said Simeon, who was actually wondering what Elisabeth might be doing at that moment.

David went behind his huge desk and sat down. "So, Simeon, tell me, how can I help you?"

Simeon told him about his research and about how much money he thought he would need to complete it.

David sat back and templed his hands. "Astrocytomas ..." he paused. "There aren't too many of those around, are there? Like, a pretty unusual kind of tumor, wouldn't you say?"

"Well, it's actually one of the commoner types of malignancy in my line of work," said Simeon. "It often affects young people and persons in the prime of life, unlike many other forms of cancer, and to my mind that gives it an added importance."

"How many new cases of astrocytoma per year, would you say, in the United States? A million? Two million? More?"

Simeon shook his head. "No. Not nearly that many. Maybe a hundred thousand, tops."

"Oh, dear." David pursed his lips. "Let me tell you about the economics of research, Simeon," he said. "First and foremost, this is not New Coventry Medical Center, and we don't think like academic institutions. Here at Thomson and Thomson, we're members of a corporate team whose primary interest has to be centered on the bottom line. Personally, and between you and me ..."—David glanced at the door as if he expected the Thomson and Thomson thought police to march in and take him away—"I despise that attitude, you know, Simeon, but there it is." He shook his head sadly. "You see, with our corporate policy being what it is, we have to allocate funds according to the scale of the projects. Diabetes, for example. We love diabetes because there are millions of these unfortunate sufferers worldwide who need our insulin, so we can put millions of dollars into further understanding of that disease. Hypertension, stroke, heart disease, these we consider to be fruitful research fields for us to be financially involved in, again because the numbers come out right."

David paused, apparently trying to figure out a way of helping Simeon. "Couldn't your research be, like, tailored to one of these more important diseases? If it was aimed, for instance, at breast cancer, which affects one out of eight American women, I'd truly jump at the opportunity to back you financially."

Simeon smiled. "I don't think so. Does the fact that astrocytomas commonly affect children in any way influence your thoughts?"

A spark of interest lit David's eyes. "Are you talking about a long-term treatment? Years? If so, we could maybe work something out."

Simeon sighed. "I don't think so. This would be, I hope, a one-shot deal. If the treatment is successful, that should be it. If not, repeated treatments would be unlikely to help."

The spark died. "I'm really sorry, Simeon. Have you tried the nonprofit organizations? The American Cancer Society? The National Institutes of Health? They are the ones, in theory anyway, who should help in orphan situations like this."

"Orphan situations?"

"I guess that's our pharmaceutical jargon. Sometimes there are treatments available for rare conditions, but if we're only talking about a few thousand people, we'd lose money if we developed or manufactured the products. We call them orphan situations, and we all stay away from them unless there are overruling financial incentives. As a physician, you would understand that, right?"

Simeon looked surreptitiously at his watch. The call should be coming at any moment, and he wanted it to come before he left. "Well, thanks anyway for trying, David. It sounds as if you really like it here."

"Yes. Life has never been better. Won't you stay for lunch? We have a really superb executive dining room here. The chef used to work at La Coupole ..."

"No thanks, David." Simeon stood up. "I'd better be getting on my way back to New Coventry."

David came around his desk. "Look, Simeon," he said

earnestly, "why don't you consider coming to work for us? Getting out of clinical surgery and coming here was the best move I ever made. No more indigent clinics, no more nonpaying patients, no more worry about malpractice suits. You'd make a great salary, with bonuses, stock options, and the benefits are superb. Look, if you like, I could have you meet one of our senior vice presidents right now."

"Thanks, David, but no thanks. I happen to like my indigent patients, and I'd feel insecure without the threat of malpractice suits hanging over my head." He grinned, trying to keep the conversation going as long as possible. "Do you ever come back to New Coventry?"

"If I never see that place again, it'll be too soon," said David, with an exaggerated shudder. "I didn't mention that you'd get almost unlimited travel, we have meetings all over the world, and there's always room for promotion if you're a good team player."

"That would disqualify me instantly," said Simeon. "Can I call for a taxi?"

"The people down at the security desk will be happy to do that for you," replied David. "And think about what I said. I'm really sorry we couldn't help with the astrocytoma project. Give my love to Elisabeth and have a safe trip back."

Something about the way David had been talking, some subliminal interpersonal vibrations, made Simeon pause. He stared at David. "Have you talked to Felix Cadwaller recently?" he asked casually.

David flushed a bright pink and turned away. "Well, yes, I have, actually," he said. "We've kept in touch. Actually I believe he gets some research money from us . . ."

At that moment the phone rang, and with obvious relief David excused himself and picked it up. His square face seemed to freeze. "HHS? Pharmaceutical Oversight? I don't think . . . Yes, of course, I'll be happy to talk to Dr. Posner."

Marsh had gone white and his eyes flickered uncertainly over to Simeon. "Yes," he said after a short wait. "Yes, I am in charge of research funding for T&T . . . an investigation?" Marsh glanced at Simeon again, licked his lips, then turned away. "I'm sure that won't be necessary," he said.

Then he stiffened, and his disbelieving gaze went back to Simeon, who had sat down again and was unconcernedly examining his nails. There was a long pause, then Marsh said, in a suddenly obsequious voice, "Yes, Dr. Posner, I'm sure we'll be able to accommodate him. Certainly. Thank you. And I'm very, very glad you can accept my assurance about the integrity of our research funding program here at Thomson and Thomson."

Marsh put the phone down slowly and contemplated Simeon for a few moments. "That was your friend Dr. Richard Posner," he said. "Chairman of the Pharmaceutical Oversight section at HHS. It sounds as if he's taking his new job very seriously. Now, Simeon, tell me again how much was it you needed for your astrocytoma project?"

An hour later, a shaken David Marsh had worked out an interim plan that would cover Simeon's research budget for six months, but because of Thomson and Thomson's inflexible accounting rules, there was no way he could make the money available until the beginning of the next month, three weeks away. Marsh was almost in tears.

"Don't worry," said Simeon, trying to keep from laughing. "I'll manage to get by until then."

On the train back to New Coventry, Simeon gazed out at the rolling hillsides, at the picture-book fields and farms nestled in green valleys, separated by long stretches of woodland. These soon gave way to more crowded suburbs, cookie-cutter brick houses jammed together; then the bleak and desolate New Jersey industrial wastelands appeared, and the yellow sky darkened in a hellish chemical twilight. Approaching Elizabeth, New Jersey, the train swayed and rattled slowly onto a high bridge over the drained marshland. Elisabeth. Simeon's internal hilarity about the brief interchange between his friend Richard Posner and David Marsh gave way to a more somber mood. He thought about his wife with a detachment that had increased over the last few weeks. Was it his growing feelings about Fiona that had done that? He didn't think so, but there was no question that his whole attitude toward Elisabeth had changed to the point that he'd soon have to do something definitive about it.

Through the window Simeon saw the old bridge's angled

network of rusty beams and bolts and wondered if there would be a train on it when it finally collapsed. Building after gray building, warehouses with trucks nestled up to the delivery bays like rows of suckling piglets, a wire-enclosed parking lot packed with dirty school buses, huddled together like a flock of dim-witted yellow sheep. In the gray, blurred distance, past the buses, Simeon could see a dark line of water, all its life and sparkle drained away by the polluted air, and beyond that the barely visible city of Bayonne. To the right he could just make out the featureless, hilly outlines of Staten Island—impersonal, still, and unfriendly, silhouetted like a hulking mastiff.

Maybe it was because of the dismal countryside, but as the train got closer to New Coventry, Simeon felt drained of all the amusement and good humor he'd felt on leaving the Thomson and Thomson campus. Even though his research would now be financially secure, there were still a lot of unresolved scientific and technical problems with the project, and his own situation was still precarious. He'd given up a good practice, one that had taken years of hard and dedicated work to build up and would not be easy to get going again. Most of his savings had already gone to finance his research, and there was not even a guarantee that the techniques he was developing would ever work.

And Cadwaller was out there, waiting for him, his incestuous heart full of malice and alert to all possibilities of damaging Simeon; he'd proved that once again by getting to David Marsh. Simeon's jaw tightened; sometimes he surprised himself with the force of his hatred for Felix Cadwaller.

Chapter 42

Simeon had left his car in the station parking lot, and after retrieving it he made his way toward the hospital. It was already getting late, the streets were full of traffic, and so many distracting things were passing through his head that he ran a red light before pulling himself together.

The lights were still on in the lab, and as usual, Edwina was there, working away at her hypercoagulable proteins.

She looked around quickly when he came in, and Simeon had the feeling that she'd been waiting for him.

"How was your trip?" she asked. She followed him through to the little office.

"Terrific," he said, smiling. He sat down at the desk and put his feet up on it. "Have you ever been to the Thomson and Thomson headquarters? No? Well, it's wonderful. Bursting with good taste and class, far above the common herd of commerce. There's so much money there, it makes you breathless. And I did manage to carve out a tiny piece of it. Unfortunately it won't be actually in our hands for about three weeks."

"Wonderful," said Edwina. "What a relief!" She paused when she saw that Simeon didn't seem as relieved as she was. "Well, isn't that going to take care of at least some of our problems?" she asked.

"Some of them, yes, of course," replied Simeon. "But the money's coming a bit late in the day, and some problems may arise just for that reason." He wouldn't tell her anything more.

"Can we go ahead and buy supplies?"

"Sure. Whatever you need. By the time they've been charged and billed we should be able to pay for them."

Edwina nodded, then her expression lightened. "Now

that that problem's out of the way," she said, "I have some good news for you. Our hypercoagulable proteins are finally checked out, purified, and ready for animal testing. We're scheduled to do some rats tomorrow morning."

Simeon smiled at her enthusiasm. "I'm glad," he said. "I wish I could say the same for the microwave probes. I have a feeling we're running into a brick wall there."

The discouraged tone in Simeon's voice must have been very obvious, because Edwina stared at him. Her eyes became bright, and she shook her head so hard that her dark hair fell over her face. "We *believe* in this project, Simeon," she said, pushing the hair out of her eyes. "All of us— Denis, Sonia, and me. We're all convinced we can get it to work, in spite of everything." She hesitated. "A week ago," she went on, "Denis was offered a senior job in another lab here, and so was Sonia, in the same lab. They didn't accept, although they'd have got more money and a lot more job security. They're staying because they're just as committed to this as you or me."

They heard the laboratory door open, and Edwina stood up and peered out through the office window to see two cleaners coming in, one pushing a wheeled bucket in front of him.

Edwina returned to her chair, looked at Simeon, and hesitated. "Dr. Paolo Mendez," she said finally. "Don't you really think he could help Andy Markle? As you said, realistically we're not going to be able to do anything for him here."

"No, I don't think he can help," replied Simeon. "You heard our discussion."

"He came back here while you were away," said Edwina. "I talked with him for a long time." She looked steadily at Simeon. "And I must tell you, I'm very impressed."

"By what?" Simeon grinned at her. "The dark, soulful eyes?"

Edwina went pink. "No, of course not . . ." She saw Simeon's teasing glance and said, "Well, a bit, maybe, but what I was *really* thinking about was his ideas about how to help people who have cancer."

"I've been thinking about that too," said Simeon. "He

seems to accept the fact that these patients are going to die. Did I get that right?"

"Sort of," said Edwina, shaking her head again. "But there's more to it than that. To me, anyway, it seems like a totally different way of thinking about patients and their illnesses."

"Yes, it is," said Simeon.

One of the cleaners came to the door of the office, looked in, then retreated with his bucket into the lab.

"What I don't like about it," Simeon went on, "is the 'acceptance' part. Our western medical ethic, our training, doesn't allow us to accept that these patients are going to die. Our job is to do our utmost to prevent that from happening."

There was a silence while Edwina gazed at him. Then that stubborn look came into her eye again. "But they *do* die," she said. "Almost all of them."

Simeon stood up. Much as he liked Edwina, he didn't want to discuss this any further—not until he had clarified some of the ideas that were growing in his mind. "I know that, Edwina," he said. "But if scientific medicine adopted that attitude, we'd never develop cures for anything. We'd still be sympathetically holding our patients' hands while they died of sepsis, or any of the dozens of other apparently incurable diseases we *have* found a cure for."

Edwina stood up too. "Don't you think it's time for both sides to get together?" she asked. "Scientific medicine and alternative medicine? They both have a lot to offer, and if we could get the scientists and the healers to stop squabbling and put their energies where it matters, it would benefit everybody, especially the patients."

"You may well be right," said Simeon. He nodded. "But you know how people are with their prejudices. And of course, the AMA isn't going to let non-M.D.'s get into the act. Not over their dead bodies. It goes against their economic interests."

"A lot of people think that's all the AMA is, nowadays, just a bunch of dead bodies," said Edwina, smiling. "But sooner or later it's going to happen, and I'd like for us to be a part of it."

"Let me think about that some more. I agree it's an interesting idea."

"Yes. Thank you, Dr. Halstead," she said, with that big, confident smile of hers. She hesitated. "May I ask you a personal question?" she asked.

Simeon stopped. "Sure. On the understanding that I may not answer it, okay?"

Edwina's face took on a curiously defiant look. "We're your team," she said. "And we're all on your side, Denis and Sonia and me. We've gotten to know you pretty well, and we worry about you. Sometimes you look so sad ..."

"What's your question, Edwina?" he asked, his tone sharper than he wanted it to be.

"Nothing, I guess," said Edwina. "We hear stuff, and we just figured that things must be tough for you at home. Like I said, we're totally on your side, if it's any help for you to know that."

"Thanks, Edwina." A curious expression came over Simeon's face. "I ... I really appreciate what you said. And you're right, things sometimes are difficult at home." His grin was strained. "Maybe that's why I like working here and being with you guys so much."

Edwina went back to the lab, and Simeon followed her.

"I forgot to tell you," said Edwina, "the data came back from the MidWest Path Labs." She pointed at an Express Mail package. "It came this morning."

Simeon picked it up. "I'll look at it tonight," he said. "See you in the morning."

The package, Simeon knew, contained the results of the rat brain microwave experiments, and he was very anxious to see the data.

Elisabeth wasn't home. He wasn't surprised, because these days she went out quite often in the evenings and was usually vague about where she had been. She came in a few minutes later, after he'd gone upstairs and opened the package.

He heard her voice from the bottom of the stairs. "Simeon?"

"I'm here. Upstairs."

"Have you had supper?"

"No. Have you?"

A moment's silence, then Elisabeth said, "Well, not really. Can I get you anything?"

"Don't bother. I'll fix myself something if I get hungry."

Elisabeth appeared at the door of his study, paused for a moment, and came in. She kissed him on the forehead. "How was your trip to Princeton?"

"Okay."

"Did you get what you wanted?"

"More or less. How was your day?" Simeon didn't like these stilted exchanges, but somehow he couldn't escape them. Well, maybe he could. Without waiting for her to answer, he went on, "Elisabeth, are you still seeing Sandra? Sandra Barry?" Simeon had learned to be very specific with her, because she had a great ability to get herself out of trouble by the imaginative use of semantics.

"Of course. I had coffee with her a couple of days ago. We're still good friends."

"Are you still lovers?"

"Simeon, that's all over, and please let's change the subject, okay?"

Simeon sighed. Elisabeth was still as slippery as a Crisco-coated piglet.

She stood next to him and put an arm around his neck. "Simeon, I do love you, you know."

Simeon nodded, a tight, angry feeling building up inside him. He didn't reply.

"I want to make love with you," Elisabeth went on. "I'm hot, and I've been thinking about you all day."

Aside from the fact that they hadn't made love for several weeks, something in Elisabeth's voice alerted Simeon. He pointed to the thick bundle of papers from the Minneapolis lab. "I have to go through this stuff tonight," he said. "Sorry."

Elisabeth came around and sat in his lap. "Don't be like that, Simeon," she said in a cooing voice. She draped an arm around his shoulders. "Come on, let's go up to bed. I'll make you forget all about your silly research."

He smiled at her and gently detached her arm.

When Elisabeth saw that her blandishments were having no effect, she became coldly angry. "That's fine, if that's

how you're going to be. I won't humiliate myself like that
again," she said and went off. He heard her footsteps all
the way downstairs.

Simeon opened the package and spread the different
parts of the report over his desk. It took him more then
an hour to correlate all the results, and the conclusions
were very depressing. The pathologists had evaluated the
damage to the brain tissue along the tracks of the microwave beams, starting at the outside of the brain, the gray
matter, then the white matter below that, all the way to
the point where the rays from the three microwave trans-
mitters met. It appeared that nearly all the microwave energy was absorbed by the brain tissue long before it
reached the focal point. At the lower energy levels, moder-
ate damage was seen in the outside two or three millimeters
of the brain, and at the higher energy levels, severe heat
damage occurred most of the way to the focal point. In
only the experiment at the highest energy level was significant damage done at the focal point. In other words, Simeon told himself, not only did the technique not work,
but there was no way to make it work. The microwave
energy was just about exhausted by the time it reached the
place it was needed, and it burned too much brain tissue
on the way there. And those were just tiny rat brains ...

Simeon pondered the data for another hour, trying to
figure out if more microwave emitters would do the trick.
He recalculated the applied energy levels if they were positioned closer to the tumor, such as inside a frontal sinus,
but it soon became obvious that there was just no way to
make it work.

He broke out into a sweat and pounded on the leather
arm of his chair. The thought of the entire project going
down the drain was simply intolerable, but unless he found
a safe and effective way of heating the part of the brain
that harbored the tumor, the project was indeed finished.
The whole theory of treating the cancer cells so that they
would coagulate with heat depended on there being a safe
and effective way of heating them. And he didn't have such
a way or, at this point, any real hope of developing one,
certainly not in the time remaining before the inexorable
return of Andy's tumor. He thought about all the work that

Edwina had done and about how flawless her results were. He put his head down between his hands and tried to think about what he should do next.

There'll be other patients, said one part of his brain. You can't expect things to go right the first time around. And when you do get a working system, there'll be other kids with astrocytomas that you'll be able to help.

That won't do, said the other part. You *have* to make it work! Get on with it! Don't just sit there like a turd on a sofa, get moving! Think of something! You're running out of time!

All kinds of ideas passed through his head, and he considered any and every possibility, even ones as esoteric as placing a tiny heating unit in the artery that supplied the part of the brain that had the tumor. But there was no way, and he knew it, even though he took the trouble to run some numbers on his computer, using a simulation of the arterial system in the base of the brain.

Then his own tired brain gave way. When that happened, it was always sudden, from one minute to the next. There was no cure for that either, so he switched off his computer, put away the rat brain report, and sat grimly in his chair for a few moments before standing up and wearily going off to bed. There, he lay dozing intermittently until daybreak, but when he got up, he felt tense and desperate, and no farther ahead than he'd been the night before.

Chapter 43

Simeon arrived at the lab at the same time as Denis and Sonia. Edwina had spent the night there and was already up, showered, changed, and ready to go.

This test was quite different from Simeon's and Denis's earlier microwave experiments that had so disastrously failed. Edwina and Sonia's rats had had astrocytoma tumors implanted in their brains. Edwina had first grown the free tumor cells in a tissue culture, then, by immersing the cancerous cells in a nutrient solution containing the specially selected amino acids, she had proved that the tumor cells took up the amino acids and combined them to form a protein inside the cell that coagulated at a temperature of 5 degrees Celsius above normal body temperature. Now they had to find out if the hypercoagulable proteins appeared inside the tumor cells. But they also had to see whether these proteins appeared in other tissues. If they did, then the team had another fiasco on their hands.

"Are you all right?" asked Edwina, glancing at Simeon, who was taking the rats out of the cages before injecting them with the amino-acid solution. Denis was loading the syringes at the other bench.

"Sure," he replied. "Why?"

"You look anxious," she replied, thinking that Elisabeth probably had something to do with it.

"I am. I got the report back on the last set of rats, and it was a disaster. The microwave beam just burns a hole in the brain and peters out before it gets to where it's aimed at. And that's only on rats. The problem gets proportionately bigger with size."

"So for a kid . . ."

"Right."

"Now you've got me anxious too. Thanks."

"You're welcome." He turned to Denis. "We're ready when you are."

Denis brought his equipment over, and Simeon did the amino-acid injections. It was a technically difficult procedure and took more than an hour to complete on the entire contingent of rats.

"How long does it take to absorb?" Denis asked Simeon while they were putting the rats back in their transport cages.

"Four hours. In that time more than ninety-five percent of the injected amount should have been converted into the protein. And it'll stay there for up to three days before it's turned over and starts to disappear. Right, Edwina?"

"Yes, sir," replied Edwina. These days she was being very polite and respectful when there were other people around, unlike her more direct manner when she was alone with Simeon.

Sonia took the cages back to the animal lab, and when she returned, Simeon went over the MidWest Path data with them. They tried to figure out a way to apply heat to the part of the brain where the tumor was located.

"How about if you put tiny pieces of metal next to the tumor?" asked Denis. "They would heat up very quickly in a microwave beam, like if you put a metal pan or foil in a microwave oven."

Simeon thought about that for a moment, then shook his head. "That's a clever idea, Denis, but I don't think it would work," he said. "For one thing, it would mean reoperating on Andy, and nobody wants that because of the dangers involved. Second, it wouldn't be selective enough."

"What do you mean, not selective enough?" asked Edwina.

"I mean it would heat up all the tissues in the area, not just the tumor cells," he replied. "And in any case, the problem is getting the microwave energy to that spot deep inside the brain. That's what we don't seem to be able to do."

They talked about different possibilities for over an hour, but nothing came up that seemed remotely feasible, and finally a depressed silence fell over the group.

"So what do we do now?" asked Denis glumly.

"Good question," replied Simeon. "I've been trying to figure out an answer to that myself." He paused. "I'll be perfectly honest with you," he said. "I don't see a way out of this right now, but we'll keep on trying. Meanwhile, to cheer us all up a bit, I decided to have a cookout at my house this Sunday."

They looked at each other.

Denis opened his mouth to say something, and Sonia jabbed him quickly but unobtrusively with her elbow.

"That'll be wonderful, Dr. Halstead," she said, smiling. "Can we bring anything?"

"Your swimsuits."

"Can we bring food?" asked Edwina. "We can't let you prepare all that stuff yourself."

"Thanks," he said. "Actually Elisabeth will be in charge of everything edible except the steaks. And we all know that grilling steaks is a man's job."

After the other two had gone back to their work, Edwina frowned at him. "We'd heard that you and Elisabeth were separated," she said.

Simeon replied rather coldly, in a tone that suggested it was none of her business. Yes, Elisabeth had left for a while, he told her, but she was now home again.

Fiona was getting increasingly concerned about Andy. For several days, his normally voracious appetite had been off, he seemed listless, and his energy level seemed to be marginally down. She told herself that she was overreacting, that this was a normal fluctuation. It was now only five months since his operation, and Simeon had said he'd probably be clear for six. Probably. A knot gathered in her stomach at the thought that this might be the beginning of his recurrence, the beginning of the end. No, she told herself, agonized. No. From time to time as he was growing up, he would lose his appetite for a day or two. Long before he'd developed the tumor. But then, on Friday, just when she thought that maybe she was merely looking for an excuse to call Simeon, whom she had not seen or spoken to for over a week, she came home from school to find Andy already home and in bed, asleep. This was totally unlike him; even as a small child he hated afternoon naps. As she watched him, he stretched an arm out; it *was* a little thinner—she was sure of it. It wasn't all her imagination.

She went downstairs, checked the time, and called Simeon at his lab. It was late enough that most people had left work, especially since it was Friday, but she knew Simeon would be there.

He picked up the phone, and when he answered, she couldn't help smiling in spite of her anxiety. How many people knew anything about the person behind that quiet, formal voice?

Simeon asked if Andy had had any headaches, any problems with his vision or his sense of balance. Fiona, who had asked Andy more or less the same questions earlier in the day, said no.

"Would you like me to see him?"

"Well, it's not an emergency. I just wanted you to know."

Simeon thought for a moment, then had an idea. "Listen, Fiona, I'm having a cookout at my house this Sunday. Why don't you come and bring Andy? About noon? Then I can have a look at him, and he can have fun, swim in the pool, and eat hot dogs. Also ..." Simeon paused and his voice became softer. "Also I'd be very happy to see you."

"Me too. Andy would love it. Thank you, Simeon."

"Are Andy and Susie Seidel still an item?"

"Yes. They're in love. It's ..." Fiona gulped.

"Good. I'll invite her too, then. And her dad. And Paolo, if he's around. It'll be fun," Simeon went on, with growing enthusiasm. "You and Andy will meet my team. They're working as hard as I am on the project, and they'd love to meet him. And you."

Fiona said, "Are you sure that it'll be okay with your wife ... Elisabeth ...?"

"No problem," he said.

There was a pause.

"Okay," said Fiona. "We'll be there. Is there anything you'd like us to bring?"

"You can bring Victor if you want."

"No, thank you," replied Fiona.

Simeon gave her instructions on how to get to his house

and hung up, happy that he was going to see her but apprehensive about what she'd told him about Andy.

Victor had suspected for some time that the people in his airline were against him, and an unofficial phone call on Friday afternoon from Bob Mulvaney, who held an important position in the pilots' union, confirmed it. Mulvaney had worked with Victor on the Cancer Society drive, knew him as well as he wanted to, and didn't waste any time.

"About that incident in the cockpit a little while back," said Mulvaney. "The company's setting up an investigation, and they advised us officially of that fact yesterday. I talked later to one of the execs on that committee, and he told me confidentially that they're going to fire you."

"That's ridiculous," blustered Victor, feeling a tightness in his throat. "I didn't do anything . . ."

"When that incident happened, you were flying with the wrong captain," said Mulvaney. "Ev Gerard is a stickler for correct crew behavior on and off the aircraft. Also, he doesn't like you."

"So what's the union going to do about it? I pay my dues, I'm entitled to the benefits, and one of the benefits is that you fight for me if I get into trouble with the company, right?"

"Right. Up to a point. But our local executive held an emergency meeting about it last night, and they decided not to fight it."

"What? Who the fuck do they think they are? I'm entitled to be protected against this kind of discrimination . . ."

"Discrimination? You turned Hispanic or black or something?"

"I mean that they've singled me out for punishment. What I did isn't any worse than what half the pilots do all the time. I could tell you some stories . . ."

"There's two more complaints of a similar nature in your record, Victor. For some reason, nobody ever said anything about it until now. But that's why the union isn't going to fight it. We just came out with a strong policy statement about sexual harassment, and obviously we don't want to look as if we're condoning it."

"That's just bullshit, and you know it, Bob. Somebody's

cut a deal. If the union agrees not to fight it, they'll get something in return from the company, some concession down the line. Don't tell me. I know how that works."

'You could be right, Victor. I wouldn't be surprised. Listen, I'm just doing you a favor by telling you this in advance. You'll get notices of hearings, appeal procedures, documents about your rights, until your head spins. But you need to know that it's all just window dressing, because the case has been decided already. You can appeal the decision as long as you want, you can spend every last penny you have fighting it, but you're out. And you can be sure they won't let you back in."

"So what do you suggest I do?" asked Victor.

"Start looking for another job," replied Mulvaney. "But don't bother trying the major airlines."

Victor went back to his apartment, shaking. His airline had a reputation for dealing generously with its employees, and when they laid people off at his level, they usually gave them a six-month cushion with pay, helped them find another job, or gave them other practical assistance. But he knew that nothing like that would come his way; he'd better start hustling. Flying was all he knew anything about, and being a pilot was the only career he'd ever wanted. Maybe he'd do like those two guys he'd read about who bought an old DC-3, took it up to Alaska, and got into the business of hauling fish to market. They'd done really well, and now they had a whole fleet of DC-3s.

But in his heart Victor knew that wouldn't work for him. He'd made lots of professional contacts over the years, but he'd rarely followed up on them, unless they were women. He also knew that his personality often put people off, and he wasn't instinctively liked the way many of his colleagues were. So he didn't have a network, didn't have half a dozen ol' buddies he could call up for help, who would tell him where to look for the good unadvertised openings.

He paced around the apartment in a fury of frustration, trying to figure out if there were any legal maneuvers he could use to keep his job, developing complicated fantasies about what he'd like to do to that self-righteous asshole Ev Gerard.

Then his thoughts turned to Colombia, as they had on a

couple of other occasions in the past. He knew of several pilots who'd flown in that trade for a year or less, then retired on more than they would have made in a lifetime working for a legal airline. It was a scary business, but none of the men he knew had ever been caught; for that, they told him, you had to be stupid or unlucky or both. The way he heard it, the pilot would take off with a full load plus one passenger from some mountain airstrip in Colombia, land for night refueling in the Turks and Caicos Islands, then fly west, low over the water to avoid the radar surveillance, to Florida. At the initial takeoff, they gave the pilot a map with a particular small area of rural Florida marked out. The pilot would find that area, fly at tree level, and circle slowly while the passenger opened the cargo door and pushed the plastic-covered bales out as fast as he could unload them. Then they could land clean in Miami, or at whatever airport they chose.

Victor poured himself a tumbler of bourbon, then went to the phone and sat looking at it for a few moments. No, he thought. None of those guys talk business on the phone. He decided to fly to Miami early next week, while he could still do it for free, and talk to some people he knew there.

Meanwhile, he was looking forward to seeing Andy on Sunday. After their last unpleasant interview, Fiona had returned strictly to the every-other-Sunday visitation schedule, as set out in the divorce agreement. He looked at the clock and picked up the phone. At least he could talk to Andy when he wanted.

Andy answered.

"Hi," said Victor. "How're you doing, kid?"

"Oh, hi, Dad. Okay. I just woke up. You all right?"

"Sure. Are you really okay? You're not getting headaches or stuff like that?"

"No. Well, hardly at all."

"Good. Listen, Sunday we're going to go up to Mystic, stop in at the Seaport, and have dinner at Bravo Bravo. That's that outdoor restaurant next to the bridge. How does that sound?"

Andy's voice sounded cautious. "Sounds fine, Dad, but I think we've already got plans to . . . Here, talk to Mom."

There was a brief silence while Andy handed the phone to Fiona.

"Victor? I'm glad you called, because Andy and I were invited to a cookout on Sunday, and he wants to go. Can you take him some other day?" Fiona's voice sounded strong and assured, but she feared his reaction. Victor didn't like changes in schedule, particularly when it interfered with what he considered his rights.

"Sunday's my day with him," shouted Victor, suddenly furious. "And I'll be goddamned if ..."

"I'm just telling you what he wants to do," said Fiona. "And please don't shout. This hasn't happened before, and the cookout would be a real treat for him. I'm sorry it's on your day, but the cookout invitation just came up. Can you take him next Sunday instead?"

"Let me talk to Andy again."

This time the silence was a little longer, while Fiona handed the phone to Andy and insisted that he take it.

"Yeah, Dad?"

"Is it true that you prefer to go to this ... cookout?"

Andy hesitated. "Well, we thought it would be a lot of fun, because there's a swimming pool there and everything, but if you want me to go with you, that's okay."

"No, you can go. Where is it? I mean the cookout?"

"At Dr. Halstead's."

Victor's grip on the phone tightened.

"Okay. Well, have fun."

"Thanks." Andy hated to have his father upset, and he was feeling desperate about it. "Look, Dad, why don't you come too? I'm sure it would be okay with Dr. Halstead ..."

"No, thanks. I wasn't invited. Listen, I'll see you next week, for sure, okay?"

"Okay. I love you, Dad."

"Yeah, right, I love you too."

Andy hung up first, and Victor slammed the phone back in its cradle so hard he thought he'd broken it.

A few minutes later, feeling angry and depressed about everything that was happening in his life, he left the apartment and walked out. The sun was low, but it was still breathlessly hot, and Victor estimated the temperature and the relative humidity and figured they were both in the nineties. He walked along Elm Street, past the long white-walled main hospital building, which made him think about Simeon Halstead. That son of a bitch ... Wasn't there something in the Hippocratic oath about alienating the affections of a patient? Well, he hadn't really done that, it was the patient's mother, but that was surely as bad. What was the law about stealing a man's wife? Even though he and Fiona were divorced, the principle still held. Maybe he should write to the local medical society and complain about it. It had to be some kind of unethical practice, but of course everybody knew that doctors stuck together and nothing would ever happen, except maybe get Halstead some bad publicity.

Mulling these thoughts over in his head, he crossed the street and went up Yale, to a small liquor store that he frequented.

There were a couple of people inside, and near the door a tall black with a small beret was waiting in line, holding a curved pint bottle of vodka.

Why was that guy wearing a beret on a hot day like this? Victor shrugged to himself. Who knew why niggers did the things they did, and who cared, anyway? He nodded at the proprietor and went over to the shelf where they stocked the bourbon. He bought a half-gallon of Old Crow. He looked at the picture of the crow on the label. It reminded him of his mother. As the crow flies ... At that moment, he decided to go to Miami the next day. Saturday was a good day to find people. And there was no point in waiting. When he got back to his apartment he made a phone call to Dan Erickson, a retired airline pilot who lived in Coral Gables. An hour later Dan called him back and gave him a number to call when he got to Miami.

Chapter 44

Victor got a direct flight from Hartford to Miami early the next morning and arrived at Miami International Airport before eleven. He called the number Dan Erickson had given him the evening before and was told to come directly to an address on Flagger Street in downtown Miami, not an area that he was familiar with.

The address was a bar. Above the door was a noisy air conditioner, and above that, a lit blue-and-green-neon cockatoo, bright even in the glaring sunlight. Several men, all Hispanic, were standing around outside. When the taxi pulled up they stopped talking and watched him get out. He checked the street number and went in. It was so dark inside that for several seconds he could see nothing, then a few dim lights appeared, a line of bare ten-watt bulbs reflected by the mirror behind the bar. The air was stale and hot, and the odor of greasy food reminded him that he hadn't eaten anything that day except a couple of packets of airline peanuts.

The bar was long, almost the entire length of the room, with a series of little booths opposite it, separated by wooden partitions.

Shadows and sounds turned into people and voices, and Victor stepped up to the bar and sat down on a black plastic-covered stool with a small triangular tear in it. The bartender, a slender shirtsleeved young man with a ponytail and a pink bow tie, was standing down at the far end, holding a cloth and talking to one of the customers. He saw Victor, but for several minutes made no move to come toward him. As Victor's eyes got more accustomed to the dark, he could see half a dozen men sitting along the bar, and he noted that several of the booths were occupied. A swinging door to Victor's left opened and a waiter with a long apron came out and headed for the booths, balancing a round tray loaded with hot, spicy-smelling food. Victor watched, tapping his fingers gently on his knee, and wondered if he was the first Anglo ever to step inside this place. An entire shelf of bottles behind the bar was devoted to rum—Barbados rum, Puerto Rico rum, Jamaica rum, and a dozen other brands he'd never heard of.

The bartender slung his towel over his shoulder and came slowly toward him. Victor ordered a double Jack Daniels, straight up.

"The end booth," said the bartender in better English than Victor had expected. He pointed. "They're waiting for you."

Victor waited for a couple of minutes, then picked up his drink and walked down to the last booth. There were two men, both in their thirties, sitting on the same side of the table and eating what looked like meat stew off big oval platters. A stack of towel-wrapped tortillas sat next to each plate. Victor slipped into the seat opposite. The man on the outside said, "You got a driver's license?" Victor reached into his pocket and produced it. The man looked at it, looked at him, and passed it back. A large parrot in a round-topped cage at the end of the bar made a loud squawking noise.

"You wanna eat?"

Victor nodded, the man snapped his fingers, and the bartender disappeared. A few moments later the waiter came up.

"I'll have the same," said Victor, pointing at the plates. "And a beer. Coronado."

The man on the inside of the booth was short, sturdy-looking, with very black hair and dark skin. He didn't pay any attention to Victor.

After a few more mouthfuls, the first man, who apparently was going to do all the talking, said, "What kind of plane you have?"

"Cessna twin. Three years old, long-distance tanks."

"Range?"

"Four and a half hours. That's twelve hundred miles or so, depending on the wind."

"Clean?"

Victor, assuming that the question referred to any previous involvement of his plane in drug traffic, replied, "Yes, it's clean."

"And you?" Both men stopped eating and looked at him.

"Yes. No arrests, no convictions, no anything."

Victor's lunch arrived. It was hot and very aromatic. "What is it?" he asked the man opposite, after a few mouthfuls of the rather stringy but tasty meat.

"*Cabra.* Goat."

They talked for about half an hour, about Victor's flying experience, about the navigational equipment on his plane, about his ability to land and take off at night in restricted spaces and on grass and rudimentary runways.

"We'll let you know," said the spokesman finally. "Within two days. Desi will call you at home. He will ask to speak to Rodrigo. You will say that Rodrigo is in Pensacola but will be back on Friday. Then after exactly ten minutes Desi will call you back."

A few moments later, Victor left, blinking when he stepped out into the bright sunlight. It occurred to him that they'd come to a conclusion pretty quickly about him, but he figured that his connections had been good enough to speed his acceptance. And of course they knew that he was a professional pilot and had all the skills they could need.

After Victor left, the two men drank Cuban coffee, strong, sweet, and black.

"Yeah," said the man on the inside, speaking for the first time. "We can use him." The other man picked up the inflection and glanced sharply at him. Then he nodded, knowing what he meant. They left the bar soon after.

Chapter 45

Simeon didn't sleep well on Saturday night. Visions of bright red, disembodied brains swelled and contracted, floated in and out of his field of vision, making crackling noises and puffs of black smoke as the internal tissues exploded. He saw himself boring holes with a hand-held brace into a living brain until it looked like a great pink jellylike slab of pulsating Gruyère cheese, and there was Fiona watching him, begging him soundlessly to stop, and hammering with both fists on the thick glass wall that separated them.

When he woke, the sun was streaming in through the wide glass doors to the balcony, and when he moved his head a little he could see the water, reflecting the sun in quick little pulses of light, intense enough to make him blink.

For once, Elisabeth was up before him, and a moment later she came into his bedroom, looking dazzling in a long, diaphanous white nightgown that hid and accented her figure at the same time. In spite of her splendid body, she always carefully avoided being naked when he was around, except for a few days after she'd first come back.

"Would you like some breakfast?" she asked.

"No, thanks," he said, as he always did when she asked that question. "But I would like a cup of coffee."

"I just have instant," she said, then went on in a gentle, firm, talking-to-a-child-or-retarded-husband voice. "Simeon, as a doctor, you know you should have something more substantial than just a cup of coffee to start the day with."

"Yes, I know, but just coffee will do nicely, thanks," he said.

"When are you expecting your guests?" she asked.

"They're *our* guests, Elisabeth," Simeon reminded her gently. "I suggested they come in around noon, so they can swim and have fun for a while before we eat. I also invited Sam Seidel and his daughter, Susie, and a young Mexican doctor who's visiting him. Also Fiona Markle and her son, Andy, who has a little romance going with Susie Seidel. Andy's a patient. I'm sure I've mentioned the Markles to you. Did you invite anybody?"

"Fiona Markle? Ah, yes." Elisabeth looked at him for a long moment, then shook her head as if her mind had been far away. "Yes, I did ask the Barrys," she went on, "but they had other plans. That's what they said, anyway. You know how polite they are, but I think they really just didn't want to come. You see, I had to tell them who else was coming."

"Of course." Simeon bounded out of bed.

Elisabeth took a quick step backward.

"You startled me," she said a moment later, putting a hand on the front of her chest. "I thought you were going to jump on me."

"Not this time," said Simeon, smiling, but his smile didn't seem to reassure her.

She stared at him. "Are you all right?" she asked.

"Fine. Or I will be, as soon as I've had my instant coffee."

"We have steaks and lobsters," said Elisabeth, watching him carefully, still disconcerted, but she wasn't quite sure why. "I'll boil the lobsters if you take care of grilling the meat."

"We'll grill the lobsters too," said Simeon. Elisabeth opened her mouth to say something, but thought better of it.

"Whatever you say," she said.

"Yes," said Simeon. "Exactly." Again something in his voice gave her a momentary twinge of uneasiness.

Elisabeth went off to make coffee a few moments later, her instincts telling her that something had happened to him, that maybe he had finally figured out what was going on. And that made her nervous and suddenly insecure. And right now, with all the things that were happening in both their lives, one thing she didn't need was to feel insecure.

Simeon got dressed and went outside. It was a beautiful day, warm, with a steady sailor's breeze coming off the sound. Next door, his neighbor, Ian Wylie, was standing on the deck of his elegant thirty-four-foot sloop, a Dufour, Ian had told him proudly, made in France and horribly expensive. Simeon walked through the grass toward him. A large rounded moraine boulder marked the property boundary; there was no fence, since neither of them wanted one.

Ian saw him approaching. "Come on up," he shouted. Ian was a red-faced, affable stockbroker with an office in New Coventry, a bit overweight and strong as a horse. "I'm sailing her over to Block Island next weekend," he said when Simeon came up. "You and Elisabeth wanna crew? We can sleep over in the Great Salt Pond and sail back Sunday."

"I'd like to," said Simeon, "but I can't, not next weekend. Listen, we're having a cookout this afternoon. You're very welcome if you and Teri want to come over."

"Okay," said Ian, brightening. "Great. Teri's away visiting her parents, and it'll break the monotony. Who else is coming?"

"Mostly people from the lab," answered Simeon. "A couple of others. you'll like them."

"Maybe some of them would like to take a ride out in the dinghy," said Ian, waving a hand in the direction of the sound. "I always like an excuse to get out on the water."

Elisabeth, dressed in a silk Givenchy beach wrap over her swimsuit, saw the first car arrive on the stroke of twelve and started off across the gravel in front of the house to welcome them. The car, an ancient but well-kept silver-colored Studebaker, came to a stop outside the garage. Edwina got out, looking very cool in short white shorts and a white-and-green-striped blouse.

Elisabeth directed her through the house to the back, where Simeon was setting up the barbecue. The pit was set a good distance back from the house, at the edge of the mown grass. Beyond it, the ground was thick with spike-grass and sedge and then fell away sharply to the water's edge, where the wavelets lapped gently onto a narrow strip of sand. Twenty miles away, the dark gray outline of Long Island hovered over the water, like a pencil sketch of a mirage.

"Hi," said Edwina, coming up to Simeon, who turned, his hands covered with charcoal dust.

"Hi, Edwina. If you want to swim, you can change inside the house."

"Not right now, thanks. Here, let me help with that charcoal."

Edwina looked around. Simeon's place was nice enough, but there was something slightly unkempt about it, a couple of cracked tiles on the edge of the pool, and paint around the windows that needed work. Edwina's father was a builder, and she'd spent enough time working with him to know the signs. Money for the mortgage was there, but not quite enough for maintenance.

Fiona and Andy arrived next. Elisabeth, watching from the kitchen, put down her wooden spoon and came out to meet them. "I hope you didn't have trouble finding the way," she said, looking curiously at Fiona, who was simply dressed in a pale blue summer outfit with white piping around the neck and hem. She was more strikingly attractive than Elisabeth had imagined; her hair was pinned up, full of big loose curls, and the highlights flashed auburn and gold in the sun. There was a palpable anxiety about Fiona, and she kept glancing at Andy. But she had big, clear, honest eyes and an engagingly direct manner. Elisabeth felt the contrast with her own self, as between a sunflower and an orchid, and she sensed danger.

"We found the place all right," said Fiona, who was just as curious about Elisabeth. "I know this area pretty well."

Elisabeth searched Fiona's eyes. "I know this area pretty well" ... Did that mean she knew other people who lived around this out-of-the-way place, or had Fiona been here before, while she, Elisabeth, was away? Still wondering, she turned and smiled at Andy. The boy appeared healthy enough until she looked more closely at him; there was a stillness about him, unusual in a boy that age, and something disturbing about his eyes, a kind of hollowness, and the whites seemed dull, almost gray.

"So this is Andy," she said, shaking hands with him. "I hear you had the nurses falling all over themselves when you were in the hospital."

Andy looked uncomfortable and mumbled something.

"Why don't you go on through the house to the pool," said Elisabeth. They went off, Andy holding his rolled-up towel under his arm, just as Denis and Sonia arrived on Denis's motorbike. Sam Seidel, with his daughter, Susie, and Paolo Mendez, arrived shortly after, in Sam's Eldorado. Elisabeth told Susie that she'd find Andy by the pool, and Susie went off with a cheerful swing of her hips.

Sam knew Elisabeth and didn't like her. He thought of her as a New England WASP-type female with icewater running in her veins. He preferred heavier-built women who liked to joke and fool around a bit.

"What that woman spends on clothes," muttered Sam to Paolo as they walked through the house following Elisabeth's directions, "would put my two kids through college, then a Ph.D. at Harvard."

Paolo nodded. He stopped to look at the peonies growing in a red, luscious clump near the patio. He took one of the flowers in his hand and stared at it.

"Come on, Paolo," said Sam impatiently, and after a moment Paolo let go of the flower and followed Sam to join Fiona and Simeon at the barbecue pit.

"I've been trying to figure out what to do about Andy," Fiona was saying. "I'm really concerned, and I've decided to . . ."

At that moment Sam came up, with Paolo behind him, wearing the same loose green shirt and thin olive-colored cotton slacks he'd worn at the lab, with the same old huaraches on his brown feet.

They all shook hands. "Hi, Paolo," said Fiona, and Simeon glanced quickly at her.

At the pool, Andy and Susie watched while Edwina did a swan dive off the board. Denis and Sonia had installed themselves in deck chairs at the poolside, each with a beer. Denis had put on a white eyeshade and sunglasses and looked rather dashing.

Edwina noticed Sam and Paolo, and immediately got out of the pool, and came up to them, looking very attractive in a one-piece black swimsuit. She stood next to Paolo, whose expression brightened noticeably.

Simeon grinned at them. "Lunch will be ready in about ten minutes," he said. "There's lobster, and that's done one way only. Steak you can have any way you like."

Paolo looked apprehensively at the lobsters still moving in the big kettle, then at the pile of floppy red steaks in a dish on the brick wall behind the grill.

"And for those who don't like meat, there's a veggie barbecue," said Simeon. "Marinated tofu, mushrooms, and green peppers on a stick."

Ian Wylie from next door appeared, his body covered with curly blond hair, and pranced joyfully across the grass in a rather flimsy pair of mauve swim trunks.

Simeon put him to work, and soon the steaks and lobster were coming off the grill. Everybody seemed to be talking at once, the beer was cold, and Paolo, Edwina, Andy, and Susie found a cooler with an assortment of soft drinks. A light breeze had risen, enough to make the brightly colored paper napkins flutter.

After lunch, Ian Wylie asked if anyone would like to go for an hour's ride in his outboard-engined rubber dinghy.

Andy and Susie volunteered, and the three of them set off toward the dock. Soon the outboard motor came to life, and with Ian at the controls, they eased gently out of the inlet, waving to the shorebound spectators.

Half an hour later, while everyone was chatting at the side of the pool, they heard the sound of a car on the other side of the house, coming up the drive. The brakes were slammed on, and the noise of flying gravel broke the sudden silence that fell over the group.

"Well, I wonder who that could be," said Simeon, standing up. Around the side of the garage came a man, well dressed in a seersucker suit that now bore traces of his passage through the tight space between the garage and the hedge that marked the limits of the property on that side.

He came up to the silent group, and it was immediately evident by the way he walked that he was drunk. Elisabeth's eyes widened, and she stood up suddenly and put a hand up to her mouth.

"Oh, God, Victor!" she said in a barely audible voice,

and when Simeon heard her and understood, a cold, dimen-
sionless fury took hold of him. He barely noticed that Denis
and Sonia had gotten up from their deck chairs and were
apprehensively gathering their things to leave.

"Well, hi," said Simeon to Victor in a voice as calm as
Arctic ice. "How would you like your steak?"

Chapter 46

Victor was about to reply when they all heard the high-pitched whine of Ian Wylie's outboard, getting louder every moment. With some kind of premonition they looked out over the water, and Fiona, standing next to Edwina and Paolo, went white. It was still too far to distinguish individuals, but the dinghy was making a bow wave like a destroyer.

Elisabeth moved over to stand closer to Simeon. He noticed that her hands were shaking. "I think there's something wrong out there," she said, looking in the direction of the boat. She seemed rather breathless. Fiona grabbed Simeon's arm, and at the same moment they heard a faint yell. Somebody, it sounded like Ian, was shouting from the dinghy, and although it was still quite a distance away, it was clear that something was indeed wrong out there.

There was a splash from behind them. Simeon turned for a second to see that Victor had fallen into the pool. Edwina was standing nonchalantly nearby, and Simeon wondered if she'd pushed him in. On the other side of the house, Denis's motorbike started up.

"We'd better get over to the dock," said Simeon. He led the way across the rough grass between the houses at a run, but to his surprise Paolo was ahead of him, running fleet as a deer, and was soon at the end of the dock. Elisabeth, Fiona, Edwina, and Sam all followed, Sam shambling along as if he hadn't gone faster than a slow walk for the last thirty years.

The dinghy came up to the dock just as they got there. Susie had one arm around Andy, and Ian passed the mooring line up to Simeon. It wasn't immediately apparent what had happened.

"Andy had a seizure," Susie said to Simeon, trying to sound cool and clinical. "It only lasted a minute, but it scared us. Him too."

Simeon stretched out a hand and helped Andy come off the dinghy. He could stand, but he seemed shaky and pale and slightly disoriented.

There was a bench at the shore end of the dock. Simeon took one of Andy's arms and Fiona took the other, and with Susie and Paolo bringing up the rear they walked slowly to the bench and sat him down.

Ian seemed more shaken than any of them. He came off last, after tipping the big outboard up to get the propeller out of the water.

He hurried down the dock toward them. "What happened?" he asked Simeon.

"I'm trying to figure that out right now," replied Simeon without looking around. He was checking Andy's eye movements and his reflexes. "Do you think you can walk back to the house?" he asked Andy.

Andy nodded. "Yes," he said. "I'm sorry. I don't know what happened."

"Don't worry, we'll figure it out," said Simeon in a reassuring voice. "You'll be fine. We'll start when you feel ready."

It took several minutes of slow walking, but they got Andy safely over to the house and into one of the bedrooms.

"Gently," said Simeon as they eased him onto the bed. Paolo put a pillow behind his head. "There. How do you feel now, Andy?"

Andy grinned, but it took an effort. "Tired," he said. Then he looked at Ian, who had come over with them. "Thanks. That was a great ride. What I remember of it."

Simeon went to get the few basic diagnostic instruments he kept at home, and after asking everybody except Fiona to leave, he spent about ten minutes going over Andy very carefully.

"Close your eyes and go to sleep for a while, Andy," he said when he'd finished. When he wished, Simeon had a very hypnotic voice, and Andy obediently closed his eyes. Simeon didn't move for a minute, just sat there, intently watching the boy. Then he stood up and silently signed to Fiona to come into the adjoining room with him.

"It's not good," he said, grim-faced. "I'm afraid that the tumor is back."

"But it's not even five months since the operation," said Fiona. Her voice was shaking. "I thought we had about six months."

"The interval varies a lot," said Simeon. "Six months is the outside."

"It couldn't have been just the heat, or something like that? Kids his age can faint for no reason . . ."

Simeon shook his head. "He's got certain signs, like an upgoing toe, called a Babinski reflex, and some eye signs that indicate there's a recurrence," he said. "Fiona, I wish to God it was just a fainting spell."

Fiona's lips were trembling, and Simeon waited a moment before saying, "Fiona, I think we'd better bring him into the hospital."

At that moment Victor came in, his clothes still damp, but the anger had left him and now he seemed completely sober and concerned about Andy.

Fiona paid no attention to him, took a deep breath, and turned to face Simeon directly. "No," she said. "I don't want him to go back to the hospital. I'm going to take him to Mexico, to the clinic in Puerto Vallarta. You've already told me there's nothing else you can do here."

Simeon was about to tell her that it would only prolong the agony, but he thought better of it.

Instead he asked, "Fiona, what do you think they'll be able to do for Andy?"

"I think that if he has only a few months or even weeks to live, Paolo can make the time that he has left more precious," she replied. "And Sam says they've had some successes with their treatment down there. I know that there probably isn't a good scientific explanation for that, but quite honestly, I'd rather try something that makes him comfortable, maybe even happy. I don't want him to die here in the hospital with tubes in his throat and on life-support mechanisms. Do you understand that? I know it may not sound completely rational to you."

"Yes, it does." Simeon took a big breath. "I think I'd feel the same way."

"I'm glad. I really need you on my side, Simeon."

"Have you already made arrangements?"

"Some. Paolo knows, because I talked to him about it a couple of days ago, and of course Sam knows."

"How are you going to get down there?" he asked. "Puerto Vallarta's a long way away."

"We'll figure it out," said Fiona.

Victor opened his mouth as if he were about to say something, but evidently changed his mind.

"I'm a bit concerned about Andy flying," said Simeon. "Cabin pressures are generally lower than atmospheric, and that could affect him ... Let me know when you're leaving. I can make some calls. Maybe we can get the pilot to maintain a higher cabin pressure during his flight."

"I'm going outside," said Victor to Fiona. "I'll see you when you're done here." Something in his tone made Fiona look sharply at him.

After he left, Fiona said, "You know, Simeon, if there was anything else I could do here for Andy, if there was any other possible treatment ... He and I would of course stay here with you."

Simeon nodded. "Let's go back to the living room," he said.

Fiona stepped closer to Simeon, and took both his hands in hers. "Simeon," she said, "I ..."

At that moment the door opened and Elisabeth came in. "How's Andy doing?" she asked, her eyes going from Fiona to Simeon. Fiona tried instantly to let go his hands, but he quite deliberately held on to hers for a few moments longer.

"He's resting," said Simeon.

Fiona stayed with Andy, and Simeon went back with Elisabeth to the living room. Ian and Edwina had left, leaving Sam, Susie, and Paolo. Susie, looking tense and tearful, was sitting close to her dad, and Sam was obviously eager to leave. Through the bay window Simeon got a glimpse of Victor, outside in the courtyard, leaning against his car.

Simeon addressed Paolo. "Mrs. Markle tells me she's taking Andy to Mexico," he said. "And as I've been taking care of him up to now, I want to know exactly how you're planning to treat him." His tone was severe, in marked contrast to the gentleness he'd shown Fiona.

Paolo put his hands together in front of him. "We'll teach him how best to use the time he has left," he replied simply. "And if our treatment makes him better, so be it. If not, at least he will learn to take life minute by minute, and take happiness from the joys of the moment."

There was such a humanity about Paolo, and such a profound and palpable humility that Simeon felt abashed.

"The worst misery in life," Paolo went on, "is fear. And too much of that fear is caused by looking ahead, by imagining the future. In our clinic we teach our friends to look at and concentrate on the present and appreciate the wonder of what they can see and smell and taste and feel." Paolo looked a little uncertainly at Simeon. He wasn't at all sure if this very awesome and distinguished surgeon understood what he was talking about.

Simeon nodded slowly. "As long as you're not pretending that you can cure him," he said. "And if that's what Mrs. Markle wants, it's okay with me."

Sam was looking up at the ceiling and tapping his foot, obviously irritated with Paolo and his weird concepts.

Simeon turned to Sam. "This doesn't sound like something you'd be involved in, Sam."

Sam shrugged. "Paolo has some interesting ideas," he said. "But as I've told him several times, that kind of idea isn't what we need at the clinic. I've been trying to teach him to read a balance sheet, but he'd rather be mixing up a bunch of herbs, right, Paolo?" Sam grinned his unamused, carnivorous grin and rubbed the side of his nose.

"Yes, sir," said Paolo, but there was a kind of blithe unconcern in his voice, and Sam frowned with renewed irritation.

"You are probably wondering what we do if Andy gets pain," said Paolo to Simeon, as if their conversation hadn't been interrupted. "I can assure you that there we have better methods to deal with pain than anything you have in western medicine—except maybe heroin."

Simeon nodded. Paolo was probably correct. He was feeling a strange kind of disorientation, as if he were being forced to revise everything he'd learned about medicine and about people, looking at them now through a different window.

Andy appeared at the door, still in his swim trunks, with Fiona behind him, holding on to his arm. Susie jumped up and went over to him. He seemed to have recovered quite well, but he still didn't look normal. "Can we go home now, Mom?" he asked Fiona.

"Yes," she said. "We were just waiting for you to feel a bit better."

They all went out to the cars. Victor, still leaning against the door of his vehicle, said to Fiona, "I'll see you when you get home," then got in and drove off. After the others had gone, Elisabeth turned to Simeon and took his arm. Gently but very firmly, he detached her hand and walked back into the house.

Driving back to New Coventry, Victor thought some more about the brainstorm he'd had when Halstead and Fiona were talking. If he were to fly Andy and Fiona to Puerto Vallarta in his Cessna, it would give him an excellent reason to be south of the border. And from Puerto Vallarta, with his long-distance tanks he could get to Colombia in two hops, refueling in Guatemala City, then back to Puerto Vallarta. And as he knew from flying Medevac missions while in the Air Force, the overworked customs and drug enforcement people usually passed ambulance flights straight through with little more than a cursory inspection.

Victor stopped at a gas station on the way and made several phone calls. The people he spoke to were quite agreeable to his plan, and by the time he pulled up outside Fiona's home, Victor had figured that he would be a millionaire after two or three such trips. And, as he gleefully reminded himself, the money was tax free.

Chapter 47

The next morning Simeon went to the lab early.

"We're supposed to get the tumor coagulation data back today," Edwina told him. "Not that it matters now, I guess." She said nothing for a moment, then said, "Thanks for inviting us to the cookout yesterday. It's a pity it ended the way it did."

"After you left," said Simeon, "Mrs. Markle told me she's going to take Andy for treatment in Mexico."

"You think that seizure or whatever he had out on the boat was a recurrence of his tumor?"

"Yes. I'm sure of it."

"I figured that too. I couldn't bear to think about that, so that's why I went home. Then I ran. And ran, for miles. Goddammit, Simeon . . ." Edwina kicked at the side of the teak bench in her frustration. Then she stopped and looked up at him. "She's doing the right thing, isn't she? I mean Fiona, taking Andy to Mexico?"

"Who knows?" Simeon's own feelings of frustration surfaced again, and he felt like kicking the bench too. "If it works, she did the right thing, if not . . . Well, maybe she did the right thing anyway. That Paolo Mendez has a very interesting way of looking at life. Did you get to talk to him?"

"Yes. I really wish they'd teach us some of that stuff in med school. He said if I wanted to, I could spend some time down there, like an elective. 'Learn about people first, who they are, what they eat, who they love and what they're afraid of. Then you can begin to understand what's happening when they get ill.' That's what he said, and it sure makes sense to me."

The enthusiasm in Edwina's voice made Simeon smile.

"Maybe you're right," he said. "But right now, if I were you, Edwina, I'd concentrate on my medical studies, and leave Mexico for later. You're already in more class attendance trouble than you need."

"I want to finish this project first," said Edwina, with a touch of her old stubbornness in her voice. "Then I'll think about it."

"It's your life," said Simeon. "I'm not telling you what to do."

The telephone rang. It was Elisabeth. The garage door was stuck, she said; he told her who to call. His face must have changed, because Edwina looked steadily at him and said, "I want to tell you something about Elisabeth, Simeon. You're wasting your time sticking with her. Didn't you see her yesterday? Even with that drunk guy, Victor? And I'm sure there are plenty more."

Simeon was by now used to her frankness, but still he was surprised that she would make such a comment. He was about to reply when Denis came into the lab, looking gloomier than usual. He was alone. Sometimes Sonia stopped off at the ladies' room along the corridor to put on makeup, but after five minutes had passed, Simeon asked him if Sonia was coming in.

"She's sick," said Denis. "She has a fever. Shaking chills, everything. Her ear was hurting, so I guess it's otitis media. She's had that before."

"I'm sorry. Maybe it was from swimming yesterday. Is somebody taking care of her? I mean medically?"

"Yes. One of the ENT docs. She has some antibiotics left over from last time, so she's starting on those."

Simeon frowned, and an entirely unrelated thought entered his mind. He seemed about to say something when a messenger came to the door with a special delivery package, and Edwina went over to take it. "It's the rat data," she said in a discouraged voice after looking at the mailing slip. "I suppose we might as well look at it."

She handed the package to Simeon, then went to clear a space on the bench. Simeon, still preoccupied, spread the data sheets over it so they could both look at them.

"Looks good," said Simeon after they had examined the data for a while. "Ninety-eight percent amino-acid uptake, over fifty percent conversion to hypercoagulable protein in the tumor cells. Now let's see what it did in the other organs. Spleen, zero uptake. Well, that's hardly suprising. Liver ... huh. Zero uptake also. That's great. I thought we might find at least some protein there. Muscle, heart, kidneys ... same." Simeon turned to Edwina, whose mind was obviously not entirely focused on hypercoagulable proteins. "Congratulations," he said. "You did an absolutely first-rate job. Nobody's ever been able to build that kind of special-purpose protein before."

"But it doesn't matter now, does it?" Edwina moved away from Simeon.

"There's one thing here I have to be quite sure of," said Simeon, ignoring her comment and scanning the data sheets. "And that's the coagulation temperature differential." He picked up a calculator and worked with it for a few minutes. "Okay," he said, "these new brain proteins coagulate at exactly 7.9 degrees Fahrenheit above normal body temperature. Edwina, would you check these numbers for me?"

Edwina shrugged, but took the calculator.

"That's right," she said after a couple of minutes. "Exactly." She pushed the calculator away from her. "But, as I said, it doesn't matter now. We don't have a way of heating the tumor to that temperature, and it doesn't look as if we ever will."

"Yes, I think we do."

It was as much the tone of his voice as what he said that stopped Edwina right where she was. Denis looked up from his work and stared at him.

"We do?" Edwina came back.

"Yes." Simeon's eyes were shining with a hard, excited light. "I can't believe I didn't think of it until now. And it was Denis, or rather Sonia, who made me think of it."

"What? For God's sake, tell us." Edwina clasped her hands together.

"Have you ever heard of fever therapy?" Edwina and Denis both looked blank. "It isn't used anymore," he went on, "but fifty years ago they used it for everything from arthritis to syphilis. They injected killed typhoid vaccine ... Let me think who would know about this ..." Simeon thought for a moment. "I know. The Pierce Foundation in New Haven. They work on body temperature regulation, and I bet there's somebody there who'd know."

Denis didn't wait to be asked. He picked up the phone and dialed New Haven information.

"7.9 degrees," said Simeon. "That would correspond to a fever of, let's see, 106.3 degrees. Wow. That's hot. But it should be feasible."

Denis dialed a number, then passed the phone to Simeon.

"I'd like to talk with somebody about fever therapy," he said, after telling the receptionist who he was. Then he waited. All three of them could feel the excitement building. "They're looking for someone," he told Edwina and Denis, his hand over the phone. "A Dr. Eugene DuBois. The guy's retired, she said, but still comes in to work . . ."

He turned away. "Yes, Dr. DuBois, thank you. I have a question I hope you can answer . . ."

Five minutes later he put the phone down.

"We're in business," he said. "They even have a small supply of that killed typhoid vaccine stored in their freezer. He said they'll do a potency check tomorrow, and I can pick it up in the afternoon and talk to him about it. He says the procedure can be quite tricky and isn't without risk."

"What kind of risk?" asked Edwina.

"Allergic reactions, hypersensitivity . . . But the biggest danger is heatstroke."

"Wow. But we can monitor him and make sure he doesn't get too hot, right?"

"Yes." Simeon was thinking hard about what would need to be done before he could carry out such a procedure in the hospital. "We'll need to get permission from the administration . . ." His voice faded. He knew that they would insist on all kinds of safety studies and animal tests before they would grant permission to use it on a patient. And that would take months, maybe years. And of course, before the administrator would even consider it, Felix Cadwaller would have to give his departmental blessing. Some hope.

"Could we do it at Andy's home?" asked Edwina, sensing the difficulties.

"No," replied Simeon without hesitation. "Absolutely not. We'd need support systems. He could go into cardiac arrest, for instance, if his body temperature went too high." He pursed his lips. "No, I guess we're not at the end of our problems yet."

"Are you going to tell Mrs. Markle?" asked Denis.

"Yes, of course," said Simeon. "But first I'll let Sam Seidel know what we're doing."

He picked up the phone and dialed Sam's number.

After a minute, he put it down again, slowly, and didn't look around for a few moments.

"They've already left," he said. "They went first thing this morning." He looked up at the clock. "I guess they're in Mexico by now."

Chapter 48

What finally convinced Fiona to let Victor fly them down in his plane was Simeon's comment that the pressure changes inside a commercial jet might harm Andy. It would take a bit longer, she knew, because Victor's Cessna didn't fly at jetliner speeds, but Victor had been insistent, he'd made a good case, and at this point Fiona just didn't have the energy to argue with him.

That evening, after Victor unwillingly left the house to go back to his apartment, Fiona made several phone calls, the first to Sam Seidel. Sam was very helpful, promised that the people at the clinic would be waiting for them, and gave her a phone number to call when they arrived at the Puerto Vallarta airport. Someone would come down from the clinic to pick them up. Sam also assured her that accommodations would be available at the clinic for all of them.

"When will Dr. Mendez be going back to Puerto Vallarta?" asked Fiona. "We're leaving first thing tomorrow, and there's room on the plane if he wants a ride."

"Thanks," said Sam, "but Paolo's gone already. He left right after Simeon's cookout." There was something abrupt about the way Sam said that, but it didn't register in Fiona's mind until much later.

When he hung up, Gloria said to him, "That's not fair, Sam. She's expecting Dr. Mendez to take care of her kid . . ."

"Vargas and his people'll take good care of him down there," said Sam irritably. "Paolo wasn't the only doctor at the clinic."

"Why did you have to fire him now?" she asked, shaking her head. "Why didn't you wait until after it was all over with Andy Markle? It would only have been a few weeks, right?"

"I couldn't. I talked to him after we left Halstead's place," said Sam. "He totally refused to go along with the medical-testing protocol we set up in Vallarta," he went on indignantly. "Damn witch doctor, that's what he is. I couldn't let him get away with that. The clinic would have gone broke before Christmas."

Fiona's next call was to Marty Seidel, her principal, at home. She told him briefly what had happened and what her plans were.

"Is there anything I can do?" asked Marty, desperate that Fiona was in all this trouble. "Would you like me to come over?"

"No, thanks, Marty. The only thing I'll need is someone to take my classes, but I appreciate your offer." Annoyed with her own weakness, she shakily pushed a tear away from her eye with one finger. Already she was feeling unsure about her decision, and the thought of not having Simeon in charge scared her.

"I want you to know that a fund's been started here for Andy," said Marty. "You wouldn't believe the support we've been getting. It's been only in the school up to now, but we went public today."

"Oh, Marty, there's no need . . ."

"Yes, there is. It's not just the money, I'm sure you know that. People love Andy, and they love you, and they're really happy to have a chance to show it."

Fiona called Wilma, who came over immediately and helped her pack and get everything ready. "I'll check on the house every day," she said, giving Fiona a big hug as she left. "It's my pleasure, actually, because you get the *Register* and I don't usually get to read it."

Victor co-owned his Cessna with two other men, an engineer who worked at Electric Boat in Groton and the CEO of a small electronics firm in New Coventry. The plane was three years old, had been carefully maintained and was in very good shape. They kept it at the New Coventry airport, in the general aviation hangar.

Victor had told Fiona to be there with Andy at seven in the morning, but by six he had already supervised the fueling and completed his preflight checks. He was always meticulous about these, even getting the ground crew to roll the plane forward so he could examine every part of the tire treads. Then he went to the control tower to file his flight plan and get the latest weather reports.

Fiona got Andy up at six, and they arrived at the general aviation terminal in plenty of time. Victor told them to go to the bathroom before getting in the plane. Andy was feeling better now, except that from time to time he saw double, but those episodes didn't last long. The plane was an eight-seater, four on each side of a narrow aisle; Andy sat in the copilot's seat to Victor's right, with Fiona behind Victor. Victor went through the checklist, which Andy read out to him, then he pushed a button on the panel in front of him. There was a high-pitched whining noise, and the left propeller started to turn slowly, then faster, and a puff of black smoke came out of the exhaust, and after that the engine ran smoothly, with only the painted tips of the propeller visible, making a yellow halo around the engine. Victor started the second engine, and they taxied out, Fiona trying to fight the hard knot in her stomach. She looked at the back of Andy's head, afraid of what was happening inside his skull. When they became airborne, and the ground fell away from under them, they looked at the wide expanse of Long Island Sound and tried to identify landmarks. They could see the harbor, a few small islands dotted just outside it, with big houses and docks.

Fiona tapped Andy's shoulder. "There's our house!" she yelled over the noise of the engines and pointed down. Andy looked, but all he could see was rows and swirls of houses, some with bright blue pools, and beyond them the long parallel ribbons of I-95 heading down toward New York. They climbed up into a bank of low cloud, and from that time they didn't see much until several hours later when they put down in a small airport at Hamilton, north of Cincinnati. They saw the straight runway looming up ahead, felt the bump, and they were down, trundling toward the terminal.

The trip took two days, and they were all exhausted by the time they flew over the last wooded mountain range and down to the coast with its continuous white rim of sandy beaches, a few miles north of Puerto Vallarta. As they circled the airfield, they could see the hazy blue of the Pacific, the harbor with two cruise ships moored at the docks, the broad white beaches, and the big hotels dotted along the shore.

Since the flight had come in from the U.S., they had to go through customs, but as Victor had foreseen, once the Mexican immigration people knew the purpose of the flight, they didn't check them or the plane, but instead helped them carry their luggage into the terminal. Victor went off to the control tower for debriefing. He would get a taxi to the clinic when he was done, he told them, but he wasn't staying, because he had to get back to the States.

Fiona called the clinic, and while they were waiting for transportation, two reporters from the local newspaper came up and started to take photos. Fiona managed to get rid of them, with the help of the clinic driver, who appeared about twenty minutes after Fiona had called.

It was hot and dusty and noisy as they left the airport and turned right, into Calle Centrale, the long street that ran parallel to the ocean and led into town.

"What's that, Mom?" asked Andy. On their left was a circular building with a cut-out metal silhouette of a bull on the parapet.

The driver spoke up, without turning around. "That's the Playa del Toros, where they have bullfights, sir." His English was good. "Every Wednesday, five p.m.," he went on. "Twenty-five dollar per person, best seats on the shady side."

The traffic was thick with taxis around the harbor, then the traffic cleared as they passed the big beachside hotels on the right, surrounded by waving palm trees and colorful tropical flowers, with occasional glimpses of startlingly blue ocean. Andy hadn't felt well during the flight and had had several episodes of double vision, but now he was perking up, and he could see normally again.

"Is that really the Pacific Ocean?" he asked his mother.

"Yes. This part is actually a wide bay, called the Bahia de Banderas."

"Have you been here before?" Andy asked.

"Yes. But it was a long time ago."

"With Dad?"

"Yes." Fiona thought about Victor for a moment. He'd been in a good mood all the way through the long flight—almost too good. She wondered what he was up to.

A few minutes later, the town a couple of miles behind them, the minivan started up the winding, hilly oceanside road, and just beyond Los Arcos, a series of three little islands with archlike tunnels passing through them, they turned inland and the vehicle whined and climbed, mostly in first gear, up a winding cobblestone road shaded by tall trees. High, irregular rocky walls lined the road, with flowering bougainvillea and jacaranda hanging mysteriously over the top. Coming around the sharp corners, they caught glimpses of tree-covered, hilly green jungle spreading inland into the blue distance.

Fiona got a crick in her neck from peering up and out of the minivan, then they came to a partially cleared area, and round the next corner, they went through a pair of high, sunlit granite gateposts, with ornamented wrought-iron gates held open by big round earthenware pots overflowing with red geraniums, dazzling in their profusion.

They still couldn't see the clinic building, but Andy and Fiona stopped talking, awed by their surroundings. To their right, down the mountainous slope, they had a breathtaking view of the bay, blue as turquoise, its arms extending far into the hazy distance. And then, coming around the corner, they saw it, the Maya Clinic, a big, two-story building of reddish stone, with a wide white-painted veranda extending out on pillars on the ocean side and above, a big, wild-looking garden with all kinds of exotic and colorful plants and flowers. Behind the garden, a stand of palm trees faded into the jungle.

The driver pulled up outside the front entrance, got out, opened a rear door, and hauled the luggage from the back.

Fiona looked around. For some reason it looked different from outside the car. The paint on the white veranda was peeling, and on it she noticed several old people in chairs, immobile, staring into space, paying no attention to the new arrivals.

A round-faced young man with long jet-black hair appeared and without a word picked up their luggage. Fiona and Andy followed him into a big, dark hall, the walls covered in cheap wood paneling. A ceiling fan rotated scratchily above. The first thing that Fiona noticed when she came through the door, was the smell, faint but pervasive, of an ammoniacal antiseptic and underneath that the sour odor of whatever the ammonia was covering up.

Andy said, "Mom, it really stinks in here!"

A large middle-aged woman stood up from a table in the far corner and came over. Her name was Dominga, she said, and everything was ready for them. Dr. Vargas, the head of the clinic, would be coming up to see them soon, as he wanted to start the tests and treatment immediately.

"Dr. Mendez is going to be Andy's doctor," said Fiona, putting a hand on Andy's shoulder.

Dominga said something in fast Spanish that neither of them understood, then motioned them to follow her into the public rooms, a large sitting room, a dining room, and the library, which looked like a converted closet with a bookshelf half full of dusty paperbacks. There was a sense of disorder, of dust and uncleanliness about the whole place that made Fiona uneasy. Still, she thought, standards are different here, and hopefully the doctors knew what they were doing. And of course she had developed a kind of personal confidence in Paolo. Then, quite suddenly, she sorely missed Simeon's supportive presence.

Dominga clapped her hands and the young Indian came over with the luggage. She led the way up the big staircase with its worn gray carpet and dark wood banister, then along a corridor to their assigned rooms. The windows opened onto a long iron-balustraded balcony with the same stupendous view of the ocean that they had seen from below. More geraniums blossomed from pots on the balcony.

The rooms were sparsely furnished, all rustic-style wood, each with a narrow single bed, two hardbacked chairs, a chest of drawers with an oval mirror above it, and a walk-in ceiling-high closet with shelves and space for luggage. A small pile of towels sat at the foot of each bed.

"Where are the bathrooms?" asked Fiona.

Dominga indicated that the bathrooms and toilets were further down the corridor.

"There is a TV room downstairs," said Dominga, "but it is rarely used."

They heard the sound of footsteps approaching in the corridor. "Dr. Vargas," said Dominga.

Dr. Vargas was rather short, with a round, dark jaw that looked as if it needed shaving twice a day. He was dressed very formally in a close-fitting dark suit, very shiny black shoes, and a gray silk tie.

"Welcome to the Maya Clinic," he said, smiling at them and coming into the room. He cast a quick, appraising look at Andy, then turned to Dominga. "You can go," he told her curtly in Spanish, and she hurried off.

Dr. Vargas put his hands together and smiled again. He addressed Fiona. "I hope you had a pleasant flight to Puerto Vallarta. You will not be disappointed here. We will make your son well." His English was good, heavily accented, and his voice was deep and pleasant to listen to. He nodded at Andy. "We will be starting off with some X-rays and other diagnostic tests . . ." Fiona listened to him rattle off a string of procedures and tests that they would carry out. Dr. Vargas was certainly impressive and appeared to know what he was doing, but Fiona wondered why all these tests needed to be repeated; most of them had already been done in New Coventry. The long trip had taken its toll, and she was so tired that her mind kept wandering off, although she tried to concentrate on what Dr. Vargas was saying. And where was Victor? It would be just like him to disappear; he'd done that kind of thing before. From the beginning of the flight she had noted a cheerfulness, a quickness, and a light in his eye that appeared only when he was up to something. And that something was usually a woman. Fiona shrugged to herself. She didn't care anymore about that, but the feeling that Victor had somehow used the flight for his own purposes angered her deeply.

"Megavitamins," Dr. Vargas was saying. "We've been successfully using doses of hyperpotent vitamins that have not yet been permitted in the United States . . ." He glanced at Fiona, and for a second his teeth flashed gold. "Your Food and Drug Administration is so cautious," he went on, "that the rest of the world is able to use important new drugs and forms of treatment long before these are permitted in your country. And, of course, that is one reason why you have come here and why your son could not receive this treatment in New Coventry."

Again Fiona wondered when Paolo Mendez was going to appear. What Dr. Vargas was talking about didn't sound at all like the treatment that Paolo had outlined to her.

"An important part of the therapy will be intravenous concentrates of organic minerals," Dr. Vargas went on. "These will tone up the normal brain cells and allow them to overcome their malignant tendency to turn into cancer cells."

"Is this a treatment you've been using for a long time?" asked Fiona. She was feeling very unsure of herself at this point; Dr. Vargas was speaking with such confidence, but she didn't really understand what he was talking about. Terms like *organic minerals* sounded slick but not quite right, but there was no way she could know and no one to ask. Simeon, of course, would know. Thinking about him, Fiona realized that she missed him, missed his nearness; in New Coventry, even when she didn't see him for a week or more at a time, there was still comfort is knowing that he was never more than a few miles away.

". . . That form of therapy has been tested with a high success rate in several different countries," Vargas was saying. "And although our own experience is more recent, we're very confident about it."

"When will we see Dr. Mendez?" asked Fiona.

Vargas frowned, and his expression showed both disappointment and regret. "I'm afraid Dr. Mendez is no longer employed by the clinic," he said. "Unfortunately neither his . . . philosophy nor his methods met our admittedly very high standards. I'm sorry to have to tell you this, because, as you say in the States, Dr. Mendez talks a good game, and my friend Dr. Sam Seidel told us that you had developed a good rapport with him. But I can assure you . . ." Vargas's voice dropped with friendly confidentiality, ". . . this way it will be very much better for our young patient here." He smiled, and to avoid any further discussion of Dr. Paolo Mendez, went on quickly, "And to consider a more useful topic, Mrs. Markle, have you ever heard of chelation therapy?"

"Yes, I have," said Fiona, and Dr. Vargas raised his eyebrows in admiring surprise. "There was a story in the papers about it a year ago. A child in New Coventry swallowed some mercury, and that's what they did for her at the medical center. Chelation removes poisonous metals from the body, isn't that right?"

"Indeed, Mrs. Markle. You are remarkably well informed." Dr. Vargas bowed slightly toward her. "Chelation is also used to remove other impurities in the body, impurities and metabolic by-products that allow cancerous growths to proliferate. Removal of these impurities permits the normal healing processes to return the cellular functions to normal."

Dr. Vargas stayed for another twenty minutes, answering Fiona's questions and discussing the details of the treatment Andy would get.

Andy had stretched out on the bed and seemed to have fallen asleep. Fiona sighed and nodded wearily at Dr. Vargas. "Okay," she said. "When do we start?"

"As you have just finished a long journey, dear lady, I suggest that you both rest quietly until tomorrow. Then we'll start with the blood tests at nine in the morning. After that we can do the remainder of the tests and start on the treatment schedule."

"Where do we go? For the blood tests?"

"The treatment rooms are on the ground floor," Dr. Vargas said and gave her directions. "You will be in room number three."

Andy opened his eyes and sat up when Dr. Vargas closed the door behind him. "Did you like him, Mom?" he asked, and from his tone she knew that he didn't.

"He was very nice," said Fiona, suddenly feeling very insecure about Paolo Mendez's absence. "And anyway, it doesn't matter if we like him or not. What does matter is whether he can help you."

"I wish we were home," said Andy. All his usual spunkiness seemed to have evaporated. "Where's Dad?"

"I don't know," replied Fiona, feeling that she was carrying more responsibility than she could bear. "Now I think we should have a rest, then we'll go down for dinner."

Fiona went to her room, but she wasn't able to sleep.

She lay on her back, staring at the ceiling, wondering if she was making the right decision, a swarm of doubts nagging and buzzing at the back of her head. Would Andy be cured here? How would he look when they all went home? And Paolo's absence deeply upset her; it was inexcusable of Sam not to tell her that Paolo wouldn't be here.

Usually Fiona could project her thoughts into the future, imagine how people's faces would look ten years from now, look ahead to events in her life and other people's lives, but now everything was blurry. She had a lot of fear, but no kind of premonition, no feeling that it would go one way or the other with Andy. It wasn't that she didn't have any hope; it was simply that she didn't know.

While Fiona was lying on the narrow bed, worrying and starting at the ceiling, one floor below, in treatment room number three, nurse Felicia Maldonado was completing her last job for the day, an intravenous treatment on Carla Locarno, the patient Sam Seidel had sent down some months before to the clinic diagnosed as a vitamin overdose, but who was in fact suffering from a severe case of hepatitis. At this time, Carla was yellow-brown, the color of an overripe lemon, and was not responding well to her treatment.

"The medication is all in, Señora Locarno," said Felicia, checking the empty bottle hanging above the treatment table. Gently, she pulled the needle out of Carla's arm and placed it in a metal kidney dish before compressing the injection site with a little ball of cotton wool. "So that's it, Señora Locarno, until tomorrow." Automatically she bent Carla's elbow over the cotton ball. Felicia didn't particularly like her job, but it brought in money. She despised her patients, mostly gringos without enough sense to die at home, who incomprehensibly came to die here, expensively, finishing up with all kinds of needles and tubes in their bodies. She turned to her thirteen-year-old son, a heavily built, dull-eyed boy who occasionally helped her with the chores in the clinic. "Remember to wash out the needles, Jorge," she told him. "We have a new patient in the morning coming for blood tests."

But Jorge's mind, which didn't focus well on anything

indoors, was far away, wandering in the jungle where his forebears had hunted monkeys and fruit, and he didn't hear his mother's words.

Unable to sleep, Fiona decided to go for a walk in the gardens and clear her head. The Maya Clinic wasn't at all what she'd anticipated. Not that she'd expected anything in particular, but there was something here that made her nervous. Maybe it was the sour nursing-home smell they'd noticed on arrival, or those immobile patients sitting on the veranda. Dr. Vargas was nice enough and seemed competent, but it was all a very far cry from New Coventry. Her head throbbing with weariness and tension, Fiona walked down the stairs and out through an open side door into the gardens. A flock of noisy black birds with yellow stripes on their wings and tails took off from the branches of a high tulip tree. Several small green parrots flew over and landed in the leaves of a coconut palm. On the downhill side, where the gardens were, black butterflies with yellow and crimson markings fluttered and danced over the beds of coral hibiscus, and she walked down to look at them and smell the pale, wonderfully aromatic yellow-centered frangipani. A gardener, an ancient, bent man with bright eyes and baggy pants barely held up by suspenders, leaned on his spade and watched her walk by. Suddenly feeling exhausted, she started to walk back to the building. Andy was still asleep when she got back to the room. She decided to miss dinner, went to her bed, and fell into an uneasy slumber.

Chapter 49

On the way home from the lab that evening, Simeon tried to calm down from the thrill of finding the solution to his project. Fever ... It would be a nerve-racking ordeal, and not just for the patient. Then he thought about Fiona and Andy, so far away, and that chilled his excitement like a cold shower. Still, he told himself, he could never have got everything ready in time to help Andy, so maybe what had happened was better than having him in New Coventry, where he would have to stand by helplessly and watch him die. And maybe Paolo Mendez *could* help him ...

Thinking these thought when he turned into his driveway, he was surprised to see Elisabeth standing there waiting for him, something so rare in his experience that he thought she must be there for some other reason. But there she was, looking her most beautiful, dressed in a simple white linen dress.

"You look as if something good happened to you today," she said as they walked back toward the house, her arm in his. And in spite of himself, in spite of everything he knew, he felt a familiar surge of something, a hope, a feeling that maybe all was not lost after all.

"Yes, something did," he replied. "I got a twenty-dollar refund on my car insurance. Just like that, out of the blue."

"Wonderful," said Elisabeth. "I knew it had to be something really major."

Elisabeth had prepared a simple but delectable dinner of grilled fresh swordfish steaks with dill, decorated with mint leaves and a single Spanish caper.

"Did you run out of capers?" he asked, picking it up with his fork and tasting it. "This one's delicious, but I crave his brothers."

Elisabeth smiled. "No, Simeon," she said. "That single caper was there on purpose. Actually, it's symbolic—like my own last and final caper . . ."

Simeon ignored that; Elisabeth had already had too many last and final capers. He decided to get down to the business he needed to discuss with her. He took a deep breath. "I've been thinking that we should get divorced," he said.

"Oh," she said, surprised. "Yes. I've occasionally wondered about that too."

"And what conclusion did you reach?"

"Simeon, there's nobody like you. And I've checked."

"You've certainly looked in some unlikely places."

"Right. I have. You pick over a lot of apples before finding the best one. The bottom line is that I love you."

Simeon nodded, his eyes fixed on her. He couldn't bring himself to reply with the expected "And I love you too." "Yes," he said, "but that doesn't necessarily mean that we should go on living together. You like other men, Elisabeth, you also like other women, but you go further, you act on those likings. Me, I have my likings and my desires, sure. But I don't follow them up. Not yet, anyway."

"It's been close, though, recently, right?"

Simeon ignored her comment. "Aside from that," he said, "we don't have any money. I told you when I stopped my clinical practice that we'd have to live on our reserves until I started up again. And now those reserves are gone."

Elisabeth said nothing, watching Simeon. She knew he didn't care much about money, and she wondered why he was approaching the topic of divorce so obliquely.

"So, as I was saying, this might be a good time to part company."

"Yesterday, after the cookout, I was wondering how far you'd got with Fiona Markle," said Elisabeth, changing the subject but still watching him very carefully. "That woman is crazy about you, as I'm sure you already know."

"Yeah, sure," said Simeon, taking care that his face didn't show what he felt. "But I'm not talking about her right now. I'm talking about you and money. You were never one for austerity, Elisabeth, and I don't quite see you starting to buy clothes at Wal-Mart or shoes at the thrift shop."

Elisabeth's pretty nose wrinkled for a second. "Well, yes, Simeon, of course money is important in a relationship. It sets the tone, and you can feel its presence there all along. And, no doubt, its absence."

Elisabeth seemed to be getting bored with the conversation.

"How did you enjoy dinner tonight?" Her tone was unexpectedly playful.

Simeon shook his head in bewilderment. "Dinner was great, thank you. But that's not . . ."

"It was a special dinner, Simeon, like a celebration. Usually you ask how my day went. Today, of all days, you didn't. I know you have a lot on your mind, but you can still ask now."

"I'm sorry. Okay, tell me, Elisabeth, how was your day?"

"Terrific. I sold a piece of sculpture, and even better than that, I got a great big commission."

"Wonderful. Which piece did you sell?"

"The bronze horseman. The rider who's just lost his horse. You remember the one I did when we came back from Tuscany two years ago?"

Simeon nodded. It was a fine piece, in his estimation one of Elisabeth's best.

"Who bought it?"

Elisabeth ignored the question. "And the commission . . . Ask me about the commission."

Simeon didn't like catechism, but he went along. "Tell me about the commission."

"It's for the new racecourse," she said, her eyes glowing. "They want a centerpiece for the stand, right outside the main entrance where everybody'll see it. It's going to be a group of wild horses running. It'll be stupendous, I've started drawings for the model already. Eight feet high, bronze casting. With the base, it'll weigh around five tons."

"At that weight, they won't need to insure it against theft, for sure," said Simeon. "Congratulations, Elisabeth. That's really wonderful." He was truly pleased for her. The new racecourse was a project that had attracted national attention, and the centerpiece would put her on the map as a sculptor of major importance.

A thought crossed his mind, and he looked questioningly

at her. "Who's the guy in charge of that development project? I mean, of the racecourse?"

A touch of color came into Elisabeth's face, and she turned away. "What does it matter?" she asked.

"Probably not at all," he said, "so you can tell me."

"It's a committee, Simeon. That kind of decision isn't made by one person."

Simeon sighed. "Who's the chairman?" he asked.

"All right," she said, tilting her head back in a defiant pose. "It's Nick. Nick Barry. I'm sure you knew that before you asked."

"Did the committee buy the horseless rider too?"

"Yes, as a matter of fact. They're going to put it in front of the stables."

"As an inspiration for the jockeys?"

"Whatever. The point is that we won't starve for a while, even if you don't go back to your practice."

Simeon looked at Elisabeth and thought what an infuriating, spendthrift, unpredictable, and unfaithful woman she was.

He stood up. "I'm going to bed," he said.

Elisabeth stood up quickly and came over to him. "I want to come with you," she said, standing very close. "I want to make love with you . . ."

"No, Elisabeth." Simeon stood back, away from her.

"This is the last time I'll ever ask you," she said. "I've said that before, I know, but this time I mean it."

Next morning Simeon got to the lab a little later than usual, and Edwina, Denis, and Sonia were there. They all looked at him when he came in. He looked cheerful, as if he'd made a difficult decision and was happy with it.

"How are you feeling?" he asked Sonia.

"Better," she replied.

There was something in her voice and in the way they were looking at him that made him pause. "What's up?" he asked, addressing nobody in particular.

"Dr. Cadwaller's looking for you," replied Denis. "He wants you to call his office as soon as you come in."

"Okay . . . What else is happening?"

"Did you see the papers? Or hear the news?" Edwina

picked up the *New Coventry Register* off the bench and gave it to him. The entire lower half of page one was devoted to Andy Markle, a brain tumor victim, and how his mother had been unable to get proper care for him in New Coventry and had been forced to seek medical help in Mexico. There was a photo, apparently taken in a Mexican airport, of a rather startled-looking Andy with Fiona standing next to him.

The editorial, on page six, was biting. How could it be, the writer asked, that doctors at the world-famous New Coventry Medical Center were unable to help this young patient? For over a hundred years, the editorial noted, NCMC had been a medical mecca; patients from all over the United States, from Europe, and from the rest of the world came to New Coventry because of its reputation for delivering the best medical treatment available anywhere on the planet. But now, it seemed, the current had changed, and the flow was reversed. Asked why she was taking her son from a world-famous center to a private clinic in Mexico, Andy Markle's mother, Fiona, said there was nothing more the NCMC doctors could do for him. She'd learned of good results that had been obtained in this Mexican clinic, where they used techniques entirely different from those employed in western medicine.

Simeon turned the page and read the next paragrah.

Dr. Felix Cadwaller, chairman of the department of neurosurgery at NCMC, stated that both he and the entire hospital were embarrassed by these revelations and that it was regrettable that Mrs. Markle should have so totally lost confidence in her doctors. Further inquiries revealed that the surgeon involved in the Andy Markle case was Dr. Simeon Halstead, a controversial figure at the medical center. Dr. Halstead was the subject of a hospital investigation two years ago, as reported in these pages at the time.

Dr. Cadwaller stated that a full inquiry would be made into these latest allegations, and appropriate action would be taken by his department and the hospital.

There was more, but Simeon put the paper down and met three pairs of eyes looking silently at him.

"So, how do you guys feel about being associated with such a controversial figure?" he asked.

"Fine with me, sir," said Denis stoutly. "Actually we're all very proud to be working with you."

"Me too," said Sonia.

"And how about you, Miss Cole?" Simeon asked Edwina, smiling.

"I'm very proud too," she said, her voice serious. "But I'm a bit scared about what might happen around here as a result of that article. What do you think they'll do, Dr. Halstead?"

There was a brief silence, then Simeon shrugged. "Who knows?" he said.

The others stared at him.

"Meanwhile," said Simeon, pulling up a chair and sitting astride it, "let's tie up a few loose ends here." He outlined a plan of action they should follow in case of certain eventualities, then mentioned that he was going to New Haven that afternoon to talk to old Dr. Eugene DuBois, the fever expert, and to pick up a supply of the fever-producing vaccine.

"Why?" asked Edwina suddenly. Her voice was loud, anxious. "We don't have money to do tests on the vaccine, and anyway . . ." Her voice trailed off, and she looked almost apologetically at Denis and Sonia for a second before going on. "And anyway, the whole idea of injecting such a vaccine is too dangerous to use on humans. You can't control body temperature that accurately. If it goes too high, the patient can get heatstroke and die. And if it doesn't go high enough, our coagulation system won't work, so it won't kill the tumor. In fact, the heat may just accelerate it." She looked at Simeon, and she felt a lump in her throat, because all this work, all their enthusiasm and effort had meant so much to her, to all of them. "Maybe, one day," she went on in a lower voice, "we'll be able to perfect something along those lines, but it'll mean years of lab work and animal testing. We just can't do it now."

Simeon nodded slowly. "Thank you, Edwina." He smiled at her, but the weariness and the pain of realization was showing in the lines around his eyes. "You all know that when we started this project I was hoping to treat Andy

Markle with this technique," he said. "It seemed like such a perfect system . . ." He paused, and took a deep breath. "But right now it looks as if Edwina's right. The best we can do is hope that everything is working out in Mexico for Andy and that Dr. Mendez's treatment is effective."

He turned to Edwina. "While we're tidying up loose ends," he said to her, "what's the status on our amino acids?"

"Status? Well, the shipment's still here." She pointed at a square cardboard box on the bench. "We could send it back for refund, I suppose."

"Good. No, don't send it back." A thought seemed to strike Simeon. "Edwina, I want to take another look at the coagulation protein data, please."

She found the papers, and he took them into the office and spent the next fifteen minutes poring over them and checking numbers on his desk calculator. The other three kept glancing through the window at him. Then Simeon put the papers away, looked in his address book, and made a number of phone calls.

"I hope he hasn't forgotten about Dr. Cadwaller," muttered Denis to Edwina. "He sure didn't look as if he wanted to be kept waiting."

Finally Simeon came out of his office and said to Denis, "If anybody needs me I'll be over at Dr. Cadwaller's office, but not for very long, I think. And I have a feeling we may both be back here soon." He paused, picked up the box containing the amino acids, and walked out, followed by Edwina, who for once was going to attend a class.

Chapter 50

When Fiona woke up, the sun was shining into her tiny bedroom. She looked at her watch, jumped out of bed, and went through to the next room, where she found Andy still asleep. She shook him awake and led him downstairs, still half asleep, to treatment room three.

The nurse, Felicia Maldonado, was already there. "Lie down, please," she said to Andy, indicating the wooden treatment table, "and roll up your right sleeve."

Fiona watched the nurse. She wore no gloves as she fitted the needle to the syringe by hand.

"Let me see that needle," said Fiona abruptly, in a tone that made Andy sit straight up.

"Please do not interfere with the procedure," said the nurse in bad English. She was astonished and annoyed that this pale-faced woman should have the nerve to challenge her. "I know what I'm doing."

"The needle," said Fiona, coming nearer to examine it more closely. Nurse Maldonado was holding in the air. "It's been used already," said Fiona, her voice high and loud with anger. "That's not a fresh needle! Look!" She pointed at the hub of the needle. "It's got dried blood on the side of it!"

"All right, then, I'll get another one," said the nurse with a sigh. She put the syringe down on the metal stand.

"Forget it," said Fiona, shaking at the thought that a moment later Andy would have been stuck with that dirty needle. She stood between the nurse and Andy. "Roll down your sleeve, Andy, and get up. We're getting out of here."

Chapter 51

After going out to the parking area and putting the box of amino acids in his car, Simeon went back into the research building and up to Felix Cadwaller's office. "Please go straight in," said Joy Grieve, the secretary. "He's been waiting for you." She looked exactly the same as the last time he'd seen her, same clothes, same shoes, same artificial smile, as if Cadwaller kept her stored in a closet and plopped her back on her swivel chair each morning.

Cadwaller was on the phone when Simeon went in, and he nodded and pointed at the visitor's chair. There was a pile of newspapers open in front of him. Simeon ignored the nod and walked around the room, looking at the photos and other mementos on the wall.

Cadwaller put down the phone. "Well, it seems you've got yourself *and* the medical center in real trouble this time, Dr. Halstead," he said coldly. He glanced at the newspapers and patted his bristly hair. "Every newspaper, every TV network, every wire service in the country wants to know why we couldn't take care of the Markle boy," he said. He paused, and his gaze became grim. "I have to report to the administrator this afternoon and tell what steps I intend to take to correct this major blow to the center's reputation."

"What blow?" asked Simeon. He sat down in the chair, looking very relaxed. "If a patient decides to try another form of treatment, that doesn't necessarily constitute a blow to our reputation."

"You may be right," said Cadwaller, eyeing Simeon, "but that's not the attitude the press and the networks are taking. Their attitude is that we must have really screwed up or Mrs. Markle would never have pulled her kid out of here. Certainly not to take him to *Mexico*." Cadwaller's lip curled with contempt.

"But as it happens," said Simeon, "Mrs. Markle may be right. There is nothing more we can do here for Andy. He's at the end of the line, from the point of view of conventional treatment."

"Hardly." Cadwaller made a quick note on a pad beside him. "He hasn't had the benefit of either radiotherapy or chemotherapy, either of which might substantially prolong his life."

"I discussed both of those possibilities in detail with Mrs. Markle," replied Simeon. He stretched his long legs out in front of him. "First of all, as you well know, radiotherapy is only marginally effective in this type of tumor, and it does serious damage to the normal brain tissue. Second, any benefits from chemotherapy would be very temporary, and the side effects are horrendous. So, as I said, in this particular case, we are at the end of the line. If they can do something for the boy in Mexico, I'm delighted."

Cadwaller nodded slowly, then picked up a folder on his desk. "And how's your research project coming?" he asked. "Have you figured out how to cure astrocytomas yet?"

"I'm working on it," replied Simeon.

"Well, it is my regrettable duty to tell you that your work is coming to an abrupt end," said Cadwaller. His expression changed, and he pulled a file out from under the newspapers. "According to this report from the university accounting office, your research grant has no funds remaining, and is in fact overspent. I discussed this matter with the senior university authorities, and they instructed me to deal with your fiscal irresponsibility as I see fit." Very deliberately, Cadwaller stood up. "Accordingly, on my authority as chairman of the department and head of research, I am closing down your research lab, as of this hour." He looked up at the clock, as if to fix the time of Simeon's destruction in his mind. "All equipment and supplies in the lab are impounded, and you and I will go up now to your lab with the building guards, who will secure it."

"Actually, you're wasting your time, Felix, because I do have funding," said Simeon, apparently not at all put out.

"From Thomson and Thomson. The money will be available in just a few weeks."

"I'm aware of that," said Cadwaller. "Our mutual friend David Marsh has kept me informed. But unfortunately there are rules that have to be followed. And as of now, you are in contravention of the most basic rules that govern the university's research programs."

"What about my staff?" asked Simeon.

"Their salaries are covered for the rest of the year," replied Cadwaller. "They will be on leave of absence until we find alternative work for them. As it happens, I might be able to find something for them in my lab."

He pressed a buzzer on his desk, and a moment later Joy Grieve appeared at the door.

"Are they here?" asked Cadwaller, and she nodded, opening the door a little so that he could see the two uniformed security guards standing near her desk, waiting. "Okay," he said to Simeon, "let's go."

"Felix," said Simeon, his casual tone hiding the rage he felt. "I'm warning you right now that you're making a big, stupid mistake. This may cost you your job here."

Cadwaller glanced at Simeon with icy contempt. "Let's go," he repeated. He was furious at the nonchalant way Simeon was taking all this; it diminished his pleasure. In silence, Cadwaller, Simeon, and the two guards went up in the elevator.

In the lab, Simeon briefly told Denis and Sonia what had happened and that everything was to be left where it was in the lab except for their personal items.

"This is just a temporary problem," he told them. "Go home and relax. I'll let you know what's happening."

But they saw the unyielding expression on Cadwaller's face and knew that this was no temporary problem. They knew, as did most people who worked at the medical center, that Cadwaller was bent on driving Simeon Halstead not just out of his lab but out of the medical center—and, if he could, out of the profession.

Cadwaller collected their keys, then gave them to the guards. He left, after giving them instructions about locking up. Denis and Sonia picked up their coats, gathered the few personal items they had in the lab, and went off after shaking hands sadly with Simeon, as if it were the last time they would see him.

The phone rang, and the guards looked at it. Simeon went over and picked it up.

"Simeon?"

With a shock of surprise he recognized Fiona's voice. He listened in silence while she told him what had happened at the clinic; not only that, she said, but Victor had disappeared with his Cessna, and there were no more commercial flights leaving that day, so they were stranded. And half an hour ago, Andy had another brief episode of blindness. His strength seemed to be going, and she was worried sick about him.

"Okay," he said, thinking fast, "now this is what I want you to do . . ."

After she hung up, Simeon made several long-distance calls, including one to an old friend in New York, while the two guards waited impassively by the door, their thumbs in their belts.

A couple of hours later, Fiona was sitting in a chartered ambulance plane and Andy was lying strapped in a stretcher next to her. The plane was rolling down the runway, on the way back to the States. It was a bigger and faster plane than Victor's, and the pilot had told them they'd have to make only one refueling stop before landing in New Coventry that evening. Fiona was pale and tense with anxiety. Simeon had been encouraging and had told her exactly what to do, but once again, she couldn't be certain that she was doing the right thing. And, looking over at Andy, she knew that time was running out.

Chapter 52

After Simeon called the admissions office and made arrangements for Andy's arrival, he left the hospital, his thoughts oscillating between Fiona, Andy, and Cadwaller. He'd stayed very cool with Cadwaller; his hatred had simmered and swelled very close to the surface, but now that he knew what his revenge would be, he calmed down. The amino acids were in their cardboard box inside his car, and he sat there for a while, thinking. Then he made up his mind and drove out of the lot, heading toward I-95 and New Haven. The Pierce Foundation lab was across the street from Yale–New Haven hospital, and he found it easily.

Dr. Eugene DuBois was waiting for him, a very frail old gentleman with watery eyes and a severe curvature of his upper back. He looked as fragile as a dead pine branch when he led Simeon into the ground floor conference room, but he was very alert and it soon became obvious that he knew his stuff.

"I tracked down the killed typhoid vaccine," said Dr. DuBois. "We haven't used it for many years, of course, but my technician and I checked it and it's still potent. Now kindly tell me what you intend to do with it."

Simeon told him.

"I'm a Ph.D., not a medical doctor," said DuBois, "so I can't comment on whether your plan makes any sense or not."

Simeon had the feeling that DuBois thought he was out of his mind, but physiologists often thought that about physicians anyway.

"Dilute it one part in ten," DuBois told him, tapping the

rubber-topped vial. "Give it as a one-quarter mil subcutaneous dose . . . Do you have tuberculin syringes?"

"No, I don't," said Simeon.

"Take these," said DuBois, taking four tiny syringes out of a cardboard box. "One-quarter mil, did you hear me?"

"Yes, sir," said Simeon. "One-quarter milliliter of a one-tenth dilution."

"Correct. Now, you have to know exactly what's going to happen to your patient from the time you inject the vaccine and the precautions you'll need to take," said DuBois. He pulled back a chair from the conference table. "I'm going to sit down because my legs are hurting. Now, please, listen to me very carefully . . ."

When the ambulance plane landed at the New Coventry airport late that evening, Simeon was waiting. He'd arranged to have an ambulance on the tarmac to meet the plane. Somehow the press had learned what was happening, and a crowd of reporters and cameramen began to gather in the main lobby of the airport, not realizing that the plane would be coming in at the small general aviation building on the other side of the main runway.

It was drizzling lightly when the plane, a modified two-engine Lear executive jet, taxied up to the small administrative building next to the general aviation hangar. As soon as the engines died, the entry hatch opened and the steps came down, and Simeon, his raincoat collar up, walked quickly out to meet them. The ambulance drove slowly behind him, lights flashing, and turned to back up to the plane.

Simeon ran up the steps, and after a hurried greeting to Fiona took a look at Andy.

"Hi, kid," he said. "Welcome back."

Andy smiled, but said nothing. Simeon saw that he looked pale and ill and had a glazed, unresponsive look about him. Simeon made only a brief examination—enough to tell him that the tumor was advancing, and rapidly.

Fiona got off the plane, and Simeon came out a moment later and told the ambulance personnel to go ahead and transfer Andy to their vehicle. He turned to Fiona. "I'm admitting him to the neuro unit," he said. "We'll let him get a good night's sleep, and meanwhile you and I have to decide whether to go ahead with the treatment I mentioned to you on the phone."

By the time the first reporters got to the scene, the ambulance, with Fiona and Andy in the back, was already heading for the airport exit and Simeon was getting into his car to follow it to the hospital.

As Simeon had arranged, Andy was put into a private room on the neuro floor, one equipped with monitoring instruments. Simeon had brought all the materials he might need up to the room earlier that evening. After Andy was settled, Simeon took Fiona down to the cafeteria, which was now almost deserted, and over a cup of coffee he filled her in on the details of the proposed fever treatment.

"So you can see that we're talking about a very experimental situation," he concluded. "It's never been tried before, and we don't even have animal studies to back it up with."

Fiona bit her fingernail. "He's getting worse every minute," she said. "We don't have time to wait for animal studies." She paused and looked at Simeon. "If you think there's a chance," she said, "I think you should go ahead. I don't see what else we can do."

"We talked about radiotherapy and chemotherapy before," he reminded her. "Those are still available."

"Are they any better than they were five months ago?" asked Fiona. "If not, we already decided not to go that route."

Simeon sipped his coffee. "Look, Fiona," he said, "you know we're at the end of the line with Andy. If we don't try this, there's nothing else we can offer. But if we go ahead, you have to understand that the treatment might kill him. First, he could get heatstroke. Even if we can avoid that, a high fever takes a big toll even in a relatively healthy person, and with Andy in the shape he's in now . . ." He left the sentence unfinished.

"Let's talk to him," said Fiona after a long pause. "It's his life we're talking about."

They went back upstairs. Andy was lying very still in bed, the TV remote switch in his hand, watching a late movie.

Simeon started to talk to him, and after a moment Fiona

turned off the TV. "Listen to Dr. Halstead," she said. "This is important, Andy. Please."

Andy, startled by the tone of his mother's voice, said, "Okay," and turned his head to face Simeon. After Simeon had explained about the injections and the fever, and that it would be very uncomfortable, Andy said, "Could I die from it? I mean, from the injections and stuff?"

Simeon took a big breath, and Fiona turned away.

"Yes, you could," replied Simeon in a matter-of-fact voice.

"That's okay," said Andy, and his eyes seemed to grow unusually large. "I'm going to die anyway."

Taken aback by Andy's words, Simeon started on a thorough neurological exam, checking Andy's field of vision, his reflexes, and his neuromuscular coordination. He chatted quietly with Andy as he worked, interspersing his questions about headaches and eye problems with comments about baseball. As he expected, he found that Andy couldn't raise his eyes above the horizontal position, that ominous Parinaud's sign, and his leg and foot reflexes were abnormal on both sides. Looking in the back of his eyes with the ophthalmoscope, he found disturbing signs of swelling around the end of the optic nerve. By the time he finished his examination, it was clear that Andy was in even worse shape than he had thought. The signs were all there; the intracranial pressure was rising, and Simeon's experience told him that Andy had only a few days left before the headaches would become intolerable and he would slip into a coma from which he would not recover.

Simeon put his instruments down and thought hard for a few moments.

"I think we should get started now," he said to Fiona. "The amino-acid infusion won't be uncomfortable," he went on. "Andy can sleep while it's running in."

Fiona took a deep breath, then went over and put her arm tightly around Andy. "That's okay with us," she said.

Simeon and Fiona helped position Andy in his bed. "Could I have another pillow?" he asked, and Fiona pulled one up. "My head is really hurting."

Simeon started the IV and hooked up the bottle containing the clear amino-acid solution.

"It looks like water," said Andy, tipping his head back so he could see the bottle.

Ten minutes later, Andy had a slight chill, but Simeon told him it was a normal occurrence with that kind of infusion. Nothing untoward was happening.

"All this is going to take a long time," Simeon warned Fiona. "This infusion will last for six hours, then we have to allow time for the amino acids to convert to protein inside the tumor cells. Then after we give the vaccine we can count on about forty-eight hours of high fever ..."

A nurse came in and looked inquiringly from Fiona to Simeon. He told her briefly what was happening, then asked her to call housekeeping to bring in a cot.

Andy's headache had improved a little, and while the infusion ran in, Simeon talked quietly with him about the All-Star game, the different players, and who should really have been chosen. Andy was surprised at how much Simeon knew about baseball. He was also beginning to understand the depth of Dr. Halstead's commitment. It felt a bit weird to Andy: Nobody, not even his mother, had ever focused such concentrated and prolonged attention on him. What Andy didn't know was that by starting this procedure Simeon had put his entire career on the line and that all kinds of problems were lying in wait for him, regardless of the outcome here.

When Andy fell asleep, Fiona and Simeon talked together in low tones. Occasionally one or the other would look over at Andy.

The night passed quietly. Fiona slept fitfully on the cot, never for very long. Morning came, and she went out and brought back coffee and doughnuts for all of them. Andy wasn't hungry, and his headache had started up again, so Simeon gave him some pain medication through the IV, which helped him to go off to sleep.

The residents came in on rounds just before seven, and they could hardly believe their eyes. But there he was, the famous Dr. Simeon Halstead, in person, unshaven, his sleeves rolled up, changing an IV while Fiona sat on the cot watching him.

At ten, there was a hesitant knock on the door, and to the astonishment of both Fiona and Simeon, Paolo Mendez, looking as unassuming as ever, put his head around the door.

"I read the paper," he said. "I thought maybe I should come here and help."

He came in, very quietly so as not to wake Andy, and Simeon told him about the fever therapy.

"We see a lot of very high fevers, out in the villages," said Paolo.

"Good," said Simeon. "We'll be able to use your expertise."

Edwina Cole appeared shortly after, and Simeon and Paolo told her what to expect after the vaccine was injected.

Simeon talked in terms of temperature-dependent metabolic rates and thermal equilibration in the different tissues, and Paolo talked about the different types of hallucinations Andy might have and how fevers affected everybody in the family. He had a totally different perspective, and to Simeon's astonishment, he felt a growing sense of camaraderie with the young Mexican doctor who saw everything in such a different way.

Andy slept intermittently. Edwina and Fiona went off together and came back with cartons of Chinese food for all of them.

By the time they got back, all the amino-acid solution had run in, and Andy was still asleep. Simeon hung up a fresh bottle of saline solution and ran it very slowly, just enough to keep the IV open.

For Fiona, the hours passed slowly and agonizingly. She spent most of the time sitting by Andy, although he dozed a good part of the time. She looked at him, so pale now, with his eyes closed, breathing so softly she could hardly see the movements of his chest. The changes in him over the last few days had been startling. She looked at his arms, how thin they had become, then at his face.

Edwina went off, saying she'd be back early the next morning.

After allowing sufficient time for the amino acids to be absorbed and integrated, Simeon checked Andy, looked at his watch, and made a notation on the log he was keeping.

"Okay, it's time for the vaccine," he said. "Paolo, let's

get the chest leads and the thermometers set up." They placed the adhesive EKG electrodes on Andy's chest, then helped him to roll over. Paolo inserted the electronic rectal thermometer probe, and they rolled him back. Simeon thought that Andy's body felt slack, that his muscle tone had deteriorated. It was clear that they didn't have much time left.

Simeon picked up the vial of typhoid vaccine, and looked at it for a moment. First he made the one-in-ten dilution, then filled the slender tuberculin syringe, checking that the amount was exactly correct. He had a momentary vision of Dr. Eugene DuBois gazing critically at him.

"This'll just take a second," he said to Andy, rubbing an alcohol sponge over his shoulder. A moment later he slipped the needle in and pushed the plunger of the syringe.

"I didn't even feel it," said Andy. His voice cracked, and he cleared his throat and said it again.

They stood around the bed—Fiona, Paolo, and Simeon—watching Andy. Each of them had the feeling that somewhere a clock had started ticking and that by the time it stopped, it would be all over. One way or the other.

Simeon glanced at the Hewlett-Packard defibrillator, on a stand next to the treatment table. "Let's check it out," he said to Paolo, partly to see if Paolo knew how to use the equipment.

Paolo did. His training at Georgetown had been good, and he remembered it. After discharging the defibrillator, they checked the recharge time and made sure it was fully operational. Now its single red eye blinked watchfully at them twice a second.

Paolo sat down facing Andy, concentrating energy into him; he could feel it passing out of him and into the boy.

For fifteen minutes, nothing happened. Then Andy sat bolt upright, his eyes staring, and Fiona rose out of her chair, feeling the panic rising in her chest.

"I feel weird," said Andy. His voice was strange, high-pitched, as if he'd become pre-pubertal again.

"What kind of weird?" asked Simeon, coming up to the table

"I don't know . . ."

Simeon could see the feverish red spots that had suddenly appeared on Andy's cheeks and forehead. On the side table, the thermometer dial, which had started at 98.6, had already reached 100 degrees Fahrenheit and was going up.

Andy lay back and started to shiver. "Could I have a blanket?" he asked. "I'm freezing." Simeon put a blanket over him, but it didn't seem to make him any more comfortable. "I'm freezing," he kept saying.

Paolo fished in the big pockets of his jacket and came up with several small plastic envelopes. He selected one. "This is powdered cinchona bark," he told Simeon. "From a variety that grows only in the state of Aguascalientes. This will make him comfortable." He hesitated. "May I give him some?"

Simeon was astonished. "Do you always carry medications around with you?"

Paolo colored slightly, then smiled and patted his pockets. "This is my work-jacket," he said. "Yes, I always have several medicines with me. It's a habit I got from my father."

"Okay." Simeon nodded in a bemused way, and Paolo half filled a glass with water from the jug, took out a tiny amount of the powder, and mixed it up. Andy drank it, and sure enough, within ten minutes he became relaxed and fell asleep, although his temperature continued to climb slowly. Simeon reinforced the place where the IV was attached to his arm. One thing they didn't need was to lose the IV, because now his veins were constricted and they would have a lot of trouble restarting it.

"Let's change his IV to five percent dextrose," Simeon told Paolo, putting down the roll of adhesive tape he'd been using. "He's going to be using a lot of energy and a lot of fluid."

Fiona sat at the head of the bed, holding on to Andy protectively. The thermometer needle kept going up, slowly but inexorably.

"I'm really scared," whispered Fiona to Simeon, when the needle indicated 104 degrees. Andy was restless, muttering and mumbling in his half-sleep. Fiona stood up, very close to Simeon, and he could feel her fear, but he could also feel something different and powerful emanating from her. She grasped his hand, and the tension became explosive.

Simeon took a small step back. "Don't be scared," he said. "So far, we're doing well." He smiled at her; she was still holding his hand. "Think of all those tumor cells starting to coagulate when the temperature goes up another two degrees."

"Are you sure the rest of his brain won't coagulate too?" Fiona's grip on his hand tightened.

"Yes, I'm sure." Simeon wished he could feel as certain as he sounded. "Heatstroke doesn't happen until the temperature goes up above 107 or thereabouts."

"That's frighteningly close, Simeon. That's only one degree above where you want his temperature to be."

"I know."

The evening turned into night. Aides came in and changed the water in Andy's bedside jug. People stopped in briefly for whispered conversations with Simeon and then left. The residents made their late rounds, but this time they stood and talked briefly outside the room and didn't come in.

Fiona looked at her watch. "It's midnight," she said. "Would anyone like anything to eat? Or drink?"

"Not for me, thanks," said Simeon.

Paolo was in the easy chair. He smiled and shook his head.

"Why don't you take a nap?" said Simeon to Fiona. "Everything's cool, and we're not going to be through until tomorrow evening."

There was a noise from the bed, and Andy turned on his side. "I need to pee," he said.

Paolo jumped up, gave him the plastic urinal, and helped him to sit up. Andy looked at his mother. "I can't do it with you watching," he said.

She turned her back, and after about a minute he managed to pass urine. Simeon took the urinal, went into the bathroom next door, poured it into a glass jar, and examined it. The urine was scanty, dark, almost brown.

Paolo came quietly into the bathroom and looked over his shoulder. "It's very concentrated," he said. "He needs more fluids, don't you think, Dr. Halstead? I would worry that in Andy's weakened condition, dehydration could lead to kidney failure."

Simeon nodded his agreement. They went back into the treatment room and he turned the IV full on. "We may need to put in a second IV," he told Fiona. "We'll decide in about an hour."

Fiona had turned off all the lights except for a small lamp, which shone a yellow light near the foot of the bed. She sat down on the cot. "I'm going to take a short nap," she said. "Wake me if anything happens."

Andy's temperature was going up more slowly now, gradually creeping up past 105 degrees. The faintly lit dial had a hypnotic effect on both Simeon and Paolo. Andy moaned, and twisted and turned restlessly, waking up from time to time, asking for something to drink, then going back to sleep.

At exactly four a.m., when Simeon and Paolo were both dozing in their chairs, Andy had a convulsion.

Simeon leaped up. "Put on the lights!" he said to Paolo, who ran over to the switch.

"Jesus Christ," said Simeon under his breath. "Damn!" The last time he'd looked at the thermometer, just a few minutes earlier, it had registered 105.6 and seemed to be holding steady. Now it had suddenly jumped up to 106.4 degrees.

Andy was shaking so hard the bed was rattling, and the veins were standing out on his neck. Simeon grabbed an ENT gag, inserted it between Andy's teeth, and gradually forced his jaw open. Paolo was ready with an orange stick wrapped in a bandage, and Simeon stuck it between his teeth to prevent him from biting his tongue.

Fiona, who had jumped up when the lights went on, stood behind them out of the way, watching, terrified, biting on the middle joint of her thumb.

Simeon, used to emergencies, had stayed calm and moved fast. He picked up a small, labeled syringe, pushed the needle into the medication port of the IV and pressed the plunger.

"IV Valium," he said to Fiona over his shoulder. "That'll break the spasms, and it'll also put him to sleep."

"What happened?" she asked once the spasms and tremors had stopped. Andy was now lying immobile with his eyes closed.

"A seizure," he replied, taking the padded orange stick out of Andy's mouth. "Probably because of his temperature, but you remember he had one out on the boat, so it could be unrelated to the fever."

Paolo had gone to the nurses' station to get ice, and when he came back they stripped the blanket and the sheet off Andy and started to put cold compresses on his body, his arms and legs, wringing out the water, dipping the cloths in the icewater and starting again. It took several minutes of concentrated work before the thermometer needle started to go down, and when it reached 106, Simeon said, "Stop. It'll keep going down a bit, even though we're not doing anything. Let's get the blankets back on him."

Andy seemed quiet now, probably thanks to the intravenous Valium, but Fiona stayed with him at the head of the bed, stroking his forehead, talking softly. He woke up half an hour later, thirsty, and she gave him water to drink through a straw.

In the next hour, his temperature crept back up, and although Simeon was worried sick that he might have another, potentially worse, convulsion, the temperature stayed in a range that was effective against the tumor cells. Talk about walking a fine line, he thought. If his temperature didn't stay high enough, there would be no effect on the tumor, and Andy would die within a week. If it went too high, there would be more convulsions, possible permanent brain damage, maybe death. Some choice.

Simeon decided that he wasn't going to relax until this ordeal was over. He was very shaken that his temporary inattention had caused a near-disaster, but the events that followed were certainly not the result of his lack of care.

At a few minutes before seven in the morning, when the sun was already lighting up the tall buildings outside, Andy, who had apparently been awake for a while with his eyes open, although he barely moved and had said nothing up to that point, said, "Mom?"

"Yes, sweetheart? I'm right here."

"Mom, are my eyes open?"

Fiona thought her heart had stopped. She knew his eyes

were open, because she'd seen the glint of them moving, but she checked to make sure. "Yes, they are. both of them. Why?"

"I can't see, Mom. I can't see anything."

He heard Simeon's reassuring voice. "That's okay, Andy. I'm not surprised. The medication and the fever make the brain cells swell up, and for a while they'll press down on the optic nerves, the ones you use to see with."

"Will it go away?"

"I expect so," said Simeon, still trying to sound confident, but with an anguished look at Fiona, as if to say. "I'm sorry, but what can I tell him?"

Andy didn't say anything more. He closed his eyes, and Fiona went on talking gently to him, the tears running silently down both sides of her face.

At eight o'clock, Andy needed to urinate again, but he didn't have the strength to sit up. His temperature at that time was steady at 106, the theoretical point of maximum effect on the tumor cells, but Simeon could see that the boy was fading. He paced up and down the room, quietly, in his stocking feet, trying to decide whether to abort, to try to break the fever with cold compresses and alcohol sponges, and hope that the tumor cells had been exposed long enough to a lethal temperature. But he knew that it wasn't a good idea. For one thing, the vaccine was too powerful, and any additional stress on his system from trying to break the fever would just add another hazard. And for a satisfactory effect on the tumor cells, it would take another eight hours, at least.

It was already broad daylight when the door opened and Edwina came in, carrying a packet of newspapers. "How is it going?" she asked Simeon.

"It's been an exciting night," he said.

She went over to look at Andy, put a hand for a moment on Fiona's shoulder, then came back.

"These are today's papers," she whispered. "This is making O. J. Simpson look like a footnote. Look at this." She pointed to the big headline in *USA Today*. ANDY'S BACK, AND THEY'RE FIGHTING FOR HIS LIFE. The *Kansas City Star* blared SURGEON TESTING SECRET DRUG—DYING BOY IS GUINEA PIG. There were half a dozen more in the same vein and Simeon merely shrugged his shoulders. There was nothing to say.

But Edwina was furious. "Those *pigs*," she raged, throwing one of the papers down on the floor. "What do they know?"

Fiona had withdrawn into a world that contained only Andy and herself. She didn't want to see the papers, or anything else. She didn't want to eat, didn't want to drink. She stayed at Andy's bedside, sometimes singing quietly, most of the time just stroking his hair with a repetitive, mechanical action.

The shadows began to lengthen as the afternoon dragged on.

"How much longer?" asked Fiona. She didn't look up, and never stopped stroking Andy's hair.

"Just over an hour," replied Simeon, checking his watch. "His temperature should come down very fast. Then we'll be able to evaluate how . . . how things have gone."

Fiona didn't answer. She started singing to Andy again, very quietly.

Paolo was tireless. He massaged Andy's legs and shoulders, fetched fresh water, helped him to take sips, and talked quietly to him, sometimes in Spanish, sometimes in English.

Simeon was working on automatic now. He remembered how during his residency he could be up for forty-eight hours at a time, but that was a long time ago, and he was out of practice. He checked the EKG monitor every five minutes, listened to Andy's chest, checked the thermometer, made sure the probe hadn't fallen out, tested Andy's reflexes, and paced, up and down and up and down, sometimes rubbing the heel of his hand against the stubble on his chin.

Andy's breathing seemed to be getting slower, and occasionally irregular. He would give a deep sigh, then wouldn't breath for close to a minute, and when that happened Fiona couldn't breathe either, and the tension in the room soared until he suddenly took a deep breath again.

After the second time Andy did this, Simeon went over to recheck the defibrillator. The metal-lined paddles were clean, the wires were clear, and the tube of conductive jelly was handy. Simeon took the cap off to make sure the foil seal had been removed.

Fiona saw what he was doing, understood the significance of it, but said nothing.

The appointed hour passed, and nothing happened. Paolo kept working gently on Andy's neck and shoulders; he too could feel how Andy was weakening.

Edwina, who could see the direction things were taking, lay down miserably on the cot, her legs tucked up under her in a fetal position, her arms wrapped around her knees.

Half an hour past the allotted time, and there was still no sign of the expected crisis. Nobody spoke. The atmosphere was already like that of a wake.

Marshall Prince, the administrator, came to the door, and when he opened it, Fiona could see the bristly-haired Felix Cadwaller standing behind him. With a sigh, Simeon went out to talk to them, closing the door behind him. After a few moments, although they couldn't distinguish the actual conversation, Fiona and Edwina could hear Cadwaller's angry tones, followed by Simeon's calm responses.

"He's going to get himself killed," said Edwina, nodding at the door.

"Who? Dr. Halstead?"

"No. Cadwaller. Nobody but a fool would take on Dr. Halstead. He can be a real mean sonofabitch when he wants."

Fiona smiled absently. She knew Edwina was very perceptive and she knew how she felt about Simeon, and was just trying to keep their spirits up. But Fiona could sense the strength of the forces gathering out there against him, and her premonition was that if anyone was going to get destroyed, it would be Simeon. Even he could not withstand the power of the medical establishment.

Feeling apprehensive and stiff from staying in the same position for so many hours, she stood up, went to the window, and stared out at the setting sun.

Simeon came back in, looking tired but unmoved by the conversation. He went over and stood looking at Andy for over a minute, and felt a growing, stifling weight of guilt bearing down on him. He'd tried an untested, unproven form of treatment without real regard or consideration for his patient, or, for that matter, his patient's mother. He had committed one of the most unforgivable sins a physician could make; he had let his own instincts and pride take precedence over the most basic and ancient tenets of medicine—*Primus non nocere*—First, do no harm.

Edwina got up off the cot and started to walk like a zombie across the room.

"There's not much more we can do," Simeon told her in a flat voice. "At this point, we're going to have to make a decision . . ."

Edwina made a sudden, loud, inarticulate noise and pointed at the thermometer dial. It was indicating 101 degrees, and going down. Andy moved his head, and Fiona ran back to him like a flash.

Then everybody was talking, shouting at once, Simeon had his reflex hammer out, Edwina was checking Andy's pulses, and Fiona was giving him little sips of water, that he sucked thirstily down. Suddenly he struggled and sat up. "What's going on?" he said, shaking his head at the sound of his own voice. His head turned toward the window, and he said, "Mom, it's getting dark."

Half an hour later, Simeon had taken out Andy's IVs, and Edwina had disconnected the temperature probe and the EKG leads. Andy was tired, but wide awake. "I'm hungry," he said. Edwina went off to get him something to eat.

"That's a good sign," said Simeon. He was watching Andy carefully, evaluating, weighing his movements, the quality of his speech, the way he moved his arms and legs, the absence of the faint tremor he'd had in his hands before the treatment started.

Edwina came back with a big mug of broth. Andy drank it down quickly, holding the mug with both hands.

Then he wanted to get out of the bed. Paolo started to help him, but he insisted on doing it himself. He stood, a little shakily for a few moments, then walked over to the window and looked out at the darkening shadows. He was obviously still very weak, but Simeon thought he could see a difference, a change in Andy's muscle tone, some kind of improvement that he couldn't quite identify. He hoped it wasn't just wishful thinking on his part.

Andy didn't have the strength to stand for long, and soon

walked back to the bed, looking at his feet as if he wasn't sure quite which way they were going. Fiona helped him back into bed, and he turned on his side and went back to sleep.

"There's nothing more we can do right now," said Simeon, straightening up after checking Andy's breathing. "We're just going to have to wait and see."

He took his white coat down from the peg on the back of the bathroom door, pulled it on, then very deliberately buttoned the three buttons, starting from the top. It seemed to both Fiona and Edwina as if he were putting on his uniform before going out to do battle.

Chapter 53

The three nurses at the station on the neuro floor were huddled together, talking in low tones when they heard Simeon's footsteps coming down the corridor from Andy's room, and they fell silent and watched him come toward them.

"Could I have Andy Markle's chart, please?"

The secretary jumped up, took the chart out of the rack, and silently handed it to him, watching his face.

As if this were just part of the daily routine, Simeon started to write his progress notes in his neat, precise handwriting.

"How's he doing, Dr. Halstead?" asked Pat Somers, the senior nurse. Her voice was nervous. "Everybody in the hospital ... we've all been hoping that he's going to be all right."

"He's doing pretty well, considering," Simeon replied without looking up. "He's asleep right now, but I think he may want some nourishment when he wakes up."

"Mr. Prince called up a little while ago, sir," Pat went on, glancing at her colleagues. "He'd like you to call him as soon as possible."

After he finished writing in the chart, Simeon picked up the desk phone and called Marshall Prince. He had been expecting such a summons.

"I'd like you to come to my office, please," said Prince. "Dr. Cadwaller has convened an emergency meeting here to consider your ... recent activities here in the hospital."

"I'll be there in half an hour," said Simeon. He put down the phone, went over his orders for Andy with Pat Somers, and walked back to see how his patient was doing.

Paolo and Edwina were leaving. Simeon thanked them,

then sat down quietly for a while with Fiona, before going over to his office to pick up a file with some paperwork he had been doing.

Marshall Prince's office was on the ground floor in the oldest part of the hospital. Large, high-ceilinged, wood-paneled, the room looked as if it had been designed to awe visitors to the nerve center of this world-famous medical center. While he waited for Simeon, Marshall glanced around the dozen or so framed portraits of his predecessors in office and fixed on the earliest sepia photo, a solemn-looking gentleman with pork-chop mustaches, a rounded collar, and the glint of battle in his eyes. Marshall seriously doubted if Ephraim L. Endicott had ever had to face problems as troublesome as the one he was faced with now.

When Simeon came in, holding the bulky file folder in his hand, there were already several people gathered around a conference table set to the right of Prince's desk, and they stopped talking when he appeared. In addition to Cadwaller and Prince, Simeon noted Dr. Desmond Rosenfeld, the senior psychiatrist who had taken care of Ted Garvey; Dr. Amon Kindness, the dean of the medical school; also Dr. Paula Cairns, one of the few female surgeons at the medical center; and Dr. Caleb Winter, a distinguished surgeon and researcher.

Felix Cadwaller's eyebrows went up in obvious distaste at Simeon's unshaven appearance.

"Come in and take a seat, please, Dr. Halstead," said Prince, standing up. "I'm sure you know everyone here." Like the others, Prince held Simeon in high esteem, and he was obviously uncomfortable at having to deal with him in any kind of disciplinary situation. He wondered why this well-established, respected neurosurgeon, already internationally renowned, would risk everything—his position, his reputation, his entire career—in such a reckless way. But if Dr. Cadwaller's information was correct, Halstead's actions had put the reputation of the entire center in jeopardy, and Marshall Prince's own job might depend on how decisively he handled the situation.

"We seem to have a very serious problem here, Dr. Halstead," said Prince after Simeon had sat down next to Dr. Caleb Winter. "Dr. Cadwaller has made an official complaint that you have broken departmental rules, the hospital bylaws, and standing FDA regulations in the treatment of your patient Andy Markle. If this is true, the implications are that the FDA will set up an investigation of this institution, and if they find that we have been at fault, they could conceivably even close us down."

Prince glanced around the table. "We're here to decide how much of a problem we have," he said, "but I understand that Dr. Cadwaller has already taken some action in the matter." He frowned. Cadwaller had a reputation for impulsiveness, and his previous unsuccessful attempts to damage Simeon's reputation had not endeared him to his colleagues. But if what Cadwaller had told him was true, on this occasion he had certainly done the right thing.

Simeon sat back. "We're using up a lot of expensive time here," he said. "Maybe Dr. Cadwaller can tell us about his problems. Or at least about the ones that relate to this matter."

Cadwaller reddened angrily, and Marshall Prince sighed to himself. He turned to Cadwaller.

"Dr. Cadwaller, would you please tell the group what you told me earlier?"

Cadwaller shuffled some papers in front of him. "Yes, certainly. I first became aware that we might have a serious problem on our hands several months ago when I was invited to give a second opinion on a patient of Dr. Halstead's, a fourteen-year-old boy by the name of Andy Markle. His parents came to me because they were concerned about the level of care their son was receiving." Cadwaller looked at the impassive faces around the table. "The first thing I discovered was that Dr. Halstead had not discussed all the possible treatment modalities with them, and that, of course, violates both local and national rules concerning informed consent."

Paula Cairns turned and said something in a low voice to Caleb Winter, who made a notation on the pad in front of him.

"Second, the parents asked me to assist Dr. Halstead during the boy's surgery, but Dr. Halstead did not permit this and engineered a very embarrassing scene in the operating room." Cadwaller took a deep breath to show how deeply that had hurt him. "But the crux of the matter is this: Andy Markle was readmitted to this hospital two days ago on Dr. Halstead's service. You've probably read in the papers that the boy has a malignant astrocytoma and is in a terminal condition. In spite of the fact that this boy was dying . . ." Cadwaller seemed to swell visibly as he spoke, "Dr. Halstead decided to try an outlandish treatment that I understand involves injection of amino acids followed by . . ." He paused, then his voice went up with outrage. "You may have trouble believing this, gentlemen, but Dr. Halstead actually proceeded to inject the boy with a vaccine made from *salmonella typhi* bacteria. In other words, he deliberately gave the boy *typhoid fever* as part of this insane and futile treatment. No animal tests of this treatment have been done, of course, and to my knowledge the vaccine has not been submitted for, or received, the necessary FDA approval for new and untested drugs. I submit that Dr. Halstead's conduct in this case has been negligent, unethical, and completely at odds with the reputation for excellence that this institution has earned."

Cadwaller paused, then his voice took on a tone of concerned sorrow. "I am personally appalled and embarrassed by this situation, which has attracted the attention of the media nationwide," he went on. "For that reason, I have been forced to take certain actions. I have closed Dr. Halstead's research lab, and as of today have suspended his hospital privileges on an emergency basis, because in my opinion his patients are at risk from his dangerous clinical behavior. In addition, I have notified the FDA by FedEx letter, as we are required to do by law when breaches of their regulations occur."

Marshall Prince's face was grim. "I understand that you have also notified the press, Dr. Cadwaller," he said. "And the medical societies and state medical licensing authorities."

"Well, I had to answer certain questions posed to me by the media," replied Cadwaller. "And the other groups must, by state law, be informed as soon as such actions are taken against a member of a hospital's medical staff."

Prince's expression became even more grim when he

turned to Simeon. "Would you like to respond to these charges, Dr. Halstead?" he asked.

"Of course," said Simeon. He pushed his chair back. "First, to deal with the question of informed consent. I discussed all the possible forms of treatment with Mrs. Markle in my office ..."

"According to the boy's father, that is not so," interrupted Cadwaller. "He said ..."

"I recorded those conversations," Simeon went on. "If anybody wants to hear them, they can."

Cadwaller's mouth opened in surprise for a second, then closed. Desmond Rosenfeld gazed thoughtfully from Simeon to Cadwaller and back.

"Next," said Simeon, "I asked Dr. Cadwaller to leave the operating room at the outset of Andy Markle's operation because in my opinion he presented a danger to the patient. Again, if anyone wants details, I'll be happy to provide them."

Cadwaller's face went red. The other surgeons around the table knew that Simeon Halstead's technical standards were of the highest level; they also knew that Cadwaller's surgical skills were not in the same class. And as top-ranked surgeons themselves, they were familiar with the often harsh meritocracy of the operating room.

"And as for using an untested new drug ..." Simeon took his folder and placed it in front of Marshall Prince. "You will find in this file summaries of one hundred and twenty-two papers written about the fever-producing effects of vaccine made from typhoid bacteria," Simeon went on. "And in parenthesis, of course these were *killed* typhoid bacteria; there isn't the slightest possibility of infecting the patient with typhoid. This vaccine has been recognized for years as a useful treatment for conditions that had no other cure."

"Let me see those!" said Cadwaller. He reached in front of Prince for the folder and quickly scanned the contents. "These reports are fifty, sixty years old!" he said. "They're not valid!"

"They most certainly are," replied Simeon calmly. "And, of course, a product that has already been used in common therapeutic practice, such as this vaccine, does not need

FDA approval, even though that use was mainly several years ago."

All eyes turned to Cadwaller, who had gone white.

After a long pause, Marshall Prince addressed Caleb Winter. "Dr. Winter," he said, "both you and Dr. Cairns have had considerable experience with FDA rules and regulations. Perhaps you would like to address this question."

"Yes," said Winter. He thought for a moment. "As I recall," he said, "the FDA rules we are talking about apply to new drugs, for instance synthetic penicillins or compounds never previously used as medicines. But they also apply to known drugs when an entirely new application is being considered, as for instance where a drug long used to treat headaches is thought to have a possible role in psoriasis." Dr. Winter looked around the table. "In this particular case," he said, "It seems that Dr. Halstead used a vaccine known to produce fever and used it for its intended purpose. Whether he used good clinical judgment in doing this, at this point I have no opinion. Only the results will show." Winter paused, and his voice hardened. "But what I can tell you is that if the facts are as stated, the FDA can have no possible interest in this case." He stared coldly at Cadwaller. "As for the other matters you brought up, these are departmental issues that you should be able to resolve without our or anyone else's assistance."

Marshall Prince looked at Paula Cairns, who said, "I agree in every respect with Dr. Winter." She tapped her pen on the pad in front of her and went on, unable to hide the contempt in her voice, "I assume that Dr. Cadwaller will take immediate steps to restore Dr. Halstead's hospital privileges, reopen his lab, inform the FDA, and do whatever else is necessary to reverse the damage he has done to Dr. Halstead's reputation."

Cadwaller licked his lips. "Yes, I suppose so," he muttered. "But I still think that . . ."

Caleb Winter stood up, ignoring Cadwaller. "Mr. Prince, I am sorry we were forced to witness this attack on the professional integrity of one of our most distinguished colleagues. We in the medical profession have enough to do resisting criticism from the outside. I'm sorry, but I consider this a truly *disgraceful* situation, and I'm appalled that it should have arisen here in our medical center. Now if you will excuse me, I have other matters to deal with elsewhere."

He left, and the meeting broke up soon after. Desmond Rosenfeld came over to Simeon. "I have my spies in the hospital," he said, "and I know the level of effort you've been putting in with Andy Markle." He looked seriously at Simeon. "I'm very pleased that you decided to join the fellowship of real physicians," he said, then walked away, a slightly bent but still commanding figure.

Cadwaller, listening to this, looked ready to throw up.

Simeon got to his feet. He turned to Cadwaller. "There's something else I want to discuss privately with you," he said. "Please come with me to my office."

As if he were in a trance, Cadwaller stood up and followed Simeon.

Simeon's secretary had long since gone home, and the office was empty.

"Sit down," ordered Simeon.

"What's your problem?" snapped Cadwaller. He had recovered fast from his humiliation. But he sat down.

Simeon went behind his desk and sat down. "I demand that you resign as chairman of the department of neurosurgery, as of tomorrow morning," he said. "I'm demanding this for a variety of reasons, but mostly because you're not morally fit to hold that position."

Cadwaller stared disbelievingly at Simeon for a moment. "How dare you!" His voice was almost a shriek. "How dare you talk to me like that!"

"I'll tell you exactly how. Let me cast your mind back a few years, to the Bahamas, and to Ann. Your sister, Ann."

"Don't you ever mention her name to me, you ..."

"Before Ann committed suicide," Simeon went on, "she told me the sordid details of your relationship with her, although at the time I didn't believe her. She told me that you had had almost daily sexual relations with her from the time she was about twelve ..."

"Have you ever heard of the laws of libel?" asked Cadwaller, making an effort to control his fury. He pulled a notebook and a pen from his pocket. "I'm warning you, Halstead, I'm making notes of this conversation."

"Good. And it would be *slander,* anyway, if it weren't true. Libel is written. Ann also told me about her abortion and that you were responsible for her pregnancy."

Cadwaller half rose out of his chair. "Halstead, you are the most despicable individual I have ever met or spoken to," he said in a tone of utter fury. He stood up. "I am going to terminate this conversation now. The next time I'll see you will be in civil court."

"Just one more thing," said Simeon. He went to the closet, pulled out a large FedEx envelope and put it on the desk. He extracted a cardboard box from the envelope and took out a plastic specimen jar with a luggage-type label attached, the same kind of label commonly used to identify corpses.

"This is yours," said Simeon, pushing the jar over to Cadwaller, who hesitated, then picked it up and examined the label. Then he dropped it on the desk as if it were red-hot and swore at Simeon. "What the hell is this?" he shouted. He seemed to have totally lost control.

"It's the products of your sister Ann's conception," replied Simeon. "Didn't you read the label? As you can see, part of the specimen was removed for DNA testing."

Simeon reached into the envelope and pulled out a typed sheet, which he passed over to Cadwaller. "The DNA in the specimen matches the DNA in a specimen of your blood presently held in the New York Red Cross archives," he said. "You remember we were both blood donors? All of which proves that everything Ann told me about you was true."

Cadwaller was holding tightly to the arms of the chair. He looked ready to have a stroke.

"In case you want to pursue the matter," Simeon went on relentlessly, "what I've just told you has been documented, tested, and recorded in New York, together with the certified originals of all documents involved. However . . ." he pushed the specimen bottle back across the desk, "that's yours. You can keep that piece of tissue as a souvenir of at least two lives that you destroyed."

"You're insane," said Cadwaller, his eyes glittering. "And you're also a blackmailer."

"Not at all. It's not blackmail, it's justice. And I expect

to find a copy of your resignation letter on my desk first thing tomorrow." Simeon stood up. "Now get out of this office before I beat the living shit out of you."

After Cadwaller left, Simeon suddenly felt so weary that he could barely move. He closed up his office and went back to Andy's room. Fiona was curled up on the cot, asleep. A nurse was taking Andy's vital signs; he looked thin and tired, but was awake and grinned at Simeon. His temperature was down to normal, and he sounded perky enough.

Simeon told the nurse to call him at home immediately if there was any problem with Andy, then he headed out to the parking lot and home.

Elisabeth wasn't there, and he didn't know whether that bothered him or not. Without even taking his clothes off, he fell onto the bed and into a deep sleep.

Next morning he found a note on the hall table. This time he recognized Elisabeth's handwriting; he had been expecting it. He sat down and tore open the envelope.

"I have left, and this time I won't be back," he read. "I know you guessed that I am pregnant, and you very cleverly made sure that you could not be implicated. Well, good for you. When I have an address I'll let you know where you can send the divorce papers. Elisabeth."

On the way to the hospital, Simeon felt shaken, saddened and relieved at the same time. In his mind he went over their marriage, the good things and the bad. He'd known about her pregnancy long enough that the shock and anger had worn off—well, mostly. He wondered who the father of her child was. There was quite a choice, just among the ones he knew about. Getting onto I-95, Simeon realized that now he had no ill feeling toward her; in fact, he didn't have much feeling about her at all. Their marriage had been a mistake, a disaster, but it certainly hadn't been all her fault. As he came off the ramp, he resolutely turned his mind to the day's work ahead of him.

Epilogue

Three days later, Simeon was working in the office of his lab when Edwina came in.

"How's Andy doing?" she asked.

"He's a remarkable kid," replied Simeon. "He's walking around, eating like a horse, asking to go home."

"You know, Simeon, that was really crazy, giving him that vaccine," she said, watching him.

Simeon nodded slowly. "Sometimes you have to take desperate measures," he replied. "But you're right. It was probably the craziest thing I've ever done."

"How about the tumor?"

"Hard to tell. He's down getting a CAT scan right now."

Edwina smiled at him. Simeon's concern was almost palpable.

"Even supposing the tumor cells are all coagulated," she asked, "The bulk of the tumor'll still be there, so won't it keep on pressing on the optic nerve and the other structures around it? Won't you have to remove it?"

Simeon shook his head. "No. There'll be a delay, then the tumor will start to be absorbed by the natural phagocyte mechanism."

"How long is the delay? I mean before the internal pressure comes off?"

Simeon stopped what he was doing and straightened up. "Seventy-two hours," he said.

Edwina looked at the clock. "No wonder you're anxious," she said.

The telephone in the lab rang, and Denis went to answer it.

"That phone's been ringing off the hook since yesterday morning," grumbled Edwina. "It's always the press or people wanting to send you patients. We can't get our work done."

"Victoria's getting somebody to come over and take care of it."

"Victoria? She's back?" Simeon's secretary, who had left because there wasn't enough for her to do in the office, was indeed back, and in over her head with work.

"Yes," replied Simeon. "By the way, I spoke to Paolo Mendez on the phone this morning."

Edwina looked up.

"I asked him if he'd like to do a year's fellowship here with us."

"What did he say?"

"He's starting at the beginning of next week," replied Simeon. "I told him you might help him find a place to stay."

"No problem," said Edwina, and a smile spread all the way across her face.

Simeon stopped off at the X-ray department to look at Andy's most recent CAT scan, then went up to his room. Fiona was there, wearing a beige linen outfit and looking rested and beautiful. She was reading a newspaper, but stood up quickly when Simeon came in. He grinned at her, then at Andy, who was sitting up in bed, and at Susie Seidel in her candy striper's uniform, sitting at Andy's feet. She stood up, embarrassed to be caught sitting on the bed.

"I just saw your CAT scan," Simeon said to Andy.

"Dr. Grant said there wasn't much change," replied Andy.

"Right. It's probably too early," said Simeon.

Fiona looked anxiously at him. She knew that they weren't out of the woods yet. "When will we know?" she asked.

"The CAT scan won't show much for another week, maybe two," he said. "But of course that's not the only indicator."

Fiona nodded. She picked up the *Register*. "Did you see the newspaper this morning?" she asked him.

"More stories about Andy?" He smiled, and looked at Andy. "There aren't too many people as famous as you are, at your age," he said.

"There's a couple of other things here," said Fiona in a strange tone. She passed the paper over to him. "Look at the top of page three."

Simeon took it. Fiona had circled the paragraph with yellow magic marker. It was about Felix Cadwaller's unexpected resignation. Simeon didn't bother to read it.

"Now look at the bottom of page one," said Fiona.

Simeon turned the page. "MAJOR DRUG BUST," he read. "As a result of a massive cooperative effort by U.S. and Mexican drug authorities, a U.S.-registered plane was impounded at the Puerto Vallarta, Mexico, airport three days ago, allegedly containing almost a million dollars' worth of cocaine. The pilot, Victor Markle, a U.S. citizen, was arrested. No decision has been made concerning extradition to the U.S., but a spokesman for the Mexican government said he would in all probability be tried there under Mexican law."

"There's another story on page two," said Fiona.

Simeon turned the page. "Huge drug shipments noted arriving in the U.S.," he read. "Our correspondent in Miami reports that record amounts of drugs came in by air to the U.S. over the weekend while the enforcement agencies were otherwise engaged. The U.S. and Mexican drug enforcement agencies had been alerted that a large drug shipment would be passing by air via Puerto Vallarta, Mexico (see story page one), and several units were pulled from the East Coast sector to set up a major interception. It is now thought that this shipment may have been a decoy. The amount of cocaine found on the plane was much less than the authorities had been led to expect and was only a small fraction of the total shipments that arrived unchallenged in the U.S. during the same period ..."

"I'm sorry," said Simeon. He turned to Andy. "I'm sure it's all a mistake ..."

"No," said Andy. "I bet it's not. Dad always wanted to get rich quickly."

Simeon took a deep breath and stepped up to the bed. "Okay, Andy, I'm going to check you out. Take off your pajama top, please." There was something in his voice that warned Fiona, and she sat up very straight.

Susie started to head for the door.

"You don't need to go," Simeon told her. "This'll just take a couple of minutes."

Simeon checked Andy's reflexes and looked into the back of his eyes with the ophthalmoscope, but after a very careful examination he couldn't detect any real changes. There was only one more test he needed to do. Simeon had told Fiona about Parinaud's sign, so she knew what was coming. She watched him, her hands clasped together, scarcely daring to breathe.

"Andy, sit on the side of the bed and look straight ahead, please."

Andy did so.

"Now look down . . . Good. Look over to the left . . . and to the right . . ."

"Now . . ." Simeon seemed to be having trouble getting the words out, and the tension in the room suddenly rose to breaking point. "Now, Andy, I'd like you to keep your head quite still . . . and look up."

For a moment nothing happened, then they all saw his eyes look upward as if it were the most natural thing in the world.

"Good. Thank you, Andy." Simeon paused. "And that tells me that you're about ready to go home."

He turned to Fiona. "If you'd like to go down to the nurses' station with me, I can sign him out," he said.

Outside the door, they started to walk down the corridor, then Simeon stopped. "I'm planning to go back to visit Florence in a few weeks," he told her. "if you and Andy would like to come, I'd love to show you the Uffizi."

Turn the page
to preview
Francis Roe's
other gripping
medical dramas. . . .

A brilliant doctor and a beautiful lawyer ... in the fight—and love—of their lives. ...

Dr. Anselm Harris is the dedicated surgeon thrust into a malpractice suit when a powerful politician mysteriously dies after a daring operation. Valerie Morse is the feisty lawyer hired to clear his name with a terrified medical community, desperate to find a scapegoat.

Caught up in a bundle of lies, betrayals, and murderous intentions, doctor and lawyer must join forces against unbelievable odds ... even as their growing feelings for one another raise the stakes in a dangerous game.

Sweeping from the high drama of the operating room to the dark corners of political intrigue and the blazing heart of passion ... this gripping novel about doctors and lawyers, medical secrets and legal manipulations will keep you turning the pages until its last shocking revelations. ...

DANGEROUS PRACTICES

The heart of a surgeon ...

Dr. Paula Cairns, young, beautiful and talented, is on the verge of making her dreams come true when she wins a fierce competition for a post at New Coventry Medical Center. In this prestigious New England institution, she can display her brilliant skill as a surgeon. More important, she can pursue research that will make medical history.

But what Paula does not count on is the sophisticated medical scam from which Dr. Steve Charnley tries to protect her ... or the unexpected overture from star surgeon Dr. Walt Eagleton, who usually gets what he wants ... or the rivalry of master manipulator Dr. Clifford Abrams, who hungers for her research funds and hard-won results.

Paula is alone but not afraid—in a medical center where base desires often come before dedication and duty ... as she fights against mounting odds for her happiness as a woman, and for her future as a doctor ...

THE SURGEON

Doctor and patient ... or doctor and lover?

Celine de la Rouche was beautiful, sensual ... and desperately ill. Dr. Caleb Winter was brilliant, dedicated, and determined to save her life. Celine was a woman who went after what she wanted: fame, a successful publishing house, and Charles, her society husband. Now she wanted desperately to live, and Caleb's experimental procedure was her only hope.

Neither doctor nor patient expected the white-hot intensity of emotions that was soon sweeping them toward a forbidden liaison and daring the world to stop them. But Caleb was locked in a battle with a rival surgeon who would use a scandal to block approval of Celine's operation. Now amid a hospital's daily high-tension dramas, a chilling tragedy and dark emotions were leading to a showdown, and time was running out.

INTENSIVE CARE

"Juicy hospital drama guaranteed to enthrall fans of medical fiction." —*Booklist*
"Startling ... a ripely dramatic denouement."
—*Publishers Weekly*

Best friends ... bitter rivals

Greg Hopkins and Willie Stringer. Best friends since medical school, they are two powerful and dedicated doctors who have it all. Until their friendship is shattered by personal and professional rivalries—and by Liz Phelan, the beautiful woman they both loved and only one man could have.

And when a child's illness brings the men together again, two decades of unresolved emotion are fueled ... and the bitter aftermath threatens to destroy both doctors and their families, as they move toward a final confrontation.

Filled with gripping, behind-the-scenes details that ring with authenticity, this masterful medical drama brilliantly evokes the lives and loves of doctors and their fascinating, high-pressure world.

DOCTORS AND DOCTORS' WIVES

"A great read." —Tony Hillerman